Plowed Over

On the Wing

Deep Creek Lake
June 2023

Ellen Ann Callahan

PARKS WELLS PUBLISHING, LLC
Gaithersburg, Maryland

This book is a work of fiction. Any references to historical events, real people, real organizations, or real places are used fictitiously. Other names, characters, places, and events are products of the writer's imagination. Any resemblance to actual events or places or persons, living and dead, is entirely coincidental.

 Printed in the United States of America. For information address Parks Wells Publishing, LLC, 110 Chevy Chase Street, #306, Gaithersburg, Maryland 20878.

Follow Ellen on Twitter at https://www.twitter.com/ECallahanAuthor
Like Ellen on Facebook at https://www.facebook.com/EllenAnnCallahan
Visit Ellen at https://www.ellenanncallahan.com

ISBN 10: 0-9962528-3-5
ISBN 13: 978-0-9962528-3-6

Chapter 1

It was one of those days when Happy Holiday couldn't make the simplest decision. Her indecisiveness began with breakfast—cereal, pancakes, or eggs? She ate all three. What to wear to work? The temperature outside was below freezing, but she often got hot inside the cab of her snowplow. She wore layers just in case.

Her decision-making ability didn't improve when she started her midnight shift. As she aimed and cocked her Sig-P232 semi-automatic pistol, she couldn't decide whether to pull the trigger.

Happy's heart was still hammering from the sudden thud against her truck, "Mack the Knife." Mack was a thirteen-thousand-pound, single-axel, heavy-duty dump truck now dressed up in its winter-wear: a plow blade, auger, and spreader. She'd been plowing snow from New Germany Road, inside the Savage River State Forest, when a deer careened full force into the driver's side of her snowplow.

A white-tailed deer with a twisted neck now lay sprawled at her feet. It was an adult buck, probably one-hundred-fifty pounds. It hadn't yet shed its horns. Wide beams, eight points. Nothing to mess with. He lay on the ground, paralyzed, his eyes wild with fear. The deer was breathing. It gazed at her, motionless except for the rise and fall of its chest.

The idea of shooting the animal repelled her. She didn't have the heart to kill the chipmunks that ran amok through her summer garden, much less a magnificent creature. But the deer was in pain. If she fired, the discovery of the gun could lead to big trouble. She had a wear and carry permit, courtesy of the U.S. Marshals Service, one of the few advantages of being in WITSEC—the Witness Security Protection Program.

The trouble was, she hadn't asked her boss, Jack Monroe, if she could carry a gun on the job. The failure to ask was intentional; if she were caught violating a no-gun rule, she could plead ignorance. There was nothing in the employee handbook about guns. Better to apologize than ask permission.

The deer's eyes teared. Unearthly noises rose from its throat. She couldn't stand to witness the suffering. *Oh, fuck it.* She pulled the trigger. The light vanished from the deer's eyes. Her shot had been true and merciful. She was rewarded with an easy-to-find shell casing she promptly stashed in her coat pocket.

"Thank you, sweet baby Jesus!" After blurting the words, she wondered where she'd heard them. Not in Baltimore, for sure. She probably overheard them in the local Walmart. The residents of Deep Creek talked nice, polite. Whenever she bumped her shopping cart against another's, her apology was met with a smile and a "you're all right, honey." Not "hon" like people said in Baltimore, but "honey" and "sweetie."

"Goddammit!"

The splatter of brains and blood covered the snow, her boots, and her pants legs from the shins down. She had no idea her little gun could make such a big mess. She climbed into her snowplow, shoved the deer from the road, and moved fresh snow over the splatter. Her worried breathing triggered an accumulation of fog inside the windshield. She opened the side-window vent to clear away the condensation.

Snow blew inside, along with the frigid air. Happy glanced at Steppie, her bichon dog, curled on the passenger seat. He was sleeping soundly under the warmth of a fleece blanket, blissfully content and oblivious to the snow raging outside the cab.

Protocol required she notify Jack about the deer strike. She gave her dog a soothing pat and whispered, "Shhh...don't make a sound."

Jack came on the line. "What is it?"

"A deer ran into me. Near the entrance to the park."

"Are you hurt?"

"No, but the deer is dead. I shoved him off the road."

"Any damage to the snowplow?"

"No."

"That's the third deer you've hit this month."

"He ran into *me*. A gigantic buck. Out of nowhere, like a guided missile. Boom! It scared the crap out of me."

He responded by giving her an updated weather report. Forty-mile-per-hour wind gusts were on the way. Probably white-out out conditions. Pull over if necessary. Wait it out. Safety first. He signed off with the usual reminder. "Cell service is spotty in the forest. Use the two-way radio."

When Happy wasn't dodging deer, she loved being a snowplow driver. It wasn't as fun as being a Baltimore City bicycle messenger, but the job had its perks. No one opened a car door into her snowplow's path. She was doored three times as a messenger and twice ended up in a hospital. No one cursed at her—Deep Creek folks were glad to see her as she rolled through the neighborhood, clearing snow from their streets. Residents blew kisses, or even better, waved her down to give her a mug of steaming hot cocoa.

Truth be told, Happy missed the speed, the daring, and the excitement that accompanied her as she biked around cars and pedestrians during Baltimore's rush-hour traffic. She grieved the loss of her former life, especially her posse of messenger friends.

There was no point in second-guessing her agreement to enter witness protection—she had her reasons. The result was a new look, a new name, and a new life in the Allegheny Mountains of Western Maryland.

After reporting the deer strike, Happy focused on the road in front of her. Any speed other than deliberate and steady could lead to a wreck. She exited the forest and entered the most challenging part of her route.

There was nothing but open farmland. Fierce winds blew across the road and whipped the snow into a blinding frenzy. Sweat rolled down her back. It was zero degrees outside the cab, but the hot rush of adrenaline coursed through her bloodstream. She dared not take her hands from the wheel. Snowflakes danced in the glow of the snowplow's headlights.

Happy kept her bearings by watching for the yellow road lines. Sometimes a forceful wind swept the road clean enough for her to see them. On the right was a metal barrier separating the road from the neighboring farmland. Drifts collected against the barrier and spilled onto the roadway. She guided the blade through the drifts to give the road a clean edge. The snowplow lurched, pushing her forward against her seat belt. A carcass rolled inside the snowplow's curved blade and exited into the drifts. *Goddammit! Another deer. Two in one night.* She dreaded calling Jack.

She slowed the snowplow to a stop. Next came donning the fluorescent safety jacket. She grabbed the tire hammer she kept under the front seat. The cab door was three feet from the ground; exiting the cab required her to climb down two ladder-like steps.

After exiting the cab, she scouted for the deer. Where did it go? A lump rested against the barrier. It took her six giant steps through the drift to reach the lump. She poked with the tire hammer. Poke. Poke. No reaction. She swept the snow from a small part of the lump to confirm she'd killed the deer. She found a corpse—but not that of a deer.

The corpse belonged to a man.

"Oh, God!"

She used two hands to frantically remove the snow from the rest of the body. She knelt over him and tried to shake his shoulders. "Don't be dead! Please, Mister, don't be dead!"

No response. His body was stiff, cold. He was half-naked. No coat, shirt or undershirt. His left hand was bare except for a gold band. The forefingers and thumb of the hand were frozen into the shape of an L. He laid on his back, staring at her with panic-wide eyes. His mouth was open as if he were trying to tell her something.

"What is it?" she pleaded, not yet accepting he was dead. "What are you trying to say? Tell me!"

Somehow the phone was in her hand. She called Jack. No cell service. Her trudge back to the snowplow seemed miles long. Frozen fingers fumbled with the radio. She sobbed her fear and frustration. Finally, she reached him.

"Jack..."

"Not another deer."

"I plowed up a dead man."

Chapter 2

Happy was at a loss. Jack ordered her to wait inside the cab until the first responders arrived. She'd protested—leaving a dead man alone in the snow just wasn't right. "Get in that cab and stay there!" Jack yelled when Happy argued. He wouldn't stop shouting until she acquiesced.

She intended to obey Jack's order until an excruciating memory speared her consciousness: the dead body of her mother, lying alone in rain and mud until discovered by a passing dog walker.

The memory compelled her to exit the cab, taking the fleece blanket with her. She planned to return before the first responders arrived. She removed her gloves and knelt beside the body in the snow drift. She grasped the L-shaped hand with both of hers.

A promise slipped from her lips, one she'd learned from Alcoholics Anonymous. "I promise to make amends to your family unless doing so would hurt them or others." She didn't owe the man an amend, but she owed her deceased mother plenty. Perhaps she could pay off a few by helping the dead man's family.

Next came the questions—why were you on the road? Where are your clothes? How did this happen?

The wind picked up. She covered the body with the fleece blanket. Snow whirled around her. Steppie barked inside the cab. Happy did her best to ignore him. The dog may be scared, but he was safe. Her chattering teeth drowned out the relentless yaps. The wind stung her eyes. Tears froze on her cheeks and eyelids. She could think of nothing to do but hold the dead man's L-shaped hand. It felt like a block of ice.

Fifteen minutes passed. She spotted the flashing lights from a Maryland state police car. The trooper parked the vehicle behind the snowplow and tromped through the snow toward the cab. She recognized the stride. It belonged to Trooper First Class James Bittinger. Her best friend.

He banged on the driver's side window. "Happy! Happy!"

Her frozen lips couldn't form words.

Jimmy walked around the snowplow with urgency. "Happy! Answer me! Where are you?"

"Here!" The word came out garbled but loud enough to get Jimmy's attention.

The trooper trudged through the snow drift until he reached her. He put his hand on her shoulder. "Happy, it'll be all right."

Jimmy lifted the blanket and stared long and hard at the corpse. His body language changed from take-charge to stunned, but only for a moment. He checked the body for signs of life. Finding none, Jimmy returned his attention to Happy. "Let's get you out of the cold."

She leaned over the body and whispered into the dead man's ear, her lips barely moving from the cold. "Tell my mother I miss her."

Jimmy stood behind her and placed his left arm around her waist. With his right hand tucked under her right arm, he gently guided her to a standing position. She was nearly upright when she balked.

"You can let go of his hand now, Happy."

He led her through the blinding snow. As they passed the snowplow, Steppie clawed at the window. She had to get him. Jimmy must have read her mind. "I'll fetch him after you're squared away."

A few moments later, she was sitting on the passenger seat of Jimmy's patrol car, a thermal blanket warming her. The car's heater blasted hot air. She took a sip of steaming coffee from a thermos she couldn't hold steady. It tasted old and bitter.

Her mind wandered. She was inside Interview Room One, Baltimore City Police Headquarters. Homicide Detective Ulysses Campbell handed her a cup of burnt coffee. "Do you know anyone who would want to hurt your mother?"

Jimmy touched her hand. "You're not going into shock on me, are you?"

Happy jumped back to the present. She smiled a little, wanting to assure Jimmy she was fine. "I'm OK, except your coffee sucks."

"If you give me a minute, I'll fire up the espresso machine I keep in the trunk. You want a nonfat, no-foam latte?"

Her favorite beverage—except for any kind of alcohol. She wasn't as picky about alcohol as she was about coffee.

She liked Jimmy. He had an easy-going way about him. Jimmy's face had some nice components to it, but he wasn't nice-looking. Rugged, maybe, but not handsome. His most attractive feature was his jaw. It was the kind of jaw that could scare a noncompliant criminal into submission.

She admired Jimmy's deep religious faith; family-lover, church-goer, community service volunteer. Her mother would've described him as a *good man*. Happy hated to admit it, but she wasn't physically attracted to him. Maybe she was only drawn to criminals.

Steppie let out a desperate howl. Jimmy opened his door. "I'll get him."

A few minutes later, the dog was asleep on Happy's lap. She nuzzled her face against him, using her cheek to caress the top of his soft, white head. Steppie opened a sleepy eye and turned over in her lap. He displayed his stomach, signaling he wanted a belly-rub. The scars from his healed gunshot wound displayed angry, red tracks. Little tufts of fur grew between them.

Jimmy turned toward her with concerned eyes. "Does your boss know Steppie rides with you?"

She shook her head. This time she *had* asked Jack for permission. He answered, "Absolutely not!" No negotiation, no further discussion.

Jimmy sighed. "Tell me what happened."

The turbulent wind rocked the police car while Happy described finding the body. She finished her story as five emergency vehicles pulled up, led by a snowplow. The Garrett County Sheriff arrived first, followed by the Southern Rescue Squad, two more state police vehicles, and a blue SUV with a placard in the windshield that read, "Forensic Investigator."

Jimmy left his patrol car and joined the others near the body. Happy watched through the windshield while the first responders attended the body. A short, round man wearing a gray parka exited the SUV. His examination of the body was quick. The paramedics strapped the body onto a gurney and loaded it into their rescue truck. The truck sped away, led by the snowplow. All the while, police took photographs and measurements. A trooper seemed to be keeping track of anyone coming to or from the area.

Once the rescue truck departed, there was a discussion between the sheriff and two state troopers who'd stepped from a car marked "Criminal Enforcement Division." The men's discussion ended with a handshake. After thirty minutes, Jimmy and the forensic investigator joined her.

Jimmy sat in the driver's seat and rubbed his hands together under the heater. "Happy, the state police are taking the lead in the investigation. This is the forensic investigator, Clayton Fleming." Fleming sat in the back behind Jimmy. As she greeted him, Fleming flipped back his parka hood. He was hairless except for the bushy, black eyebrows obscuring his eyes. He held a small spiral pad with an attached pen. It reminded her of the spiral pad held by Detective Campbell while he interviewed her about her mother's death.

In an instant, she was back inside Interview Room One.

"What's your full name?" Campbell asked.

"Lucy Prestipino."

Jimmy sucked in a breath. Happy suddenly realized she wasn't talking to Campbell, but to Fleming. "Oh shoot! I just gave you my wrong name. My real name is Happy Holiday."

Fleming's bushy eyebrows raised enough for her to see his hazel eyes. "That's your real name?"

"Yes."

"You're sure?"

"Yes, sir. I'm sure."

Fleming shot Jimmy a puzzled glance.

"WITSEC," Jimmy said. "Say nothing. Ms. Holiday's handler will be in touch with you."

Fleming acknowledged and continued with his questions. "Do you know how old you are?"

She had to think about that. Her birthday was changed when she entered WITSEC.

"Yes, sir. I'm twenty-three."

"You're a driver for Garrett County?"

She shook her head. "I work for Mountain Lake Landscaping. It has a roads contract with the county. I'm assigned to Garage A."

When Fleming finished his questions, he asked if she had any. She had a million, but none came to mind.

There was a short rap on the driver's side window. It was Jack. Jimmy lowered the window, and a blast of snow and wind blew into the car. Jack lowered his head, so he was eye-level with Jimmy. "Are you done with Happy? The clock's ticking."

"What clock?" Happy said.

"You're a commercial driver, remember? Federal and state regs. There's a two-hour window on the drug and alcohol tests. I'm taking you to a collection facility for the lab work."

Fleming said he was finished. Jimmy gave Happy's arm a quick squeeze and said he'd call her.

As Happy climbed into Jack's snowplow holding Steppie, she could see from Jack's expression that her life would soon become a dumpster fire. The drive to the collection facility was silent. She glimpsed at Jack, hoping to figure out how hot the fire would be.

Everything about Jack was long—his limbs, his eyelashes, and his nose. He wore his hair in a braided pony tail that trailed to his belt. She guessed he was in his forties. The only thing short about him was his sense of humor. The one time she'd caught him smiling, she noticed he had long front teeth.

Jack's face was longer than usual. She wouldn't be surprised if he fired her on the spot. Riding with a dog was a safety violation, no exceptions permitted. She'd also disobeyed his order to stay in the cab. Two strikes. Maybe he'd allow a third strike before firing her.

During the drive, Jack didn't mention a word about the dog. No lectures, no questions. His only inquiry was whether there was anyone who could stay with her overnight. "No, just Steppie." Wrong answer.

"I told you 'no dogs.' Why was he in your snowplow?"

"I can't leave him alone. He has a severe anxiety disorder."

"I'm not surprised. You're giving me one, too."

She laughed out loud at the joke. It was a welcome release from her crushing anxiety and grief. Jack's icy glower choked her silent, mid-laugh. Apparently, he wasn't joking.

"You think this is funny?"

She shrank into her seat. "No. It's horrible. I'm sorry I laughed. I thought you were making a joke."

"I don't joke about my drivers plowing up bodies, whether they're dead or alive."

Jack didn't stop shouting until they reached the lab. His last words were, "Don't come back to work until further notice."

Chapter 3

Happy stripped away her soaked outerwear as soon she crossed the threshold of her front door. She secured her gun and said a prayer of thanks no one discovered it during the blood test. She turned on the television and streamed an old episode of *Xena: Warrior Princess*. It was her favorite show as a child. She'd watched it every Saturday with her mother, Debbie Prestipino.

She imagined herself cuddled against Debbie's shoulder, but the image didn't expel intrusive thoughts. Her mind kept flashing the bizarre appearance of the frozen man. The L-shaped hand, the wide-opened eyes, the half-naked body. She remembered the way he smelled. Whiskey. He'd been drinking. She knew the smell of alcohol well enough—she'd been clean and sober for nearly eight years, but she'd never forgotten the alluring scent of alcohol. A craving rose inside of her.

It was seven o'clock in the morning. There were many hours to fill before going to bed. She worked the night shift—midnight to eight in the morning. Her usual bedtime was three in the afternoon. Until then, she had to keep busy. Idleness allowed her mind to dwell on the people and events that landed her in WITSEC. What would Deputy U.S. Marshal Peter Etchers say when he found out she'd blown her cover? She already knew. "Pack up. We're moving you."

No! No matter what he said, she wasn't leaving Deep Creek. It'd taken too long to make her new life. She wasn't starting over. Even if she did, she'd just mess up again. She wasn't witness protection material. Simple as that.

"Stupid, stupid, stupid," she muttered to herself. How could she have made such a dumb mistake? Every morning she studied the details of her new identity and practiced her signature. It should be automatic by now, but it wasn't. It was getting harder as the lies piled up.

Just yesterday, a driver on the day shift commented she talked like she was from Baltimore. She had to think fast. "No, I'm from Norfolk, Virginia. My mother was from Baltimore. I talk like her." To keep her lies straight, she wrote the details of each one on an index card and added them to her "Lie Box." She studied the index cards, so she could remember who she told what. The box was getting heavier with cards by the day.

While Happy waited for Jimmy's call, she began making the grocery list for the next monthly senior citizens' dinner at Jimmy's church. She wasn't a church member, but she helped out when she could, and food shopping was right up her alley. She based the menu on the tall stacks of food coupons she collected during the previous month. In addition to newspaper ads, there were coupons on apps, e-mail subscription lists, and all manner of social media. Whenever she presented Pastor Nelson with a pittance of a grocery receipt, he'd laugh and say, "Are you sure the grocery store doesn't owe *us*?" And Jimmy always said, "Happy, you're a wonder."

What would she do without Jimmy? He was the only one, other than Etchers, who knew the circumstances surrounding her entry into WITSEC.

Steppie pawed her leg. He needed to go out. She checked the weather through the great room window. The storm had passed. It was clear, and the sky had the soft glow of morning twilight. She dressed Steppie in his winter gear, including the boots he hated. Following the beam of her flashlight, they walked the length of her hundred-foot driveway and turned right onto a gravel road.

They headed toward a rolling field, snow-covered and soon-to-be decorated with the tracks of snowmobiles. The field produced corn, oats, and soybeans during Deep Creek's summer months.

Distant headlights lit the sky. It was probably Deputy Etchers coming to snatch her from her home. When she disappeared from Baltimore, she wasn't allowed to say good-bye to anyone, not even her posse of messenger friends. Were they looking for her? She'd bet good money her old AA sponsor was. She tried not to think about her past life. *Move forward*—that's what Jimmy always said.

Red and blue lights flashed for a moment, accompanied by the short whoop of a siren. It wasn't Etchers, thank God. He never announced his arrival. It was Jimmy, signaling he was on the way. Her heart lightened. He pulled his patrol car beside her. "Get in."

The patrol car crunched down the gravel road and her tar-and-chip driveway. Happy's home was a modest, two-bedroom fix-up, hidden by four acres of woods. She'd bought it for the privacy and the view. The house sat on a steep hill overlooking a valley of fields and working farms. On a clear day, she could see the ridges of the Allegheny mountains from her screened-in back porch.

Jimmy and Happy kicked the snow from their boots against the threshold of the front door. The door opened to a great room with dining and living areas. A granite countertop separated the great room from the kitchen. She'd completed the dry wall in the dining area and was deciding on a color scheme. A dozen paint chips hung from the walls. Flea-market finds furnished the living area.

Jimmy settled on the sofa while she fixed him a cup of coffee. Good coffee—not the syrup of ipecac she'd gagged on in police stations. He chugged it down. She offered him dinner. He declined. Never in the eighteen months since she'd met Jimmy had he ever turned down one of her home-cooked meals.

He rested his forearms on his knees. No hearty smile. No goofy jokes. His whole body telegraphed sadness. His weary expression told her it'd been a rough night. She sat next to him and waited. Minutes passed before he spoke. "I came by to give you an update."

She sat motionlessly.

"His name was Bernie Singleton. The body is on the way to the ME's Office. The investigators found his Ford Explorer approximately two miles away. He'd run out of gas. They believe he tried to walk for help, got lost, and wandered around until the cold got him. He'd been drinking. The investigation is ongoing."

For a fleeting moment, she contemplated her own alcohol and drug addictions. If it weren't for her mother's devotion, she could be somewhere in Baltimore, dying on an icy sidewalk.

"Do you know anything about him?"

"He was married, fifty years old. Two kids...boys...fourteen and ten." Jimmy slapped his hands against his knees. "His boys needed him. Now they'll grow up without a father. All because he ran out of gas."

Jimmy was more emotional than she'd ever seen him.

He turned to her. "Don't worry about the FI. I talked to him. He won't say anything about Lucy Prestipino."

"Thank you." Her eyes welled with gratitude. "What happened to the man's clothes?"

"I asked the FI that question. He said it's a phenomenon that's not understood. It's called paradoxical undressing. One of the first signs of hypothermia is irrational thinking. Sometimes, this irrationality prompts a victim to remove his clothes. Any other questions?"

"Are you off-duty now?"

He nodded. "It's been a long day. I need to get going."

"Don't drive. You're exhausted. Stay here."

She took his silence as a "yes." Jimmy secured his Glock with a trigger lock. By the time she gathered a pillow and blanket, he was sprawled on the sofa, still in uniform, and sleeping soundly.

Covering Jimmy with the blanket brought her back to her conversation with Jack. She realized Jack never mentioned her failure to stay inside the cab. Why not? She'd disobeyed his order. Another reason to fire her. There was only one explanation; Jack didn't know. Jimmy covered for her—he didn't tell anyone he'd found her sitting next to the body. She owed Jimmy big time. As usual. She had the urge to caress his fuzzy, cop-style hair.

Her bedtime was six hours away. Being home at this hour threw her; she didn't know what to do with herself. There was always the news to catch up on. Happy cozied into the love seat. Steppie curled into his place in the crux of her knees. She opened her iPad and clicked her way to the front page of the *Los Angeles Times*. There was an article entitled, "Sanchez Cross-Examination Continues."

She glanced at Jimmy to confirm he was still asleep. He objected to her reading anything about her ex-boyfriend, Romero Sanchez, or the ongoing Roach trial. Roach was the notorious gang behind the endless onslaught of violence plaguing the country. There were eight defendants—each of them shot callers. Romero Sanchez, former gang kingpin, was the star prosecution witness. He'd testified every day for a grueling three weeks. Now it was the defense's turn to pick him apart.

The racketeering arrests had swept up most of the gang members, but a few still roamed the streets. As far as Happy was concerned, the most vicious gangster was missing from the defendant line-up: Fernando Flores AKA "Peeps." He'd been Romero's treacherous driver. Peeps was on the lam with a single mission: find Happy and use her as leverage to stop Romero from testifying.

Last week, when Jimmy discovered she was following the trial, he gently removed the iPad from her hands. "Happy, don't read about that. Don't think about Romero. It's bad for you. You'll get mired in an awful part of your life. Move forward. Your future's here, in Deep Creek. Let go of the past." His blue eyes bored into her as he spoke. The way he looked at her physically hurt. His advice made perfect sense. But within a few days, she was reading again but discreetly.

She'd sacrificed a lot to keep Romero safe. While visiting Deep Creek, they'd made an agreement: she persuaded Romero to turn state's evidence against the gang. Romero, worried about her safety, agreed to do so only if she entered WITSEC. Once the deal was struck, Happy didn't know what to do. She sensed time was of the essence. Romero could change his mind. She'd met Trooper Jimmy Bittinger the day before; he seemed trustworthy. She called him for help. It was the smartest thing she'd ever done.

The story wasn't over, and she had to know how it ended.

Funny thing, the trial transformed Romero into a celebrity superstar. He had a fan club; his mug shot was an international sensation that set records for the number of downloads. Romero's testimony riveted the country with descriptions of the internal workings of the gang. Cool, charming, and composed. Occasionally, his ruthless nature surfaced sending shockwaves through the hearts of thousands of women who'd developed crushes on him.

Happy didn't pay much attention to any of that. She only wanted to know if he was alive and healthy.

That's all.

Chapter 4

Happy awoke to find herself coiled on the love seat, her arm around the dog and her iPad on the floor. It took a moment before her mind cleared. Romero, that's who she'd been dreaming about. He was screaming. Trapped and bloody beneath the blade of her snowplow.

Jimmy sat on the edge of the love seat, gently shaking her. "Happy... wake up. You're having a bad dream."

She was breathless and sweating.

He brushed the hair from her face. "Are you OK?"

"Yeah...more embarrassed than anything else."

"Don't be." He kissed the top of her head. "Want to talk about it?"

"No, it was just a stupid dream."

Jimmy's face was whiskered and full of sleep. There was the faint scent of aftershave on his undershirt. He smelled nice. Without thinking, she sat up and hugged him. His return hug was as soft and comfy as a warm sofa. "You're the best friend a girl could ever have."

He pulled away. "I'm looking at a busy day. I gotta go."

"Do you have time for breakfast? I'll fix you anything you want."

Jimmy declined. A minute later, he was out the door.

"Well, that was a quick exit," she said to Steppie.

Happy took the stairs to her bedroom to get ready for the day. There was a rag doll positioned against her pillow. A Christmas gift from Jimmy. It had black button eyes and dark string hair. A banner across the doll's chest read, "Happy Holiday." It was a typo—there should've been an "s" at the end of Holiday. Jimmy was pleased with himself for spotting the doll at a flea market. "It's named after you," he said. "It looks just like you." Happy pretended to love it.

The truth was, the doll was ugly and gave her the creeps. And it certainly *did not* look like her. Lucy Prestipino had strawberry-blonde, wavy hair and mismatched eyes. Her left eye was blue; the right was a mottle of browns rimmed in blue. WITSEC had given her a makeover; short, brown hair and brown contact lenses.

The afternoon brought Happy's WITSEC handler to her doorstep—Deputy Peter Etchers AKA "Uncle Peter." He was a nice-looking man, in his mid-fifties, with a propensity for teasing and lame jokes. His hair was brown with a dash of gray at the temples. He had a dignified presence about him until he opened his mouth.

His tirade started before he stepped inside her home. "You're the most high-maintenance protected witness I've ever handled. Giving your real name? How could you have made such a dumb mis—"

She was nearly able to close the front door before Etchers planted his foot on the threshold. "Go away! I warned everyone I'm not cut out for witness protection."

Etchers waved an envelope through the six-inch gap between the door and the door frame. "I brought you something you need."

"Keep it! I don't care if you're shipping me off to Paris. I'm not going, and you can't make me."

"Take a look."

She snatched the envelope from his hand. It was heavy paper, embossed with raised print that read, "Deep Creek Nail and Body Salon." Inside she found a one-hundred-dollar gift certificate. She opened the door. "What's this?"

"Finding a dead body can stick with a person. I thought a little pampering might make you feel better. Now let me in. I came all the way from Pittsburgh for a cup of your fine coffee."

A few minutes later, they were sitting at her kitchen table across from one another. Etchers sipped his coffee while patting Steppie, now parked on his lap. "Tell me, other than plowing up a body, how's the rest of your life going?"

She gazed at the gift certificate. "I'm worried you're softening me up before telling me I'm on the wing again."

"You can stop worrying. Bittinger saved your ass. He told the FI some cockamamie story about your just being released from an insane asylum. Nothing will—"

"What?"

He smiled as if he'd just gotten her good with a joke. "I spoke to the FI myself. Told him if he spilled the beans, it would find its way back to Roach. First, they'd ask him nicely where you were. Then they'd torture the information out of him. Either way, they'd kill him in the end. I scared him shitless. He'll keep his mouth shut, believe me. The next time you plow up a body, save me some trouble and keep your name straight."

A wave of anxiety washed through Happy. Etchers scared her shitless, too.

"I can't do this…I just can't." She returned the gift certificate to its envelope. "I'm trying really hard to make this work, but Lucy keeps trying to pop out. Last night she finally did."

"Don't be so hard on yourself." Etchers spoke with the paternal tone he adopted whenever she became discouraged. "I know it's been a difficult adjustment. Some protected witnesses struggle—especially witnesses like you. Innocent people who somehow got mixed up with the wrong person. You're doing well, better than most. Don't give up. It won't be long before Lucy completely disappears. You'll see."

Etchers's pep talk made her feel worse. If Lucy disappeared, who'd be left? Happy Holiday, the stupid twit who jumped at the sound of a bullfrog. The only trait Happy shared with Lucy was her addictions. Soon, those addictions would be all that remained of her former self.

Etchers eyed her. "What are you thinking?"

"Jack's gonna fire me."

"No one's going to fire you. What happened last night could've happened to anyone."

She braced herself for the flack she was about to get from Etchers. "Steppie was riding with me. I've been sneaking him into the snowplow for a month."

Etchers's eyes flashed. "Jesus! Do you have any idea how many strings were pulled to get you that job? Why would you risk it over a dog?"

He knew the answer; why did she have to keep repeating it?

"Steppie got shot trying to protect my mother. I have to do right by him." She pushed the envelope to Etchers. "You can have this back."

The gesture seemed to smooth out his ruffled feathers. He slid the gift certificate toward her and returned to his professional demeanor. "Talk to me."

His softened eyes encouraged her to keep talking. "Ever since I started working the night shift, Steppie gets anxious. He's a city dog. He's used to sirens and traffic, not fox screams and deer bawling. I've tried everything...crating him, a thunder shirt, lavender...nothing works. I don't want to sedate him. It'll make him dopey, and I don't want drugs in the house. I can't get a sitter because of the hours."

"What can I do to help?"

Her employment troubles would be solved if she could find Steppie a sitter. Someone nice and reliable.

"Assign a Deputy Marshal to handle Steppie while I work."

Etchers's chest and stomach started bouncing. That's how he laughed—never out loud.

"Ha! I'd take that assignment myself. Steppie's got it pretty good around here." The dog was sleeping on his stomach with four paws hanging on either side of the deputy's lap. "I can't get Steppie a handler, but I can give you some advice. I've had dogs all my life. They're sensitive creatures. He's probably picking up his anxiety from you. You need to work on controlling your emotions. Why don't you take up yoga or something?"

With a quick turn of the wrist, Happy flicked the gift certificate across the table. It hit Etchers in the chest. "Yoga? Are you kidding me? Maybe if you'd stop terrorizing me, I'd feel better. Every time you come around, you harp about me getting hunted down and killed. Now you've added FI's getting tortured to the nightmare. Yoga! Geez. Anyone ever tell you you're a jerk?"

His chest and stomach were bouncing again. He'd been teasing her.

"Why'd you upset me like that?" Happy sighed her exasperation. "That's just plain mean."

"C'mon, Happy, buck up." He stopped smiling. "I'll give you the point about the scare tactics. I'll try to watch it. But I worry about you. Right now, you're afraid, but most of the time, you act as if you don't understand the jeopardy you're in."

Of course, she did. She just couldn't accept a life of living in fear. Rather than exploding into another rant, she decided to pacify him. "How can I do better?"

"Do what I always tell you. Be mindful, careful, and keep your head down. I'm going to offer a suggestion, and I don't want you getting mad at me.

She nodded a *go ahead, say it* signal.

"Have you considered maybe Steppie's a wee bit spoiled? Leave him alone for a few nights. Put him in a room where he can't get into anything. He might howl at first, but he'll get used to it."

Happy had to admit that Steppie was spoiled rotten.

"I'll try it." She picked up the gift certificate. "If it doesn't work, he's getting a soothing mani-pedi."

Chapter 5

Jack called two days later. "Meet me in my office. Tonight. Eleven-thirty, sharp." The time struck her as odd. The work shift changed at midnight. From eleven-thirty to midnight, Garage A was a madhouse with drivers coming and going. She'd be waiting in the reception area full of mingling colleagues. Jack wanted to add humiliation to her punishment.

Her mind wandered to high school. It was soon after she finished rehab. A new school, a new start. A boy she liked invited her to Homecoming. Her mother made her a pretty dress. The day before Homecoming, the boy cancelled, explaining his mother didn't want him associating with a drug addict. She called her mother from the school's health room, crying.

The first words out of her mother's mouth were *shit, shit, shit.* Then she said, "Lucy, you are *not* going to walk around school with weepy eyes. Blow your nose. Wash your face. Put your chin up. You're going to behave like Xena, the Warrior Princess, even if you have to pretend. And...don't *ever* give that boy the time of day."

After disconnecting with Jack, she stroked the dog. "It'll be tough love for you tonight. You're gonna stay by yourself."

Steppie was quiet until she shut the front door. The ensuing howls haunted her—not howls, exactly, but terrified screams at a pitch she'd never heard. She ran to her 4Runner holding her hands over her ears. Once inside the SUV, she wondered if Bernie Singleton screamed as he lay dying. Did her mother scream while her killer chased her? Happy pressed her head against the steering wheel. *Don't think of it, don't think of it, don't think it.*

At eleven-thirty, Happy entered the garage. She sat with Zen-like serenity during the shift change. At twelve-fifteen, Jack called her into his office. The office was small. There was barely enough room for a desk and two chairs, much less two people having a conversation. The office had no window. It had a two-way radio, a filing cabinet, and a locker with Jack's name on it. The desk held a coffee cup, a pen, and two files. The place looked cluttered despite the minimal furnishings and supplies.

Jack pulled a chocolate-chip cookie out of a bag. He snapped off a hunk with his long teeth.

"I got your toxicology results. You passed. Now I need to decide what to do about you."

She breathed deep and said nothing.

"I specifically told you 'no dogs allowed.' You disobeyed my direct order. Is that a fair summary of what happened?"

"Yes, sir."

"Any explanations you'd like to offer?"

She wanted to say, *"Yes! I couldn't leave my dog alone and afraid. He got shot trying to protect my mother. I owe him."*

WITSEC silenced her. All she could say was, "No, sir."

"What if you'd hit someone who wasn't dead? Like some pedestrian walking on the shoulder. Even if the dog didn't cause the accident, the company would've been hit with a big, fat lawsuit. Maybe even run out of business. I can't ignore that."

She waited for the hammer to fall.

"I'm suspending you for thirty days, without pay."

Happy swallowed hard. It was now mid-February. "Snow season will be over by then."

"I know that. When your suspension is over, you'll go back to where you came from, working in the company's billing department."

"For how long?"

"For as long as you work for this company. Bad timing was the only thing that saved you from getting fired. Management doesn't want people thinking you got canned for plowing up a dead man. You're welcome to quit."

"I'm not going to quit." No sense crying over the matter. She'd taken a chance and intentionally disobeyed her boss, knowing the risk. It would be best to remain on good terms. "If there happens to be a weather emergency, call me. I'll come in, and when the emergency's over, I'll go back on suspension for the rest of the thirty days. OK?"

Jack shook his head. "Not happening."

The farther away Happy drove from the garage, the worse she felt. She didn't want to go back to billing. It was the most boring job she'd ever had. Even after she'd gotten her CDL license, it'd taken her six months to get out of that department. Jack would never let her plow again. He was done with her. She didn't blame him; she was done with Happy Holiday herself. Lucy Prestipino was fierce and persistent; she would've talked her way out of a suspension. Happy sat there, polite and quiet, like a passive fool.

When she arrived home, the house was eerily quiet; no enthusiastic barking greeted her. Where was Steppie? She launched a search and found him quivering under the sofa.

"Mom," she prayed while calming the dog. "I'm doing my best here. Please send me some help."

She decided to go to bed, put the covers over her head, and stay there. As she entered her bedroom, she spotted the rag doll. Pseudo Happy Holiday. She picked up doll and regarded its brown eyes. "I'm not *you*!"

No reply.

"Happy Holiday, get on outta here." She tossed the rag doll out of the bedroom.

A star-bangled quilt covered the bed. It was her first quilting effort. The squares weren't square, and the points didn't point, but the quilt was stuffed with batting. She snuggled under its warmth, simmering with regret. She hated the name "Happy Holiday." What was she thinking when she'd picked it?

She knew exactly what she'd been thinking. William Holiday was her Baltimore AA sponsor. He'd served as a special-ops parachutist with the 101st Airborne. She'd affectionately nicknamed him "Floater." He taught her how to fight and shoot; she loved him like a father. She gave herself his surname, so she could pretend she was his daughter.

WITSEC gave her a new life, a chance to forget the sorrows of her life in Baltimore. She named herself "Happy," believing if she said it enough times, she'd be happy. What a joke.

Happy lasted about five minutes under the covers. She couldn't sleep. Idling with nothing but her thoughts prompted a craving for alcohol. An

Irish car bomb would be perfect—a shot glass of Bailey's and Jameson Irish Whiskey dropped into a mug of Guinness stout. *Stop it!* She forced herself out of bed. It was three o'clock in the morning. She needed a distraction.

Happy downloaded the latest edition of the *Garrett County Republican.* Mr. Singleton's death notice appeared in the obituary section. He was a musician and composer. He'd taught music in Washington County's high schools and gave private lessons. The viewing was tomorrow, the funeral the day after.

She wanted to pay her respects to the Singleton family. A card or note wasn't good enough; it had to be in person. She wasn't sure how she'd be received, but it was important she try.

Chapter 6

Humphrey's Funeral Home was an elegant place. The Singleton family lived in Cumberland, Maryland, about forty minutes east of Deep Creek. The Victorian-style building was on a street lined with old, but well-kept houses in the heart of Cumberland. As Happy approached the parking lot, she spotted throngs of people walking toward the front door.

There were a surprising number of young people, maybe high-school age. The line of mourners extended to the sidewalk. Happy joined them, not knowing what she was supposed to do. The only viewing she'd ever attended was her mother's. She had little memory of it other than being hugged by a lot of forlorn people.

Once through the front door, she found a receiving line. Mourners were comforting family members. Mrs. Singleton stood between her two sons. She was a large woman, not in an overweight way, but tall and big-boned. Highlights streaked through her short, dark hair. She wore a black sheath dress, pearls, and a black cardigan sweater.

Happy recognized the expressions on Mrs. Singleton and the children. The faces were blank, except for dazed, polite smiles. Happy knew the look; a *Baltimore Sun* reporter had taken Happy's photograph as she walked away from her mother's funeral. When she saw it in the next day's paper, she didn't recognize herself. Small, faded, and zombie-like. She couldn't have identified her own self in a police lineup.

She thought about what to say to Mrs. Singleton when it was her turn to speak. Sorry I plowed up your husband? It didn't matter. Chances were good that Mrs. Singleton wouldn't remember anything said to her today.

Happy remembered few of the expressions of sympathy she'd received during the days following her mother's death.

Jimmy stood ahead of her, wearing his uniform. When he moved forward, his shoulders blocked her view of the Singleton family. Funny thing, she saw Jimmy nearly every day but never noticed his broad shoulders.

As Jimmy approached the casket, he removed his felt, Stetson hat. He leaned over and spoke to each child at eye level. Mrs. Singleton, who'd been stoically greeting visitors, wept when Jimmy put his arms around her shoulders. It occurred to Happy that Jimmy was more than an attentive law enforcement officer; he was a family friend.

Mrs. Singleton left the receiving line taking her children with her. The funeral home director announced the family was taking a brief break. The line dispersed with some mourners moving into a parlor room, others moving outside. Happy needed fresh air and followed the outside crowd.

There were two men standing on the sidewalk. They were in their early-fifties. Each wore a suit, tie, and various levels of hair coverage. At first, their conversation was quiet, but it became incrementally louder until the men were yelling at one another. "We have to tell her!" the bald one said. Happy was horrified. Who argues at a viewing? She moved toward the men with the intention of telling them to...well, she wasn't sure.

Jimmy beat her to it. He flew down the sidewalk and faced them.

"Show some respect," was all he said. His voice was calm, but there was a *don't tangle with me* edge behind it that silenced the men. They exchanged shameful glances and murmured a round of *sorries* before departing the premises.

Jimmy joined her. "So, what exactly were *you* planning to do?"

"No plan. Whatever it took to shut them up."

"Happy Holiday doing whatever it takes. Frightening."

His expression was serious, but his eyes glinted humor. Odd, she'd never noticed how blue his eyes were. They reminded her of Deep Creek Lake on a sunny, cloudless day. Maybe a paint company should name a sample chip, "Deep Creek Blue."

"I'm surprised to see you here," he said.

"I didn't know if I should come. My mother always said if you're not sure what to do, do the positive. So here I am."

He peered at something over Happy's left shoulder. "Mrs. Singleton is on her way over here."

Within seconds, the widow stood before them. She was nearly a head taller than Happy—a good five-eleven without heels. "Jimmy, please introduce me to your friend."

Jimmy did so. The widow's first name was "Olivia."

Mrs. Singleton appeared to recognize Happy's name. "Jimmy told me you found my husband. He said you held his hand while you waited for help."

Mrs. Singleton's eyes watered.

Happy's eyes watered, too. "I'm so very sorry for your loss."

Mrs. Singleton turned toward Jimmy. "I'm glad to see you without a big crowd around. I need to talk about my husband with someone who knew him. I don't understand how this happened. He wasn't a careless man. You know that about him, don't you, Jimmy?"

"I know him to be a responsible man. A good teacher and father. I don't understand how this happened either."

"He wasn't a drinker. The last time he had a drink was on our anniversary. Our twentieth, a little over five months ago. I keep thinking about it."

Jimmy was making motions to exit the conversation, but Happy sensed Mrs. Singleton wanted to reminisce. "You and Mr. Singleton must've had a nice celebration."

Mrs. Singleton showed a fleeting, soft smile. "He surprised me with a Smith Island cake. Do you know what that is?"

"I had a slice a long time ago," Happy said. "It was delicious."

"It's my favorite cake. Bernie was traveling and happened to find one. We ate it and washed it down with champagne."

The widow became quiet and pensive. "Ms. Holiday, when you found my husband...when you first saw him...could you tell if he suffered?"

Happy pictured the half-naked man, his mouth open, fingers distorted. Fear and desperation radiated from his eyes. Should she comfort Mrs. Singleton or tell her the truth? She hedged.

"I felt like he was trying to tell me something."

The color in Mrs. Singleton's face drained away. "What did he say?"

"He didn't say anything. He'd already passed before I found him. It was the expression on his face that made me think that. I kept talking to him, asking him questions, hoping he'd answer, praying he was still alive...but he wasn't."

Mrs. Singleton wandered away from the conversation and into the funeral home.

Jimmy slipped his arm around her waist and gave her a quick hug. "Tough question."

She wasn't sure she'd said the right thing. Sometimes avoiding the truth was the best of bad options. Her mother taught her that.

The viewing ended at three o'clock in the afternoon. Visitors streamed from the funeral home. Jimmy headed to work. Happy sat in her SUV for five minutes while her heart ached for Mrs. Singleton. She understood what the widow was going through. Happy had almost grieved herself to insanity when her mother died. She thought about her promise to Mr. Singleton, but what could she do to help his wife and children? She couldn't think of anything.

The cold steering wheel prompted her to reach for her gloves. Missing. Maybe they'd fallen to the floor of the coat room. She returned to the funeral home. She heard Mrs. Singleton weeping as she pulled open the front door. The woman was sitting in a wing-back chair, elbows on her knees and hands covering her face. The funeral director stood beside her resting his left hand on her right shoulder.

Mrs. Singleton looked up when Happy entered the room. Her eyes were swollen and red-rimmed. Blotches of sorrow covered her face. The woman tried to compose herself. Happy remembered the struggle to confine own tears of grief to private moments. She didn't want anyone feeling sorry for her. Mrs. Singleton was doing the same. Happy slipped into the matching wing-back chair next to Mrs. Singleton.

The widow mopped her tears with a tissue. "I thought everyone left."

"Everyone's gone except me. I came back for my gloves."

"You're right about Bernie trying to tell you something."

Happy's heart quickened. "What do you mean?"

"Bernie called me the night he died. He was on his way home from Pittsburgh. Every year, he meets up with his college friends to go to a Steelers game. He's crazy about those Steelers."

Happy remembered the game. She'd been wearing her long-sleeved Ravens shirt the night she'd found Bernie. "They played the Ravens that night."

"You're a football fan."

She nodded. "I like the Ravens."

Thirty seconds passed before Mrs. Singleton could continue. "The snow got bad, and he stopped to get some coffee, to wait out the storm. He was celebrating something, and whatever it was, it made him absolutely giddy. He wouldn't tell me over the phone. It had to be in person. I know this is silly, but that's all I've been thinking about."

"Did you tell Jimmy?"

The widow nodded. "The night he told me about Bernie. He didn't seem too interested. He promised to keep track of the police investigation and let me know if anything came up about the phone call."

"If Jimmy made a promise, he'll keep it."

Mrs. Singleton looked toward the front door and answered in a wistful voice. "Maybe."

"You don't believe him?"

The widow's gaze returned to Happy. "Did Jimmy tell you he took guitar lessons from Bernie? For five years. He came to our house every Wednesday after dinner. Bernie said Jimmy was the best student he ever had. One day, he called Bernie and quit." She threw up her hands. "Just like that. It was like he didn't want anything more to do with Bernie. He still doesn't."

Happy was appalled. That wasn't the Jimmy she knew. She couldn't let this nonsense go by without saying something. "Mrs. Singleton, Jimmy wanted to make sure you heard the awful news about your husband from a friend. He traveled in dangerous conditions to tell you, personally. He was terribly upset afterward. Today, he came to pay his respects. He didn't have to do any of that. He cares deeply about you and your sons."

Mrs. Singleton said nothing.

Happy broke the silence. "Have you considered hiring a private investigator?"

"Investigators cost money I don't have. It's silly to pay a lot of money to someone just to find out why my husband was so happy."

"It doesn't sound silly to me. I'd think it'd be a comfort to share someone's final happiness." Happy gently touched Mrs. Singleton on the arm. "Would you like me to ask around? I'm off from work for a while, and I live in the area."

Mrs. Singleton raised her eyebrows in surprise. "Why? Because you plowed up my husband's body? I don't blame you for that."

"Not long ago, someone close to me died. It was sudden. One day I was talking to her, the next day she was gone. I had so many questions. I thought I'd lose my mind if I didn't get answers. But people helped me. Some were friends; some were people I hardly knew. In the end, I got my answers. Helping you would be a way for me to pay it forward."

"Were you satisfied with the answers you got?"

"Satisfied? No...I hated the answers. But they gave me some peace."

Mrs. Singleton took Happy's hand and squeezed it. "I'd like you to find out what you can."

As Happy drove home, she decided not to tell Jimmy and Etchers what she was undertaking. She could hear it now: too risky, don't draw attention to yourself, Roach will find you, torture you, kill you. *Blah, blah, blah.* No, this time she was going to do the right thing—help the Singleton family. Besides, she was only looking into Bernie's surprise.

That's all.

Chapter 7

It was shortly after midnight. Happy's phone sounded the arrival of an e-mail with an attachment. Mrs. Singleton had done her homework; the e-mail described everything the widow could remember about her last conversation with her husband. Happy downloaded the attachment and found a full-body photograph of Bernie Singleton. His left hand held a calico cat, and his right hand pointed to an overturned Christmas tree.

When Bernie wasn't dead and frozen, he was attractive in a bad-boy sort of way. He could've passed for a perfect mash-up of the lead singer in a rock 'n' roll band and an uber-cool high school teacher. At fifty-years old, he was physically fit enough to look good in jeans. He wore his baldness boldly; no comb overs, fringe, or toupees. Dark eyes, olive skin. A mouth enhanced by a mischievous smile. A small, gold earring hung from his left ear.

Mrs. Singleton's recollections of the phone call were spotty. Bernie called his wife at eleven o'clock in the evening. He told her the roads were impassable; the snowplows couldn't keep ahead of the snow. He was in Somerset, Pennsylvania, waiting out the storm.

Mrs. Singleton heard a television in the background. There were voices and glasses tinkling. Bernie had something wonderful to tell her. An awesome surprise. She'd tried to guess. No guessing, he said—he'd tell her in person. He laughed. She begged him to stay put, to find a place to stay the night, and come home in the morning. He promised he would.

Happy searched online for a map of Somerset. The small town was a two-hour drive from Deep Creek. What kind of restaurant would have tinkling glasses and a television? A sports bar. Somerset had several. If Bernie were on his way home from Pittsburgh, he probably drove south on the Pennsylvania Turnpike. There was a sports bar close by the exit to Somerset.

She patted her dog, now on her lap. "Steppie, tomorrow we're taking a road trip."

The dog answered with an ear-splitting series of barks, whines, and yaps. A siren sounded a short whoop. Blue and red lights flashed. It was Jimmy. The dog continued his excited antics as the patrol car made its way down the driveway. She opened the door.

Jimmy sloughed the snow from his boots against the threshold. "Quiet, Steppie."

The dog went silent. Happy shook her head in amazement. "How do you do that?"

Jimmy answered with a blasé shrug. Once inside, he used one foot to anchor the heel of the other while he slipped off his boots. Off came his hat, gloves, and coat. Steppie trailed him into the kitchen. Jimmy had worry written all over his face.

"What's wrong?" she said.

He leaned against the kitchen counter. "I heard Jack suspended you."

She let out a mournful sigh. Sometimes Deep Creek was too damned small. In Baltimore, she could do anything she wanted. If it wasn't a crime, no one would know or care. She reported only to her own conscience.

"For thirty days. You're not surprised, are you?" She opened the refrigerator and gathered leftover vegetables, rice, and meat from the refrigerator. "Are you hungry?"

"Why didn't you tell me?"

Jimmy's inquisitive eyes made her squirm. "Are you hungry or not?"

"I thought—"

"Stop!"

She disengaged by moving to the living area. Jimmy continued leaning against the kitchen counter until she took a seat on the sofa. He joined her on the sofa, took her hand and held it. "C'mon, Happy. I thought we were friends."

He kept his silence while she took a few deep breaths. She hated Happy Holiday. Lucy would go on a nice, long bike ride until she got the blues out of her system. Her comforting bike rides were over; Etchers made her give them up. "It's your distinguishing feature," he said. "Roach will be on the lookout for a pretty, elite bicyclist."

Honestly, she wasn't sure why she was feeling unsettled. She'd known she would be suspended; she was lucky she wasn't fired. Maybe it was the day's painful reminders of her mother. She focused on her right hand, now nestled in Jimmy's left. It was the first time he ever held her hand. She liked it. His hand was large, warm, and strong. It felt nice. She knew from the sturdy grip he wouldn't let go until she asked him to.

"Don't you get tired of all my drama?" she said. "I do, and it's *my* drama."

He brought her hand to his lips and gave it a peck. "No."

She turned to face him. "I don't want to lean on you for everything. It makes me feel…icky…like I'm helpless and dependent."

Jimmy's lips curved upward. "You're not helpless and dependent; that's for sure. It's all right to lean on me."

"You say that now. Just wait—Etchers keeps telling me I'm trouble."

Jimmy's smile turned wide. "Deep Creek is a small town. I could use some trouble. It makes life interesting."

"Friendship is a two-way street, you know."

His blue eyes registered surprise. "What do you mean?"

"You took guitar lessons from Bernie Singleton. For five years, no less. Why didn't you tell me?"

"I was worried about you. You seemed overwhelmed. Who wouldn't be? I didn't want to add to it."

"Why did you stop taking lessons?"

Jimmy's eyebrows furrowed together as if he were confused. "Baseball. When I was fifteen, I went to a baseball camp and loved it. I quit the guitar, so I could play ball. How did you know I took guitar lessons?"

"I talked to Mrs. Singleton after the viewing. She also told me about the last phone call she had with Bernie. Why aren't you helping her figure out Bernie's surprise? She said she asked you to."

Jimmy released her hand. "Oh, geez…I'm the only cop in my family, in my neighborhood, and in my church. People come to me all the time, wanting me to investigate something. It's always the same—I go down a rabbit hole, only to end up with nothing but disappointment and frustration. That's what'll happen here, I guarantee you. He probably bet on the game and won. Maybe he was just a happy drunk. If there's anything to find out, the investigators will find it. But no matter what they turn up, it won't change the fact that Bernie Singleton is dead."

Happy knew there was more to the story of Jimmy and Bernie. Never had Jimmy used so many words to answer a question. She didn't mind Jimmy keeping his secrets; she had her own.

Her most shameful secret had to do with money. She had a lot of it—over two million dollars. Her mother's death had landed Happy a hefty life-insurance payoff. It was tucked away in an investment account that Happy refused to touch.

Blood money, as far as she was concerned. She told no one about it.

Chapter 8

It was eleven o'clock the next morning. Happy traveled north on New Germany Road toward Somerset, Pennsylvania. She had alternative routes available but intentionally chose to repeat her snowplow route. The sun was bright and warm enough to melt any snow residuals. The road was wet. Passing cars sprayed slush against the windshield of her 4Runner.

Steppie watched the scenery from his perch in the passenger seat. Driving in daylight on a snow-cleared New Germany Road struck her as unnatural. It was a completely different road—the yellow center lines were clearly visible, as were the road's edges. The sun shimmered through the forest's trees. Even the deer stayed in their wooded territory.

Her hands sweated as she approached the spot where Bernie had taken his last breath. It looked like any other part of the road, except for a memorial wreath hanging on a nearby tree. She parked on the road's shoulder, wiped her hands on her coat, and stood before the wreath. How could Bernie have died like that? Happy dismissed the question from her mind. She'd go crazy trying to answer it. Finding explanations was up to police investigators. Her only mission was to uncover Bernie's surprise.

She walked a half-mile on the shoulder, first heading north, crossing the road, then heading south. What she was looking for, she didn't know. The police would've recovered anything important—the cell phone, his wallet, the clothes he'd stripped from his body.

On the night Bernie died, Jimmy told her the investigators found Bernie's Explorer two miles away from his body. He didn't say exactly where. Maybe it would be obvious as she neared the area. She returned to her 4Runner.

Two miles later, her eyes caught the flicker of a single strand of yellow crime-scene tape. She'd seen that tape before. In Baltimore—inside Patterson Park, to be exact. She'd biked to the park to find her mother. Instead, she found homicide detectives and Rick McCormick, the ambitious gang prosecutor she grew to detest.

There was a muddy area not far from the yellow tape, surrounded by footprints. Deep tire tracks led from the muddy area to the road. This had to be the area where the police found the Explorer. She guessed a tow truck had made the tracks. Why didn't Bernie buy gas? It was a terrible night. Jimmy said he was a responsible man. It would make more sense if Bernie lost his gas after hitting something that damaged the vehicle's gas tank.

She dropped to her hands and knees and began sniffing the ground. It was cold and soggy. The mud oozed through her fingers as she moved around the area. Her hair fell forward into her face. She brushed it back vowing to add a hair barrette to her 4Runner's emergency equipment kit.

Her attention turned to the sound of an approaching vehicle. A Dodge Ram truck parked behind her 4Runner. Alarmed, she jumped to her feet and instinctively put her hand on her chest to verify the presence of the gun hanging between her breasts in a flash bang holster. She didn't intend to draw her weapon—not yet, anyway.

A chubby, bearded man with a weathered complexion exited the truck. "Ms. Holiday?"

She didn't acknowledge him. The man looked familiar, but she couldn't place him. He had thin lips and fat jowls. Green eyes squinted from beneath a red and black plaid flannel hat. His brand of coat was Faded Glory, most likely purchased from Walmart. His jeans were baggy and dragged on the ground as he walked toward her.

"I'm Milo Sullivan. I'm a substitute driver for Mountain Lake Landscaping."

Happy held out her hand and immediately withdrew it when she saw the mud caked between her fingers. She gave herself a quick once-over. Mud smeared her arms, knees, and shoes. "You must think I'm crazy rummaging around in the mud like this."

"No, I don't." He gave her a sympathetic smile. "I come here every day."

"Did you know Bernie Singleton?"

"No. I worked the shift before you came on duty." Milo's voice wavered. "I keep wondering how many times I passed that dying man and didn't see him. Had to be three or four times…I could've saved him." He cleared his throat. "I'm sorry this fell on you. It should've been me."

"If Bernie Singleton was in a place where he could've been found, you would've found him. And that's the truth."

A sedan passed them on the road. Happy and Milo greeted the driver with a wave, as was customary in Deep Creek. The driver returned it.

"If that's the truth, why are you here?" Milo said.

"I'm not sure…just trying to make some sense of it, I guess. I'm mystified about the gas. A responsible family man drives into a snowstorm without filling up. Does that make sense to you?"

"I heard he was drinking."

"I heard that, too. The thing is, he drove from Pittsburgh, got to Somerset and called his wife. He wasn't intoxicated when he made that phone call. I thought maybe he hit something and lost his gas."

"Does it matter why he didn't have gas? Either way, he's dead."

"I suppose you're right." Happy brushed some mud from the knees of her pants. "Anyway, I thought I would sniff things out. Literally."

Steppie began barking and pawing the window.

Milo smiled. "There was an office pool about how long it would take Jack to bust you for driving with your dog."

"Everyone knew?"

"Everyone but Jack."

"Well, thank them for not ratting me out." She looked toward Steppie. "He's lonesome. Want some hot chocolate? I have a thermos in the car."

Happy stashed Steppie into the back seat to make room for Milo. She poured the hot chocolate and topped it off with a squirt of whipped cream she kept in a cooler in the SUV's cargo area. She handed it to Milo, now in the passenger seat. "Want a biscotti to go with it?"

"Sure." He grinned. "You have a regular café in here."

She handed him a biscotti, broke another in half, and tossed half into the back for Steppie.

"Happy, I'm sorry you got busted for your dog, but I'm glad you're the one who found that poor soul. I heard you took real good care of him that night."

"Where'd you hear that?"

"I have a friend on the rescue squad. He said they found a blanket on the man. Something tells me you're still looking after him."

Milo's words warmed her heart. They were the first sweet ones she'd heard from anyone at Mountain Lake Landscaping. No one ever disrespected her, but she was an outsider. A young woman in an occupation dominated by men. A lifetime city resident plopped into a rural community. A protected witness forced to keep her head down and her mouth shut. Try as she might, she could never find a common denominator for a meaningful conversation.

She handed Milo another biscotti. "Tell the drivers they can visit my café any time."

Milo's eyes focused on Happy, then Steppie, then back to Happy. He seemed to be working out a puzzle inside his head. "You've had a hard time of it, haven't you?"

He was staring at her, with the kindest eyes she'd ever seen. She wanted to tell him about Romero Sanchez, the criminal she once loved, and about Rick McCormick, the prosecutor who tried to strong arm her into becoming an informant. But mostly, she wanted to tell him how much she missed her mother. She could say nothing.

"Who won the office pool?' she said.

"I did."

"How much?"

He grinned and opened the passenger door. "Thanks for the hot chocolate." When he had one foot on the ground, he turned. "Happy, don't worry about your job. You'll get it back after Jack cools down."

Happy finished her mud-sniffing without detecting a whiff of gas. She drove out of the forest, turned right onto Chestnut Ridge Road, and eventually crossed over Interstate 68. From there it was a straight shot on Route 219 to Somerset, Pennsylvania.

A question occurred to her. If Bernie was driving home from Somerset, why didn't he merge onto I-68 toward Cumberland? Instead, he crossed over the interstate and drove into the forest. What was his destination? Maybe he missed the interstate entrance because he was drunk and disoriented.

After a few miles, Happy discovered Route 219 was *not* a straight shot to Somerset. It was winding, mountainous, and at some points, very steep. Portions of the road were under construction. Sometimes the blind, circular merges put her on roads without yellow lines. She drove cautiously, hugging the right shoulder, in the event she was unknowingly driving on a two-way highway.

The road wasn't all bad—there were interesting sights. She passed near a farm of magnificent wind turbines, so close she thought she could touch them. A few miles later, there was a series of towering concrete piers on her left. She guessed they belonged to a superstructure bridge, yet to be completed.

As she entered Somerset County, Route 219 became "Flight 93 Memorial Highway." Happy's throat tightened as she remembered the courageous passengers and crew of United Flight 93. On September 11, 2001, Al Qaeda terrorists hijacked the plane to use as a bomb against the U.S. Capitol. The passengers and crew lost their lives resisting the hijackers. During their brave effort, the plane crashed into a small field near Shanksville, Pennsylvania. She promised herself to soon visit the Flight 93 Memorial.

She arrived at the Borough of Somerset. As she waited at a red light, she came to the unmistakable conclusion that a drunk Bernie Singleton couldn't have driven that route. She doubted even the hand of God could have spared him from a crash.

Happy passed through the town toward the Pennsylvania Turnpike. She found N. Center Street, which accessed the turnpike, both east and west. She spotted a Ruby Tuesday restaurant, parked, and made her inquiries.

"We were closed during the storm," the hostess said. "Try the Somerset Bar and Grill. I heard it was open that night. Down the street, on the left."

She spotted the bar a block away. It was a stand-alone, red-brick building that had seen its better day. From the curb, it looked like a typical sports bar, except for a hand-written poster taped to a window of the wooden front door. *Closed.*

Happy stood on tiptoes and strained to see inside the bar. The lights were on. A soap opera was playing on a flat-screened TV hanging on the wall. The place was deserted, except for a young woman covering table vases with newspaper and putting them into a cardboard box.

Happy pushed on the door. It wasn't locked.

The woman stood, and with a screaming, "*screw you,*" hurled a dish straight at Happy.

Chapter 9

Happy ducked. The dish sailed over her head and smashed against the door. Dish shards rained on her head and shoulders before landing on her feet. When the glass storm ended, Happy found herself in a crouched position peeking through her fingers.

She stood and shouted. "What the hell? The door was open!"

The woman ran to her. "I'm sorry! I'm sorry! It was an accident."

Happy began picking glass out of her hair. "Accident? You threw that dish at me on purpose."

"I *did* throw it on purpose. I just didn't mean to throw it at you. I didn't know you were there. Oh, God! Are you hurt?"

Happy gave the woman a quick look to make sure she wasn't armed. She was more of a girl than a grown woman, maybe in her late teens. Her platinum-blonde hair was teased into the texture of a cotton ball. Brown eyes were red-rimmed, and mascara streaked her cheeks. Silver chandelier earrings dangled to her shoulders. The name tag on her apron identified her as "Christine." No apparent weapons.

"No…I'm all right." Happy brushed the glass from her coat. "Why are you throwing dishes in the first place?"

Christine slid into a booth covered with balled-up paper napkins. She took a few breaths before launching an angry tirade. "I'm totally pissed-off. That's why. I've worked here since I was fifteen." She held up her right hand with her thumb and forefinger nearly pinching one another. "I was this close to having enough money to get my own place, and now I'm out of a job."

"That really sucks."

"Yeah, it does." She pulled a fresh napkin from the dispenser and wiped her eyes. "This morning, I came in and found the 'closed' sign and a note telling me to pack up my shit and get out. They didn't even tell me in person. A stinkin' note, that's all I got."

"Your bosses sound like jerks."

"Al and Zeke Hershberger. Assholes is what they are. There are no good jobs around here, and I'm sick and tired of living with my aunt Violet. And she's sick and tired of me living with her. Now we're glued to one another with no end in sight."

Happy stretched for a coffee cup on a nearby table and handed it to Christine. "Here."

Christine stood as if she were on a pitcher's mound, wound up, and hurled the cup underhanded across the diner. The cup soared through the door's window. She turned to Happy, smiling.

"Nice arm." Happy meant it.

"I used to pitch for my high school softball team. We won State."

"Cool." Happy held out her hand. "By the way, I'm Happy Holiday."

Christine shook the offered hand and giggled. "That's a funny name. Were your parents stoned when they named you? Do you know you're covered with mud? I'm Christine White."

Happy had forgotten about the mud. She picked up the metal napkin dispenser and checked her reflection. Mud was smeared all over her face. She ignored the questions—she didn't feel like explaining either the mud or her name. "I'm here about a customer who came in on the night of the big snowstorm."

Happy fired up her cell phone, pulled up the photograph of Bernie Singleton and showed it to Christine. "Do you remember him? I think he stopped in here on the way to Cumberland."

Christine studied the photograph while fiddling with an earring. "I remember him. How come you're asking?"

"He died on the way home. I'm here on behalf of his widow."

Christine's hand flew to her mouth. "He died? How?"

"Froze to death."

A man wearing jeans and a Steelers sweatshirt burst through the front door. He was oversized in every way, especially his stomach. With his reddish complexion and swath of white hair on head and face, he was a ringer for Santa Claus.

"Goddammit, Christine! What did you do here?"

Christine crumbled into the booth, put her head on the table, and cried into her folded arms. "Al—"

"We showed up at the same time," Happy said. "This is how we found it. Somebody must've broken in."

Al turned to Happy. "Who are you?"

"Happy Holiday."

"Ms. Holiday, we're closed. Can't you read?"

Christine glanced up from her crying spell. "Al, do you remember the customer who came in here the night it was snowing so bad? He's dead, frozen to—"

"I know, I know. The cops were here. I didn't tell you because I knew you'd get upset." He kicked a half-broken dish on the floor. "Why do you think I'm getting rid of this goddamn place? The recession nearly bankrupting us, Zeke getting pneumonia, and then that man dying after leaving here. This cussed place." Al looked at the broken door window and the glass pieces on the floor. "And now a break-in."

He turned his attention to Happy. "What's your interest in this?"

"I'm helping out the man's widow. She asked me to look into a phone call he made while he was here."

"I don't remember no phone call. That's what I told the cops."

"What's the story with the phone call?" Christine said to Happy.

"The man told his wife he had a surprise but wouldn't tell her anything about it. He wanted to tell her in person. It would be a comfort to her to find out what it was. Did you have a conversation with him?"

Christine wiped her eyes. "Not much of one. When he came in, he said he was glad we were open. We talked about the nasty weather. Then he sat at a table and ordered a cup of coffee. That's all he said to me. Then he moved to the bar. He was watching TV. Don't you remember that, Al? You were talking to him."

"I remember him being at the bar, watching TV. I don't know nothin' about any phone call he made. My brother got sick that night. Zeke... he's the cook, and he left early. I spent the night running back and forth between the bar and the kitchen. The only call I remember was the one I made to the Pleasant View Inn, right down the street. I told the man not to drive. I made a room reservation for him. I told all this to the cops."

"Was anyone else here at the time, like any customers or other employees?"

"Just Zeke. He wasn't here for long, getting sick and all."

"Where's Zeke?" Happy said. "Maybe he heard something you didn't."

"He's in the hospital. Like I said, he's got pneumonia. He's too sick to talk to anybody. He couldn't have heard anything. He was in the kitchen all night, coughing up his lungs until he went home."

Happy directed the conversation back to Christine. "How long was the customer at the bar?"

"I don't know. About an hour, maybe more. He was—"

Al took a step closer to Happy, occupying some of her personal space. "Miss, as the door sign says, we're closed. I'm real sorry about the man who died, but we have a lot of cleanup to do. Please give the widow-woman my sympathy."

"How can I reach Zeke?"

Al walked to the door and opened it. "I'm asking you nicely to leave. If I have to ask again, I'm calling the cops."

She left.

Happy smiled to herself as she opened the 4Runner's door. Al was a bully, and she was glad she spooked him. She knew about the dram law from her drinking days. Bartenders were liable for damages to third parties for accidents caused by customers who were over-served alcohol. Maryland didn't have a dram law, but Pennsylvania did. She wondered whether the widow of the intoxicated person counted as a third party. Al could probably see a lawsuit flying his way.

Happy glanced at the ramshackle bar. A lawsuit wouldn't do Mrs. Singleton much good. Even if the widow won, she probably wouldn't collect anything. From the looks of it, the bar and anyone associated with it was probably judgment-proof. She spotted Christine walking toward her 4Runner.

Happy lowered her window. Christine squealed when she saw Steppie. The dog shot across Happy's lap and stuck his head out the window. Christine held out her hand. "Hello there. Who are you?" Steppie licked his introduction.

"His name's Steppie. It's short for Steppenwolf."

Christine kissed the dog's head. "I used to have a dog like this. When he died, my aunt Violet wouldn't let me have another one."

Steppie's front half was now hanging out the window while he stretched for Christine. Happy clung to his torso to keep him from falling. "Christine, come inside and visit for a while."

When Christine slid into the passenger seat, Steppie became nearly apoplectic with joy. The dog curled his way into her lap.

"Did you remember something, Christine?"

"I remembered the man was really nice. He gave me a twenty-dollar tip on a cup of coffee."

Christine reached into her coat pocket and handed Happy a piece of paper. "Here's the hospital information where Zeke's at. Don't tell anyone I gave it to you. If Al finds out, he'll give me a bad job reference."

"Thanks. When Mr. Singleton was at the bar, did he and Al talk much?"

Christine cuddled with the dog. "They mostly watched the weather on TV."

"What was Mr. Singleton drinking when he was at the bar?"

"Coffee. He brought his cup from the table. I saw Al give him a refill."

"Did he ever seem intoxicated to you?"

"No. Al's very careful about how much alcohol he serves people. He got sued one time."

Jimmy was probably right. This investigation was going nowhere. A waste of time.

Christine let out a sweet laugh. She was playing patty-cake with Steppie's paws. Maybe this excursion wasn't a waste of time, after all. If Happy got her job back, she'd need a dog sitter. She evaluated Christine's appearance. Good teeth, nice skin. Well-groomed. Clear eyes. No track marks. Chances were good she wasn't an addict or a criminal. She liked Christine; maybe they could help each other.

"Christine, would you consider a job being a sitter for Steppie? I work nights. He's a good dog, but he's afraid to be by himself when it's dark out. All you need to do is keep him company, feed him, and walk him. The hours are eleven-thirty at night to nine in the morning. You can live with me if you want. I'll give you room and board, plus minimum wage. You would still have time for a day job or school if you want to."

Christine's eyes grew large. "Really? You mean it? Where do you live?"

"I live in Deep Creek, and I absolutely mean it. There are some rules, though. No smoking, drugs, or alcohol inside or around the house. And no matter how mad you get, you can't throw dishes or anything else. Are you OK with that?"

Christine was more than OK with it; she agreed to move in the day after tomorrow.

After Christine exited the car, Happy read her note. Zeke was in Laurel Hill Hospital, about four miles west of Somerset. Happy considered a visit until she called the patient information line. Zeke was in intensive care. ICCU visitors needed permission from the charge nurse. No dogs allowed. She didn't want to leave Steppie in the car, out of her sight, for the time it would take to have a productive conversation. She'd come back later, alone.

On the way home, Happy called Etchers and requested a background check on Christine. He was pleased. "You're getting the hang of WITSEC. If there's anything negative about Ms. White, we'll find it."

"What do I tell her about me being in WITSEC?"

"You tell her nothing. Not a thing."

"Why? Doesn't she have a right to know? If I'm at risk, so is she."

"You're not at risk as long as your identity is secret. Understand? Do not reveal yourself to her, ever. Are you clear on that?"

Happy said she was clear but felt sick saying so.

Chapter 10

Two days later, Christine sent Happy a text message; she'd be arriving within an hour. Happy fluffed the pillows on Christine's bed, positioned a bouquet of flowers on the night table, and set the correct time on the wall clock. Christine's background check had turned up nothing. Etchers approved of the dog-sitter.

Happy was delighted. Not only could she return to work without dog worries, but there was also the possibility of female friendship. Other than her mother, Happy's closest girlfriend had been Mary Louise O'Brian, AKA "Crackhead." She'd earned her nickname by fracturing her skull during a delivery. Mary Louise was a world-renowned bicycle messenger, having won competitions at the Cycle Messenger World Championship three years in a row.

Did Mary Louise compete last year in Montreal? The question took Happy back to her Baltimore messenger days. She was with her redheaded messenger friend, Fireball. They were straddling their bikes, waiting at a red light on Charles Street, competing in their own track stand contest. Their feet were on both pedals, daring one another to put a foot on the ground. The winner was the biker who balanced the longest. Bragging rights was the only prize, and it could shift as early as the next light. Fireball let go of his handlebars. "Look at me, Lucy." He used hands to sweep his Fabio-like red hair into a bun and secure it with a rubber band, all the while keeping his balance. "Girl, you are toast."

She blinked her eyes shut and willed herself to stop reminiscing about her old life. *Look forward,* like Jimmy says. She concentrated on the joyful possibility of a new female friend.

No more fussing with the house. Jimmy and his older brother, Matthew, would be arriving within thirty minutes to help with the move.

Happy settled on the sofa with her phone. She owed Olivia Singleton a progress report. She'd been procrastinating because there was no progress to report. Happy could hear her mother's voice running through her head, "Stewin' ain't doin'!"

The widow said nothing as Happy told her no one overheard the telephone conversation she had with her husband or knew of anything leading up to it. Mrs. Singleton's silence bothered her. Wanting to report something nice about Bernie, Happy mentioned the twenty-dollar tip he gave the waitress on a cup of coffee. She expected Mrs. Singleton to be pleased to learn of her husband's generosity.

Mrs. Singleton huffed. "Let me guess. The waitress was young, pretty, and big-boobed."

A flare shot from Happy's stomach to her mouth. "The waitress was a hard-working woman who served a cup of coffee to a stranded customer during a God-awful snow—"

"I'm sorry." Mrs. Singleton's voice cracked. "Please forgive me. I'm not myself."

Regret extinguished Happy's flare. "No, I'm sorry. You're allowed to be as angry as you want over anything."

Fifteen long seconds passed before Mrs. Singleton replied. "My husband was a Peter Pan. He never grew up...no sense of money or financial responsibility. It was a problem throughout our marriage. When you told me about the twenty-dollar tip, it triggered something in me."

"Mrs. Singleton, I wouldn't have brought it up if I knew it would add to your sorrow. Do you want me to keep looking? I haven't spoken to his college friends yet. Maybe they know something."

"I think they know a lot."

"How so?"

Mrs. Singleton began to cry. "In many ways, they were closer to my husband than I was."

"Have you asked them about your husband's surprise?"

"I tried, but they wouldn't talk about it. It's all so painful. I haven't heard from them since the viewing. I think they're avoiding me. They don't know what to say."

"Do you blame them for your husband's death?"

She answered in a teary voice laced with anger and bitterness. "No, Bernie's the one who forgot to get gas. He's the one who got drunk and didn't stay put like I told him to. The blame for Bernie's death is on him, no one else."

Jimmy and Matthew could pass for twins, although Matthew was two years older than Jimmy's twenty-seven. They shared the same blondish-red hair and penetrating blue eyes. It was their voices that distinguished them. Matthew's was light and cheerful; Jimmy's was the voice of command. Everyone listened to Jimmy and did what he said, even Happy. Which was why she didn't tell Jimmy she met Christine in Somerset or that she went to Somerset to check out Bernie's surprise.

"So, how did you find Christine?" Jimmy said. "Did Etchers help you?"

Dammit. He always knew what she was thinking. Maybe she should stop thinking when Jimmy was around.

"Etchers was a big help."

Steppie ran to the door, barking and spinning. A blue Honda Civic eased down the driveway. Christine stepped from the car wearing the silver chandelier earrings that glittered through her cottony hair. Happy made the introductions ending with, "Christine, where are your things?"

Christine fidgeted with her earrings. "My aunt Violet is driving the rental truck. We were ready to go when Al called wanting me to get my things from the diner. Violet went to get them, and I drove separately so I wouldn't be late." She looked at Jimmy and Matthew. "I'm sorry for the delay. Thanks for helping me move in."

"You're welcome," Jimmy said. "How did you and Happy meet?"

"She came by the restaurant where I used to work."

"Which one?"

Happy got nervous. She kept telling herself Jimmy was her friend, not her nanny. She didn't have to report every detail of her life to him.

"Somerset Bar and Grill."

Jimmy's eyes shifted to Happy's, loaded with a hundred questions. She was saved from answering by the sight of a U-Haul truck crawling down the driveway.

"There's Aunt Violet," Christine said.

The truck was huge—twenty-five feet long, minimum. Happy would've bet good money she could pack the contents of her entire house inside of it. Christine seemed to shrink as the truck drew closer. She toyed with her earrings and gazed at the garden bird bath, now filled with ice.

The driver's door opened. Four-inches of a stiletto boot heel appeared first, followed by a left leg that seemed miles long. It was covered in a skin-tight black legging that emerged beneath a black leather coat.

The Bittinger men appeared gob smacked as the whole of Violet alighted from the truck. She was a svelte blonde who looked to be in her early thirties. Happy vowed to learn how to exit a vehicle the way Violet just did. She wondered if she could achieve the same dazzling effect while climbing out of a snowplow.

Violet glided across the driveway toward the group. She smiled as if she were about to be photographed. "It's a big day for you, Christine. You finally get to live on your own. Be polite and introduce me to your friends."

Christine froze, apparently forgetting everyone's name.

Jimmy introduced himself and his brother.

Violet flashed the brothers a sultry look. "I'm very glad to meet you. I was afraid I'd have to unpack the truck wearing these." She placed her stiletto-heeled boot forward, touching Jimmy's shoe and displaying the full length of her leg.

Happy had seen the woman for less than two minutes but had the urge to punch her in the face. She'd never learned how to flirt. It was silly; that's what her mother always said. Be clear and direct. That's how to get what you want. Whenever Happy wanted sex with a man, she just said so. It worked every time.

Happy put her leg forward until her foot, wearing scuffed-up boots, touched Violet's boot and Jimmy's shoe. "I'm Happy, your niece's employer. Nice boots."

"Thanks." Violet lifted her foot an inch off the ground. "I got them on sale at Nordstrom."

"I got mine on sale at the 219 Flea Market."

Violet released a smoky laugh. "I wish Christine told me your driveway was tar and chip. I feel very unbalanced."

Happy could see the family resemblance. Violet was the same make and model as her niece, only fancier. "I understand you're Christine's aunt."

Violet swayed. She touched Jimmy's arm, ever so slightly. "Oops. Lost my balance for a second."

"Next time you're in Nordstrom, you should buy gravity boots," Happy said.

"It's getting late," Matthew said. "Let's get to it."

Matthew walked away from the conversation. When he raised the truck's back gate, he shot a look at Happy. There was something about his disturbed facial expression that drew her to him.

When she reached the back of the truck, she glanced inside but noticed nothing. All she could see was Jimmy laughing at whatever Violet was saying to him. She had never seen him flirt. What a disappointment—Jimmy was just another man smitten by a skinny blonde.

"Jimmy," Matthew said.

Jimmy sauntered to the back of the truck, smiling until he faced Happy. The smile disappeared. "Why the snark?" he whispered.

Snark? She hadn't been snarky. She was mentally crafting a sarcastic response when she saw Jimmy's jaw drop. What was he looking at? She shifted her attention to the inside of the truck. It was crammed with file cabinets, loose papers, stacks of magazines, newspapers, American Girl dolls, calendars, and bags of flour. As she stared at the endless contents, she remembered Al's nasty note to Christine, "Pack up your shit and get out."

Happy felt sick. From the looks of it, her home was about to become a landfill.

A large Hefty bag rolled off the truck. Jimmy picked it up, peeked inside, and showed it to Happy. The bag was stuffed with dryer lint. "This is bad," he said. "What're you going to do?"

Violet was now standing beside Happy. "Whatever you're going to do, Christine isn't coming back to my house. I don't mean to sound harsh, but she needs to live on her own." With that, Violet walked back to Christine, gave her a quick hug, and took the car keys. She spoke across the driveway to Happy. "When you're done, call me. I'll come back and get the truck." A moment later, Violet zoomed off.

Happy didn't know who she was most angry at—Christine, Violet, or herself. Why didn't she investigate Christine a little more? *Always know who you're dealing with.* She'd learned that hard lesson from Romero.

She couldn't look at Jimmy. If he said anything that started with the words *you should have,* using either his voice or his eyes, he'd end up being the unjustified target of her anger. Jimmy's arm slipped around her waist. She felt no judgment or criticism. She leaned against his shoulder.

He kissed the top of her head. "What do you want us to do?"

"Set fire to the truck."

She felt a silent chuckle rise in his chest. The chuckle pruned away her budding despair. "I need to talk to Christine. Go home. I'll call if I need you."

How could Christine's hoarding have gotten past WITSEC? Maybe hoarding wasn't considered a negative.

Now it was Etchers she wanted to punch.

Chapter 11

Christine sat slumped on the step of the deck's walkway leading to the house. She stared straight ahead, hands folded in her lap. No tears, no watery eyes. She didn't turn her face when Happy sat beside her. There was no sound except for the harsh cawing of an overhead crow.

Christine broke the silence. "Have you changed your mind?"

"I don't want to. We need to figure something out." Happy stood. "Want some cake?"

Christine followed Happy to the kitchen and plopped into a chair at the table. Her eyes settled on the tall cake sitting on a glass cake stand in the middle of the table. "What kind of cake is that?"

"A Smith Island cake."

"Never heard of it."

"I'm not surprised. It's named after a little island in the Chesapeake Bay. Not many people west of the Bay Bridge know about it. For some reason, the cake seems to be a big secret. You can't even buy it around here. I hope you like it. I got the recipe off the internet."

Happy sliced through ten thin layers of vanilla cake, iced with chocolate frosting. She'd embellished the top of the cake with fresh strawberries. As she handed the slice to Christine, she smiled with pride. "Want some coffee to go with it?"

Christine nodded as she scanned the kitchen and the great room. "It's really pretty in here. Your cake is pretty, too."

"Thanks. After we eat, I'll show you to your bedroom."

Happy poured Christine's coffee and took a seat with her own serving of cake and coffee. Christine picked at the cake as if a single wrong bite would explode and take her head off. Happy didn't want to prolong Christine's anxiety. The hoarding issue had to be settled, here and now.

"Christine, the thing is...I'm a neat-nick. Clutter makes me crazy. I have a shed in the back. If we store most of your things there, do you think you can keep the house neat?"

"Will my things be safe?"

"The shed's got a sturdy lock. No one's ever broken in. You can't store food, birdseed...anything like that. Mice and chipmunks will get into it. Bears, too, if you're not careful. There's no electricity. If your things can't stand the cold, you can rent a storage unit in Oakland. My house must be kept orderly. Can you live with that?"

Christine stopped eating. "Bears?"

"There's wildlife all around, that's the beauty of this place. I'll teach you how to be safe...So what do you think?"

"I'll try."

"Christine, 'trying' is a deal breaker. You have to do it."

"I'll do it."

"Good."

Christine stared at the fork in her hand. "I'm sorry I didn't tell you about how much stuff I have."

Happy gathered her courage for her first foray into a real friendship with Christine. "I have something I should've told you, too. I hope when you hear it, you won't change your mind about living here." Happy's heart beat faster as Christine's eyes got wider. "I started drinking when I was thirteen. I was a full-on alcoholic and drug addict by the time I was fifteen. I've been clean and sober for almost eight years."

Christine sat without sound or motion. After interminable minutes passed, she said, "How'd you get over it?"

"A juvenile court judge ordered me into rehab. I got counseling. I go to AA. I'm careful who I hang with." Happy sipped her coffee. "It's still hard. Sometimes, it's really hard. I'll never get over my addictions, but I learned to manage them day-by-day...that's why I can't have any drugs or alcohol anywhere on the property, not even cooking wine...so, do you still want to stay here? I really want you to."

Christine nodded. "Maybe we can help each other."

"Maybe we can." Happy wanted to hug her. "All right, then. Let me tell you more about the house. I have a security system. The neighborhood is very safe, but we're out in the boondocks. I figured it wouldn't hurt to get one. I'll teach you how to use it. Are you bothered by that?"

"Nope."

Happy showed Christine the cheery, yellow bedroom on the first floor. The flowered bedspread splashed colors of pink, yellow, and white. There was a dresser, two nightstands, desk, TV, and large closet. Christine smelled the flowers on the nightstand and tested the queen-sized bed. As she stretched, Steppie leaped up and snuggled against her.

Christine smiled for the first time since Violet left. An emotion Happy wouldn't acknowledge filled her. It was the same one she'd felt earlier in the day when Violet flirted with Jimmy. Now Steppie was flirting with Christine.

"I have a feeling Steppie will be sleeping with you," Happy said, forcing a grin. "It's getting late. We need to unload."

Happy had to admit, there were plenty of interesting stories behind Christine's belongings. They sorted the property into three piles: house, shed, and trash. After four hours, the trash pile consisted of a few McDonald's wrappers, used paper coffee cups, and a bag of flour filled with weevils.

Happy held up a large, plastic bag filled with dog fur. "Trash or shed?"

"Shed. I'm going to make a sweater out of it."

"How?"

"I had a bichon, just like Steppie. Whenever he got groomed, I kept his fur. I'm going to spin it into yarn and knit a sweater."

"You know how to spin and knit?"

"No, but I'm going to learn."

Happy showed her the bag of lint. "Trash or shed?"

"Shed. I'm saving it for a paper mache project—Mardi Gras masks!"

Next came a bag of old lottery tickets and paint chips.

"That goes in the shed," Christine said. "I'm going to weave them into wallets and sell them."

"Have you ever done that before?"

"No, but I saw it on Pinterest."

Happy found a box filled with table vases. They were the vases Christine was wrapping when she visited the Somerset Bar and Grill. "Don't these vases belong to the Hershbergers?"

"No, they're mine. I found them during Somerset's recycle day. They were free."

"How many did you take?"

"Twenty. I'm going to use them for wedding reception centerpieces whenever I get married. I let Al and Zeke use them in the meantime."

Happy strained to lift a large trunk, but it was too heavy. "What do you have in here? Dumbbells?"

Huffing and puffing, they lowered the trunk onto the driveway. Christine opened the trunk and revealed a trove of photo albums. A vase, covered in newspaper, was tucked beside the albums. A small jewelry box occupied the remaining space. Christine unwrapped the vase. "I'm glad this didn't get broken. I haven't looked at it in years." She began looking around. "There's a matching teapot somewhere. Have you seen it?"

"I unloaded a box of dishes," Happy said. "Maybe it's in there."

It was. The cream-colored teapot was made by Lenox. The porcelain handle was worn, the lid taped shut.

"It's beautiful," Happy said.

"My mother used it all the time. I got it after my parents died. Everything in the trunk came from them. I keep the teapot out so I can look at it every day."

Christine was matter-of-fact, but the air sucked from Happy's lungs. "I'm sorry, Christine."

"I don't remember them much. They died in a car crash when I was five. And my older brother, too. That's when Violet became my guardian. She's my mother's younger sister."

"Violet took you in? How old was she?"

"Eighteen. There wasn't anyone else who could do it."

Happy was ashamed of her thoughts about punching Violet. How many youthful opportunities had Violet sacrificed to raise her niece? She thought of her own mother, who'd given birth to Happy when she was barely fifteen. Happy and Christine had something in common—both lost parents too young to die.

Asshole. That's how Happy had acted toward Violet. She felt sick about it. After berating herself, Happy returned to the conversation.

Christine caressed the teapot. "Sometimes I worry I stole an important part of Violet's life. You know, the part where you date and have fun, and figure out who you are and who you want to be."

"Let's bring the trunk inside," Happy said. "We'll put these treasures where you can enjoy them." She looked at the property still in the truck. "We need to finish unpacking before dark. Would you like to invite Violet for dinner?"

Christine called Violet and then turned to Happy. "She wants to know if Jimmy and Matthew are coming."

Happy gulped down her dismay. "Good idea. I'll invite them."

"She also wants to know if Jimmy's your boyfriend. She said you were giving off weird vibes. She doesn't want to poach on your territory."

Jimmy, her boyfriend? No, but...but what? But nothing—she had no claims on him.

"No...we're just friends."

Dinner was the longest and most miserable meal Happy ever endured. Violet went gaga when Jimmy arrived wearing a uniform for his later shift. Violet flirted with him, full throttle. He responded with more enthusiasm than Happy thought possible. Was he just being polite? For some reason, she hoped so.

Matthew and Violet left the house by nine, but Jimmy stayed behind. He walked Steppie while Happy cleaned the kitchen and Christine unpacked her belongings. When Jimmy returned, Steppie trotted into Christine's bedroom, his tail wagging.

Happy was bemused. "That little traitor."

"Steppie knows how to play the ladies." Jimmy let out his soft laugh. "How about we go for a walk? It's a nice night."

He was going to ask her about her visit to Somerset; she knew it. Might as well get it over with. Besides, she'd rather have the conversation outside. If it turned ugly, she could escape inside her own home.

The overcast day had transformed into a beautiful, clear night. The stars glowed against the pitch-black evening sky. The moon was rising, full and luminous. It was warmer than she expected, but still cold enough to lace the gravel road with patches of ice. The air was clean and crisp. No air freshener could capture Deep Creek's lovely scent.

"It's a little slippery." Jimmy placed her hand on his forearm. "Hang on to me. I won't let you fall."

She waited for the lecture. Not for long.

"Why'd you go to Somerset?"

"I wanted to find out if anyone knew anything about Bernie's surprise."

"Get anywhere?"

"No, but it was still worth the effort. I found Christine."

"Does Etchers know about your investigation?"

"It's *not* an investigation." Happy heard the exasperation in her voice. "I'm just asking around. And no, I haven't told Etchers—and don't you tell him, either. He'll bombard me with tales of killings and torture. No wonder I have nightmares. Being cooped up in Deep Creek is not part of the WITSEC deal and never was."

"C'mon, Happy. You have to tell—"

Happy didn't want to argue. "It's been a long day. Let's go back."

She turned and headed for home. Jimmy matched her stride, step for step, trying to catch up, until he said, "Hold up a sec!"

She stopped and turned. "What is it?"

A zinging snowball hit her in the chest. She was dumbfounded into silence. Seriously? Did Jimmy just hit her with a snowball? She laughed out loud. "This is war!" She gathered two handfuls of snow and lobbed a snowball. Jimmy ducked. Her snowball missed him by a mile. Another snowball headed her way. She tried to dodge, but it smacked her in the back of the head.

Jimmy ran toward her. "Oh no! I didn't mean to hit you like that."

A moment later, she was standing in front of Jimmy, leaning against his chest, his arms surrounding her. He touched the hair on the back of her head.

"Are you all right?" he whispered. "I'm sorry."

"That was fun. I haven't been in a snowball fight in years."

Jimmy's body radiated heat. Sweat gathered in her armpits, but she didn't want to move from the cozy nook inside his arms.

"Gosh, Jimmy. You're as warm as a furnace. Are you getting sick?"

"I guess my pilot light's been lit up."

Happy pulled away. "What are you talking about? That doesn't make any sense."

"No, it doesn't. Never did."

Jimmy said nothing more as they walked to the house.

Chapter 12

The next morning, Happy experienced the strange sensation of reading the news without Steppie's warm company. The dog was with Christine, who was still sleeping.

Happy downed a tall glass of orange juice and popped some vitamins. Whatever Jimmy had, she didn't want to catch it. She perused her daily to-do list. First on the list was calling Bernie's football friends, Hank Tinker and Randall Kennedy. No answer at either number; she left messages. The next item was getting a copy of any police reports.

She'd learned a lot while investigating her mother's killing. Police reports in pending investigations are privileged and not easily available to the public. Luck, nerve, and prayer had gotten her what she'd needed.

This time, she knew enough to start by looking up the pertinent legal statute. It wasn't as if she could understand the law and all its nuances, but she could get the gist—and the gist was if she were named in the report, she was entitled to a copy.

She drove twenty minutes to the Maryland State Police Barrack W in McHenry, a community on the northwest edge of the lake. She submitted her written request to the trooper behind the glass window and waited for him to retrieve the report.

A door on the left of the glass window led to the secured area of the barracks. She watched the door open and close, hoping one of the troopers who exited would be Jimmy. After five minutes, an older man in uniform entered the lobby from the secured door.

"Ms. Holiday, I'm Corporal Harold Friend. I'm investigating the death of Bernie Singleton. I'd like to speak to you for a few minutes."

Friend led her to an interview room with yellowish walls, turquoise woodwork, worn gray carpeting, and an artificial ficus plant. There were two desks. Friend took a seat at the desk in front of the plant. He directed Happy to sit in the adjacent chair.

She asked her standard question. "Am I in trouble?"

Friend shook his head. "No. I'm sorry we need to use an interview room. The Troopers Room is too busy for a chat."

The corporal was petite and thin with flawless skin the color of milk. He could've been a model for Dove soap. He looked at her with sympathetic eyes. "I'm sorry about your mother."

Her jaw dropped in surprise. "Thank you, but she died many years ago."

He leaned back in his chair and appeared conversational. "Listen, I know your situation. When you called Trooper Bittinger for help with Romero Sanchez, I was the officer on duty. I coordinated the law enforcement needed to protect Sanchez while he was in Deep Creek meeting with the feds."

"Thanks for telling me. I don't know who knows what around here."

"Only a few of us know the details. We keep in touch with the U.S. Marshals Service." Friend handed her a copy of the report she'd come for. "What's your interest in the Singleton investigation?"

"Thanks." She glanced at Jimmy's two-page report. "I'm interested in knowing how Mr. Singleton ended up under the blade of my snowplow. But that's not why I'm here. I'm just helping his widow." Happy explained the mystery of Bernie's surprise. "Has your investigation turned up anything about that?"

"No. If something comes up, we'll let Mrs. Singleton know, but she ought to hire a private investigator."

"She can't afford one."

"Are you a licensed PI?"

"Who, me? No, I'm just a free helper."

"Maybe you can help us."

Friend pointed to a large box sitting on the other desk. "We released the Explorer to Mrs. Singleton, but the personal property found inside wasn't yet processed. We're done with that now. We've called Mrs. Singleton several times to pick up her husband's belongings. This morning, I offered to have someone bring them to her home. She told me to throw it all away. As far as I can tell, there's nothing valuable, but there could be something sentimental in there. I would hate for her to regret her decision later."

"Give it to me. I'll take it to her."

"I can't give it to you without her authorization."

Happy called Mrs. Singleton. As soon as she mentioned the personal property, Mrs. Singleton interrupted. "Oh, for God's sakes, I told the corporal to throw it away."

"There might be something important in there."

"There's nothing important, believe me. It's all junk I don't need to look at it. If the corporal won't throw it out, will you?"

"I'd be glad to. Send an e-mail to Corporal Friend authorizing him to give it to me, and I'll take care of it."

The corporal received the authorization in less than a minute.

"Thank you, Ms. Holiday," Friend said while writing a number on a business card. "That's my cell phone number. If you have any problems... *any*...call me."

Within minutes, she was driving home, wondering why Olivia was adamant about throwing the box away—it could contain a clue to the surprise.

Maybe there was something in that box Olivia didn't want to see.

Happy found a note from Christine resting against the cake stand. "Gone job hunting." As she read the note, the cardboard box called her name. Would it be unethical to open it without Olivia's permission? She'd been instructed to throw her husband's belongings away—not examine them. Her gut told her she shouldn't open the box, but maybe she could think of a way to change her gut's opinion.

Happy settled at the kitchen table, holding a piece of cake with one hand and the police report with the other. Jimmy's narrative of the events was exactly as she remembered, with one exception—he'd omitted the fact that he found her sitting beside the deceased, not in the snowplow's cab.

Reading the report disturbed her. Every night, as she dropped off to sleep, the grotesque sight of Bernie Singleton slipped into her dreams. Left hand twisted into the shape of an L, wide eyes staring ahead, mouth formed as if he were struggling to be heard. What was he trying to say? His desperation haunted her. She could see it, feel it, and hear it in Jimmy's written words.

She needed to get her mind off of Bernie Singleton. Next on the to-do list was visiting Pastor Nelson. She had an idea for the March senior citizen's dinner and wanted to run it by him before buying the groceries.

The town of Bittinger was slightly west of the Savage River State Forest, fifteen minutes from Happy's home. Happy always thought the building that housed the Meadow Mountain Community Church was a lovely mix of old and new. The structure was sleek and modern, while the windows were old-fashioned stained glass. The church had a skylight that seemed to shed grace on the interior, even during inclement weather.

Jimmy and his extended family were active members of the church. His faith clearly brought him joy. He trusted God to make things turn out as they should. Whenever Jimmy asked her to help with an event, she gladly did so. The church services were foreign to her; she had no formal religious training. Her sense of right and wrong came from her mother, along with the TV show, *Xena: Warrior Princess.*

As she pulled into the driveway of the church, she spotted Jimmy's Jeep. He was outside, wearing jeans and a coat, talking to Pastor Nelson. An extension ladder leaned against the church. The men greeted her as she stepped from the SUV. Nelson was tall, thin, and wore a high and tight haircut. She suspected he was a military man in a previous life.

"Hello, Happy," Nelson said. "Always a pleasure to see you. What brings you here?"

"I have an idea I want to run by you for next month's dinner. Do you have time?"

"Now's a good time. What's your idea?"

"The dinner falls on St. Patrick's Day. I thought we could make it a little holiday party." Happy kept glancing at the ladder. "We could have everyone wear green. Maybe even a DJ to play Irish music, get some dancers."

Happy paused, distracted by the ladder. "What are you two doing?"

"Getting ready to clean out the gutters," Jimmy said. "Water's overflowing onto the foundation."

Happy estimated the gutters were thirty feet up. "Need some help?"

Both men shook their heads.

"Well, I can help hold the ladder."

Jimmy put on work gloves, approached the ladder, and hesitated. He took a quick look toward the gutters. He breathed deeply for a few seconds and grabbed a rung. Happy was struck by a sudden realization: Jimmy was scared.

"Pastor," she said. "May I have a private minute with Jimmy?"

"Of course. Let me know when you need me." Nelson stepped away from the conversation and went into the church.

"Jimmy, you're afraid of heights, aren't you?"

"No."

She nudged him with an elbow. "You're such a liar. Look, I clean my house gutters twice a year. Heights don't bother me at all. I'm dressed for it. I know what to do. Let me do this for you."

"No, I'm not—"

Happy folded her arms across her chest. "You're not going all macho on me, are you?"

No reply.

She held out her right hand. "Give me those gloves, and hold the ladder."

Happy climbed the ladder with ease and began scooping muck from the gutters. As she dropped it by the fistful, she shouted, "Bombs away!" They moved the ladder around the church, four feet at a time until the task was done. She descended the ladder for the last time.

Jimmy smiled at her through the mud, decomposed leaves, and slop that covered his face and upper body.

"Oh no!" she said. "What happened?"

"The last 'bombs away' got me. You've been gotten, too."

Happy discovered she wore sludge from the neck down. Jimmy laughed from his belly. His deep-blue eyes danced as she wiped the gook away from his face with her hand. Gosh, he was handsome. Why hadn't she ever noticed? She leaped into Jimmy's arms and kissed him—squarely on his lips, her arms thrown around his neck. His arms encircled her waist and drew her body flush against his.

Chapter 13

Jimmy's lips were soft. He tasted...well, the Smith Island cake came to mind. Their height difference was perfect; she felt feminine looking up to him, but not so much that it hurt her neck. Jimmy's mouth was right-sized for hers. A perfect fit.

She pulled away to take a breath. Jimmy pulled her back. More kissing. Her arms tightened around him as his lips toyed with hers. Jimmy's hands found her lower back and pressed her body closer to his hips. She longed for him to caress her breasts. *More, more, more.*

"Where's the pastor?" she blurted, pulling away.

Jimmy drew her body back toward his. "Don't know, don't care."

"Jimmy!" she said while he kissed her again. "You're shameless."

His tongue grazed her lips, and his hand found the zipper of her coat. "I'll confess it to the Lord...later."

She broke the kiss by laughing hard. A quick glance around revealed the pastor was nowhere in sight. Jimmy stood in front of her, smiling through the muck that covered him, his eyes now conveying a serious mood. He nodded toward his Jeep. She followed, looking forward to a more intimate session.

Once inside the car, her heart began to race. Would Jimmy dare initiate sex on the church premises? She said nothing and waited for him to take the lead.

Finally, Jimmy began. "We need to talk."

Talk? Her racing heart geared down to a crawl.

"I'm crazy about you, Happy. I have been since the moment I met you."

She was astonished. Jimmy had given her no sign. "Why'd you wait so long to tell me?"

"I worried you were still hung up on Romero. I waited for you to show some sign you've left him behind. Today, you kissed me. It gave me hope you're finally done with him. Are you?"

A knotty question. "I don't hate him. I don't wish him dead or hurt."

"Do you ever think about him?"

"I think about him whenever I think about my mother being dead, which is every single day. He's part of that whole ball of misery, along with the prosecutor and the police. Remember the nightmare I had the night I found Bernie? I dreamt Romero was trapped under my snowplow's blade. He was bloody and screaming."

Jimmy looked almost gleeful until he saw Happy's shocked expression. "Sorry. It's just that...well, you couldn't have given me a better answer."

"This is painful for me, Jimmy."

He reached for her right hand and kissed it. "Please, allow me one more question. It's been on my mind since the day I met Romero."

"Go on, ask it. But I don't want to talk about him ever again."

"How did you get mixed up with him in the first place? You're so smart and pretty. You could have any man you want. Why him? I just never understood it."

It was complicated; she'd been a pawn in a war between a gang kingpin and an ambitious prosecutor. Most of the time, she didn't know what the hell was going on. She could only give Jimmy the bullet points. If he wasn't satisfied, she'd walk away from whatever potential relationship he seemed to be aiming for.

"I met him during a messenger delivery. He had that handsome-charm shtick going on. Like a dope, I fell for it. I knew he was in a gang but had no idea how deep. There was a 'don't ask, don't tell' policy between us. It was a casual thing, superficial. All heat, you know what I mean?"

She could tell by the expression on Jimmy's face that he understood.

"One day, Rick McCormick, the Baltimore City gang prosecutor, told me the truth about Romero. I broke up with him, and it wasn't pretty, believe me. That was the end of it, as far as I was concerned."

Her breathing became ragged. Her voice cracked. "Then my mother... died. Everything went to shit—"

Jimmy jumped in, his voice filled with regret. He clearly wanted to put the worms back into the can. "Stop, Happy. You don't have to tell me anymore."

"OK." Happy stared through the windshield, depleted and exhausted. "I need to go home now." She pulled the latch on the Jeep's door. It wasn't until he squeezed her left hand that she realized he was still holding it.

"I shouldn't have pushed you. I'm sorry. It's none of my business...and everything you did to get rid of Roach...well, Happy, you're the bravest person I've ever met."

No, Jimmy. Lucy was the brave one, not Happy.

They sat in silence, holding hands across the console. She kept her other hand on the latch.

"Please, don't go," he said. "Will you wait here a minute?"

She acquiesced. Jimmy bolted into the church. Five minutes later, he came running out holding a gigantic bouquet of flowers and handed it to her. The bouquet was so enormous it blocked her view through the windshield.

"These are beautiful, Jimmy. Where did they come from?"

"I told the Pastor I needed flowers in a hurry, so he sold me the ones by the altar."

Happy giggled. Her hand was no longer on the door latch.

After a few minutes, Jimmy cleared his throat. "I've probably already blown my chances, but I'm going to finish what I started. I want more than friendship. If you're open to that, let's go for it. If you want to stick with just friendship, then that's what it'll be. But if you'd like to explore a committed relationship, just tell me you're in."

The aroma of flowers filled the police car. He didn't say it right out, but if everything went well, he was offering the future she always wanted—a good man, a loving marriage, children to raise, and a home to care for. But his concern about Romero worried her. "I need to think about it."

Jimmy smiled at her. "Take all the time you need. If you're willing, I'd like to kiss you again, good and proper, to give you more to consider."

"I'm willing."

He exited the car and opened her door. She placed the flowers on the driver's seat. Jimmy grasped Happy's hand, guided her from the car to her feet. His right hand caressed her cheek and the hollow of her throat. The kiss began with a gentle brush across her lips and became more intense until she was breathless and wobbly-kneed. Somehow, he had opened her coat. His hand drifted to her right breast and stopped.

He tilted his head and raised an eyebrow. "You're carrying?"

She touched the tip of her tongue against the tip of his. "Don't worry, the decocker is on."

"Happy—"

"Shhh...more kisses," she whispered.

"There's lots more where they came from. Think about what I said." He placed a tender kiss on her forehead. "Can I take you to lunch...on a date?"

She gave Jimmy a once-over and then scanned herself. "Where? The dump?"

"Go home. I'll pick you up in an hour."

They entered Brenda's Pizzeria, an Italian restaurant located above Trader's Coffee House on Garrett Highway. The irresistible scent of garlic, bread, and olive oil greeted them. They shared a pizza at a table next to a long glass window; the sweeping view of the lake was one of Happy's favorites. She saw fishing huts, snowmobiles, and the colorful sails of ice boats skimming across the lake.

She also saw Jimmy. Broad shoulders, blue eyes, strong jaw, gentle manner, wide smile and wide heart. How could she have been so blind? She wanted him.

She was *all in.*

When the check arrived, she put her hand on his and whispered. "Jimmy, I'm not armed."

Happy loved Jimmy's home. When they entered, she could feel the rich history of a loving family life. It was a small cabin, not too far from the church, decorated with the worn furniture his parents had replaced after raising eight rambunctious children. Jimmy had a story for every piece:

"That's the sofa Matthew and I tried to jump over. I made it; he broke his arm."

"I did my homework on that table every night."

"That's the 'time-out' chair."

Jimmy's great grandparents built the cabin. His paternal grandfather grew up in it, as did his father until he married. It later served as a transition home for each of the Bittinger children as they launched their way to independence. It was now Jimmy's turn to occupy and care for it.

The only thing she didn't like about the cabin was the cold. The window and doors allowed drafts. The insulation was thin. Jimmy was slowly improving the cabin as his budget allowed. She never complained but drank a lot of hot tea whenever she visited.

Jimmy flicked on the gas fireplace. "It'll warm up in a minute."

While Happy waited to take off her coat, she remembered a question she meant to ask him earlier. "Jimmy?"

He turned to her.

"When you're on the job, do you ever have to climb high?"

"Yeah, sometimes. Why?"

"How can you do that if you're afraid of heights?"

"Never thought about it. I just do what needs to be done."

"Anything else you're afraid of?"

He showed a tentative smile. "At the moment, I'm a little afraid of you. I want things to go well."

"Oh, Jimmy." She threw her arms around his torso. He responded with a kiss that made her wobbly-kneed for the second time in a single day.

He led her to his bedroom. It was filled with unlit candles and flowers. The fragrance was almost intoxicating. "I bought another bouquet off the altar."

Jimmy undressed her as she stood before him. When he finished, he laid her on his king-sized bed. He opened the side table drawer, removed a condom and a pack of matches. Soon all the candles in the room flickered. As he unbuttoned his shirt, he gazed at her nakedness. "You're so beautiful, Happy." He apparently noticed the goose bumps popping up on her arms. "You're still cold."

Before she could answer, Jimmy spread a blanket over her. He tucked the blanket in around her body and folded it under her feet. His nurturing moved her in a way no man ever had.

"Comfy?" he said.

"Yes."

She discovered a new pleasure—watching Jimmy as he undressed. He had a sturdy, muscular physique with shoulders strong enough to lift her above her addictions. His loving arms would hold her tight and rock her babies. His hands...well, her body responded with heat as she thought of them. Looking back, she couldn't understand why she didn't find him attractive at first sight. Funny thing; the more she got to know him, the more handsome he got.

Jimmy was sexy, but not in a blatant sort of way. He wore loose-fitting T-shirts that concealed his defined arm and shoulder muscles. Walmart jeans suited him fine. He made no effort to impress anyone. Just a regular guy at ease in his own skin. He belonged to her. His sensual body was her secret to keep and enjoy.

After Jimmy removed his clothing, he slipped onto the bed and covered her with his arms and legs. "Warm enough?"

"Jimmy, I'm burning up, and not just from the blanket."

Off came the blanket. He crawled on top of her and began with a sensuous kiss. His gentle manner eased her into releasing her inhibitions. His tongue and tender touches ignited her passion. She wrapped her legs around his torso and submitted to his lead. Her imagination flew. Soon the wind was caressing her hair, and she was breathing hard, soaring on her bike, never wanting to stop, pumping and careening in waves, edging ever closer to the downward glide until she cried out in a prolonged apex of mutual pleasure. When Jimmy raised himself from her, she locked her legs.

"No, stay a while," she whispered.

Jimmy complied as she drifted into a satisfied sleep. When she awoke, Jimmy was watching her, still nestled between her legs, perched on his elbows. His fingers were stoking her hair with the slightest of touches.

"What're you thinking, Jimmy?"

"I'm praying."

"You don't have to pray...just tell me what you want."

Jimmy grinned at her. "I'll keep that in mind, but I'm not praying for anything. I'm saying prayers of gratitude." He kissed her gently on the lips. "I'm thanking the Lord you're with me."

He rolled over, leaned on his elbow, and propped his head on his hand. "What're you thinking about, babe?"

Ugh. Romero always called her "babe."

"Jimmy, please don't call me 'babe.'"

His expression darkened. "Is that what Romero called you?"

"Every boyfriend calls every girlfriend 'babe.' I want you to call me something that's special only to you and me. Something no one else in the world will ever call me."

"That's quite a challenge. Sweetheart? Honey? Cupcake?"

Happy giggled. She couldn't imagine anyone ever calling her one of those pet names. "I want you to call me 'Lucy.' Just when we're in bed... together...like this. Please?"

He stroked her cheek. "You know I can't call you that. I won't be able to keep your name straight. I'll make the same mistake you did. Besides, you're not Lucy anymore."

"I am on the inside."

"I'll keep thinking about what to call you, and you keep working on being Happy Holiday, outside and *in.* OK?"

It wasn't OK, but she agreed to it anyway.

Chapter 14

Happy awoke before dawn, in her own bed. She'd fallen asleep fantasizing about Jimmy and his sexy ways. If she knew that *good men* were so hot, she would have included them in her dating pool long ago. She lingered in bed, relishing her fantasies until they become too fiery to bear. A cold shower threw water on her sexual inferno. She dressed and fixed herself a cup of coffee.

By eight o'clock, she was on her way to Somerset. She had two stops on her itinerary; the Pleasant View Inn and Laurel Hill Hospital. The weather was misty dank, and the roads were sloppy. She repeated the previous route, including a stop at the turnoff where police found Bernie's Explorer. Milo Sullivan was pacing the area with his hands in his pockets. She pulled beside his Ram and parked. He stopped pacing.

"Milo, are you OK?"

He shrugged. "I guess I'm like you…can't let it go."

His face was unshaven and his hair unkempt. Based on the odor wafting from his mouth, he hadn't brushed his teeth. No shower either—he was wearing the same baggy pants, the hems still caked with mud. His eyes drooped. She doubted he'd gotten any sleep since she'd last seen him.

"You can't beat yourself up like this," Happy said. "I don't understand why you think you're to blame."

"I was his last chance." He took a handkerchief from his coat pocket and wiped his eyes. After a few seconds of throat-clearing, he continued. "Did you find anything out?"

"No...it's a dead end so far. I'm still looking." She gave him a reassuring smile. "Something will turn up, it always does. You'll see it's not your fault. So please, go home. Get some rest."

As Happy walked away, she had a thought and turned around. "Milo, what's your cell number?" When he gave it to her, she sent him a text with her address. "Now you have my contact info. Call or visit me whenever you want to talk, OK?"

"You're a good girl, Happy."

She put the key in the ignition and thought about Milo's compliment. She always tried to do the right thing; it seemed to Happy that her efforts went sideways more often than straight.

Al Hershberger was right—the Pleasant View Inn was just down the street from the Somerset Bar and Grill, a five-minute walk at most. The inn was a one-level building that appeared to have been transplanted from the Caribbean. Happy remembered the pastel décor of houses in St. Lucia that she'd seen in a *National Geographic* magazine. Coral was the primary exterior color of the inn, accented by sea-green woodwork and aqua shutters. The wet parking lot was larger than the building, giving the illusion that the inn faced the Caribbean Sea. The same pastel colors decorated the interior. Tropical plants provided botanical accents.

She approached the reception desk. It was loaded with textbooks and computers. The dark-haired clerk minding the desk was in his mid-twenties. He wore Bermuda shorts and a flowered, short-sleeved shirt. A name tag identified him as "Danny." Danny was abuzz with multitasking.

"This place is really cool," Happy said.

"Thanks." Danny smiled. "We think so, too. How can I help you?"

Danny's smile displayed a mouthful of overlapping, twisting, and crooked teeth. She wondered how he could eat and talk. As unsightly as the teeth were, the smile was stellar. She smiled back because she couldn't help it.

"I'm here about a guest of yours, Bernie Singleton. He checked in the night of the big storm."

Danny winced. "Oh, the man who froze to death. The police have already been here."

"I'm not police. I'm a friend of the family. I'm looking for anyone who might've spoken to him. Were you on duty when he checked in?"

"I was here all night, but he never checked in. I told that to the police."

"Was anyone else here?"

"No one but me. Management sent everyone else home because of the weather. Mr. Singleton was never here."

The front-desk phone rang. Danny answered, "Pleasant View Inn. Reservations." While he spoke about rates and available dates, Happy noticed a bulky textbook next to the phone entitled *Technology Solutions for Homeland Security.* It looked interesting.

"What are you studying?" Happy asked when he disconnected.

"Cybersecurity. What does that have to do with the frozen man?"

"Nothing, just curious, that's all. In case I go to college." She leaned over the desk. "Are there any guests still here who were here that night?"

"No, they've all checked out."

He gave her another stellar smile, although this one was sympathetic. "I'm sorry I can't be more helpful."

Another dead end.

She needed the restroom before heading to the hospital and asked where it was.

Danny pointed to the long hallway. "Three doors down, right next to the water fountain."

As she walked to the restroom, she passed the "Bar None Lounge." It wouldn't be open until five o'clock. The door was unlocked. She slipped inside the bar and perused the menu she found on the hostess stand. The bar served appetizers as well as every kind of alcoholic drink imaginable.

Her eyes rested on her favorite, the Irish car bomb—the drink that had given her much more sorrow than pleasure. Cravings surged. She could smell the drink, taste it, and feel it slide down her throat. For a moment, she considered waiting until the bar opened.

Danny came through the door, no longer smiling. "Did you get lost?"

"No, I got hungry."

"The restaurant is closed until five." He pointed to a door across the hall. "The ladies room is right there."

As Happy washed her hands in front of the bathroom mirror, she sent a prayer of gratitude to her mother. She'd been hungry, all right, but not for food.

Happy wasn't quite done with the Pleasant View Inn. She walked every square foot of the parking lot searching for the rainbow colors of spilled gasoline. Colorful spots of fuel floated in the puddles, but nothing large enough to indicate a gas tank spill.

Danny stood at the inn's entrance watching her. After a few minutes, he interrupted her search. "If you're not checking in, could you please go away? The guests think you're casing the place."

"Have you cleaned up any gasoline spills since the night of the storm?"

"No. Leave or I'm calling the police."

She left, wondering why everyone wanted to call the police on her.

Laurel Hill Hospital was a plain, red-bricked building, embellished with beige bricks. When Happy passed through the front entrance, she found the hospital smelled clean and the beige-marbled floor tiles shined. Soothing cream-yellow walls were accentuated by the woodwork's blues and greens.

A friendly receptionist directed her to the B section of the third floor. Happy approached the nurse's station, identified herself, and asked to see Zeke Hershberger. "Oh, yes," said the charge nurse. He's expecting you." She was directed to Room 308B. It occurred to Happy that her own health might be at risk. "Is Mr. Hershberger contagious?"

"He doesn't have that kind of pneumonia. You don't need to worry."

That was news to Happy—she had no idea that there were different kinds of pneumonia. She found her way to Zeke's room. It was a two-patient room, but the second bed was empty. Zeke greeted her with a raspy voice. His effort at politeness set off a deep, phlegmy cough. From the look of his glazy eyes, he was feverish. Happy handed him a Styrofoam cup of water with a straw poking from the plastic lid. After a few sips, Zeke managed to get control of his cough.

"Sorry," he said. "These spells sneak up on me."

"Thanks for seeing me when you're feeling so poorly."

"Anything for Christine." He took a long sip of water. "What kind of name is 'Happy Holiday'?"

She shrugged her shoulders and smiled. "A stupid one."

"It *is* stupid. How'd you get it?"

"Well...you see, my parents—Mr. and Mrs. Holiday—they won't tell me the whole story. Something to do with sex, drugs, and rock 'n' roll."

"Must be a great story."

"Knowing my parents, I seriously doubt it."

Zeke swallowed a bit more water. "Christine told me you might be visiting. I wish I could help, but I can't. I've never talked to the man or seen him until I passed him on the way out the door. Al told you I was sick. I can't be cooking when I'm sick." He tried to make a sweeping gesture with his hand but was interrupted by another coughing spell. Eventually, the spell abated, and he completed his grand movement. "So here I am, coughing up my insides in a hospital."

"When you passed him, was he talking to anyone?"

"Just watching TV."

"Could you hear anything going on at the bar from the kitchen?"

Zeke shook his head while enduring another coughing episode. His eyes and nose streamed liquid.

Happy offered him a tissue. "How in the world did you get pneumonia?"

"Corn chowder. I was making corn chowder and took a taste. A little piece of corn went down the wrong way. Now the damned thing is swelled up and won't go anywhere without some surgery. That damn corn kernel has nearly killed me."

Sweat collected on Zeke's face. Happy found a facecloth and ran it under cold water from the bathroom. She placed the cloth on Zeke's forehead. "How long will you be here?"

"I'm getting a bronchoscopy tomorrow morning. They're gonna put me under and try to extract the thing...Ms. Holiday, I'm feeling real bad. You need to go. Tell Christine I'm sorry I didn't say 'good-bye.'"

Happy made her exit. The sounds of wretched coughing followed her until she entered the elevator. She had the uneasy feeling Zeke wasn't going to make it—all because of a kernel of corn.

Funny, how little mistakes can kill a person.

Chapter 15

Happy awoke the next morning knowing it would be a good day.

It was Steppie's fifth birthday. A special dinner was on the menu; beef tenderloin, green beans, and carrots—which happened to be Jimmy's favorite meal. He was coming for dinner. She got the tingles just thinking about it.

She launched into her morning routine. She studied her WITSEC history for the umpteenth time, practiced her signature, and reviewed the index cards in her Lie Box. She spent the next thirty minutes catching up on the news. Not much interesting these days. The weather forecast was always the same—cold with a chance of snow. On a rare winter's day, the weather might be sunny and clear, but it was always cold with a chance of snow.

Out of habit, Happy clicked on the *Los Angeles Times.* There was nothing about the Roach trial; she didn't expect to find anything. After Romero's testimony, every defendant pleaded guilty to multiple murder-related crimes. Federal prosecutors agreed to remove the death penalty in exchange for life imprisonment without parole. The guilty pleas eliminated the right to an appeal. The prosecution case was over and final. Now she could finally move on from this sorry chapter in her life.

As she disconnected her computer, she spotted the box of Bernie's belongings in the dining area. It had been tempting her since she'd brought it inside the house. Why shouldn't she open it? The contents were nothing but trash to Olivia. She'd instructed Happy to throw it all away. What difference would it make if Happy examined the contents first? Maybe that's what Olivia expected her to do.

Steppie romped into the kitchen from Christine's bedroom. He stood on hind legs and pawed Happy's knees demanding his rightful place in her lap. She picked him up and snuggled her face into his fur. "Happy birthday, you little traitor."

Christine shuffled in wearing a blue robe and fuzzy pink slippers. The *Garrett County Republican* was tucked under her arm.

"Good morning, Christine. Sleep OK?"

She answered with a stretch and a wide yawn.

"There's a pot of coffee on the counter."

Christine poured herself a cup. She joined Happy at the table and opened the paper to the jobs classified section. The box caught Christine's attention. "What's that?"

Happy explained.

"Aren't you going to open it?"

"I'm not sure I should. I'm only authorized to throw it out."

"Of course, you should open it. Mrs. Singleton wants you to help her. The surprise might be in the box, or there could be a clue."

That was all Happy needed to hear. She pulled open the interlocking flaps and spread the contents onto the dining room table.

"See a cell phone?" Happy said.

"Nope." Christine picked up two identical Steelers T-shirts. "Do you think this is the surprise?"

"Oh, God, I hope not." Happy took the shirts from Christine. Each T-shirt had a sticker marking the price as fifteen dollars. They were poorly constructed and made of thin cotton. She examined the size tags printed onto the neck bands. One adult-medium, another youth-medium. "These are for his boys."

"How about this?" Christine held up a plastic Ravens Christmas ornament.

"Nope. I'm sure the surprise is more than a cheap ornament."

The ornament surprised Happy. Why would Bernie have a Ravens ornament? He was an avid Steelers fan.

Happy found Bernie's slightly-damp wallet in a paper bag. It was a tri-fold style, brown, and made from some sort of synthetic material. The wallet's exterior was stretched and worn, especially around the folds. The interior was empty. She showed Christine the empty cash slot. "Nothing inside."

Christine spotted two envelopes, both labeled "Singleton wallet contents." They were tagged "One" and "Two." She handed one envelope to Happy and kept the other.

Christine discovered nine credit cards, mostly expired; photographs of the boys, driver's license, health insurance card, six loyalty retail cards, and a membership card to a music society. "That's odd. There's not a single picture of Mrs. Singleton."

Happy's envelope contained nothing but receipts. There were over thirty, some of them months old. How had Bernie stuffed the contents of the two envelopes into his wallet? The man was an organizational mess. He must've driven his uber-organized wife crazy.

The receipts were crisp and slightly ruffled. She guessed they got wet in the snow and later dried by police. The centers of some receipts were unreadable. They were probably stuck together and pried apart during the investigation. Only the tops and bottoms were discernible.

Happy handed Christine half of the receipts. "Let's arrange the receipts chronologically, so we have a timeline. Pull out everything for the day Bernie died."

There were no receipts for any purchases before or during the game.

"I wonder where the T-shirts came from," Happy said.

"For fifteen bucks apiece, he must've gotten them from a vendor outside the gate. He probably paid cash and didn't get a receipt."

"I don't see any receipts for food, do you?"

Christine looked through her receipts a second time. "No, nothing for alcohol either. I've been to a couple Steelers games. You can bring food into Heinz Field, but not alcohol."

Happy considered the implications. Olivia was thrifty; she probably packed Bernie a lunch. She also said Bernie wasn't a drinker. Maybe his football friends could fill in the gaps.

Steppie yapped the arrival of a visitor. Happy peeked through the window and groaned when she spotted Etchers's Ford F-150 truck rolling down the driveway. Now what? She hadn't spoken to him since he reported that Christine's background check was perfect. The next time someone asked him to do a background check, he should add hoarding to the checklist. She smiled in anticipation of telling him exactly that.

"It's my Uncle Peter."

Happy opened the door to Etchers. He greeted her with a smile, decidedly fake. "How's my favorite niece?"

"She's fantastic, thank you very much. What's up?"

"Glad to hear it. I was in the area and thought I'd stop by for a cup of coffee."

He joined Christine at the dining room table. "You must be Christine."

They introduced themselves while Happy prepared a cup of coffee the way Etchers liked it. She noticed Etchers observing Bernie's belongings on the tabletop.

Etchers smiled and focused his attention on Christine. "What're you girls working on?"

Christine left nothing out, beginning with Happy's visit to the Somerset Bar and Grill. Christine had an eye for detail, a bear-trap memory, and a gift for gab. She was still talking after ten minutes. Etchers listened wearing the male-equivalent of a Mona Lisa smile.

Happy interrupted. "Want something to eat, Uncle Peter?"

"Shhh. I want to hear Christine's story. It's fascinating." Etchers turned to Christine. "Tell me everything."

Christine continued for another excruciating two minutes. Happy sighed. Yeah, Christine was a talker.

Etchers answered Happy's diversionary question. "Let's go out for breakfast. We can catch up."

The queasy feeling in Happy's stomach sounded an alarm. Etchers was on a mission and needed to speak to her alone. Her heart sank; the conversation was about to end her good day. "Good idea. Want to come, Christine?"

Her expression told Happy she was aware of Etchers's need for privacy. "No, but thanks. I'm still job hunting."

Etchers drained the remainder of his coffee and stood. "Very nice meeting you, Christine." He turned to Happy. "Ready?"

Absolutely not.

Chapter 16

As they drove along New Germany Road, Etchers asked only one question, "What the hell are you doing, Happy?"

She explained the whats and the wherefores of Bernie's surprise. It didn't seem to register. Etchers's mind was clearly elsewhere. He said nothing more until they reached the Brenneman Road entrance to the Meadow Mountain Trail in the Savage River State Forest. The day was clear and bright, but the temperature hovered near freezing.

Happy wasn't dressed for extended time outdoors. Hypothermia came to mind. "We're going hiking? What's going on?" She wrapped her arms around herself. "It's freezing out here!"

"I've got some warm clothes for you in the trunk."

She put on an extra layer of heavy outerwear and a pair of sturdy boots. The clothing was stylish and upscale. "Who do these belong to?"

"One of my daughters."

"You have daugh—?"

"Four daughters and a son." Etchers did a global scan of the surroundings. "Enough chit-chat. We need to have a serious discussion. We're having it here because I want to show you something."

He began walking. The trail was muddy, but visible through snow residuals and fallen leaves. Happy walked beside him. Her legs trembled with every step. "I'm not leaving. Nothing you say can—"

Etchers stopped short. "I'm not here to move you anywhere. Just listen and answer my questions." He resumed walking. "This is unrelated to the topic—today was the first time I've ever heard you say you're fantastic. What's happened?"

"Jimmy and I are together."

Etchers's eyebrows flew up. "As in, romantically?"

"Yes."

Etchers exhaled as if a weight had been lifted from his shoulders. "Well, it took you two long enough. I'm happy for you. Jimmy's a fine, young man. The timing couldn't be better."

He picked up the pace. There were no more words spoken until they reached a small wooden platform at the lookout on the trail. Safety rails surrounded the platform on three sides. They stood on the platform and looked out over an expanse of mountain ridges that seemed endless.

Happy was enthralled by its beauty. "Wow. I never knew this was here."

"It's one of my favorite spots. On a clear day, you can see Maryland, Pennsylvania, and West Virginia." He pointed in the direction of each state. "I want you to contemplate this view as if it's a representation of your future. Bright, beautiful, and unlimited. That's what your future can be if you exercise good judgment in your decision-making."

Fear found its way to Happy's sweat glands. She shivered when the cold seeped through her coat to her torso. "You're scaring me. What's this about?"

He gestured at the wooden platform beneath their feet. "Sit."

She sat crossed-legged on the platform. He did the same. A wrinkle occupied the space between his eyebrows, his lips pressed into a straight line, and his eyes focused. "I'm making a request on behalf of Tony Gilkerson, the Attorney General of the United States."

Happy blurted a laugh. "Quit teasing me."

Etchers shook his head. "I'm sure you understand the Roach trial has national, if not international implications. There are only a few Roach members on the loose—Peeps being the most dangerous. Romero's testimony has effectively dismantled the gang. Now that the trial is over, he'll be leaving prison and going into WITSEC."

She felt the goose bumps rise on her arms. "What does that have to do with me?"

"Romero wants to see you before he disappears."

It took a beat for the information to sink in. What could Romero possibly want?

Etchers anticipated her question. "We don't know what he wants. Romero's keeping that to himself. He's insistent, threatening to recant his testimony if he doesn't see you."

Happy was incredulous. "Can he do that?"

"He can do whatever the hell he wants." Etchers's voice leaked contempt. "Whether he gets away with it or not is another story. At the very least, it'll set off a legal shitstorm—hearings, appeals, motions to set aside plea agreements. It'll cost the taxpayers millions."

"What's the Attorney General want me to do?"

"He wants you to meet with him. If you agree, you'll be taken to a meeting point, to be determined."

Etchers leaned toward her. "But me? I don't give a rat's ass about Gilkerson and his Roach problems. My only concern is for you and your safety. Tell me you won't do it, and I'll let the AG's office know. They can't force you to see Romero."

"What'll happen then?"

Etchers shrugged. "I have no idea. You're the one who knows Romero. Would he recant his testimony if you refuse to see him?"

"If he recants, do all the deals go away? Witness protection for him? For me?"

"He'll be tossed out of WITSEC, and so will you."

"Then he won't recant. Ever."

"Smart girl." Etchers pulled a document and pen from his coat pocket. "I want you to sign this."

She reviewed the document. It stated she'd been informed of Romero's request for a meeting and that she declined. Intuition told her there was something fishy was going on. On the one hand, she hadn't seen or heard from Romero in over eighteen months. Now he wanted to see her. Why? The reason must be important enough to stir up a hornet's nest of trouble.

"Something's not adding up." She twirled with her hair while she formulated her question. "Romero wouldn't make threats unless his request to see me was denied. Why would the AG refuse to let him see me?"

"I don't know, but I can guess—money and security. I suppose the AG changed his mind to avoid a lot of grief."

Grief. The vise of grief squeezed out a terrible memory. She could see herself leaning over a mirror, a straw in her hand, ready to snort a line of cocaine. Romero appeared out of nowhere and flushed the coke down the toilet. He held her while she begged for more. *"No, Lucy, I will not get you any coke."*

Romero saved her from a grief-induced relapse. She owed him the small courtesy of listening to what he had to say. Happy handed the document back to Etchers. "I'm not signing this. I'm going to see Romero."

Etchers's eyes bulged, and his skin flushed. "Don't be stupid!"

"I think Romero wants to tell me something important, something I need to know."

Etchers stood from the platform and leaned over her. "What if he tells you something you shouldn't know—like the existence of a pot of money he got from Roach activities, money that should have been forfeited to the government? Will you disclose that and betray Romero, or will you keep your mouth shut and become a co-conspirator? Why risk putting yourself in that position?"

"He'd never tell me such a thing." She stood in front of him, close enough to signal she wasn't intimidated. "He knows I'd turn him in."

"Are you sure about that? He'd go to jail for the rest of his life. Do you have it in you to turn him in? I don't think you do."

Etchers picked up a stray stick resting on the platform and hurled it over the railing into the vista. "You're throwing away your future, just like that stick. You've worked hard to make a new life for yourself. It hasn't been easy, but you've done it. You have a nice life here—you're putting it all at risk."

"It's something I have to do."

Etchers grasped the platform's railing and stared out at the glorious panorama. He muttered a string of profanities under his breath. When he finished his self-talk, he turned to face her. "Listen to me." Etchers's vexation seeped into his voice. "Think about Jimmy. He loves you. I know he does. You have a future with him. He'll give you everything you want, but he'll walk if you see Romero."

"That's ridiculous! He helped Romero turn state's evidence. Jimmy sat by his side for two weeks while a deal was being negotiated. He would want to know what this is about, too."

"You'll regret this, I'm telling you. You're risking everything good in your life. And for what? Curiosity? Old times' sake? Promise me you'll talk to Jimmy before deciding."

"I'll talk to Jimmy, but I've decided. I'm meeting Romero."

Etchers stuffed the unsigned document back into his coat pocket. “Have it your way.” He stomped down the trail so fast she had to run to keep up.

The ride home was long and silent.

As she opened the truck’s door to exit, Etchers warned. “Just don’t come crying to me when your life turns to shit.”

Chapter 17

Etchers called an hour later. The meeting was set for eleven o'clock the next morning, location TBD. He would pick up her at eight. She wouldn't return until the afternoon. Etchers's prickly tone told her that wherever they were going, she'd be getting the silent treatment on the way there.

It was four o'clock; she had an hour to finish Steppie's birthday meal before Jimmy arrived. Etchers's angry warning looped through her mind. She wasn't worried. Jimmy might be surprised, but he'd be his calm and logical self. They'd talk it out. He'd understand this was something she had to do.

Happy snapped the beans, peeled the carrots, and checked on the beef tenderloin roasting in the oven. She glanced at the clock. The vegetables needed to go into the steamer in twenty minutes. What could she do for twenty minutes? Happy re-opened Bernie's box of personal belongings.

There was a pile of commercially-sold CDs plus four CD-Rs with home-made covers. She found a black umbrella, windshield squeegee, and an ice scrapper. The Steelers T-shirts Christine discovered yesterday triggered a flashback. Bernie was half-naked, his eyes beseeching her, left hand frozen in a strange L-shape, mouth locked open. Happy pressed her hands to her eyes to block the frightening sight from her mind. *Don't think of it, don't think of it—*

Steppie's yaps interrupted her mantra. Jimmy. Two deep breaths later, she answered Jimmy's rapid knocks on the door. She greeted him with a smile and quick hug.

Jimmy kicked off his boots. "The house smells great! What's on the menu?"

"Beef tenderloin." She kissed him tenderly. "I'm for dessert."

He returned the kiss as only he could. "Are we celebrating something?"

"It's Steppie's birthday."

Jimmy's face fell. "What's wrong, Happy?"

The oven timer buzzed, and she took the roast from the oven. The meat had to rest for fifteen minutes. The time had come to talk to Jimmy. Everything will be OK, she told herself. He'll understand.

"Etchers came by this morning. Sit down, and I'll tell you about it."

Jimmy sat on the sofa, still wearing his coat. Happy settled next to him. "Romero asked to see me. No one knows why. Etchers is picking me up tomorrow morning."

"To see Romero?"

She nodded.

Jimmy trained his steely cop's eyes on hers. "Tell me about your conversation with Etchers, word-for-word."

She repeated the conversation with every detail she could remember, ending with, "The request came from the Attorney General." Jimmy listened without any interruptions or questions. A long, nearly-unbearable silence followed. He stood and paced the length of the great room. He stopped in front of her.

The silence ended with a shout. "What the fuck, Happy?"

Jimmy's tone and volume made her jump. The profanity shocked her. She'd never heard him curse at anyone. And now he was cursing at her.

"Jimmy?"

His clenched jaw betrayed his fury. "I don't understand this. You could've said 'no.' Why didn't you? And don't give me any bullshit about making sure Romero doesn't recant his testimony. He won't recant, and you know it."

"The Attorney Gen—"

"Fuck the Attorney General. No one, not even the AG, can force you to meet with Romero. The decision to see him is on you, so own it."

A wave of intimidation swept through her, soon replaced with a wave of anger. She rose from the sofa, planted her feet in front of Jimmy, and looked him in the eyes. "Romero wouldn't ask me to see me unless it was important. There's something he thinks I need to know. He's always looked out for me."

"Looked out for you?" Jimmy let out a sarcastic laugh. "Are you joking? Now you're in WITSEC, worrying about the target on your back, complaining about the secrets you're forced to keep, and the lies you have to tell."

"Romero was a good friend at a sorrowful time in my life. I owe him."

"You saved his life. He owes *you*. Collect that debt by keeping him out of your life. You owe him nothing."

Yeah, she did. It had been over eighteen months, and she could still sense the lines of coke that nearly finished her—the alluring smell, the intriguing texture, the promise of exhilaration. She could hear the powder sounding its siren's call.

Come to me, Lucy. Let me comfort you. I've missed you.

She couldn't stop herself. Romero did. That relapse would've been the end of her. She knew it then, she knew it now.

"I saved him; he saved me. I can't just blow him off."

"So, this is just a matter of etiquette? Or you don't want to hurt his feelings? Jesus!"

"No, of course not. I thought you and Romero were friends. You stayed by his side for two weeks while he turned state's evidence."

Jimmy scoffed his contempt. "You have it all wrong. For some reason, my presence calmed Romero. The feds noticed he was more cooperative with me around. They called the Superintendent of the Maryland State Police. The next thing I knew, I was babysitting Romero for the longest two weeks of my life. I was doing my job, nothing more. I wasn't his friend, and I never will be. There's no room in our relationship for Romero."

"I agree, one hundred percent. I don't want that either."

"You're making room for him, don't you see? You're giving him your time. You're giving him time that belongs to us. He's in our lives right now because we're talking about him. I want him out of the room."

Happy entered the kitchen and placed the roast on the cutting board. She cut off a couple of beef slices before looking back at Jimmy. He was on the sofa, hunched over, forearms on knees. She wondered if he were praying. Why would he do that? Sometimes, you have to figure things out for yourself. A new approach was required—address his worries.

"Jimmy, what exactly are you worried about? Do you think I'm going to run off with him?"

"What I worry about is worse. I think he's going to fuck with your mind. You'll come back, but you won't be the same. I worry Romero matters more to you than you've led me to believe, maybe more than you know yourself."

A few seconds later, Jimmy was standing beside her, turning her face toward his with the fingertips of his left hand. "Please don't go, Happy. You've been doing great since you left him behind. You've worked hard to get past a terrible time in your life. Leave it all behind, leave him behind."

"I *have* left him behind, but I need to see this through."

Now both of Jimmy's hands were cupping her cheeks. His gaze into her eyes was so penetrating it felt like he was reaching for her soul. "The man's a narcissist. He's manipulative; he'll do what it takes to get what he wants. In the end, he'll hurt you, and your life will be trashed. Please listen to me. Don't go."

"How can he hurt me? Etchers will be there. So will other deputies. Nothing's going to happen. I'll be back in Deep Creek tomorrow afternoon, and everything will be fine."

"No, it won't be fine." Jimmy looked defeated. "Is there anything I can do or say to change your mind? I love you, more than I could ever tell you, but I can't live with this."

She could've sworn she saw tears in his eyes. She shook her head. "It's a matter of conscience for me."

Jimmy walked away from her, toward the door, and put on his boots. When he grasped the doorknob, he turned. "Happy, your conscience needs some fine tuning."

With that, he walked out.

Two quiet hours passed. Only Steppie ate the beef tenderloin, carrots, and green beans. Happy was alone with her conscience. She was determined to see Romero but knew she would hurt Jimmy. There must be some way to resolve this. How could she reassure him that Romero wouldn't *fuck* with her mind, as Jimmy so surprisingly put it? Maybe Jimmy could go with her—even be part of the conversation with Romero. Romero may object, but if she insisted, it would be up to him to cancel. She called Jimmy.

"I have an idea how to solve our issue."

"Does your idea involve you seeing Romero?"

"Yes, but—"

"No. You decide what you want. Goodnight."

The phone disconnected. She wanted a drink; anything would do. Her mind automatically scanned the house for the presence of alcohol. There'd be nothing in the pantry, not even cooking wine. Maybe Christine used mouthwash with alcohol. Just a few swishes needed.

Where was Christine? If Happy could hang on until Christine came home, she'd be fine.

She clung to Steppie and called her sponsor. No answer. Left a message.

Out of habit, she pulled up the list of AA meetings she kept on the phone. The next one wasn't until tomorrow. Happy clicked her phone to the folder of alcoholism apps. One tracked how many days she'd been sober. She was now on day five-thousand two-hundred sixty-nine. An argument with Jimmy wasn't worth breaking her nearly eight-year streak. The next app led to prayers and meditations. Cravings kept intruding into her readings.

Christine breezed through the doorway five minutes later, carrying a plastic bag from Discount Depo. Steppie leaped from Happy's lap and raced to greet her. She laughed while he licked her face. "Happy, guess what. I got a job today."

"Congrats." Happy glanced at the plastic bag. "Discount Depo?"

Happy shopped at the massive retail store every week. It sold groceries, clothing, auto goods, electronics, and pharmaceuticals.

"I start tomorrow."

She joined Happy on the sofa. "See what I bought?"

Christine opened the bag and displayed two small turtleneck sweaters, one purple, one pink. "I got a great deal. There was a coupon in the paper for thirty percent off. And I got to use my employee discount, even though I don't officially start until tomorrow. Isn't that great? Guess how much I paid."

"Ten dollars?"

"They were three dollars each."

"Are they for you?" Happy took a sweater from Christine's hands and held it up by the shoulders. "They seem kinda small."

"No, they're gifts for next Christmas. I don't know who I'll give them to yet, but come Christmastime, I'll be glad I saved so much money." She folded the sweaters into perfect squares and slipped them into the plastic bag. "I'm going to go put them in the shed."

By the time the door shut behind Christine, Happy had stopped thinking about alcohol and started wondering about how many more of Christine's *great deals* the shed could hold.

Chapter 18

Happy stared at her closet. What does one wear to meet someone who was just released from prison? Appearance-wise, everything about her was different. When Romero last saw her, she had blonde hair, mismatched eyes, crooked teeth, and a muscular body. She'd gained ten pounds over the last eighteen months—a consequence of driving, not biking, for a living. She considered removing her brown contacts but thought the better of it. Romero had to understand she was no longer the Lucy he knew.

She selected jeans and a red-checked flannel shirt. No makeup. No jewelry. She hated fuss—Lucy's *no fuss* trait remained with Happy. When she entered WITSEC, Etchers arranged for a personal stylist to advise her. She passively acquiesced to trading in her scraggly mess of hair for a short, curly pixie cut. Next came the new hair color—mousy brown replaced the blonde. Her mismatched eyes disappeared under brown contacts. Her facial features transformed under makeup.

When she first saw herself in a mirror, she tearfully asked the stylist, "Where did Lucy go?"

"Dear, the point of all this was to make Lucy disappear."

Etchers arrived at eight o'clock. He looked her over, apparently surprised by her casual appearance. "I thought you'd dress up."

"There's nothing to dress up for. Where're we going?"

"U.S. Marshals Service in Pittsburgh."

Etchers was polite but made no attempt at conversation during their drive. When they crossed Liberty Bridge, Happy got her first view of the city. She perked up; the city reminded her of Baltimore, her beloved hometown. The sunlight reflecting off the skyline windows was familiar and comforting.

She smiled at the sound of blaring car horns. It occurred to her that she had never heard the honk of a car in Deep Creek. She lowered her window and inhaled the city's aroma—a mix of car exhaust, food trucks, and the Monongahela River. Not as fragrant as Baltimore's Chesapeake Bay, but pleasing enough. Pittsburgh was busy and exciting.

Etchers turned onto Grant Street. Happy learned the Marshals Service was located inside the federal courthouse serving Western Pennsylvania. The building shared the same imposing architecture and gray exterior as the federal courthouse in Baltimore.

The deputy drove his truck through a security gate to an outdoor parking lot, found a space, and took the keys from the ignition. After he unbuckled his seat belt, he turned to her with a paternal demeanor. "Happy, there's still time for you to change your mind."

"I know."

"I don't want to see you get hurt."

"I know that, too." She smiled at him. "But if I am, I promise I won't come crying to you."

He gave her a long look before opening his door. "Let's go."

A rectangular, wooden table with eight matching chairs occupied most of the conference room. There were no decorative seat cushions. Much to her disappointment, the office was on the second floor; she had hoped to enjoy a bird's eye view of the city. No pictures, books, or table lamps. The stark nature of the décor sent a message, loud and clear—all business. Get in, get done, get out. An overhead fluorescent light gave Etchers's face a pasty appearance. Happy knew she shared the anemic complexion, probably made worse by her red flannel shirt.

Etchers gave her final instructions. "If you change your mind, or this breaks bad in any way, call out for me, you hear? I'll be right outside the door with another deputy. Scream if you have to."

Happy affirmed. Etchers left. She was alone.

Anxiety crept into her stomach and spread to her lungs, triggering a bout of rapid breathing. Nerves tingled beneath her skin. She pushed the hair from her face with sweaty hands. Was her body warning her she was making a grievous mistake?

She was about to call for Etchers when voices sounded outside the door. Male voices. The silky one belonged to Romero. Next came the turn of the door knob. The door opened.

"Romero," a deputy said. "You have thirty minutes."

"Yes, sir," he said while giving Happy a wink and a grin. The door shut.

They stared at one another for a moment. Romero was still sinfully handsome, but jail and trial testimony had aged him. Streaks of gray ran through his dark hair. His eyes and mouth were surrounded by deep creases. He wore an ill-fitting dark suit and a white dress shirt. She recognized the outfit from the courtroom sketches that appeared in the newspapers during his testimony. The tie was different—too wide, too short, and too colorful. Not his style. He must have borrowed it. She regretted not putting more effort into her appearance. Although she wanted to send the message that their relationship was over, she didn't intend to disrespect him.

He grasped both her hands and turned her around. "Let me take a look at you."

When the turn was completed, he smiled his approval. "You're absolutely gorgeous; more beautiful than I remember." Romero gestured to the table. "Come sit with me."

After she took the chair next to him, she leaned into him and whispered, "Romero, is this a booty call?"

He threw back his head and let out a deep-throated laugh. "Oh, Lucy! You can still tickle me." He laughed for another thirty seconds before grabbing a tissue from the box on the table and wiping his eyes. "It's been a long time since I've had a good laugh. Thank you."

She laughed at her own joke, as she always did. It occurred to her she hadn't told many jokes recently. "It's been a long time since anyone called me 'Lucy.' Thank you for *that*."

Happy surveyed the room from her seat, looking for anything that could hold a microphone or video camera. "Do we have privacy?"

"I've been assured we do, but let's assume we don't." He reached for her hand and held it. "God, I'm so glad to see you again. How are you?"

"I'm doing well. Are they treating you right? I worry about your safety."

"You do?" He kissed the back of her hand. "You shouldn't. The Bureau of Prisons kept me safe. I was isolated from the prison population, but the guards worked hard to keep my mind sharp. I had access to reading material. They used to have conversations with me. We played cards, talked politics, current events, joked around. They wanted to make sure I didn't lose my mind before I testified."

"And now?"

"We'll see." He shrugged. "I'll be on my own, except for my WITSEC handler. I'm glad you came. I wasn't sure you would."

"Of course, I'd come. Why did you think I wouldn't?"

"It's been a long time. I heard you had a good job and were in a serious relationship. Is that true?"

"Yes, to both. But you and I are friends. Why did you want to see me? And don't tell me anything that'll get me into trouble."

"Of course, I won't." He squeezed her hand. "I'd never put you in a bad spot."

Chapter 19

Happy didn't like the feel of his hand resting on hers but said nothing. The sooner Romero told her what was on his mind, the sooner she could leave.

He must have sensed her mood. He removed his hand and used it to gesture while he spoke. "You saved me, in too many ways to count. I never thanked you. I wanted to express my gratitude, in person. I'm deeply indebted to you."

"You're welcome. I owe you thanks as well. Let's declare our mutual debts 'paid in full.'"

He readily agreed. Now her Romero slate was clean. She could finally move on.

Romero continued. "My obligations under the plea agreement have been met. The trial's over. As soon as I leave this room, I leave the protection of the Bureau of Prisons and enter WITSEC. I wanted to find out what it's like."

"It takes some getting used to, but it's fine."

He slowly shook his head. "Lucy, you're a terrible liar, always have been. That's why I'm asking *you*. So, tell me what it's really like. I want the God's honest truth."

She opted for a truthful, but optimistic answer. "It's OK. I like my handler, Deputy Etchers. I feel safe under his watch. The whole identity thing is complicated. It's hard keeping it straight—Lucy pops out at inopportune times."

His slight nod signaled her to continue.

"Every morning I study up on Happy Holiday and practice her signature. I keep track of what lie I tell who. About two weeks ago, I blew it. I was driving a snowplow and found a dead body. I was so rattled I told the forensic investigator my name was 'Lucy Prestipino.' Etchers had a conniption, but he didn't yank me out of Deep Creek."

Romero's eyebrows flew up. "Holy shit, Lucy. How'd the body get there?"

"The man froze to death. The police said he'd been driving drunk, ran out of gas, and tried to walk for help." Happy put her elbows on the table and folded her arms. "But, the thing is, he drove on curvy and mountainous roads for two hours and never crashed. It's weird, don't you think?"

Romero gave her a concerned look. "I'm sure the police will figure it out. How'd you get into snow plowing?"

She told him about getting her commercial driver's license and her job with Mountain Lake Landscaping. She omitted the fact she'd been suspended.

"What do you do when there's no snow?"

"The blade comes off, and it becomes a dump truck. I haul tar, dirt, gravel, whatever is needed for a roads' project."

He chuckled. "I'll bet you could terrorize someone with that truck."

"What? Why would I do that?"

Romero stopped chuckling. "Of course, you wouldn't. I made a bad joke...sorry."

She didn't reply and let the apology sit there.

Romero spoke first. "Anything else I should know about WITSEC?"

"Sometimes it's really hard. I'm not allowed to ride a bike anymore. Etchers said bike-riding is a red-flag—Roach will be looking for a skilled, female biker." She made an effort to keep her voice steady. "I miss my bike. It was part of me, but now it's gone. The marshals will figure out your signature trait and take it away from you. Be ready for that."

Apprehension crossed Romero's face. "I know. I'm scheduled for plastic surgery. I'm getting a new face."

Happy cried out with horror. "Oh, Romie!" Her eyes glistened while she stroked his cheek. The marshals were right—his movie star looks were his signature. Roach would find him in a New York minute if his face weren't changed. She felt small for mentioning her bike prohibition. At least she got to keep her face.

"What about your tattoos?"

"They'll be removed." He looked at her with eyes filled with anxiety. "Lucy, the plastic surgeons could turn me into…a monster."

This horror was worse than the last. "They wouldn't do that!"

"They could if they wanted to. There's plenty of law enforcement who think I got a free ride, that I wasn't punished enough for my crimes. And they're right. I wasn't. They could fix that by making me spend the rest of my life as a freak."

She wanted to weep for him but didn't dare. He needed reassurance and encouragement. She cupped his face in her hands and stared into his eyes.

"Romie, listen to me. No matter what you look like, you'll always have that way about you…I can't explain it, but it's magic. The way you hold yourself, how you look at a woman, your smell, the smile. You won't ever lose that. You have *it,* and *it*'s not going anywhere, no matter what you look like."

She pulled his face toward hers and kissed his lips, sweetly but without passion. Afterward, she caressed his cheek. "Do you know what your name will be?"

He shook his head.

"Where will you go?"

"No one's told me anything. When they asked me if I preferred a warm or cold climate, I said 'cold.'"

"Why? You hate the cold."

"That I do, but I figured if I said 'cold,' they'd give me warm."

Happy commented on his cynicism with a small shake of her head. "Is there anything else you want to know about WITSEC?"

He nodded. "The most important thing of all. I want to know if you'll go with me." Romero got down on one knee and pulled a small ring from his pocket. "Will you marry me? This isn't much of a ring…I made it in the prison workshop. I'll give you a better one once I get on my feet, I promise. I've always been good at making money. I'll support you. Give you everything you want and need."

She gazed at the ring. It was a narrow, silver-colored band. Whatever it was made of, she knew it wasn't silver. The offered ring was an apt symbol of the life she'd have with Romero—not a genuine marriage in the way she needed it to be. He'd be unfaithful to her. Somehow, she understood there'd be no children. It would be an unsatisfactory, empty marriage.

She wanted to be married to a man like Jimmy. No, not *like* Jimmy. She wanted Jimmy.

Happy touched the ring but didn't take it. "This is a fine ring. I love Jimmy Bittinger. He's the one I want to marry."

Romero's eyes displayed surprise. His face hardened for a moment, followed by half-smile. "He's a steady man. Solid as they come. Best of luck."

There was something about his tone that annoyed her. It was almost contemptuous, but not enough for her to call him on it.

"There's something you need to know," he said. "The marshals didn't want me to tell you. They're afraid you'll spill it. I assured them you won't. I had to kick up a fuss to get you here, but they gave in."

"Don't tell me anything I can't tell Jimmy."

Romero paused a beat. "I prefer you not tell him, for reasons that'll be obvious, but I trust you'll be discreet and use your good judgment."

He settled into his seat and leaned toward her. His voice dropped to a near-whisper.

"The marshals will stage my death. It'll be in the news. I wanted you to know it's all a lie. I don't want you living your life thinking I was dead, because I know you'll find some way to blame yourself."

Happy was mesmerized into silence.

"Only a few people in the Marshals Service know about this. The fewer people who know, the safer it'll be for me. You may get interviewed about this meeting by people who don't know. If you tell anyone, they'll gaslight you—they'll say you're crazy, that you can't face reality. Save yourself a lot of trouble, and keep this to yourself."

He leaned in close enough to kiss her lips but didn't. His right hand found a place on top of her left. "This is the most important thing. Don't forget who you are, Lucy Prestipino. The only thing that's changed is the superficial stuff. Your name, your looks, your occupation. None of that matters. Don't let Lucy disappear. Promise me."

"I promise."

"Be careful, Lucy. Peeps is still out there, and he's practically in your backyard. He's building an opioid network in West Virginia, Kentucky, and Ohio. Be on the lookout wherever you go."

"Why would he come after me? You're done testifying. He can't use me as leverage anymore, especially if you're 'dead.'"

"I betrayed Roach and Peeps blames you. He wants revenge. He's never going to stop looking for you until one of you is dead. Make sure it's not you. There are other Roach members floating around. Some might want to kill you for bragging rights. Promise me you'll never let your guard down."

"I promise. Now, I need a promise from you."

"Anything."

"I need to get on with my life. I can't do that if you're in it. Promise me you won't contact me again. If you try to, I won't respond."

The deputy marshal entered the room. "Time to go, Romero."

"Promise me, Romie!"

He nodded his promise and stood. After taking a few steps toward the door, he hesitated. "Please, one more minute," he said to the deputy.

Romero turned toward Happy. The concerned look reappeared. "The man you found with your snowplow—you're not looking into that, are you?"

She gave him her best lying shrug. "No, of course not."

Chapter 20

Happy found Etchers waiting in a chair outside the conference room. He spoke only of logistics while they walked through the building. The exit's this way, the elevator's down the hall, the ladies room is on the left, the truck's over there, buckle up.

Etchers turned the ignition. "Now we can talk privately. Tell me what Romero wanted."

She shook her head. It would take a while to process the conversation. She didn't want to share it with anyone until she reviewed the conversation, bit-by-bit, and understood it. One thing was plain to her—Romero's life was going to suck. A lifetime of lies and pretense. Relationships built on falsehoods. But he'd been a criminal. Maybe the lies and pretense would come easily for him.

It didn't for Happy, but Jimmy knew her truth. She could have his love without the lies. But she couldn't stop fretting about Christine.

"Are you sure I shouldn't tell Christine the truth? It doesn't feel right. She's telling me all these personal things...confidential stuff and all I'm sharing are lies. How am I supposed to have true friendships when nearly everything I say about myself is a lie?"

Etchers turned off the ignition. "Does Romero have something to do with these questions?"

"Indirectly." She gazed through the passenger window for a few seconds. "I had friends in Baltimore, like my messenger posse and my AA sponsor. They knew the real me. I could have heart-to-heart talks with them. I'll never have that with Christine. It's lonely. I think Romero knows how lonely his life is gonna be. He proposed to me. That was the main reason he wanted to see me."

"What did you say?"

"I turned him down."

Etchers smiled his approval. "Good. As for Christine? Don't tell her anything. She's young and immature. Your friendship with her is not a lifetime commitment. She'll move on. One day, she'll be at a party, have a few too many, and entertain the crowd with the amazing story about her former employer with the funny name who was in witness protection."

Happy sighed her acknowledgment that Etchers's scenario was likely correct. Christine was a yapper. "Thanks, Marshal."

"Uncle Peter." He persisted with his Romero questions. "What else did he want?"

She pulled her phone from her backpack. "One of Bernie's friends works in Pittsburgh. I'd like to meet him." She paused for effect. "There's more."

"Maybe." He glanced at her. "Tell me what else and I'll think about it."

"He wanted to know what WITSEC was like. I gave him a little pep talk."

"Anything more?"

"I made him promise not to contact me again."

"Smart girl. Keep talking."

She told him about Peeps. "That's it, nothing more."

"Go on and set up your meeting."

She called Bernie's friend, Randall Kennedy. He agreed to meet for lunch at the Pittsburgh Palace, a restaurant on the bottom floor of his office building. Etchers drove through the city until they arrived at the valet parking stand in front of the restaurant. A plaque outside the door displayed the menu along with the three-star Michelin rating. A tall, curvy blonde wearing a clingy, black dress greeted them.

"We're meeting Randall Kennedy," Happy said. "Is he here?"

"He just arrived. Follow me."

As the duo followed the hostess to a table in the back, Happy admired her stylish French twist. She caught Etchers admiring her other features. The smell of sizzling steak floated through the restaurant. White linens covered the tables. Place settings gleamed with crystal glasses, bone china plates, and polished silverware.

Kennedy was bald and had the craggy look of an outdoors man. Ruddy cheeks, chapped lips, and squint-wrinkles around the eyes. He wore navy blue slacks and a tan knit polo shirt. She estimated he was in his fifties. Etchers appeared to size him up as they approached the table. Happy made the introductions ending with, "Mr. Kennedy, thank you for coming."

Kennedy shook Etchers's hand with a demeanor telegraphing suspicion and caution. "Law enforcement?"

"U.S. Marshals Service," Etchers said.

"He's my uncle," Happy said. "He happens to be a Deputy U.S. Marshal."

"Of course," Kennedy said, with a knowing smile that perplexed Happy.

Etchers's cold glare wiped the smile from Kennedy's face.

A server approached the table. "May I get you something to drink?"

Kennedy ordered a Manhattan. Happy imagined the taste of a Manhattan—the lovely mix of the sweet vermouth and the dash of bitters. Would the bartender make it with rye, bourbon or scotch? She'd love a drink now; she deserved one after meeting Romero.

Etchers ordered two iced teas.

Kennedy dispensed with the small talk. "How's Olivia?"

"Not good," Happy said. "Managing."

The server arrived with the drinks. Happy couldn't take her eyes off the Manhattan. She considered asking Kennedy for the cherry garnish. The erotic taste of whiskey would cling to the little, red fruit. The few molecules of whiskey would go down nicely. Etchers cleared his throat, yanking her attention from the cocktail. Temporarily.

Kennedy drained his Manhattan. Happy mentally joined him.

"What can I do for you, Ms. Holiday?" Kennedy said as he raised his empty glass to signal the server for another drink.

Happy explained the mystery surrounding Bernie's phone call to Olivia.

He fished the cherry out of his empty glass and popped it into his mouth. "Olivia mentioned it at the viewing. I told her I didn't know anything. Sorry."

Another Manhattan appeared on the table.

She kept her eyes on Kennedy's to distract herself from the drink. "Bernie's death was so sudden, such a shock, maybe you just didn't remember anything at the time. I'm hoping you remember something now."

"I've been trying to forget everything."

Happy pressed. "Don't you want to help Olivia? Maybe you know some small thing that will lead to something important. Will you try? I know it's painful to—"

Kennedy shook the ice cubes, so they clinked in his glass. "I'll try... for Olivia's sake. But I'm telling you, Bernie didn't say anything about a surprise, not a single word."

"Did he buy anything at the game?"

"Not at the game. On the way into the stadium, we passed by one of those freelance vendors. He bought his kids T-shirts."

"How'd he pay for them?"

"Cash."

"He didn't buy anything inside the stadium? Like food or beer or something?"

"We bought it for him. That was standard operating procedure."

"How so?"

"Olivia kept him on a short leash. She was the money maker in the marriage and doled out a weekly allowance. He usually ran out of money before the end of the week."

"Did he ever ask you for money?"

"All the time."

"For what?"

Kennedy shrugged. "I stopped asking."

"Did he complain about the allowance?"

"What difference could that possibly make?" He removed the napkin from his lap and tossed it on the table.

Etchers jumped into the conversation. "You're right...it makes no difference." He shifted his eyes to Happy and spoke with a voice loaded with reprimand. "None at all."

Another Manhattan appeared on the table. Happy imagined how it would warm her toes. "Mr. Kennedy, I'm sorry for my clumsy question. Please forgive me. And I'm sorry about your loss. It's clear you were a good friend to both Bernie and Olivia."

"I tried to be. Ever been married, Ms. Holiday?"

She shook her head.

"You're naïve." Kennedy used the glass to gesture while he spoke. "Sometimes good people aren't compatible. That's how it was with them. He was a free spirit. She wasn't. They clashed. That's how it can be in a marriage. Isn't that right, Marshal Etchers?"

"It can be that way, sure."

"How about you, Marshal? Are you married?"

"Divorced."

"You are?" Happy said. "I didn't know that."

Both men turned their heads in her direction; Kennedy leered, Etchers glared. Happy shrank with the realization she'd just blown her cover. It took her a moment to re-focus on the conversation. She fretted about the stern lecture from Etchers heading her way. How could she have made such a stupid mistake?

Kennedy sipped his drink and gazed at Etchers from above the rim of the cocktail glass. "Odd your *niece* doesn't know you're divorced."

Happy's fists knotted as she envisioned landing a three-star punch into Kennedy's face. Asshole. Etchers spoke, but she couldn't hear a word. The heartbeat pounding in her head deafened her.

"Hey," she said, interrupting whatever Etchers was saying. "How dare you insult my uncle? He's a decent man who's looked after me ever since my mother was—"

"Happy, that's enough," Etchers said.

"No, Uncle Peter, it's not enough." She turned to Kennedy. "Why'd you agree to talk to me? Did you think it was a chance to eat at a fancy, schmancy restaurant on someone else's nickel? Maybe have a few drinks while you're at it? What do you think Olivia's gonna say when I hand her the bill?"

Happy became aware that the low background noise in the restaurant had vanished. Other diners were no longer eating and drinking but watching their table.

Kennedy dropped the leer and looked at Happy with eyes now red and glazy. His ruddy complexion turned ashen. "Olivia's paying for this?"

"Of course, she is. And I'm gonna tell her all about you getting drunk and acting like a sleazy creeper. What's the matter with you?"

Happy hailed the server and asked for the check.

"There's no need to involve Oli—"

She leaned across the table, put her face near Kennedy's, and hissed. "Then act like a fuckin' gentleman. Stop drinking and start talking. Answer my questions."

Kennedy's eyes widened. He glanced at Etchers who raised his hands, palms up. "You're on your own, buddy."

"My apologies to you both." Kennedy pushed the drink away. "Yes, Bernie complained all the time. What else do you want to know?"

"I saw you at Bernie's viewing. You and Hank Tinker were arguing. What were you arguing about?"

"We weren't arguing...we were blaming ourselves, blaming each other. I live in Pittsburgh, Hank lives in Keyser, West Virginia. Either one of us could've invited Bernie to stay the night, but we didn't. Just didn't think of it. We said good-bye and let him drive off into a snowstorm... and now he's dead."

"I heard you say to Mr. Tinker, 'We have to tell her.' What did you have to tell Olivia?"

Kennedy shifted in his seat. He gripped his cocktail glass as he stared at the cherry inside. It occurred to Happy he was either trying to remember or trying to make something up.

Thirty long seconds passed before he slurred his answer. "Bernie talked about a song he wrote. He played it for us on his phone. I wanted to make sure Olivia knew about the song. Maybe she could sell it and make some money."

"Why was there an argument about that? It seems like a reasonable thing to do."

"The song was bad...to our ears, anyway. But what do we know about music? Hank didn't want her to waste any time or money on it." He shrugged. "That's all."

The server arrived with the check.

Kennedy glanced at his watch and stood. "I have to get back to work. He grabbed the check and pulled out his credit card. "I'll pay on the way out."

"Are you all right to drive?" Etchers said to Kennedy.

"No, but I can walk. My office is upstairs."

"Thank you for your time, Mr. Kennedy," Happy said. "May I call you if something comes up?"

"Please don't."

Etchers was quiet during the return to Deep Creek, but Happy felt like talking. "What did you think of Randall Kennedy?"

"He's a man carrying a lot of guilt. It would be a kindness if you left him alone."

"He knows more than he let on, don't you think?"

Etchers paused while he glanced into his side mirror to yield onto the Pennsylvania Turnpike. "Whatever else he knows, it doesn't make a bit of difference."

"Why not?"

"You said your mission was to find out Bernie's surprise. His marital problems have nothing to do with that. If you have any feeling for Mrs. Singleton, you'll walk away. Digging up painful history isn't going to help her."

Etchers was probably right. Bernie had called his wife while he was happy. Those happy moments could've been few and far between. Maybe Bernie's happiness was something Olivia could hold on to. "You're right. Thanks for the reality check, Uncle Peter."

"You didn't need to defend my honor to that idiot."

"Of course, I did." She smiled at him. "You're the only uncle I got. So, why did you get divorced?"

"Which time?"

"You got divorced more than once?"

"Three times." He turned to her with raised eyebrows. "Not that it's any of your business, but I'm not marriage material. All of my wives were lovely women. They deserved better than me. I'm friends with them, and they're friends with each other. We have Thanksgiving together every year with the kids."

"Wow." Happy couldn't imagine such a Thanksgiving, but it sounded like fun.

Etchers put on his paternal demeanor. "I need to tell you something because I don't want you to be surprised when it happens. I'll be retiring soon."

"How come? You're too young to retire."

"The mandatory age of retirement for U.S. Marshals is fifty-seven. I'm almost there."

"Don't you have a choice?"

"No, but even if I did, I'd retire. I'm getting old, and I'm not as quick as I used to be. It's for the safety of those I protect, including you. Don't worry, you'll be assigned another handler."

Happy didn't know whether to laugh or cry. Etchers got on her last nerve, but the thought of him being gone made her heartsick. "I know

I'm supposed to say 'congratulations.' Do mind if I say it later? I need to get used to the idea."

"That's fine."

The conversation ended. Her thoughts shifted to Jimmy. She'd call him as soon as she got home. They'd make up, and things would get back to normal. She closed her eyes and listened to the eighteen-wheelers thunder by. Soon she'd be kissing Jimmy, touching him, loving him until he released his own thunder.

Chapter 21

Etchers dropped Happy at home at three o'clock in the afternoon. When she opened her front door, Steppie shot out and greeted her with his usual gusto. She tried to play with him, but he was more interested in exploring her 4Runner. He circled it, sniffed it, ran to her, and returned to the SUV. Some animal must've left its mark during her absence. She lured Steppie into the house with a slice of beef tenderloin. Now she needed to take care of Jimmy. She called him. He didn't pick up.

She fidgeted while fifteen minutes ticked away. The Manhattan had stirred up a craving. There was an AA meeting in twenty minutes at St. Peter's Catholic Church in Oakland. "Sorry, Steppie," she said as she kissed the dog. "I gotta go out again."

She unlocked the SUV and took her spot behind the steering wheel. The hair rose on her arms. She snapped her head to the right. Looked at the backseat. No one there. Steppie wasn't barking from inside the house. No one was on the premises. Her heart pounded warnings even though her brain assured her she was safe.

There was something different about the 4Runner, but she couldn't put her finger on it. Nothing was missing from the glove compartment or the console. She exited the vehicle and circled it, searching for anything unusual. The SUV's exterior appeared untouched. The door locks showed no sign of tampering. Nothing was amiss in the rear cargo area. Her arm hairs settled down. Romero's warning about Peeps must have made her edgy.

Steppie yelped. Happy jumped, half-expecting Peeps to come at her with a machete. Jimmy's patrol car nosed down the driveway. She gave

Jimmy an exuberant wave and raced to greet him. He stepped from the car wearing a grave expression that stopped her short. Momentarily. She threw her arms around his chest and hugged him tightly. "Jim—"

He unhooked her arms, stepped back and stood facing her, arms at his side. "Before you say anything, did you see Romero?"

"Yes. Come inside so I can tell you about—"

He held up his hands signaling her to stop talking. His eyes filled with pain. "I need to talk to you. This will be a difficult conversation. I've been up all-night praying about it."

"What is it?" Her voice trembled. "Has someone died? Tell me."

Jimmy took a couple of deep breaths. "I begged you not to see Romero. If you saw him after everything I said, you either don't care about my feelings, or you care about Romero more. You'll always be at his beck and call. I won't spend the rest of my life looking over my shoulder for Romero Sanchez. I refuse to wonder if the woman I love cares for someone more than me."

"You don't have to wonder—"

"I don't want to hurt you. I really don't. We're not meant for each other. Let's leave it at that."

She stared at him, mouth agape, speechless for a full fifteen seconds before she sputtered questions. "What are you saying? Are you breaking up with me?"

"It's important to me that we part on good terms."

"We don't have to part at all. You'll understand if you let me tell you what—"

He shook his head.

"Don't do this," she said. "What do you think happened? We met at the Pittsburgh office of the U.S. Marshal. There were deputies all over the place. Etchers was right outside the—"

"It doesn't matter what happened, or what was said. It's the fact you saw him. No amount of talking will change that."

"You don't know that. Just listen—"

"I need to put boundaries around Romero. I don't want to talk about him. I don't want to think about him, and I certainly don't want my girlfriend having anything to do with him. As for you and me? I just want our relationship to end. Peacefully, if possible. Can we do that? End it in a civil manner?"

"How can you put an end to us without hearing what I have to—"

"You broke my heart."

"How? By visiting Romero? That makes no sense."

"Please, Happy. Let's end our relationship in a dignified way."

Dignified? Her dreams were exploding in her face. She wanted to shout, "You controlling asshole!" She kept her mouth shut. It may take some time, but Jimmy would eventually see things her way. In the meantime, she wouldn't say or do anything that would sabotage their reconciliation.

She grasped his hand and held it against her heart. "Let's not end our relationship at all. I'm going inside. You go home. We'll talk later."

He pulled his hand away. "We're done, Happy."

Happy stared at the oven. She'd entered the kitchen intending to do something, but now she couldn't remember what it was. Something about the oven. After she spent some time meandering around the kitchen, it came to her—she'd meant to set the oven timer for an hour. Her mother always said, "Whatever disappointment comes your way, an hour of tears is enough. Then leave the pity-party and go help someone." There were no tears; Jimmy would come around. She was sure of it. All would be good. In the meantime, she would follow her mother's advice and help someone. Olivia.

Olivia answered the phone on the first ring. Happy updated her on the conversation with Kennedy, omitting her opinion that the man was a sleazy, creeper-asshole.

"Randall mentioned Bernie wrote a song," Happy said. "Do you know anything about that?"

Olivia's first response was a long exhale. When words came, her tone was hard and bitter. "Yes, I know all about that damned song."

"Randall guessed Bernie might've sold it. Could that have been the surprise?"

"No. If it got sold, I would've known before Bernie did."

"How so?"

"Bernie worked on that song for weeks. Revising, tinkering, obsessing. He'd hide out in his music room all night while I cleaned the kitchen, folded laundry, and helped the boys with homework. Finally, he made a demo, but he wouldn't let me listen to it. He said it needed more work. I couldn't stand it anymore. When he wasn't looking, I sent it to a friend of mine in the music business. Bernie was livid, but I didn't care." Olivia's voice cracked. "I needed his help, and the stupid song kept getting in the way."

The cracked voice became a sob. "That's not exactly true. I got rid of the demo because I missed Bernie. The songwriting consumed him. It took him away from me. I loved my husband and wanted him back."

Olivia's sob melted into a torrent of tears. Happy could offer no comforting words, so she said nothing until Olivia stopped crying.

"Excuse me," Olivia said. "Anyway, if the song got sold, my friend would've called me."

"There's no need to excuse yourself. You're in Grief Hell. You're allowed to do whatever it takes to get out."

Olivia responded by blowing her nose.

Happy continued. "I'd like to follow up with your friend, just in case there was a missed communication."

Olivia gave Happy the contact information for Bluesy Cruise. Happy intended to call, but she doubted that a song that caused so much misery could lead to Bernie's happy surprise.

Chapter 22

Happy shivered, either from the chill in the house or from the sadness that permeated her bones. She spotted Jimmy's flannel jacket hanging in the front closet. He'd forgot it weeks ago, but it had become her go-to jacket whenever she needed warmth. It was soft and carried the faint scent of Old Spice aftershave. As she removed the jacket from its hanger, she nixed her intention to wear it. She was confident Jimmy would come around, but there was no sense beating herself up with reminders of him.

Reminders were everywhere; a pair gloves in the closet, a toothbrush in her bathroom, a Pittsburgh Pirates baseball cap on a hat rack, a bible in her bookcase. Where was the creepy Happy Holiday doll? The last time she'd seen it, the doll was laying on the hallway floor outside her bedroom. Now it was missing. She gathered Jimmy's belongings, tossed them into a plastic storage container, and walked to the outside shed.

A dump greeted her; not a single square inch of clear space. There was no path to an area where she could store Jimmy's belongings. Happy stood in the doorway and heaved the storage container with all her strength. It flew across the heaps and landed behind a mound of junk somewhere on the far side of the shed.

The sudden landing jostled other mounds and set off a chain reaction of trash displacement. A pile near the door tipped, spilling its clutter beyond the doorway. Happy began shoving the mess back into the shed with her foot. During the final shove, her foot connected with a clear plastic bag. It contained the remains of a smashed cell phone.

The phone looked as if it'd been run over by a car. It was old. A Nokia flip top. Why, oh why, would Christine save the pieces of a dinosaur cell phone? She intended to ask her.

As soon as Happy returned to the house, she settled on the sofa, emotionally spent. Etchers had warned her—if she wanted to keep Jimmy, she shouldn't see Romero. Her dreams of marriage and children faded before her eyes. Had she just sentenced herself to a life of loneliness? Steppie circled in the space beside her. She caressed his fur until she slipped into sleep.

Bernie Singleton pleaded with his eyes. She smelled his fear, his desperation. His L-shaped hand clung to her. He was screaming words she couldn't understand.

Tell me, Bernie! Tell me!

Help my family. You promised.

Happy bolted awake, startled and disoriented. During her restless slumber, the sun had set. The house was dark for lack of lights; the moon was absent. What day was it? She reached for her cell phone and discovered she'd been asleep for only two hours. It was seven o'clock in the evening on the same lousy day.

Usually, a nap refreshed her, but not tonight. Even turning on the house lights required effort. She dragged herself to the kitchen and made a cup of coffee. Her stomach rumbled. She crunched down a bowl of Cocoa Puffs, all the while ruminating about Bernie Singleton. She wished the man would leave her the hell alone.

Steppie scratched the front door. She slipped on her coat. Once outside, she immediately regretted not wearing a hat and gloves. Bitter cold greeted her. Steppie discovered some interesting tracks and took his time investigating.

"C'mon, Steppie. Hurry up."

During the ten minutes it took the dog to locate his perfect spot, the cold revived her. The coffee kicked in. Once inside the house, she vowed to uncover Bernie's surprise. That'd be the only way to get rid of him.

There were voices outside and noisy footsteps on the walkway steps. Steppie barked with a wagging tail. It was someone she knew. Christine entered, followed by Al and Zeke Hershberger. Zeke wore a blue medical mask across his face. When Christine took his coat, baggy pants drew attention to his thin torso.

Christine laid an overstuffed Discount Depo bag on the counter. "Remember Al and Zeke? I ran into them at work. They wanted to see my new place."

"Welcome," Happy said. "I'm glad you're out of the hospital, Zeke."

"It was touch 'n go for a while, but I pulled through."

"Thank the Lord," Al said. "I thought that little kernel of corn would be the end of him. My baby brother."

A heavy silence followed until Zeke said, "Christine, give us the tour you promised."

Happy watched and listened from the dining area table as Christine led the Hershbergers throughout the house. The tour was thorough; Christine showed them every room, the crawl spaces, and the utility room. They asked questions about the septic system and furnace. After the house tour, they asked to see the outside. Happy watched through the window as Christine walked them around the house, carrying a flashlight. The outside tour included a visit to the shed.

When they returned to the house, the trio joined Happy at the table. "You have a nice home," Al said. "It's way out here, isn't it?"

"Where's your nearest neighbor?" Zeke said.

"A quarter-mile down the road."

"How long does it take the police to get here?" Al said. "We just want to make sure our Christine is safe."

"About twenty minutes, at most," Happy said. "It depends on where the patrol cars are when the call comes in. You don't need to worry. There's no crime in this neighborhood. And no one comes near my house or property without me knowing about it. We have an alarm system." She smiled. "Even better, my dog's yapping will split an eardrum."

Christine piped up. "Happy's boyfriend is a state trooper. He's here all the time. And he's really nice."

Happy didn't correct Christine. As far as she was concerned, Jimmy may be angry with her, but he was still her boyfriend.

The Hershbergers leaned back in their chairs, apparently satisfied with Christine's new living arrangements.

Al eyed the smashed phone on the table. "That man who froze. Did you ever find out his surprise?"

"No, but I'm still working on it."

"And I'm helping," Christine said, brimming with enthusiasm.

Zeke was eyeing the phone, too. "Christine, isn't that the phone you found in our parking lot?"

Christine picked up the plastic bag and examined the phone. "Yes...it is." She looked at Happy. "Where'd it come from?"

"I was putting something in the shed, and it fell when I opened the door. Do you remember when you found it in the parking lot?"

"When I was packing up the restaurant. I guess it got moved here by accident."

Happy boarded a train of thought. Bernie had called Olivia using a cell phone. The box of Bernie's personal property didn't contain a cell phone. Either the police found one and weren't releasing it pending the investigation, or they'd never found the phone in the first place. Maybe the Nokia phone belonged to Bernie.

Al must've been on the same thought train. He held out his hand. "I'll take the phone. It shouldn't have been moved from our property."

Happy turned to Christine, who was still holding the phone and cooked up a lie. "When I found the phone, I wondered if it was Bernie's. I called the police. They never found his phone and wanted me to bring it to them. I told them I'd bring it by tomorrow."

Christine turned to Al. "I'll tell the police to give it to you if it turns out not to be Bernie's."

Al glowered but said nothing.

Funny thing, Happy was never any good at lying until she entered WITSEC.

Chapter 23

By eight o'clock the next morning, Happy was preparing her 4Runner for the day's travel. It was a habit she'd acquired during her messenger days. Cell phone, charger, emergency tools, hazard triangles, snacks and water—each had its assigned place.

When she grabbed her empty water bottle from the console to replace it, she realized what had disturbed her yesterday about the SUV. It was the water bottle. She always put it in the console holder closest to her. Now it was in the holder near the dashboard. The discovery was a surprise but easily explained. The last time she'd sipped water, she inadvertently put the water in the wrong holder.

Twenty minutes later, Happy spoke to the female trooper minding the lobby window of the state police barracks. The trooper, whose name tag said "Miller," wore her technicolor red hair in a tight bun at the base of her neck.

"I'm here about the Bernie Singleton investigation. I'm not sure, but I might have found his cell phone." Happy held up the plastic bag to show Miller the demolished phone. "Could you give this to Corporal Friend?"

Miller's eyes widened. "I'll let him know you're here."

The trooper placed a phone call, nodded at what she heard, and returned the phone to its receiver. "He'll be out in a minute."

There was a seating area in the lobby. Happy made herself comfortable and watched Miller answer a string of phone calls. A door to the barracks' interior opened. Happy stood, expecting to see Friend. It was Jimmy. Maybe Miller told him she was in the lobby. Happy's spirits soared;

Jimmy wanted to see her. Everything would be all right. She smiled at him. The smile was not returned.

He stood in front of her, his eyes blazing, his jaw clamped in interrogation mode. "Happy, this is not the place," he said in a fierce voice that was deceptively soft.

"I'm not here to see—"

The interior door opened a second time.

"Ms. Holiday," said Corporal Friend. "Come with me."

Jimmy stepped away. She could feel his burning gaze follow her as she exited the lobby. Along the way to the Troopers Room, she gritted her teeth. How could Jimmy think she'd ever go back to Romero? Her mother's voice spoke to her as clearly as if she were walking beside her. "Don't give that boy the time of day."

The Troopers Room looked like a place for administrative business. There were desks, chairs, stacks of forms, supplies, and computers. Friend pointed to a chair. "Please sit down." He positioned a wheeled chair close to hers and took a seat.

"Is this Mr. Singleton's phone?" Happy said, handing him the plastic bag.

He examined it through the plastic, turning the bag over and over. Friend fired up his iPad. After a series of clicks, he was apparently reading a report.

"Maybe," Friend said. "He owned a Nokia phone. Where'd you find this?"

"In my shed." She explained her connection to Christine and how her roommate found the phone in the parking lot of the Somerset Bar and Grill. "I wondered whether he dropped it the night he died. It looks like a car ran over it, don't you think?"

"Something happened to it, that's for sure. I'll send it over to forensics for a look."

"What could forensics tell from it? It's pretty smashed up."

"Yes, it is. Thanks for bringing it in."

As Happy headed for the building's exit, Trooper Miller hailed her to the reception window. Miller smiled and leaned in close to the speaking hole. "Want me to call Jimmy?"

"No...but thank you."

Happy stomped to her car. Jimmy was right; they were done. Before pulling out of the parking lot, Happy deleted Jimmy from her life in every way she could. Phone number, e-mail, social media—all gone with a couple of taps on her phone. Where was that creepy Happy Holiday doll? She had to get that goddamn thing off her premises.

Happy didn't remember much about her drive home.

Fifteen-pound Steppie rushed to Happy when she entered the house. He was wild-eyed and barking relentlessly. She knelt on the floor to pat him. Instead of rolling on his back for his usual stomach rub, he leaped against her with such force he knocked her over. She sat on the floor, stunned; Steppie was getting worse. Since coming to Deep Creek, his anxiety had been limited to the nighttime when he was alone. Christine's presence had solved that, but now the anxiety was spreading to the daylight hours.

How could she fix this? Pay Christine to watch him during the day? She now had a full-time job at Discount Depo. Hire two dog sitters? Ridiculous. Give him anxiety-relieving drugs? No, she would end up taking the pills herself. Steppie quivered in her lap while she mindlessly stroked his fur. Her eyes settled on the front door. It was rather shabby. The paint was scratched off at the bottom.

Wait a minute! She'd painted the door less than six months ago. She rose from the floor to examine the damaged door. The damage was fresh and limited to the height of the dog's reach. She fingered through Steppie's paws. Flecks of paint were buried in his nails, not only the white paint of the door but the gray paint of the walls.

She carried the dog with her as she checked the windows. Steppie wasn't large enough to reach the sills, but the paint below them showed deep trails of nail scratches—all new.

"Oh, Steppie." She held the dog close to her chest. "I don't know what to do about you. What are you so afraid of?"

Chapter 24

Happy researched everything Google had to offer about Bluesy Cruise before calling about Bernie's demo. Bluesy was well-known in the world of rock 'n' roll. Wikipedia described her as "an icon in the music industry." She'd discovered dozens of famous musicians and revived the careers of many fading artists. As Happy tapped in Bluesy's phone number, she anticipated enduring many layers of assistants screening her call.

Bluesy answered the call herself on the first ring. Her hoarse voice had the sound of a lifetime cigarette habit. Bluesy recognized Happy's name as soon as she identified herself. Olivia had sent her an e-mail introducing Happy.

"I'm glad you called me," Bluesy said. "I didn't want to talk to Olivia about Bernie's melody, especially after what happened to him. How can I help you?"

As Happy searched for words, she realized she didn't have the vocabulary to ask an intelligent question about music. She'd never taken music lessons, studied music appreciation, or attended a concert. Why hadn't she studied up on the fundamentals of song writing before calling? She had no choice but to muddle through ignorant questions.

"Is Bernie's song any good?"

Bluesy laughed softly into the phone. "I like your direct approach. I take it you're not a musician."

"I sing along with songs if I like them. Sometimes I dance. That's the extent of my musical experience. I don't know a chord of music from a cord of wood."

"That's all right," Bluesy said, a smile in her voice. "I appreciate your frankness."

Happy heard the inhale of smoke from a cigarette. She knew that sound; her mother smoked. Her mind wandered. She could envision Debbie relaxing on the back deck of their Baltimore home, puffing away, the smell of tobacco seeping into the kitchen.

Following a long and breathy exhale, Bluesy interrupted Happy's roaming thoughts. "You've asked a very complicated question. Let's start at the beginning. By way of definition, Bernie's composition is not a song. A song has both lyrics and a melody. The demo Olivia sent me has only a melody. It's an instrumental, piano to be specific. By the way, the melody is titled, 'Melody Rocks.'"

"So, is 'Melody Rocks' any good?"

"It depends on what *you* mean by 'good.' When *I* mean 'good,' I'm talking about whether I can make money from it. Is it marketable? Will people buy it? In those terms, 'Melody Rocks' is not good. If you think *good* means a melody that's interesting to listen to, then it's good."

"Why won't people buy it?"

"It's a mix of genres. It's basically romantic style for classical piano, with a mix of pop, country, and rock 'n' roll thrown in. It's very eclectic and complex. Fast tempo, especially at the end. What radio station would give it play? None that I can think of. It's a remarkable piece of music. I was astounded by the level of Bernie's piano-playing. Breathtaking talent. He could've performed in concert halls. But, in my opinion, his melody won't sell."

Happy wasn't surprised. Bernie struck her as a man who couldn't seem to get things right. "Bernie called Olivia the night he died and told her he had a wonderful surprise. Could this melody be the surprise?"

"I never spoke to Bernie. Any encouragement he might have gotten didn't come from me. Maybe he was experimenting or just having fun. Frankly, I don't think he intended to sell his composition. I'm sorry."

"I'd like to listen to it. Can you make that happen?"

"I can email you the melody. Best of luck, Happy. And keep singing and dancing."

A few minutes later, Happy received "Melody Rocks." After listening to the melody, she understood what Bluesy was talking about. It began soft and sweet. Then it transformed into something else. She recognized many of the classical parts, although she didn't know the titles. Bernie's composition leaped to pop music, then country, and back to classical. There were several repeats, each faster and louder than the one before. Happy could visualize fingers flying across the keyboard, sweat collecting on Bernie's brow. Then it ended. Boom. Over.

Happy stared at the computer screen. What had she just listened to? An amazing mishmash of weirdness. If she ever heard it on the radio, she'd switch to another station. She didn't want to listen to "Melody Rocks" again; once was enough.

In her humble and uneducated opinion, the melody was a loser.

She turned her attention to the box of Bernie's belongings. She studied a receipt timed thirty minutes after the game ended. Bernie made a forty-dollar cash purchase at Taste Buds, located near the stadium. He must've stopped by the establishment for something to eat on the way home. Even if he'd eaten lunch at the stadium, he would've been hungry by the time the game ended.

Like some of the other receipts, this one was damaged in the middle. She couldn't decipher what Bernie purchased. Maybe he bought something for Olivia and a short while later, called her in excited anticipation of giving it to her.

Some food chains sold their own logoed merchandise. Maybe the restaurant sold Smith Island cakes. Bernie had surprised Olivia with the cake on their anniversary; maybe he planned to surprise her again. On second thought, if he'd bought a cake, where was it?

Happy found a faint transaction number and website address on the bottom of the receipt. She tapped in the website. Surprise! Taste Buds was not a restaurant, but a gas station with a food mart. If Bernie were at a gas station, why didn't he buy gas? Maybe he bought food and simply forgot. In a snowstorm? Receipt in hand, she called the gas station and spoke with the manager. She gave him the transaction number.

"The customer bought regular gas," he said. "Paid forty dollars in cash."

"How many gallons?"

"At the time, regular gas was $2.50 a gallon. He purchased sixteen gallons."

Happy googled Ford Explorers. The SUV typically got sixteen miles to the gallon. Bernie should've been able to drive two hundred fifty-six miles. MapQuest revealed Cumberland was one hundred miles away from the Taste Buds. There was plenty of gas to get Bernie home, including getting-lost gas.

Did Corporal Friend know this? Of course, he did. The State Police had processed the receipts before giving them to her.

She was back where she started; something must have happened to the Explorer. There was no evidence of a catastrophic gas tank failure. Maybe there was a problem with the gas line. Could someone have pinpricked invisible holes in the gas line to make it leak fuel, ever so slowly?

Happy pulled out her to-do list and added: "Examine the Explorer's gas line."

Chapter 25

At nine o'clock the next morning, the phone jolted Happy from a deep sleep. She'd had a restless night of strange dreams, each accompanied by Bernie's melody playing in the background like a horror movie. She was half-awake when she answered.

"Did I wake you up, honey?" The caller was her colleague, Milo Sullivan.

"I'm glad you did." She stifled a yawn. "I overslept. What's up?"

"I'm on my way home from work. Are you up for a visit?"

"Sure, I'd love to see you." She meant it; she missed her job. Maybe Milo knew how she could worm her way into Jack's good graces. A peek through her bedroom window encouraged her. The snowplow season wasn't over; six inches of snow covered the ground. Christine had already left for work—there were tire tracks on the driveway.

Happy hustled up some coffee and pancakes. There was a soft knock on the front door. Milo had the post-nightshift look of fatigue—tired and whiskered—but he appeared healthier than the last time she'd seen him. "I made you a little something. Want some coffee?"

"I would, indeed." Milo settled into a kitchen chair while she placed breakfast on the table.

"How was it last night?"

"Routine, nothing to tell. So, we all want to know—when are you coming back?"

She passed him the platter of pancakes. "Jack said I'll never plow for the company again. When my suspension's over, I'll be back in billing."

Milo forked pancakes from the platter to his plate. "Maybe not for long. We miss you, even Jack."

Hope leaped into her heart. "Jack? I don't believe it."

"He says you're a royal pain in the ass, but you make life interesting." He poured syrup on the pancakes. "You know, Happy, you're a mystery to us. There's a five-year waiting list for the job. When you showed up, we thought you had a high-dollar connection." Milo smiled. "Either that or you blackmailed someone. Turns out, you're a real good driver, better than most. Reliable, too. We've been getting on Jack to bring you back, so don't give up."

"OK, I'll try not to."

Milo glanced around the kitchen. "My wife and I looked at this place when it was first on the market. Kids are gone, we gotta downsize. Right off, she talked about paint and wallpaper. I told her, 'Forget it. Too much work.' I'm too old to be climbing ladders and crawling around on my knees painting trim. I hope she never sees what you've done. It looks real good."

"Thanks."

"Care to give a tour to someone who missed the boat?"

Happy loved giving tours of her house. She was proud of her home-improvement skills. The classes she'd taken with her mother at Home Warehouse came in handy. She was skilled in plumbing, tiling, painting, and plastering.

Her mind strayed to her first home-improvement lesson. Happy was five years old, and her name was Lucy. Life was simple then; there were no addictions, school suspensions, or sorrows. She was helping her mother, Debbie, wallpaper the dining room of their Baltimore house. Her job was to snap the plumb-line. Debbie stood on a ladder, held the blue-powdered string to the ceiling and slowly lowered the plumb. The plumb twirled and danced. Catch it, Lucy!

She grabbed it, held it tightly against the wall, and snap! A perfect plumb line. Debbie didn't mind that Lucy ended up looking like the Cookie Monster. Her mother laughed and wiped her face and hands. Debbie taught her how to sew, knit, and crochet. There wasn't anything her mother couldn't do, except staying alive beyond the age of thirty-seven.

Milo interrupted Happy's reminiscing. "Happy?"

She felt her face flush. "I'm sorry. I started thinking about my mother. We used to wallpaper together."

"Does your mother live near here?"

She deflected. "Let's go for a tour."

Milo followed her from room-to-room while she explained the work that was done and the work that was planned. Christine's bedroom was not on the tour. Happy feared that the bedroom would look like the shed. "This is my roommate's bedroom. I owe her privacy."

When they returned to the kitchen, Milo's eyes showed concern. "Did you find the answers you were looking for about Bernie Singleton?"

She shook her head. "The only thing I found were more questions."

"Maybe you should stop looking. You'll drive yourself crazy."

There was a pause in the conversation while she toyed with her hair. "You're right. I should stop. If the answers can be found, the police will find them."

The concern in Milo's eyes ratcheted up a level. "The police are still investigating? I thought it was cut and dry. The paper said he was drunk, ran out of gas, and froze to death."

Happy needed to back pedal. She didn't want to start any rumors, especially ones that could get back to Olivia. "Nobody said it didn't happen that way. The police are just being thorough, I guess. It probably has something to do with life insurance."

"Yeah, that sounds right. I'll bet the widow made a claim, and the insurance people are fighting it. You know how they are—you pay premiums your whole life, and then they won't pay."

Milo's complaint reminded her to review her latest financial statements. Her mother's life insurance policy paid off right away. Maybe the U.S. Marshals Service had something to do with that. Probably not; she wasn't as cynical as Milo.

He leaned across the table toward her. "If you hear anything, please let me know. I still have trouble sleeping. I keep thinking I could've done something...if only I'd been paying attention."

His words poked a wound inside of Happy. Police, counselors, and bereavement groups had tried to convince her otherwise, but she still believed she could've saved her mother. If only she'd been paying attention.

"I will, Milo. I promise."

Chapter 26

During the night, blustery weather plummeted the wind chill temperature to single digits. Steppie wanted nothing to do with his morning walk. The area beside the road was covered with ten inches of frozen plowed snow, topped with ice dense enough to hold Happy's weight. She discovered she could walk on the snow and leave no trace.

Happy tugged on the leash. "C'mon, Steppie, don't make me carry you home." He refused to budge. She picked him up and held him close against her chest.

She was grateful to reach her home without a slip-and-fall mishap. Etchers's truck was parked at the bottom of the driveway. How did she miss him? He must have taken the back entrance through the development. She could see him watching her through the rearview mirror. His door opened as she approached.

"Couldn't stay away from me, could you?" she said.

No banter, no jokes, no smile. Something was up, and it was bad.

She invited him inside. He sat at the kitchen table wearing his coat. His expression was grim and his eyes intense. Happy placed a cup of steaming coffee in front of him. She took the opposite seat and placed Steppie on her lap. "Tell me."

"Is your roommate here?"

"No, she's at work." Happy grew anxious. "Don't make me wait."

"Romero's dead."

His words punched the air out of her stomach. She'd been waiting for the news of Romero's death, but so soon? Happy clung to the dog and rubbed her cheek against the fur on his head.

Etchers cleared his throat. "I'm sorry, Happy."

Did Etchers know Romero's death was a ploy? Apparently, not. Either that or he was a great actor. He'd barely choked out the news that Romero was dead. His pained facial expression mimicked the one worn by the throngs of friends who expressed their sympathy after her mother was killed. No, Etchers was clueless about what was really happening.

So how did WITSEC kill off Romero? She had to know. "How?"

The tremble in her voice shocked her. There was nothing to be upset about. Romero was safe and settled into his new life. His "death" was a good thing.

Distress spread across Etcher's face. "He hanged himself. No one was expecting it. His handler found him last night."

She sat in stunned silence. Etchers said nothing while she processed Romero's death. Her thoughts turned to her mother. She was viewing the screen of Rick McCormick's iPad, staring at a death photo of her mother taken by the medical examiner.

Etchers must have misread her sorrowful facial expression. "Don't grieve for Romero. Be done with him."

"I was done with Romero the night I broke his nose."

"I'd like to have seen that."

"It's just that...my mother's been on my mind a lot...ever since the night I found Bernie Singleton." She rubbed her forehead. "Please excuse me for a minute."

She rinsed her face in the bathroom sink. Hard questions were coming; she needed to brace herself. How much should she tell Etchers about her conversation with Romero? Romero warned her that few people in WITSEC knew about the plan. A safety precaution; the fewer who knew, the better. Obviously, Etchers wasn't one of them.

She guessed his reaction if she told him; he'd tell her Romero had planned his suicide all along but wanted her to believe he was still alive. If she insisted Romero wasn't dead, Etchers would tell her she was in denial. She'd endured enough of the *denial* crap from Rick McCormick when she insisted her mother's death investigation was on the wrong track. McCormick didn't believe her then. Etchers won't believe her now. No, she wouldn't tell Etchers about WITSEC's plan. When she returned to the conversation, Etchers was armed with an iPad.

He studied her as if he were gauging her state of mind. "I need to talk to you again about your meeting with Romero."

"You want to know if Romero told me he was going to kill himself. Of course, he didn't."

"Did he say—"

"Nothing, not a word. What kind of a person do you think I am? Do you think I'd just ignore something like that? If he'd even hinted at it, don't you think I would've told someone? He was my friend. I would've done anything and everything to stop it. Don't you know that—"

"Yes...yes, I do. I know you would—"

"Jesus, God. I wouldn't let a stranger go off and kill himself if I could stop it."

"I know...it's all right. Please don't cry."

She didn't realize a tear had slid down her face. "You know, you can be a real jerk sometimes. I don't want to talk about this anymore."

Etchers said nothing as she wiped her eyes and blew her nose. When she finished cleaning herself up, he spoke. "Please help us, Happy. Everyone is terribly upset. No one saw it coming. We're trying to figure out what went wrong. We're hoping you can shed some light."

"All right, but this is the last time I'm talking about it."

"Tell me what you and Romero talked about. Everything you can remember."

"At first, it was awkward. I think we were each surprised by how the other looked. He looked older. My hair and eyes are different. In the beginning, there was minor chit-chat, mostly about my job. After that, he said his prosecution obligation was over, and he was going into WITSEC. He asked what it was like. I put a positive spin on it. He thanked me for helping him. He asked me to marry him. I said no. Then a guard came and said, 'Time's up.' We said our good-byes. That was it."

"Tell me about the marriage proposal."

"He got on one knee and offered me a ring. It was sweet. I declined and told him I wanted to marry Jimmy Bittinger."

Etchers smiled for the first time since he'd pulled into her driveway. "You do?"

"I thought I did, so that's what I told Romero." She glanced at her left hand, focusing on the ring finger. "You were right...Jimmy dumped me. But see? I didn't come crying to you. I want you to be clear about that."

Etchers nodded slightly. "Do you want me to talk to Jimmy?"

"No, no, no! If you do, I'll never speak to you again. Let's get back to Romero. He wasn't surprised when I said 'no.' He wished me the best of luck."

"What was his mood, his state of mind?"

"Upbeat, even funny at times. He was his same old, charming self. The only difference being he looked older. There was nothing he said or did that alarmed me."

Etchers pulled his hands away from the iPad and leaned back in his chair. He looked directly into her eyes. "You're holding something back. What is it?"

She stopped breathing for a second. How did he know? She needed a lie that would pass his truth radar. What truth could she sprinkle in? "Are you writing a report?"

"Yes."

"There's something embarrassing I don't want in it. It's not relevant to anything."

"You need to tell me. If it's not relevant, I won't put it in the report."

She stroked Steppie's fur and barely looked at Etchers, pretending to be embarrassed. "In the first few minutes, when we were alone, I asked Romero if it was a booty call. It was a joke. He laughed. That's all."

Etchers chuckled softly. "Funny joke. You're embarrassed to have that in the report?"

"Well, yeah. It could be misinterpreted. You know how flat a joke can be on paper. I can just see some asshole leaking it to the press. If Jimmy ever spoke to me again, how would I explain it?"

"He won't see it." Etchers gave her a faint smile. "I won't put it in the report."

"Or tell anyone?"

"My lips are sealed. Don't worry."

"Romero thought it was funny, too. Why would he laugh at a joke if he was thinking about killing himself? I know how this looks. People at WITSEC are going to think he killed himself because I wouldn't marry him."

"Do you think that?"

She shook her head with vigor. "No, do you?"

"Of course not. You had nothing to do with it. Don't forget that."

Etchers handed her a tissue. "Are you all right?"

She waved off the offered tissue. "I don't need that. I'm done crying. Do you have any more questions?"

"Not now. Maybe later."

"No later. Once I'm done talking to you, I'm done talking. I'm moving on from Romero, just like you said. Like everyone's said."

"I wish I can promise the questions are over, but I can't. The powers-that-be are not going to let this go easily."

"Why would they care? He was a criminal. Romero dead saves the government a lot of hassle and money."

"The reputation of WITSEC is at stake. We may not like our cooperating witnesses, but we're sworn to take care of them. And we do. If the public gets the impression we're lax or don't care, why would future witnesses cooperate in criminal prosecutions in return for protection? They wouldn't. WITSEC would cease to exist. It's a very valuable program."

She leaned back in her chair and crossed her arms. Her next words spilled out through gritted teeth. "If I refuse to talk about Romero, what would happen?"

"The AG could launch an investigation. You could be subpoenaed to testify. Romero's death could prompt Congress to get involved."

She envisioned Monica Lewinsky, Anita Hill, and Hillary Clinton. Her life was not going to be torn apart. She pretended to relent. "I remember something else."

Etchers nodded for her to continue.

"Romero told me he was getting a new face. He was worried the surgeon would turn him into a monster. I asked him why a surgeon would do such a thing. He said a lot of law enforcement felt he wasn't punished enough. Maybe he's dead because someone thought he needed the ultimate punishment."

A look of horror passed across Etchers's face. "No, no, not poss—"

"That's the God's honest truth. And that's what I'd testify to."

She leaned toward Etchers. "Are you sure it's not an inside job? Could there be some kind of cover-up going on? Those are the questions I'd pose to the press, starting with my friend at the *Baltimore Sun*."

"Jesus!"

"Uncle Peter, tell the powers-that-be to leave me the hell alone."

Chapter 27

As soon as Etchers left, Happy paced the great room looking for a distraction. She didn't want to think about Romero or her mother. Bernie's box called to her.

She rifled through the box and retrieved the four CD-Rs with home-made covers. A given name labeled each cover. She selected "Henry" and popped it into her laptop. It took her only a few seconds to realize Henry was one of Bernie's trumpet students. Henry was terrible. Happy was no musician, but she knew when someone blew a string of wrong notes. She took Henry out of the player and put in Frances.

Frances was a flutist and a perfectionist; whenever she made a mistake, she started over. After several takes, Frances began to cry. "I can't do it, Mr. Singleton." From the sound of the tearful voice, Happy guessed Frances was about nine-years old.

A gentle, patient voice answered. "Sure, you can. You're very talented, Frances. No one is perfect when they start playing an instrument. It's hard, and it takes a lot of practice."

"I hate it. I don't want to do it anymore."

There was an interval of sobbing before Frances spoke. "All I want to do is play soccer."

"I heard you're an excellent soccer player. What do you like best about it?"

"I like running fast."

"Does your mother have any movies of you when you were learning to walk?"

Silence.

"I'll bet you fell down a lot, maybe even hurt yourself. You kept trying. And look at you now. You play soccer. Running makes you happy, doesn't it? Learning an instrument is the same thing. Once you get the hang of it, playing an instrument will bring you a lot of happiness."

Silence.

"Frances, have you ever met Eleanor, the Elephant?"

"No."

"Here she is."

Frances giggled. "She's cute."

"Eleanor's going to sit right next to you. And guess what? She's magical. She never hears mistakes. Last night, Eleanor told me she wanted to hear you play. I need to step out of the room for a few minutes. Can you play for her while I'm gone?"

"OK."

A door closed. Frances made it through the piece, mistakes and all.

Happy changed her mind about Bernie being a loser. Maybe he could've been a concert pianist; but he chose to be a music teacher. What could be a worthier use of talent than that?

Steppie let out a howl. He charged around the house, barking and re-bounding off furniture. Happy peeked through the window. A state police car. Jimmy. He knocked as he usually did—four quick raps on the door. She was determined to be dignified and civil. Whatever Jimmy thought of her, he was going to remember her as a class act. She opened the door. Steppie shot out. The barking reached a higher decibel.

"May I come in?" Jimmy could barely be heard over Steppie's greeting.

"Now's not a good time."

Jimmy's eyes were soft, and his voice was kind. "Happy, I just I heard about Romero. I came over to tell you I'm sorry for your loss. I know Romero meant a lot to you."

"Not as much as you think."

Jimmy's eyes narrowed; he didn't believe her. She renewed her determination to be civil. "Thanks for your sympathy. I put your belongings in the shed. Give me a few minutes."

She put on a coat and left Jimmy waiting outside. The bitter cold air felt good on her face. As she trudged along, she focused on her footing to avoid slipping on the ice-covered snow. When she reached the shed, she looked behind her. No footprints; no trace of her at all. She unlocked and opened the shed.

The contents looked different than they had just two days ago. She couldn't put her finger on exactly how, but she knew it was so. Had someone been in there? She walked around the shed. No footprints. Nothing seemed out of place. Nothing had been disturbed. Perhaps Christine had added to her collection of *good deals*. Perhaps it was all in her imagination.

Jimmy appeared. "I couldn't wait any longer." He stood behind her as she stared at the contents of the shed.

Apparently, he was staring, as well. "This shed's a fire hazard."

"It's just a mess, that's all. There's nothing combustible in there."

She entered the shed and found a slight path. She was positive it wasn't there before. After snaking over boxes, under clothes racks, and a workbench, Happy found Jimmy's box of belongings under a pile of Discount Depo bags. She abandoned the effort and made her way back to the door.

Jimmy smiled when he saw her. "You've got fluffy stuff all in your hair."

She remembered the bag of upholstery stuffing she had to wiggle past. "I can't reach your things. I'll get them later and drop them off at the barracks. Don't worry, I won't ask for you."

They walked side by side toward the house. At the half-way point, Jimmy said, "Why don't you make Christine clean out her junk? You can't even use your own shed."

"You don't get it, Jimmy. Christine had some terrible losses in her life. When a person loses everything, maybe they just want to hold on to something, even if other people think it's junk. She'll let go when she's good and ready, not before."

Jimmy stopped mid-stride. Happy kept walking

"Happy, wait." He ran to catch up. "I hate how things ended with us."

She answered with a shrug.

"I miss you. Do you think we can go back to being friends?"

Happy stopped short. "Now that Romero's out of the way?"

"C'mon, Happy."

"The dumpee sets the terms of friendship. That's a rule. I'll let you know, if and when."

"Wait! You think this is my fault?"

"I don't believe this." She shook her head in disgust. "Just go away and leave me a—"

She continued walking, annoyed the ice slowed her pace.

Jimmy overtook her and stood in her path. "I didn't come to argue with you. I just wanted to check on you."

"Why?"

"I still care about you."

She stepped closer to him. "Let me make sure I understand this. You came to visit an ex-girlfriend to check on her because there's a part of you that still cares. Do I have that right?"

"Yes, I'm worried—"

"Do you have any idea how ironic that is? Now get out of my way. Don't come back again. Ever."

Jimmy swallowed hard and moved from her path.

Chapter 28

Bernie's friend, Hank Tinker, was an elusive man. Whenever Happy called his cell, she left a message that was not returned. She'd tried his office and home land lines; no response. Her messages got more detailed with each call. After five attempts, she concluded either the man wasn't getting his messages or simply didn't want to talk to her. She decided to show up, unannounced, at his place of work. If he didn't want to talk to her, she would tell Olivia she tried...

Tinker was the manager of the Home Warehouse in Keyser, West Virginia. MapQuest gave her a couple of travel options. She could drive to Keyser by way of I-68 or take the winding Route 135 across Backbone Mountain. She decided on Route 135; traveling across a mountain named "Backbone" was too intriguing to resist. Besides, she might need a boost of backbone to have a productive conversation with Tinker.

Happy caught Route 135 in Swanton, a town less than five miles from Deep Creek Lake. Her winding ascent toward the mountain's ridge line began shortly afterward. The road became straight and wide. She enjoyed the serene views of farmland but felt mildly disappointed that the mountain didn't live up to its name. The disappointment was short-lived.

Warning signs appeared along the road, advising truck drivers of the upcoming nine-percent grade for the next five miles. Trucks were limited to ten miles per hour. The speed limit for cars was forty.

When she reached the descending slope, the view downward seemed endless. She shifted into lowest gear. She descended behind an eighteen-wheeler. The logging truck behind her filled her rear-view mirror. She imagined herself as the meat in a Happy Holiday sandwich squished between two layers of trucks.

There were three signs directing truckers to check their truck's brakes in the up-coming pull-off areas. The eighteen-wheeler pulled over, as did the logging truck. Now that her view was no longer obstructed, she could see the cars in front of her leap-frogging around the plodding trucks as they crawled down the mountain. Soon she was leapfrogging as well. It was fun once she caught on to it.

A sign alerted drivers to a sharp right turn at the bottom of the mountain. *Sharp* was an understatement. The turn was right-angled in front of a massive mountain wall. There was a traffic signal marking the turn. As Happy waited at the red light, she counted the number of white crosses painted on the mountain wall. Twenty-four.

As Route 135 became flat, she fantasized about plowing Backbone Mountain. What an adrenaline rush that would be! Soon she meandered through the town of Westernport. The town was dark from the shadows of mountains blocking the rising sun. She crossed the Potomac River and arrived in West Virginia. Keyser was a few minutes away.

The Home Warehouse was much smaller than its counterpart in Baltimore. Happy's knees shook as she walked toward the front door. Her mother had been the assistant manager of the Baltimore Home Warehouse. The smell of freshly-cut lumber took her back to the summer days when they'd built a small deck off the back of her mother's house.

Happy walked through the store hunting for the customer service desk. She could see her mother in every aisle and hear her voice on the loudspeaker. She arrived at her destination with a closed throat.

A young man wearing a blue Home Warehouse vest approached her. "How can I help you?"

She choked out an unintelligible answer, followed by a minute of deep breathing while she tried to collect herself. The man looked stunned and helpless. Happy guessed employee training didn't include how to deal with customers going mute for no apparent reason. Within a few seconds, she was surrounded by women wearing blue vests.

"Oh honey, don't worry," said a woman with silver hair. "Whatever's broken, we'll help you fix it."

"We'll take anything back," said a young blonde wearing a messy ponytail and hipster glasses. "Even if you don't have a receipt."

A brunette with green eyes led Happy to an employee break room. "Sit here for a bit. Someone will be right with you."

A Medicare-aged man sat at a long table eating fried chicken from a Popeye's box. The bulk of his hair was on his chin. He wasn't wearing a name tag or a vest.

The chicken's delicious aroma set off a rumble from her stomach. The scent reminded her of the fried chicken sold inside Baltimore's Lexington Market. The man held up a chicken drumstick. "Want some?"

Unexpectedly, the only thing Happy wanted in the world was fried chicken. "Yes, I do."

He handed her the chicken leg, a napkin, and a can of root beer.

They ate chicken in silence until Happy wrapped her gnawed chicken bone in her napkin. "Thank you. You have no idea how much I needed that. You're an angel."

He gave her a friendly smile adorned with yellow teeth. "If I make it to Heaven, St. Peter will make me the Chicken Drumstick Angel."

His remark struck her funny bone, and she laughed.

The lunchroom door squeaked open. A tall, angular man wearing slacks and a dress jacket entered and sat next to Happy. "I'm the manager. Customer Service alerted me that you might be having a medical emergency."

Happy's face pivoted toward his name tag. Hank Tinker.

"Nah, she's all right," said the chicken man.

"Who are you?" Tinker asked. "And why aren't you wearing your blue vest?"

"I'm Allen. I don't work here."

"You don't? Why are you eating in our break room?"

"I always eat here. It's quiet."

"This room is for employees only." Tinker turned his attention to Happy. "Has this man been bothering you?"

"No, sir, not at all. Actually, he's been a comfort to me."

Tinker redirected his attention to Allen. "Leave the store and take your trash with you. Don't come back unless you're shopping at this store."

As Allen gathered his chicken bones and trash, he smiled at Tinker. "You should put a TV in here. And some plants to oxygenate the room. It could be a really nice break room."

After the door shut behind Allen, Tinker shook his head in disgust. "Can you believe some people? Coming into our break room to eat lunch." He gave Happy a concerned smile. "Miss, are you all right?"

"Yes, sir. I was just having a bad day."

"May I get your name? I have to fill out a report."

"Happy Holiday."

Tinker shot her a glare that would've killed her if it were weaponized. His voice lowered as he snarled. "You manipulative little—" He interrupted himself, apparently considering the consequences of what he was about to say. "You staged histrionics and upset my staff, just so you could get me in here? You must've called me a dozen times. Tell me why I shouldn't go to the police and swear out a warrant for stalking."

Happy's jaw dropped. Stalking? Manipulating? "I wasn't sure you were getting my messages," she said politely. "When you didn't return my calls, I thought I'd drop by, maybe talk to you in person. What else was I supposed to do? I wasn't stalking you. Why didn't you call me back? And just so you know—my upset wasn't faked. My mother took a lot of classes at Home Warehouse. She died recently. This place reminded me of her."

He tapped on his cell phone. "No woman by the name of Holiday has ever taken a class here."

"No, not *here*. In a different location."

He said nothing as he gazed at her with no expression. She couldn't tell if he believed her.

"Mr. Tinker, if you want, I'll leave right now. I won't bother you again. But I gotta say, I don't understand you. You were friends with Bernie since college. Now he's dead. His widow needs your help. Why won't you help her?"

Tinker leaned back in his chair. "My helping will hurt Olivia more. I like her. She was a good wife to Bernie. Much better than he deserved."

During the lunch with Etchers, Randall Kennedy hadn't said anything negative about Bernie, other than he was bad with money and wrote a bad song. There must be more.

"Because he was a bad husband?" Happy saw the surprise in Tinker's eyes. "Randall Kennedy told me."

Tinker raised his eyebrows. "Goddammit. Randall and his big mouth. We agreed to keep it between us."

It occurred to Happy she was missing something. Something big. She needed to keep Tinker talking. Maybe he would spill what he was really talking about.

"Sounds like you and Randall are very protective of Olivia."

"I never understood Bernie and Olivia. She's smart, works hard, good-looking. Why would a man disrespect a woman like that? He was irresponsible. A Peter Pan, who never grew up. And why did Olivia put up with him? She should have kicked him to the curb a long time ago."

Peter Pan. That's how Olivia described her husband. Had they been talking?

"Did you ever ask Olivia why she didn't?"

"Just once." Tinker had a wistful look on his face. "My question wasn't welcomed. She said she loved him despite his faults."

"When did you meet Olivia?"

"College, Penn State. We all lived in the same co-ed dorm—Bernie, Olivia, Randall and me. We hung out together. Randall and I had crushes on Olivia, but she only had eyes for Bernie. She had a lot of female competition, but long story short, they got married after college."

"At the football game, did Bernie say anything about a surprise for Olivia?"

Red color crept upward from Tinker's neck until it covered his face. His eyes flashed. "Yes, he talked about it. Totally pathetic. I flat out-refused to help him."

"Why?"

"I wasn't going to cover for him. If he was going to lie to Olivia, he'd have to do it without my help."

"Did he ask Randall to cover for him?"

"No, Bernie's wouldn't ask him. He doesn't have any money."

"What was the money for?"

Tinker opened his mouth and shut it again. He studied Happy's face. "You don't know what I'm talking about, do you?"

Busted. She took a shot at lying. "Of course, I do."

Tinker laughed to himself. "Shit. You've been sitting here, faking knowledge, hoping I'll reveal something. You've got game; I'll give you that."

He stood. "Ms. Holiday, we're done here. Don't call me, don't come around here again. If you do, I'll swear out a warrant."

Chapter 29

It was two o'clock. Examining the gas line in Olivia's car was the next item on her agenda.

US-220 was a straight shot from Keyser to Cumberland. Happy crossed the Potomac River and entered the town of McCoole, Maryland. Her gnawing stomach set off a yearning for more fried chicken. She surveyed both sides of the highway for a restaurant that could satisfy her craving. No KFC, no Popeye's, no Denny's. US-220 climbed upward. Midway up the hill, she spotted a sign atop a tall pole. Minnie's Kitchen was on the right.

The free-standing building was one level, brown-bricked, with a flat black roof. Parking was readily available—the lot surrounded the restaurant. Behind the tall sign, was an American flag waving atop an even taller pole. The place looked as Americana as baseball and apple pie. It would be a crime if it didn't have fried chicken. She considered getting apple pie for dessert.

The interior was an appealing combination of browns: brick walls, leather, and wood. Daylight streamed through the many large windows, complementing the various shades of brown. The greenery of live plants abounded. Happy's salivating mouth told her she'd made a good choice. The hostess seated her at a booth facing the door.

An elderly woman with a slight limp approached the table, menu in hand. "I'm Beth. I'll be taking care of you."

"Hi, Beth. I don't need a menu. I'd like a big plate of fried chicken and an apple pie for dessert."

While Happy waited for her meal, she ruminated on her anticipated conversation with Olivia. How would she explain her need to examine the Explorer's gas line? The conversation would be dicey. She didn't want to inadvertently interfere with a pending police investigation. The police knew Bernie purchased gas on his way home; Friend gave her the receipt proving it. They must have examined the gas line while they processed the car. If it were leaky, they wouldn't have let Olivia drive it home. Something was wrong; she could feel it in her bones.

And what about Hank Tinker? Tinker admired Olivia. Maybe he loved her. He was protecting her for some reason. Did Olivia know why? Was Bernie having an affair? Happy envisioned what would happen if she asked Olivia those questions. The widow would toss her down the front steps.

Bernie had a surprise, all right—a hurtful, ugly secret. A secret that jeopardized college friendships of almost thirty years. Whatever the secret was, it wasn't the surprise he'd called Olivia about. That call announced a wonderful surprise. Bernie was a weak man with many faults, but Happy didn't believe he would joyfully hurt his wife.

Anxiety flooded her. The hair on her arms stood. Her neck hairs rose. Her breathing shallowed and quickened. The only sound she could hear was her heart pounding. Why was she having a panic attack? She froze in her seat. Instinct compelled her to stay still, be silent, and not to look around.

Deep breathing tamed her heart. She could see nothing unusual straight ahead. Had she heard something? She closed her eyes to listen. There was the din of usual restaurant noise. Someone was talking on the restaurant's phone, accepting a reservation. There was the sound of clacking utensils on plates. Laughter. Footsteps.

Spanish.

Her eyes shot open. It was the voice. Deep, rich, guttural. She knew that voice. It belonged to Peeps. She guessed he was sitting behind her, about two tables away. He was talking with another man. Also Latino. Did Peeps know she was there? Had he been following her? Her hands were shaking.

She recalled what Romero had said. Peeps was "right in her backyard," building an opioid network in West Virginia, Kentucky, and Ohio. Maybe he was expanding his criminal enterprise into Maryland. If their presence together in the restaurant were a simple coincidence, she didn't want to do anything to bring to attention to herself—like flee the restaurant or get a phone call. She muted her cell phone. If she'd been found and targeted, her safest bet was to stay in a public place.

She sent a text to Etchers. *need help peeps mccoole rt 220 minnie's kitchen*

Peeps was talking. Maybe she could get a clue about what he was up to. Romero had tried to teach her Spanish. She didn't have the ear for it, but there were some words she recognized. Maybe Peeps would say them, and she could catch the gist of the conversation.

"Westernport." She understood that word because it was in English. The rest of the words were a muddle. Two words were conspicuously absent from the conversation: Lucy Prestipino. She guessed Peeps and his companion were planning some sort of criminal activity in the town.

Plates clattered on her table. She jumped.

"I'm sorry, dear," said Beth. "I didn't mean to startle you."

A split second passed before Happy comprehended the plate of fried chicken in front of her. She smiled at Beth and nodded. *It's OK.* She dared not say a word. Peeps would recognize her voice as she'd recognized his.

She checked her phone. No return text from Etchers. Now, what should she do? She didn't want to risk a phone call fearing her voice would be heard. She sent a text to 9-1-1 and promptly received a bounce back message informing her that Text-to-9-1-1 was not available. She texted Corporal Friend, hoping he'd contact the McCoole police with all necessary explanations. No reply.

There was movement and rustling at Peeps's table. They were getting ready to leave. Beth walked past Happy's table while ripping a page from her order pad. Peeps told Beth, in English, to keep the change. Beth thanked them for their business and urged them to return soon. It wouldn't be long before Peeps and his companion walked by Happy's table to leave. Should she make a dash for the women's room? No, that would draw attention.

She considered sending a text to Jimmy. She'd almost rather die than ask for his rescue. Almost. She was about to send the text when she got a reply from Friend.

Protect yourself. Help on way.

She reached under her shirt. Removed the gun from the holster. Released the decocker. Clutched the grip. Held the gun in her lap with her right hand.

Her left hand fished through her backpack and found a can of pepper spray. Parked it by her left hip. Touched the coffee with her pointer finger. Still hot. Something else to use. Her fingers glided along the blade of her dinner knife. Dull. She doubted it would be effective, but she slipped it from the table and added it to her short collection of self-defense weapons.

The men's footsteps got closer. She ate a chicken drumstick with her left hand, thinking it would look more natural for a customer to be eating than sitting still while sweating bullets.

Peeps walked by, talking to his companion on his left, facing away from her. The exit door opened and closed. She eyed them through a window as they entered a black, Silverado pickup truck. They made a right from the parking lot onto US-220 heading southeast. That was the way to Westernport.

Happy re-holstered her gun, slipped out of her seat, and grabbed two clean napkins from a neighboring table. She sauntered over to the table that had been occupied by Peeps. Using the napkins, she grabbed the dirty utensils. Once back in her seat, she snuck the napkin packages into her backpack.

She sent a second text to Friend. *Peeps gone SE on 220 black silverado westernport a guess peeps + 1*

"Would you like your apple pie now, honey?" Beth said.

Happy looked at her plate of bones. She didn't remember eating the chicken. "Yes, with lots of vanilla ice cream."

After a few minutes, Beth returned with a slice of apple pie piled high with ice cream. Happy put a spoonful of ice cream into her mouth. She caught the muffled sound of sirens in the background. The sirens grew louder and more urgent. A half-dozen police vehicles flew past the restaurant. One vehicle careened into the parking lot and screeched to a halt. A state trooper exited the vehicle. Soon he stood at her table, hulking over her. She was astounded by his size. Large, broad, sturdy. The personification of a Mack truck.

"I'm Trooper First Class Michael Rhodes. I've been deputized by the U.S. Marshals Service to protect you. Are you all right?"

"Much better now that you're here."

"Anyone in here I should know about?"

"Only me, but I'm guessing you already know plenty. Please sit down."

He sat, unsmiling and as serious as a jackknifed snowplow.

Beth was staring at them. Happy waved her over. "Please bring the trooper some pie and put it on my check."

The pie appeared on the table instantly. "Trooper," Beth said as she placed a fork and napkin in front of him. "What's going on?"

"There's nothing you need to worry over, ma'am. We've got a warrant for someone we're trying to catch."

Beth collected Happy's empty plate. "I hope you catch him quick."

Rhodes ignored the pie while he surveyed the restaurant and its perimeter with watchful eyes. "How were you able to identify Peeps?"

"His voice."

Rhodes gave her a doubtful look. "Did you see him?"

"No."

Rhodes leaned into his seat. "You texted he had a companion. Did you hear his name spoken?"

"No."

"Your identification is based solely on his voice."

Happy's chest expelled the air from her lungs. Without warning, she was in Baltimore, inside the prosecutor's office, knowing her mother's murder investigation was on the wrong track, telling him so, him not believing. Rhodes was appraising her with eyes that revealed nothing.

"I know his voice," she said. "It's gravelly, deep. His street name's a joke. He used that voice to tell me he was gonna throw me out of a car going eighty miles an hour on a freeway. He used that voice to tell me to 'shut up' before he hit me. Yeah, I know that voice."

"Did he see you?"

"No, I'm positive he didn't.

Rhode's cell chirped. He answered with a business-like demeanor. He glanced at Happy with a grimace while he spoke. He ended the conversation with, "Understood."

Happy sat silently waiting for the results of the call.

"State police stopped the Silverado at the Westernport city line. There was only one occupant, the driver. He denied anyone was in the truck with him."

Happy's voice trembled with exasperation. "I'm telling you it was Peeps. The sirens—he knew you were coming. He got out of the truck. He's somewhere nearby. Do you have his picture? Show it to the waitress. She talked to him. I heard her."

Rhodes approached Beth who was stacking menus at the hostess desk. Happy watched but was too far away to hear the conversation. Rhodes handed Beth a paper, presumably a photograph of Peeps. Her face turned scarlet. There was fear written all over her. Beth shook her head.

Happy grabbed her backpack and rushed to the hostess desk. "Beth—"

Beth's eyes were red and rimmed with tears. "I've never seen this man before."

"How long have you lived in Western Maryland?" Happy said.

"My whole life. What's that got to do with anything?"

"There's an opioid epidemic going on here. Heroin. Fentanyl. It's everywhere; people are dying. Good people. Mothers and grandmothers are watching their children die. Some die themselves." Happy pointed to the photo. "This man's a distributor. Get him off the street. How will you feel if someone you love, or a friend's child, OD'ed and you did nothing to help stop it?"

Beth was crying.

"Look, I know you're afraid, but you don't have to say anything. Just nod your head if this is the man you waited on. That's all you have to do."

Beth studied the photograph with shaking hands. Looked down at her feet. Shook her head.

"No?" Happy said. "You're a li—"

"That's enough," Rhodes said to Happy.

He pulled out two twenty-dollar-bills from his wallet and handed them to Beth. "Will this cover it?"

She took the money and ran to the women's room.

"Shame on you, Beth!" Happy called after her. "How can you live with—"

Rhodes grabbed Happy by the forearm and hauled her from the restaurant.

Chapter 30

Happy struggled against Rhodes's grip. As they neared his patrol car, she shouted, "Let me go! I'm going to be sick." She vomited her chicken and apple pie onto the parking lot inches from the trooper's boots.

"Go on," he said. "Get it out of your system."

After her stomach emptied, Rhodes handed her a bottle of water. She doused her mouth, spitting the rinse water onto the ground. She spotted Beth limping through the parking lot. Coward. She took a step forward.

"Don't even think about it," Rhodes said.

She stopped in her tracks. "Let me talk to her again. I can convince her. I know it."

Rhodes opened the passenger door. "Get in."

She got in, adrenaline still blasting through her bloodstream.

"Settle down," Rhodes said in a voice that stilled her.

She folded her arms across her chest and let loose a string of profanities.

"Happy, how old do you think she is?"

"Old enough to have acquired some spine."

"She's more than seventy, don't you think? Did you notice her limp? Waitressing is hard, physical work. On your feet all day, carrying heavy trays. She's probably got someone depending on her, maybe grandchildren. Judging from Beth's reaction to your lecture, you're probably right—someone close to her has an addiction. Maybe Beth stepped up to care for her grandchildren. What would happen to them if something happened to Beth?"

Happy squirmed.

Rhodes glanced at her while he punched a number into his phone. "It's a lot easier to be brave when you're the only one at risk."

He turned his attention to the phone and spoke. "Sergeant, Peeps is probably wondering who identified him. There's a waitress at Minnie's, Beth Watkins. She was the only one who had direct contact with him. I suggest patrol look in on her every day until the U.S. Marshals Service says otherwise. Same with the restaurant."

Restaurant? The word reminded her of the utensils sitting in her backpack. She pulled out the napkin-wrapped package and handed it to Rhodes. "After Peeps left, I swiped these off his table. I don't know who ate off which utensils, but I'll bet they're both in CODIS."

Rhodes popped open the car's trunk. Using the side mirror, she watched him place the napkin and utensils into a paper bag and label it. He returned to the passenger seat and sat quietly. After a few seconds, he shifted so he could face Happy directly. His steel-gray eyes hooked onto hers like a pair of handcuffs. "Why'd you give that waitress a hard time when you had those utensils in your backpack?"

She had to admit, it was an excellent question. Why did she? Frustration, that's what it was. Topped off by the vivid sensation of *déjà vu*.

"It felt like Baltimore all over again," she said. "After my mother was murdered, the police investigation headed off in the wrong direction. I knew it, but no one would listen to me. The prosecutor said I was in denial, that I couldn't face the truth. He even threatened me with prosecution if I interfered. But it turned out I was right."

She turned her head and gazed through the windshield, staring at nothing. "Today the same thing happened. You didn't believe me when I said I could identify Peeps by his voice. I could see it in your face, hear it your questions. If Beth wouldn't confirm she saw him, the DNA on the utensils in my backpack would mean nothing—it would end up on the bottom of a pile somewhere and never be tested. Then I'd be on my own again. I'd have to catch Peeps myself. That's what I was thinking."

Rhodes turned the ignition. "I want to show you something."

They drove toward Westernport. A trooper waved Rhodes through a roadblock as they entered the city. She spotted police cars, both Westernport Police and Maryland State Police, swarming the neighborhoods. Troopers were on foot, knocking on doors, talking to residents who opened their doors. Police were going in and out of local businesses.

Rhodes drove the perimeter around the town. More police, holding dogs, were searching open spaces. The sound of a helicopter caught Happy's attention.

"Trooper 5 is assisting," Rhodes said.

Eventually, Rhodes returned to US-220 and headed toward Cumberland. Rhodes turned on the public radio. There was a special news report coming out of Westernport. Police were searching for a dangerous fugitive, Fernando Flores AKA "Peeps." An announcer gave a physical description and instructed residents to call 911 if they saw him. Exercise caution. Report anything unusual. Stay sheltered in place until further notice. The same announcement looped three times before Rhodes turned it off.

The drive ended in Cumberland at the Maryland State Police Barrack C. She stayed close to Rhodes while he logged in the utensils. He asked for her vehicle key, explaining her SUV would be driven to her home by another trooper. Rhodes would take her home and search her house and its surroundings.

Rhodes stayed silent until he parked the car in her driveway and unbuckled his seatbelt. "Who was the Assistant State's Attorney in Baltimore assigned to prosecute your mother's killer?"

"Rick McCormick. Know him?"

"I've had a couple cases with him."

Rhodes's flat voice and body language said everything she needed to hear. Rick had his positive moments, but they were rare. He was an ambitious dick, plain and simple. Rhodes apparently agreed with her assessment.

"I'm not McCormick," Rhodes said. "I believed you, every word you said. Do you think the police would be tearing apart Westernport looking for Peeps if I didn't?"

Shame heated her face. "No."

Rhodes dropped the topic but began another conversation. "I assume you're going to tell Jimmy Bittinger?"

Goddammit! Rhodes must be a friend of Jimmy's. She shook her head. "We're not together anymore."

He seemed disappointed, but not surprised. He muttered under his breath, "Romero Sanchez, still fuckin' around with Jimmy's life."

Her attention zeroed in on Rhodes. "What do you mean?"

"I was part of the team providing security during Sanchez's proffer session. It took him two weeks to describe his involvement with Roach. The security team was mostly outside; Jimmy was inside babysitting Sanchez. He heard every word. When the proffer session ended, everyone who participated—prosecutors and FBI investigators alike—went into group therapy, including Jimmy."

Happy was shocked; the only thing Jimmy ever said about the session was that it was the longest two weeks of his life. "Why didn't Jimmy tell me?"

Rhodes focused his eyes on hers. "Didn't he? In his own way?"

Chapter 31

It was four thirty. The 4Runner was back in the driveway. Rhodes was gone, but his words churned inside of her. Happy had no idea that Romero's proffer session had been so horrific.

She contemplated her last conversation with Romero. Was learning that he'd be *killed off* as part of the WITSEC plan worth losing Jimmy? Learning the plan saved her from a lifetime of sleepless nights, heart palpitations, and anxiety sweats. Her conscience hurt about a lot of things, but at least it wouldn't ache over Romero's death. Now her conscience hurt over Jimmy.

Christine came through the front door, sparing Happy from a guilt-induced downward spiral. Happy expected Christine to sit on the love seat and display the great deals hidden in the Discount Depo bags she carried into the house. Instead, she opened the freezer and pulled out a quart of ice cream. She parked the quart on the kitchen table and loaded ice cream onto a large spoon.

"What's wrong, honey?" Happy said.

Christine ate two spoonfuls of ice cream before she answered. "I made a big mistake at work."

"What happened?"

"The manager called the sheriff's department. A deputy questioned me to see if I was in on it."

Happy was dumbfounded. "In on *what*?"

"Today was my first day as a cashier. This lady customer came through my line. She was real pretty and dressed nice, you know...classy. Talked nice, too...like she was educated and brought up with good manners.

She bought a can of chicken noodle soup and gave me a twenty. I tried to hand her the change, but she didn't want any coins, so she handed me two quarters and asked for fives and ones."

Christine demonstrated the money transaction with her hands. "Then she changed her mind and asked for a ten. She had a little boy with her, maybe about three-years-old. The whole time, he was screaming for a candy bar."

Christine's voice began shaking. "She told me to hurry up because she had to pick up her kindergartner from the bus stop. I hurried as fast as I could." She looked at Happy with sorrowful eyes. "You can't leave a child stranded on the street, right?"

"No, you sure can't."

"Then the lady said she wanted the fives, after all. She got mad because I wasn't going fast enough. Called me 'stupid,' asked me how far I'd gone in school. I ended up giving her fifty-five dollars. I didn't even realize it until after she left. I called my supervisor right away. She made me talk to the store manager...then a deputy sheriff came."

Christine put down the spoon and stared straight ahead, looking like she'd lost her best friend.

"It's OK, honey," Happy said a dozen times. "Go on."

Christine's eye filled. Happy handed her a tissue. "The deputy asked me how long I knew her, how I first met her. I couldn't understand why he was asking me those questions. Then I realized he was trying to figure out if I was her partner. Oh, Happy...everyone was looking at me. The other employees and customers. No one in my whole life ever thought I was a criminal."

Happy fed Christine more tissues. "She was a professional thief, wasn't she?"

Christine nodded while dabbing her eyes. "My supervisor scolded me for forgetting my training. If a customer starts confusing you with money, slow down and call the supervisor. I'm so dumb."

Happy was infuriated. A con artist had scammed and humiliated sweet Christine. She jumped to her feet. "You're not dumb! Get that thought out of your head right now." She paced around the great room. "What does the thief look like? Let's go find her."

"Find her? Why?"

"We'll beat her up. Get that fifty-five dollars back. Teach her a lesson."

Christine let out a horrified gasp. "What? No! I don't want to beat anyone up!"

Happy returned to her seat with a quiet, maternal demeanor. "I know you don't—I was just trying to make a point. If you don't want to beat anyone up, you gotta stop beating *yourself* up. That woman was a professional con artist. She did her research—studied the cashiers for an inexperienced employee, someone nice and conscientious. Someone who would want to please a customer. She pegged you as her mark. Once you started changing-up the money, she distracted you with her crying kid. Then she bullied you. I'll bet she taught that kid to cry on command. You didn't stand a chance."

Christine sat silently, staring at her fingers folded around her ice-cream spoon.

Happy continued her encouragement. "Now you're more experienced. Next time, you'll spot it right away. This is how people learn to do their jobs well. Sweetie, you're a more valuable employee now because of this experience."

Christine looked at her with water-filled eyes. "Do you think I should ask for a raise?"

It took a slight grin from Christine for Happy to realize she'd made a joke. Happy laughed so hard she shed her own tears. "Oh, Christine. You're awesome, you really are."

"Have you ever made a dumb mistake?"

"Oh, boy...Can I have some of your ice cream?" When Christine nodded, Happy fetched a spoon and took a dip out of the quart. "I've made plenty of mistakes, and not just dumb ones. Mistakes that hurt people... especially when I was in the throes of addiction." She moved the spoon to her mouth but put it down. "But now...when I hurt someone...I try to make an amend. If I can't do that, I try to help someone else."

"Is that why you're helping Olivia?"

"Pretty much. My stack of outstanding amends is as tall as the Washington Monument."

Christine was quiet for a long thirty seconds before she spoke. "Gosh, that's a terrible burden to carry. You have to find a way to reduce the stack. Maybe doing big amends can reduce the need for smaller amends. You know, like weighted averages in algebra."

"Weighted averages." Happy smiled. "I'm going to bring it up at my next AA meeting. It's brilliant. Speaking of brilliant, how come you're not in college? I hope you don't mind me asking."

"Too expensive. I got a scholarship, but it wasn't near enough. Violet can't help me—she can hardly pay her own bills. Discount Depo has a tuition reimbursement program. The thing is, I have to take the class before I can get a reimbursement. I'm saving up for my first class."

Happy didn't sense that Christine was looking for suggestions. She reached for Bernie's box. "Want to help?"

Christine nodded with gusto.

Happy explained she listened to the CD-Rs of students' music lessons found inside Bernie's Explorer. She replayed the recordings of Henry and Frances.

"What do you think, Christine?"

"I think Bernie's a very good teacher."

"Me, too." Happy retrieved the last two CD-Rs from the box and slid the one labeled "Nick" into her laptop. Nick was a drummer who played well-enough to prompt Bernie to cheer, "Bravo!" Nick responded with "Thank you, Mr. Singleton." Based on the pitch of Nick's voice, he was older; maybe a high school junior or senior.

"I want to meet Nick," Christine said. "He sounds hot. Is he in a band?"

"I don't know anything other than his name is on the label." Happy held the last CD-R. "This one doesn't have a label."

Happy slid it into her laptop. She recognized the melody immediately. It was the introduction to "Melody Rocks." She braced herself for the exploding music yet to come. It didn't. The pleasant melody continued with many repetitions. Before long, both women were nodding their heads and humming along. Happy could sense the rhythm; one-two-three, one-two-three. She felt herself slide toward sleep.

"That was Bernie playing," Happy said when the melody ended. "I think that was an early draft of a later song. Listen to this one."

Happy clicked on her laptop, and the full "Melody Rocks" began playing. As before, the lovely rhythm morphed into a raging mix of tempos and genres. "What do you think?"

"Wow, that was pretty weird. I don't know whether to drink a cup of coffee or a shot of Fireball. But Bernie sure can play the piano."

Sadness fell over Happy. Bernie died, and his outstanding talent flew into the wind. What did he leave behind? A melody that made no sense, a bitter wife, friends he couldn't count on, and Jimmy—a guitar student who distanced himself from Bernie for reasons he wouldn't reveal.

Bernie also left behind a surprise. Happy vowed to find it, no matter what.

Chapter 32

Happy woke up groggy; Peeps's gravelly voice played inside her head throughout the night. An investigation concluded her brush with Peeps was coincidental. Etchers reminded her, "Keep your head down, be alert to your surroundings, and for the love of God, keep your name straight." Despite Etchers's assurance that WITSEC wouldn't uproot her, she worried the deputy would materialize and announce, "Pack up."

She didn't need a clock to tell her it was seven in the morning. The programmed coffee pot perked its brew and floated a wake-up scent throughout the house. She listened to Christine shower, fix breakfast, and leave the house. Rain clacked on the roof. A dreary day. That's how it was in Deep Creek—some form of precipitation throughout the winter and spring, with an occasional sunny day.

Checking the alarm system was the first item on the day's to-do list. The alarm worked fine. She spent the next half-hour cleaning her gun. If the sun came out, she'd go to the firing range. She holstered her gun under her sweatshirt. Bernie's box whispered her name. "Oh, stop it!" she said to the box.

At nine fifteen, she called Olivia, not sure how she would explain her desire to examine Bernie's car.

Olivia didn't ask. "The Explorer's gone. I sold it."

Happy was taken aback. "Sold it? Did it pass inspection?"

"Of course, it did. I couldn't have transferred the title if it didn't."

"I spoke to Bluesy—"

"I know. She called me."

"Oh. Did she tell—"

"She told me Bernie's song was worthless."

"Those weren't the words she used with me."

"Whatever way Bluesy said it, that's what she meant."

Happy pulled back from the conversation, surprised at the level of hostility. What was going on? "Mrs. Singleton, has something happened since we last spoke?"

"Corporal Friend called. They've closed the investigation. It was an accident." She cleared her throat as if choking back a sob. "I don't know why this is so upsetting. I knew it was coming. I was just hoping...I don't know what I was hoping for...that somehow it wasn't Bernie's fault...that my boys wouldn't have to grow up knowing their father died because he was drunk."

Happy stayed quiet to allow Olivia to continue venting. A few seconds of silence passed and Happy ventured forth. "Mrs. Singleton, I haven't given up on the surprise."

"Well, *I* have to. It's like Bernie's making fun of me from his grave. A surprise, a promise, a hope. And that's it, nothing more. Like always. I have to forget all that and take care of my kids."

Happy mentally begged Olivia. *Don't give up, please don't give up, I can figure it out. I know I can.*

"Happy, thank you for your efforts."

Before Happy could reply, Olivia disconnected.

The disconnection shot through her body like a bullet. Now Happy had little reason to get up in the morning. No job, no social life, no family, no Jimmy. The only compelling task remaining in her day was taking care of her dog. It wasn't enough; life was no fun without a mission.

The more her mind re-played the conversation, the more she realized Olivia hadn't ended the mission. Not exactly. Olivia said *she* had to forget about the surprise; she'd said nothing about Happy doing so. Olivia had simply thanked Happy for her efforts. Happy was sure Olivia meant *past* efforts, not *future* ones.

There was only one interpretation: carry on but leave Olivia out of it.

To Happy's delight, the great room brightened as the rising sun chased away the rain. The warm rays shined through the chalet windows directly onto the floor by the sofa. Steppie, laying at Happy's feet, crawled into the sunlight and rolled on his back. That struck Happy as a wonderful idea. She sat down beside him in the sunbeam and rubbed his stomach.

"What shall we do now, Steppie?"

She answered for him. A nice, long walk. As they strolled down the gravel road, the weather was remarkably mild. It was one of those unseasonably warm winter days that teased Deep Creek residents into thinking an early spring was on the way. Perfect for target practice.

Happy drove down Glendale Road heading toward the Sure Shot Shooting Range south of Oakland. As she approached the light at Garrett Highway, she slowed for the emergency triangles positioned on the shoulder. She spotted a disabled Jeep obstructing the intersection. Drivers were maneuvering their vehicles around the Jeep while observing the traffic signal. A traffic jam was in the works; before long, there'd be a line of cars clogging both Garrett Highway and Glendale Road.

The Jeep was gray, and its front bumper displayed the distinctive West Virginia University blue and gold sticker. It was Jimmy's. He stood on the shoulder, talking on his phone, and pressing his free hand against the opposite ear.

Happy parked her 4Runner on the road's shoulder and walked toward Jimmy. He was wearing jeans and a heavy, black sweatshirt that drew attention to his broad shoulders. His golden-red hair glinted in the sun.

"Need help?" she said.

When he looked up from his phone, his face revealed surprise. "No, I got this."

"OK." She turned around.

She'd nearly reached her SUV when she heard Jimmy's rapid footsteps behind her.

"Wait!" he said, giving her a tentative smile. "I *do* need help."

She acknowledged with a nod. "What happened to your Jeep?"

"I was waiting at the light. When it turned green, I hit the gas, and it stalled. Now it won't start."

"How was it running before you stopped at the light?"

"Rough."

"Why don't you clear up the traffic while I give it a look?"

Jimmy returned to his disabled Jeep and pulled out a florescent-green vest, two traffic batons, and a whistle. Happy gathered an apron and tools from her 4Runner. Before long, they were both immersed in their respective tasks.

Based on Jimmy's description, she concluded the problem was a dirty idle air control valve. After locating the valve, she lightly tapped it with a wrench, hard enough to shake loose some of the dirt. It would be a temporary fix. Replacing the valve was a ten-minute job, but she needed the replacement part to do so. The Jeep restarted on the first try. She pulled the vehicle onto the shoulder and kept it running.

Jimmy untangled the traffic knot. Traffic flowed through the intersection. He walked to his repaired Jeep, grinning. "You're amazing. Thanks for the rescue."

"You're welcome. You need to replace the idle air control valve right away. Who works on your car?"

"Team One."

Happy was familiar with the car dealership in Oakland. "You should be able to make it there, as long as you don't stop. Want me to follow you?"

He hesitated for so long she thought he hadn't heard her. She could see him weighing the pros and cons. He was making her offer to assist much too complicated.

"Yes or no?" She immediately thought of an alternative. "Or I can follow you to Advance Auto Parts. You buy a new valve, and I replace the old one. I can do it right in the parking lot."

He gave her an appreciative smile that radiated warmth and possibilities. "I'd be very grateful if you could fix it."

The Jeep made it to the auto parts store, seven miles away. Jimmy purchased the replacement valve. Happy leaned over the engine to locate the idle air control valve. Jimmy stood to her left, his right arm reaching across and over her head, bracing his hand on the raised hood of the Jeep. His breath was warm and smelled like mint.

Happy moved slightly away from the engine. "Jimmy, step back. You gotta give me some space."

"Oh, sorry. I just wanted to see what you were doing...in case I ever have to do it myself."

"Come here, then. I'll show you."

Jimmy stood beside her, closely, his hand still on the raised hood. Her heart jumped into fourth gear as her body reacted to his proximity. No, she wasn't going to kiss him. Not even a peck.

She pointed to the valve. "Here's the idle air control valve. 'IAC valve' for short. It tells the computer how much air to let in at idling speed. If it doesn't work right, the engine runs rough or stalls."

She glanced up from the engine to make sure he understood. He was looking at her—not the IAC valve. He turned pink and averted his eyes toward the engine. A quick touch on the engine block told her it had cooled. She envisioned laying across it, beckoning Jimmy to climb on top of her, granting him a lingering kiss if he complied. And more.

Happy continued her explanation. "Sometimes the valve gets dirty. When your Jeep was stalled, I tapped the valve with the wrench to loosen up the dirt. That's how I got the Jeep to start. It's only a short-term emergency fix." She handed him a socket wrench. "Now you try it, so you know what to do."

Jimmy gave it a good whack.

Happy frowned. "You don't have to bash the hell out of it. Just a tap, OK?"

He grinned sheepishly and nodded.

"This is very important. Disconnect the battery before you start." She disconnected the battery. "There are two bolts holding the valve in, top and bottom. Use the socket wrench. The bottom bolt is hard to reach. I have an extension bar if you need it. Once you get the bolts out, put them in your pocket. Losing the bolts would be bad news. Then remove the connector wires and the valve." She gave the wires a little shake to show him where they were.

It took Jimmy a while to execute the instructions due to a struggle removing the bottom bolt.

"Good job." She displayed the new valve. "See how clean it is compared to the old one?" After he examined the valve, she continued. "Now put in the new one, doing the reverse of everything you just did."

Her imagination soared as she watched his fingers insert the IAC valve. Gently, slowly, accurately. She was not surprised when he easily replaced the bottom bolt. He reconnected the battery.

"Let's fire her up," she said.

He easily started the car. She gave him two thumbs up and walked toward her 4Runner, parked ten feet away, giving herself a mental pat on the back. She'd been civil to Jimmy; maybe karma would finally give her a break.

Chapter 33

Jimmy lowered the Jeep's driver's window and shouted. "Happy! Wait!"

By the time she turned around, Jimmy was standing in front of her. His eyes sparkled with hope.

"I miss you," he said.

"I miss you, too."

"What are we going to do about it?"

"We're not going to do anything about it."

He smiled tentatively. "You don't mean that."

"Yes, I do." She stepped back to claim her personal space. "Jimmy, you were right. We're not a match. It just took me some time to catch up to you on that."

"We were good together until—"

"No." She shook her head. "We're not gonna have this conversation."

They stood silent and still, not looking at one another until the daylight darkened. She looked upward and saw the sun was no longer shining brightly but was blocked by a patch of swiftly-moving clouds. A chill flew though her. Before long, she was shivering. She lost her grip on her tools, and they clanked onto the asphalt parking lot.

Jimmy picked them up. "Let's get out of this cold. I have coffee in my car."

She didn't want his stinkin' coffee. It was always bitter and burned. Police coffee, that's what it was. Toxic enough to kill everything in her garden's compost pile. It'd probably been sloshing around in his thermos for days.

He must have read her expression. "I got it from Traders. Just now, along with a chocolate-chip cookie."

She shook her head, more slowly this time.

"It's the large-sized cookie. Right out of the oven. I'll bet it's still soft and warm."

Her favorite coffee shop, her favorite cookie. She couldn't resist.

Once inside Jimmy's car, he passed her the cookie and coffee. She split the cookie and handed him half. Thanked him for the treats. Sipped on the coffee and nibbled on the cookie. Waited.

The cookie was gone by the time Jimmy spoke. "I never understood why you met with Romero. Will you explain it to me?"

She shook her head. "I'll never be able to."

"Please try." He gently placed his right hand over her left.

"The same reason you visited me the other day. To see if I was all right." Her eyes met Jimmy's. "When I saw Romero, I knew he'd be OK... not great, but OK. I didn't have to worry anymore. He's fine. So am I. Seeing him gave me peace of mind. Now I can move forward. Just like you always say."

She didn't notice Jimmy squeezing her hand until she stopped speaking. He was staring at her, lips parted, brows knitted together. His face displayed creases she'd never seen.

"Happy," he whispered. "Do you realize you're talking about Romero in the present tense?"

She stared through the passenger window while she sorted out her conundrum. Should she tell Jimmy that Romero was alive? Romero had given her permission, but she and Jimmy were no longer a couple. Jimmy's contempt for Romero was palatable.

If she disclosed, would he put Romero at risk by telling someone? Jimmy was initiating a renewal of their relationship on the assumption Romero was dead. If she wanted Jimmy, she had to tell him the truth. It was a matter of integrity. Fear paralyzed her; what if Jimmy told?

He was still holding her hand, but now caressing her fingertips with his thumb. His touch was gentle, loving, reassuring. The warmth from his hand radiated to her heart. She made her decision.

"That's why Romero demanded to see me...to tell me his death was going to be faked. He didn't want me feeling guilty about it."

Jimmy dropped her hand. His worried face was replaced with one reddened with anger. "What exactly did he say?"

"He said the Marshals Service would fake his death and use news and social media to spread false information. He didn't know how he'd die, but he knew it was coming. WITSEC had arranged for plastic surgery on his face so no one would recognize him."

"Did Etchers confirm this with you? Did anyone in law enforcement?"

"Romero said only a few people knew. That's why there was such a fuss when he insisted on seeing me. His handlers were afraid he'd tell me, and I'd blow his cover. Did I just blow it? Are you going to tell anyone?"

Jimmy hit the steering wheel with both hands. He muttered a soliloquy of profanities, some of which she'd never heard before, ending with, "That cowardly motherfucker!"

He leaned toward her. "Romero is dead. Dead! He hanged himself. Rick McCormick viewed the body. He called to tell me. That's how I found out. Don't you see what Romero's done? He couldn't face not being an alpha dog. He kills himself, but not before he sets you up, so you're always thinking about him, always wondering what he's doing. Plastic surgery? Now you'll be looking for him around every corner. You'll see someone down the street and think, 'Could that be Romero?' What he's done is the ultimate act of a ruthless narciss—"

Happy yanked opened the passenger door. "You arrogant, self-righteous ass—"

Jimmy grabbed the sleeve of her coat. "This is exactly what I was afraid of. Romero fucked with your mind."

Happy glared at the hand grasping her sleeve. Her eyes followed the arm upward, across the shoulder, up the neck until her fury and contempt pierced Jimmy's eyes. "Take your hand off me."

He released her sleeve.

Jimmy hurt her; she was going to hurt him back. "Who's the one fucking with my mind? You're the one who used the power of prayer to turn me into a one-night stand. You're dispic—"

His jaw dropped in apparent shock. "What? You know that's not what hap—"

"You said you prayed to God for guidance. Then you dumped—"

"Happy! Have you lost your—"

"Now you're trying to gaslight me. It won't work. Better people than you have tried and failed."

She didn't remember running back to her 4Runner. As she stood in front of the driver's door, she discovered her right hand was balled into a tight fist.

Chapter 34

Happy wanted to base her life on truth, she really did. She could hear her teenage lies now: No, Mom...I only had a sip! I didn't take the ten out of your purse; I swear! I have no idea where that baggie came from—someone must have put it in my backpack as a joke. Don't you believe me?

Truth-telling was a fundamental component of addiction recovery. She promised herself to live truthfully. What happened to that promise? It disappeared the moment she entered WITSEC. Everything was a lie after that. At this point, she couldn't keep the lies straight. Look what happened when she told Jimmy the truth about Romero. A giant backfire.

She considered the bike stored in her shed. It reminded her of everything WITSEC had taken from her. Enough was enough. Now that Romero was "dead," what was the point? None that she could see...other than Peeps. Yes, there was that. She thought of Floater, her Baltimore friend, and AA sponsor. He'd schooled her in street fighting, gun shooting, and a host of other life skills. He had the special ops background to protect her. If that didn't work out, she had the money to go someplace where Peeps could never find her.

She called Etchers.

He greeted her as he always did. "How's my dear niece?"

"I want out of WITSEC, right now. What do I have to do?"

A long silence followed before Etchers spoke. "What's happened?"

"Nothing's happened. I'm done. Get me out of WITSEC."

Etchers cleared his throat. "There's paperwork you have to sign. It'll take a couple of days to get it pre—"

He was stalling, buying time needed to convince her to stay. She was having none of it. "Then I'll just up and leave. You can't make me stay."

Pause.

"You're right," he said. "I can't make you stay. I'll come by tomorrow. Happy, get yourself a lawyer to explain the documents and the consequences."

"I'll wait for you until the end of tomorrow, that's all."

"Promise me you won't disappear or do some cockamamie thing before I get there."

"I promise…no disappearing, no cockamamie things." She held up her left hand and gazed at the back of it. "See you tomorrow, Uncle Peter."

A mani-pedi, that's what she needed. The next available appointment was in two hours. Thinking of nothing better to do, Happy retrieved the receipts from Bernie's box and reexamined them, hoping to find where the Singletons regularly purchased gas. The family gas station would've been a likely place to have Bernie's car inspected. There were three gasoline receipts from a Sunoco in Cumberland. Google informed her the gas station was six blocks from Bernie's home. The list of services on the station's website included car inspections.

When Happy opened her phone to call the station, she was dismayed to see Olivia had left three voice messages. The first was a cryptic, "Call me." The second was an annoyed, "Where are you?" The third was an irate, "Stay away from me and my personal business or I'm calling the police."

Happy tapped in Olivia's number.

She answered with a voice roiling with sarcasm. "So very kind of you to return my three calls."

"I'm sorry. I just got your messages."

Olivia was silent.

"Mrs. Singleton, why are you angry at me?"

"You humiliated me. Pried into my personal business. Lied your way into a conversation with a dear friend."

"Wait…what?"

"You went into Home Warehouse, pretended to have an emergency, upset the staff, just so you could corner Hank into talking to you."

"No! That's not what happen—"

"Then tried to discuss my marital difficulties. Old history that has nothing to do with Bernie's phone call to me." Olivia's voiced ratcheted up a decibel.

"You must be crazy. Leave me alone, leave my friends alone. Stay away, you hear? If you bother anyone again, I'll tell Jimmy what you did. Got that?"

"Please let me expl—"

"*You* got that?" Olivia shouted.

"Yes, I got—"

The phone disconnected.

Happy leaned back in her chair and stared at the clutter on the table, thinking nothing, feeling nothing. Rain and wind raged against the window behind her. She felt a gentle scratching on her thigh. Steppie was standing on his back legs and pawing her. She picked him up, held him against her chest, and whispered her love for him. Did he understand?

Love. It began with the letter *L*. Bernie's left hand was formed into the shape of an L. He died with his mouth open, making a last desperate effort to communicate. What was he trying to say? No one cared, except for her. Maybe, if she accomplished the mission, the tower of outstanding amends she owed to her mother would be reduced. Weighted averages.

No, she wasn't giving up. And she didn't care how Olivia felt about it.

Happy spent the next hour scanning and photographing the contents Bernie's box. She copied all CDs and created organizational folders. She wanted a digital backup. Just in case.

There was a thud on the front doorstep, followed by a loud knock on the door. The mailman. Happy found a box addressed to her with no return label. The package originated in Seattle, Washington. Who did she know in Seattle? Not a soul.

It was an ordinary brown box. Medium-sized. Sealed with mailing tape. She shook it. Nothing moved or rattled. She smelled it and detected nothing but the scent of cardboard. It was mysterious enough to be worrisome. Should she open it?

Maybe it was a bomb from Peeps.

She scolded herself for being paranoid. It was silly to even think that. She opened the box, wincing with every rip of the tape. The box was loaded with packing peanuts. Happy dug through the peanuts and found an object covered in wrapping paper depicting helmets and bicycles. A sealed envelope was taped to the wrapped object.

She opened the envelope.

It was a bomb, all right. Not the kind that would explode, but the kind that could blow her life apart.

Chapter 35

The envelope contained a selfie of Romero holding the *Talkeetna Good Times*, an Alaskan newspaper, dated two days after his "death." The wrapped object was a prepaid cell phone. He included a hand-written note. "Call me."

Happy dropped the cell phone like a hot steamed crab. Romero promised he would never contact her again. Why had she believed him?

She studied the photograph. It was awkward and off-centered. She imagined Romero trying to take a selfie while positioning the newspaper to show the location and date. He hadn't had his surgery; he looked the same. Handsome, sexy, alluring. She envisioned an Irish car bomb. No, she wasn't going to have anything to do with him.

She peered out a window. The rain was lifting, but not by much. "Steppie, we're going for a car ride."

Happy's destination took them west on Glendale Road, a curvy, two-lane road that led to Glendale Bridge. The bridge spanned the southern part of Deep Creek Lake. The approach to the bridge was tricky; the grade of the road was six-percent. An S-shaped curve, immediately before the bridge, surprised drivers unfamiliar with the roadway. Dark scrape marks scarring the bridge's barrier railings revealed the negligence of inattentive drivers.

After parking her SUV on the road's shoulder near the bridge, Happy walked the dog along the bridge's bicycle lane until she reached its raised center. The rise allowed boats to pass under the bridge. She paused and beheld the panoramic view of Deep Creek Lake. It was frozen, except for the fast current of water flowing beneath. Distant snowmobile tracks embellished the lake's icy surface. The tiny huts of ice-fishermen dotted the lake.

Happy pulled the burner phone from her backpack. She leaned over the bridge's barrier rail and held the phone above the swift current. She briefly considered showing Jimmy the newspaper and the burner phone. Why bother? She didn't want to be with a man who needed proof that what she said was true. That was no way to live and no way to love.

"Good-bye, Romero."

The phone splashed into the water below.

The next stop was the Refuse and Recycle Site. Happy tossed Bernie's box into the dumpster bin. Next came the mani-pedi. Steppie sat on her lap while her nails were painted orange, black, and white—the team colors of the Baltimore Orioles.

Her errands finished, she returned home. Lit the fireplace. Flames consumed the *Talkeetna Good Times* and Romero's cryptic note. While Happy watched Romero's proof of life go up in flames, Christine entered the house. "It sure is cozy in here tonight."

"It sure is."

That night, Happy slept through the night and dreamed of Baltimore.

Happy awoke light-hearted. In a few more hours, she'd be free. She could live where she wanted and do what she liked. The destination was Baltimore; the occupation was bicycle messenger. She wanted her old life back.

It was nine o'clock. The day was sunny, and the house was quiet. Christine was spending the weekend with her aunt. She had borrowed the 4Runner and taken Steppie with her. Happy had an hour to kill before Etchers arrived. She called the Cumberland Sunoco. The inspection mechanic was a woman named "Laura." Happy felt a kinship with Laura; they were both employed in traditional men's jobs. Laura knew the Singleton family and had done the pre-sale inspection on Bernie's SUV.

"Are you looking to buy the Explorer?" Laura said.

"No, I'm the snowplow driver who found Mr. Singleton."

"Oh, my lord. What can I do for you?"

"This is a long shot...I was hoping you could give me a little peace of mind. You see, the way Mr. Singleton looked when I found him...well, I just can't shake it. I'm trying to find out what happened."

"The paper said he ran out of gas."

"I'm trying to figure out why he ran out of gas in the first place. Did you inspect the fuel line? Could there have been some problem with the Explorer?"

"I inspected the whole fuel system, along with everything else. I know that SUV. I always did the maintenance on it—the alignments, oil changes, brake linings. The vehicle was old but in very good condition. There was nothing wrong with it."

Happy thanked the mechanic and disconnected.

Where'd the gas go?

Etchers arrived at ten. She greeted him with a smile, a cup of coffee and a cinnamon bun. When he asked her to join him at the table, she nearly skipped to her seat.

He took a slow sip of coffee while he studied her. "What's going on, Happy?"

She shrugged. "I want to go home."

"Home being Baltimore."

"That's right."

"What about your life here?"

"I haven't been able to get one started. I want to go home."

"You *have* started a life. A very good one. Is this because of Jimmy?"

"No. He has nothing to do with this. I want to go home, that's all."

"What will you do when you get to Baltimore? How will you earn a living?"

"I'll go back to messengering."

Etchers's face wrinkled from forehead to chin. "Home always changes when a person's gone. Baltimore won't be the same. Bike messengering won't be the same. Have you ever heard the expression, 'You can't go home again'? That's what it means."

"It couldn't have changed that much in eighteen months. Give me the paperwork to sign."

"What about Peeps? You had a close call. And there may be more Roach gangbangers looking for you. You have people here who care about you.

Your AA friends care. So do the people you work with. Jimmy loves you. I know he does. They'd be devastated if something happened to you."

"My old AA sponsor will protect me. My posse, too. Besides, the people who care the most about me are in Baltimore. I want to go home."

Ethers sighed and said nothing while he drained his coffee. He plunked his cup on the table. "All right, let's go bike riding in Baltimore. We'll go wherever you want, talk to whomever you want. At the end of the day, if you still want out, I'll give you the papers to sign."

"Seriously?" Happy laughed. "You want to bike around Baltimore with me? You're too old. You'll have a heart attack or get hit by a car. I'll be protecting you instead of the other way around."

Etchers stood. "Get your bike and gear."

She wheeled her bike outside and was surprised to find another bike inside the truck's storage bed. It was a black Marin Four Corners touring bike. Sleek. Solid. She placed her helmet inside the bed alongside his.

"You bike?" she said, amazed.

"Some."

She placed her iPad in the cab's front. As expected, the conversation during the drive to Baltimore was minimal. She intended to use the quiet time to review what she'd digitalized but now didn't have the heart for it. Happy turned on the radio and sang along with her favorite tunes. At the end of an off-key rendition of "Bohemian Rhapsody," she sighed. "I wish I could sing."

Etchers broke his silence. "So do I."

She hadn't been west of Cumberland since she moved to Deep Creek. There were new billboards advertising retail shops. More antique stores populated the highways. The interstate speed limit had been raised. The traffic near Hagerstown and Frederick was more congested. She saw a sign heralding the arrival of a new Prime Outlet Center in Clarksburg.

They drove I-695 around the suburbs of Baltimore and exited onto I-95. Baltimore City was a few minutes away. The Baltimore skyline appeared in the distance. Happy's heart pounded with anticipation. She spotted the Transamerica Tower and the Bank of America Building. Her heart swelled. She was home.

Etchers turned to her. "You're the tour guide. Where do we go?"

"Lexington and North Charles. Messengers call it 'Ground Zero' because it's in the middle of the city. That's where they hang out between runs."

Etchers parked in a nearby multi-level garage. As soon as Happy exited the truck, she could smell the Patapsco River feeding the Inner Harbor. She didn't remember it being quite so pungent; a little diesel oil, more than a little pollution, and spiced with salt from the Chesapeake Bay.

They mounted their bikes and coasted down Charles Street to Ground Zero. It was noon, the perfect time to find her messenger friends. Her old posse would be eating lunch, practicing the track stand, trading insults and quips. She hoped they wouldn't be angry that she disappeared without a word.

While she fantasized about her messenger reunion, Happy inadvertently strayed too far into a traffic lane. She was greeted with a lengthy horn blast that nearly stopped her heart. The driver zoomed around her while flicking the one-fingered salute.

"Doing OK, Happy?" Etchers called from behind her.

"Yeah." She wasn't. Now she was scared.

Ground Zero was deserted, except for a few pedestrians waiting for a bus. Where was everyone? There must be a lull between runs. She began practicing the track stand to pass the time until someone showed up. "Watch this, Uncle Peter!"

She put her feet on the pedals and promptly fell over. Tried again. She lost her balance a second time. Tried a third time.

Etchers laughed. "What exactly are you trying to do?"

She gave up. "Oh, never mind."

A lone bicycle messenger rolled up to Ground Zero. He wasn't one of her posse, but she recognized him. His name was Paul. He was in his forties, grayed-haired, and muscular.

"I know you," Paul said. "You used to pedal. I haven't seen you in a while."

"Where is everybody?"

"Scattered around, here and there. Some are waiting outside restaurants to deliver lunch orders. Some are at the new Amazon fulfillment center in southeast Baltimore making one-hour deliveries."

"Have you seen my friends Floater or Crackhead? How about Pringles? Fireball?"

"I heard Floater's somewhere in Colorado. Haven't seen or heard about anybody else. Sorry."

Paul's cell phone buzzed. He spoke a few words and pedaled away on a delivery run. Happy looked toward the Inner Harbor feeling out-of-sorts.

She longed for a latte from her favorite coffee shop, Café No Delay. She put on a faux smile for Etchers. "Can I buy you a cup of coffee?"

"Sure."

Café No Delay was five blocks away; a steep, uphill-climb north for three blocks followed by a downhill, two-block glide east. After pedaling two uphill blocks, Happy lost her breath and walked her bike up the third. Etchers biked in front of her during the downward glide. He wove easily in and out of traffic. Happy was slow and cautious. She berated herself for biking like an *old lady*. They arrived at Café No Delay, but it was now a Starbucks. Happy's latte desire dissipated. She handed Etchers his coffee.

"Thanks," he said. "Anywhere else?"

"Loaves and Fishes. Near Highlandtown."

It was a soup kitchen. For years, she'd been a cook, along with her mother. The court-ordered community service had been a lifeline that helped her manage her addictions. Sister Donna, the manager, treated Happy with respect, even when she showed up as a resistant and surly teenager. Happy wanted to see Sister Donna. Maybe she could resume her weekly stint as a volunteer cook.

Etchers followed Happy as they cycled through the neighborhoods of Baltimore City. The city was dirtier than she remembered. Angrier, too—probably the result of underlying tensions inflamed by the fatal injuries sustained by Freddie Gray in the back of a police transport van. She never before noticed the stark economic inequities between neighborhoods. Either Baltimore changed since she left, or she had been oblivious.

As they pedaled near her old neighborhood, Happy detoured to avoid the street of her former home. She didn't want to see the tiny row house in Canton that she'd loved but lost to foreclosure.

Etchers and Happy arrived at Loaves and Fishes. She straddled her bike and admired the appearance of the building. The exterior was fresh and clean; no graffiti scarred the brownstone exterior. The front door was newly-painted. It was two o'clock. The volunteers wouldn't arrive for another hour. They would cook the night's dinner in time for the four-thirty opening.

The front door was locked. Happy knocked, knowing that Sister Donna always answered. The door opened. A petite woman with short, brown hair and no makeup greeted them. There were mutual introductions. The woman's name was Sister Esther.

"Is Sister Donna here?" Happy said. "I used to be a cook and wanted to say 'hello.'"

"No, dear. She was so successful managing this soup kitchen the church sent her to Chicago to start another one."

Happy's energy drained away. She fell silent.

"Do you have Sister Donna's contact information?" Etchers said, pulling a little notebook and pen from his jacket pocket.

"Of course."

Happy passively watched while Etchers noted the phone number and address. As they re-positioned themselves on their bikes to leave, the sister called to Happy. "We'd love to have you back as a volunteer."

Happy gave her a weak smile but said nothing. As she biked away, she knew she wouldn't be coming back to Baltimore.

Chapter 36

Happy couldn't look at Etchers as they pedaled toward the parking garage. He was right—there was no going home.

They waited for the red light at the intersection of St. Paul and E. Lexington. The light was long. A large, gray rat crawled from a nearby street grate, onto the sidewalk, and crossed her path inches from her feet. Etchers hollered and kicked at the rat. The rat artfully dodged the attempted assault and scurried away. The rat seemed fitting; this was the intersection where, a lifetime ago, she crashed her bike into Romero's Suburban.

She automatically reverted to her old messenger ways and began practicing the track stand. The bike refused to balance when she placed her feet on the pedals. Over it went. She tried again. And again. The light turned green. Etchers crossed. She stayed, determined to regain a skill that had seemingly disappeared overnight. She normally didn't care about her ten-pound weight gain but wondered if it were responsible for her inability to balance. Etchers called to her. She ignored him and tried again.

The traffic resumed. Etchers dodged his way through traffic and returned to her side of the intersection. "Happy, what're you doing?"

She didn't answer but remained stationary, feet on the pedals, determined not to move forward until she could do the track stand. Etchers watched as she tried again, and again. How could she have kissed the Romero-rat? She knew better but kissed him anyway. So stupid.

Etchers, also straddling his bike, pulled a handkerchief from his coat pocket and offered it to her. "You're not stupid. Let it go, cry it out."

No, she wasn't going to go crying to him.

A red-haired, black woman approached Happy. She was wearing a fitted, mocha coat accented with a peach scarf. She eyed Etchers suspiciously. "Hon, do you need police?"

The woman was pure Baltimore. No one in Charm City said, "the police." It was simply "po-lice."

"No...thank you." Happy wiped her eyes on her coat sleeve. "Just having a bad day, that's all."

The woman continued giving Etchers the once-over.

Happy nodded toward Etchers. "He's police."

As the woman walked away, Happy felt better knowing one thing hadn't changed—a passing Baltimorean would still inquire after a distressed woman on the street.

"What was that all about?" Etchers said.

"I can't do the track stand anymore."

After a two-hour drive, Etchers's truck approached a gap in the Allegheny Mountains known as "Sideling Hill." During the construction of I-68, a section of the mountain range had been blasted away to facilitate easier access to Western Maryland. They pulled into the rest area at the top of the mountain ridge.

"Hungry?" Etchers said. "I have a cooler in the back."

She nodded. He retrieved the cooler and handed her a ham sandwich and a bottle of water. From her vantage point, she could see the magnificent rock strata patterns on the south side of the Sideling Hill gap. She took a few bites of her sandwich. "Did you mean it when you said I'm not stupid?"

"I meant it. You're foolish and bullheaded, but you're not stupid."

"Thanks...I guess."

He gave her a paternal grin. "You remind me of my middle daughter. She's twenty-six and is having a hard time finding her way in the world. But she's got something special inside her. Her mother and I can't even guess what she's going to do for a living, but I'll bet the job hasn't been invented yet."

Etchers's facial expression reverted to its grim resting position. "Are you done with Baltimore?"

"Yes."

"Adjusting to WITSEC is hard. You're through the worst of it—it'll get better now."

Happy fell silent. She agreed with him; things would get better as soon as she was out of WITSEC. Her new life wouldn't be in Baltimore, but wherever she landed, she'd live her life as Lucy Prestipino.

"Thank you for taking me to Baltimore," she said.

He answered with a smile and kind eyes.

As they resumed their westward drive, Happy's emotional exhaustion lulled her into a deep sleep. She awoke to the refined voice of the truck's navigation system announcing an incoming call. It was four o'clock in the afternoon. They were fifteen minutes from her home.

Etchers immediately pulled onto the shoulder and answered with his cell. As he listened, his posture straightened; he became more intense and focused. Happy strained to overhear the caller on the other end, but all she could make out were numbers that sounded like police crime codes. Etchers signed off with, "ETA thirty-minutes."

He turned to her and cleared his throat. "We're heading to the state police barracks in McHenry. Your house was broken into and vandal—"

"Christine!"

"She's fine. Upset, but fine. Steppie's fine. Your house was ransacked. Christine discovered it and called 9-1-1. The police are at the scene. We're wanted at the barracks. Christine's there with her aunt. Steppie's there."

By the time he finished the rundown, they were rolling down Glendale Road toward the bridge. It wasn't raining, but the weather was dank and cold enough to freeze any moisture on the roads. Happy squirmed in her seat; Etchers was driving too fast.

"Slow down. This road is steeper than it looks." She pointed ahead. "Coming up is a wide curve to the right, followed by a sharp curve to the left. Then you go across Glendale Bridge. The bridge gets slippery in weather like this."

Etchers followed her instructions.

Happy spotted Violet as soon as Etchers pulled into the barracks' parking lot. She was leaning against her car, smoking a cigarette, wearing the same slinky outfit she wore the day Happy met her.

"Where's Christine?" Happy said.

"Inside, talking to a trooper," Violet said.

Etchers showed his badge to the trooper seated behind the glass. The trooper buzzed them into the interior of the barracks. A small, rubber ball bounced toward Happy's feet. Steppie chased it until he stopped short. He barked, twirled, and bounced off her knees. The dog grabbed the ball and returned it to the trooper who threw it. Jimmy.

"Happy," Jimmy said without smiling, his eyes soft with concern. He gently lobbed the ball toward Happy. Steppie chased it and was soon in her arms.

Corporal Friend greeted them.

Happy held Steppie to her chest. "Where's Christine? I want to see her."

"Just for a minute," Friend said. "She's being interviewed."

Friend led Happy to the interview room with the ficus plant. Christine, who was sitting with a female trooper, jumped to her feet when she saw Happy. Her mascara was the only makeup left on her face, and it streaked Kiss-style down her cheeks. Happy hugged her friend and asked if she were all right.

Christine sobbed. "Why would someone do this?"

"I don't know. All I know is you're safe; that's the most important thing."

Friend popped his head in the door. "Ms. Holiday, please come with me."

He led her to the Processing Room. Her knees shook as she crossed the threshold. Why was she so wobbly? Everyone she cared about was safe. Her ransacked house and personal property were just *stuff;* it could be replaced. She'd lived through worse, she told herself.

Inside the room were a couple of machines Happy presumed had to do with fingerprinting and DUI testing. Friend took a seat at the lone desk and directed Happy to a chair opposite his. There was a large eye bolt near her chair. She hoped she wouldn't end up handcuffed to it. Etchers was already in the room, standing by the fingerprinting machine.

"I need to ask you some questions," Friend said.

"Please give me a minute."

She patted Steppie, now on her lap, and imagined a serene place. Her mother's garden. She was nine, and it was summer. She was standing by the daylilies, watering them with a hose. Rainbows appeared in the water's spray. Her mother kissed her on the cheek. *You're doing a great job, sweetie.*

"I'm ready."

Friend was efficient and pointed with his questions. His main interest was whether she had anything valuable in her house. She knew he was asking about drugs. Why wouldn't he? He knew her history. She answered the question he didn't verbalize.

"No drugs, if that's what you're worried about. Not even aspirin."

"And Ms. White?"

She shook her head vigorously. "No way."

"Any valuables, money?"

"Only my gun."

"The Sig-P232?"

"Yes. It's secured in a locked safe inside my bedroom closet."

"Trooper Bittinger told us about it. The safe is gone. Any idea who took it?"

"My gun is missing?" she said.

He confirmed.

"I don't know who would take it. No one knows about it, except for police."

"Does Ms. White know about the gun?"

"No."

"Is there something special about it?"

"I shot someone with it. Didn't kill him though."

Friend glanced at Etchers before continuing. "The crime scene hasn't been cleared. The CSI's took photos of each room in the house. I want you to look at them and tell me if anything's missing."

Finally, there was a pause in the questions allowing her to ask her own. "Corporal, my house has an alarm system. How could this happen?"

"We're looking into that."

He handed Happy an iPad and gave her instructions to swipe through the photographs. There were probably a couple of hundred. Happy studied each one, not only for missing objects but for gang tags spray-painted on the walls.

The exterior photos came first. The front door had been smashed in a brutal, but unsuccessful, attempt to gain access to the house. The bolt lock was intact; the front window was not. A gaping hole stood where the glass had been. The window grills were gone. The sashes hung in splinters.

She swiped through the interior photographs, room-by-room. The damage seemed random and odd. Coffee grounds were strewn on the kitchen floor, and the crumpled coffee bag tossed into the sink. The drawers were empty, utensils on the floor. Pots and pans were thrown about. Pantry emptied. Pictures yanked from the walls. Every bed torn apart, every bureau drawer emptied. So was the laundry basket, the cabinets, the medicine chest, the utility closet. There was no end to the chaos and disorder. There were no gang tags anywhere.

Her laptop was missing. She told Friend and then reassured Etchers. "No one can get into it without my password. Even if they did, there's nothing on it that would reveal I'm in WITSEC."

She turned to the last batch. The shed. The area surrounding the shed looked like a garbage dump. Christine's bags of treasures and *good deals* had been emptied and the contents tossed like trash. Papers had blown through the woods, even beyond the range of the camera's view.

She handed the iPad back to Friend. "The laptop is the only thing missing. I can't speak for Christine."

"We're done here," Friend said to Etchers. "I'll keep you informed of any developments."

Happy spoke up. "Corporal, did the investigators see any evidence of gang involvement?"

"The investigation is ongoing."

Happy gritted her teeth. Why can't cops just answer a direct question? She remained seated when Etchers stood to leave.

"Happy, we're going back to my truck."

"Not until the corporal answers my question." She looked directly at Friend. "I understand the investigation is ongoing. Did your investigators see any evidence in my house of gang involvement? It's a *yes* or *no* question. Please tell me."

"He's given you his answer," Etchers said. "Don't be difficult. Let's go."

She relented and stood. "Go where?"

"I'm taking you to a temporary safe house."

"How temporary?"

"Until WITSEC makes the necessary arrangements. Someone will collect your things as soon as your house has been cleared by investigators."

The horror of what he said made her gasp for air. "Wait! Collect my things? Why?"

"We're moving you to another location, to be determined."

"You've spent all day convincing me to stay, and now you're telling me to leave?"

"Circumstances have changed."

"No, they haven't." She was choking on her words. "I want out of WITSEC. Whether I go back to my house is *my* decision."

"You just told me you weren't going back to Baltimore."

"And I'm not. I never said I was staying in WITSEC." She thrust out her open hand. "Hand over those papers, like you promised."

Etchers smacked the desk with both hands. "That's enough!"

She was now in front of the door. "You're right. I've had enough—the lies, the disappearing acts, the fear. I'm through with all of it."

She yanked open the door and stepped into the hallway.

"Get back in here!" Etchers shouted.

She returned the shout. "If Roach wanted to kill me, why didn't they just do it? Why tear up my house?"

"Roach?" said a throaty voice behind her.

Happy spun on her heel and found Christine and Violet facing her.

Chapter 37

Happy hadn't seen eyes saturated with such fury since the night she confronted her mother's killer. Unnatural panting flowed from Violet's mouth; Happy could feel it on her face.

"What do you mean, 'Roach?'" Violet said.

Happy froze.

"Answer me!" Violet screamed. "Are you in a gang?"

Happy found her voice. "No...never. I once knew someone who—"

"Happy!" Etchers bellowed from behind her. "Shut the hell up!"

"You put my niece in danger from someone you knew in a gang?" Violet shrieked. "Christine could've been killed!"

Steppie growled at Violet. Happy turned to calm him. She caught a glimpse of something out of the corner of her left eye. Movement. Coming at her face. Fast. She flinched. Before she could duck, the movement abruptly stopped. Violet's right hand was inside of Etchers's left. Violet struggled against Etchers's grip. He terminated her resistance by cuffing her hands behind her back. "Behave," he said.

Happy stared with an open mouth, finally comprehending Etchers had saved her from a brutal face-slap. Troopers flooded the hallway.

"What's happening?" Christine cried. "Someone tell m—"

Etchers held onto Violet and pointed to Christine. "I need to speak to these two. Take Happy someplace else."

Jimmy led her to a large conference room at the front of the barracks. "Are you hurt?"

The question barely registered. She knew Etchers was giving the women a version of the same horrifying lecture he'd given Clayton Fleming, the forensic investigator who examined the frozen body of Bernie Singleton.

If you reveal Happy's identity to anyone, it'll find its way to Roach. First, they'll ask you nicely where she is. Then they'll torture the information out of you. Either way, they'll kill you in the end.

Happy remembered her dog. "Where's Step—?"

"Hear him?"

She quieted. Steppie was romping around on the other side of the conference door. She smiled to herself. "For a little dog, he's got heavy feet, don't you think?"

"Like a Tyrannosaurus Rex."

Happy fiddled with her hair. "Etchers told me not to say anything to Christine. I wanted to tell her. I should've told her anyway. She had a right to know. Now all her treasured things are gone."

"You don't need to explain."

"I want to. What you think matters to me. I didn't disrespect Christine or lie to her...I'm getting out of WITSEC, no matter what Etchers says."

Jimmy spoke gently. "Don't make a life-changing decision right now. Give it a few—"

"I decided a while ago. I don't want to live like this anymore."

There was familiar scratching at the door. Jimmy opened it. Steppie pranced in, his face lit with fun and excitement. Happy scooped him up and settled into a chair. She patted him, thinking of nothing, searching for a modicum of peace. The door flung open, and Etchers entered with a gruff clearing of his throat. He aimed his voice at Happy. "We leave for the safe house in five minutes, sharp. Get your—"

"No." She didn't shout or curse. She only patted the dog and refused Etchers's order.

"Goddammit, Hap—"

"Not now, Deputy." Jimmy's voice was tranquil but fortified with a ferociousness she'd never heard from him.

Etchers's mouth fell open. He glared at Jimmy, who returned the glare with a resolute gaze. Happy hadn't seen this kind of stare-down since she left Baltimore.

To her surprise, it was Etchers who blinked. "A moment of your time, Trooper?"

The men exited the room, slamming the door shut, most likely by the hand of Etchers. A heated discussion began in the hallway. Happy could make out the tone, but not the words. Etchers's voice was angry, punctuated by what she knew was profanity. Jimmy's voice was the usual calm. A second door slammed. The voices disappeared, thwarting Happy's efforts at eavesdropping.

She passed the time by staring mindlessly through the window. Light snow flurries marred the twilight. Christine and Violet were making their way through the parking lot. Christine was weeping. Violet's arms surrounded her as she guided her niece, occasionally skidding in her fine leather boots. Christine paused, bent over, and heaved. Violet held Christine's hair and rubbed her back. Happy turned away; she couldn't watch any longer. Five more minutes elapsed before the men re-entered the room, this time joined by Corporal Friend.

Jimmy spoke first. "Circumstances have changed since Deputy Etchers said he would give you your exit papers. If Peeps or his ilk is behind the ransacking, you'd be foolish to walk away from WITSEC now. It's too risky. Give us time to investigate. We should be able to rule gang-activity in or out by the end of the weekend."

Etchers spoke next. "This is what we're going to do, but only if we get your word that you'll cooperate. I'll be back here Monday morning. If you continue with the program, you'll come with me to the safe house. If not, you'll get your exit papers. In the meantime, Jimmy will provide you with protection."

Jimmy's turn again. "You must agree to follow my instructions exactly. No arguments or negotiations. No going off on your own, no crazy stuff. If you don't agree, you can stay here and fight it out with Deputy Etchers. Any questions?"

Happy pictured the calendar. It was Friday. She'd have to endure WITSEC for the rest of Friday, along with Saturday and Sunday. "Jimmy, are you going to spend the weekend punishing me about Romero?"

Jimmy's face reddened. His eyes looked as pained as if she'd poked them with a stick. "No, we won't talk about him at all."

"What about Steppie? Are you going to protect him, too?"

A collective groan filled the room as the men exchanged glances. Friend answered. "Burdening Trooper Bittinger with Steppie is a risk.

The dog will be distracting and a red flag to anyone looking for you. The state police will kennel him."

"No, I won't leave him."

"Goddammit!" Etchers shouted. "I'll take him."

"Are you going to be nice to him?"

Etchers picked up Steppie and cuddled him. "Your precious dog will have the time of his life; I guarantee it."

"Then I agree to all of it. You have my word."

Next up was Corporal Friend. "The State Police higher-ups have reluctantly agreed to this. Jimmy's risking his life for you. Do you understand that?"

"Yes, sir."

Etchers deputized Jimmy.

As Etchers put on his coat, he addressed Jimmy and Happy. "I'm about to retire. I've never lost anyone. I don't want my last protected witness to be my first loss. Be careful."

Chapter 38

Within minutes, Happy and Jimmy left for parts unknown. Investigators were still processing the crime scene; she couldn't return home, even to get a weekend's worth of clothes and toiletries. Their first stop was Jimmy's house where he exchanged the police cruiser for his Jeep. The second stop was the Grantsville Shopping Center for Happy's clothes and toiletries.

"Where're we going?" Happy said when they got back on the road.

"Haven't decided yet."

"Let's go to the Caribbean."

"This isn't a date."

"I know that. There's a hotel in Somerset that looks like it belongs in the Caribbean—the Pleasant View Inn. Look, just because you have to protect me, doesn't mean you can't do it in a nice place."

He considered. "Somerset should be far enough away."

They traveled the same route Happy took when she made her visits to Somerset. She said nothing while they traveled through the Savage River State Forest. Her mind was on her wrecked house and smashed belongings, but her heart was on Christine. A lifetime of Christine's treasures and memories lay demolished inside the house. Happy had introduced fear into her roommate's life. How could she ever make amends? It was too overwhelming to think about.

Jimmy drove past the sign welcoming them to Pennsylvania. There was little progress on the road construction. The roads were still serpentine and mountainous; the traffic signs still confusing. As they passed the turbine farm and the towering concrete piers, Jimmy drove cautiously, giving the road his full attention.

"How could Bernie have driven this road while intoxicated?" Happy said. "A social drinker with a .2 blood alcohol concentration." She didn't expect Jimmy to know the answer; she only wanted him to think about it.

Apparently, he *had* been thinking about it. "Maybe his guardian angel helped him drive."

"That guardian angel ought to be fired. How many people have you arrested with a BAC that high? I'll bet none of them could even walk, much less drive. And another thing—if Bernie could drive well enough to make it to I-68, why didn't he take the exit to go home? Why did he drive over the interstate and into the forest?"

Jimmy said nothing. She let the topic rest until they reached Berlin, Pennsylvania. "Have you seen the police investigation reports?"

"No."

"Why not? Aren't you interested? You knew Bernie."

Silence.

Happy let out an impatient sigh. "I don't understand you at all. And I sure as hell don't understand how Bernie's death was an accident."

"It's pretty simple, Happy. He was intoxicated, ran out of gas, and froze."

She didn't like the condescending tone in his voice. "It's not so simple. He bought a full tank of gas after the game."

Jimmy jerked his head in her direction. "How do you know that?"

"I saw the receipt and called the gas station with the transaction number. They confirmed the gas purchase. He bought a full tank."

"Does Friend know this?"

"Of course, he does. He's the one who gave me the gas receipt."

Jimmy's eyebrows furrowed, but he made no comment. Happy knew he was nipping at the bait when he drifted over the shoulder's rumble strip. The Jeep's sudden vibration prompted her to speak. "He had plenty of gas to get himself to Cumberland."

"The car must've been damaged and lost the gas."

"That's what I thought, but Olivia just sold the Explorer. I spoke to the mechanic who did the pre-sale inspection. The car was in perfect condition."

Another rumble strip drift ensued.

She turned to Jimmy with the most innocent eyes she could muster. "You seem to be having a hard time staying on the road. Want me to drive?"

"No. I want you to stop talking about Bernie Singleton."

The Pleasant View Inn hadn't changed, except for the staff. A bright-eyed receptionist in her early-twenties greeted them. She wore the hotel uniform: a flowered shirt, Bermuda shorts, and inviting smile.

After check-in, Jimmy unloaded a pile of books. He issued the prime directive—stay inside the room and don't answer the door.

It was a nice room, with two queen-sized beds. The walls were turquoise, as were the bedspreads, drapes, and shower curtain. The framed artwork displayed Caribbean houses rimmed in pastel colors, sitting on hillsides of green. The landscape scenes emphasized the smallness of the room. The room was pretty, but not spacious enough for two people to stay inside for an entire weekend.

At first, she was bored and then antsy. Jimmy ignored her fidgets and read. It was seven thirty at night. She hadn't eaten since consuming the ham sandwich on Sideling Hill. Her stomach complained with a resounding growl. Jimmy looked up from his book. "Let's get something to eat."

She jumped off the bed, smiling, grateful for a reason to leave the room.

"Relax." Jimmy handed her the menu. "We're getting room service. What do you want?"

Deflated, she perused the menu. "Let's see...order me broiled salmon, sautéed green beans, and brown rice with dried cranberries. For dessert, I'll have pecan pie."

Jimmy called room service. "Please bring up two hamburgers with lettuce and tomato."

She flopped backward on the bed. He added, "And two slices of pecan pie."

An hour later, there was a knock announcing room service. Jimmy stepped into the hallway and returned a few seconds later. Happy guessed he verified the identity of the food deliverer. A young man stepped into the room, carrying a tray. He greeted them with a spectacular, teeth-mangled smile that Happy recognized immediately.

It was Danny, the receptionist she'd quizzed during her last visit. He recognized her as well. His mouth clenched while his eyes darted from Happy and settled on Jimmy. She was certain Danny figured Jimmy for a cop.

He resumed his smile, now obviously bogus. "Ms. Holiday, welcome back."

"Thank you."

He placed the tray of food on a side table. As soon as the door shut, Happy steadied herself for whatever angry words were coming. Jimmy asked only a simple question: "How do you know him?"

"We met when I came to Somerset asking questions about Bernie's surprise."

"What'd you find out?"

"Not much. Right after Bernie called Olivia, the owner of the Somerset Bar and Grill called this hotel and made a reservation for him. Danny was working the desk that night. Bernie never showed."

"He looked rather hostile."

"I was persistent. Looking around, asking questions. He told me to leave. I must've gotten on his nerves."

Jimmy gave her a straight-faced gaze. "I find that shocking."

He handed her a plate of food. "Eat and pack up. We're not staying anyplace where someone recognizes you." His facial expression turned hard. "I don't appreciate your manipulating me into coming here. I'm not getting involved with your Bernie Singleton investigation."

Ouch. Jimmy was right. She'd manipulated him but coming to the inn wasn't her purpose. She wanted him to drive the route. "I'm sorry, Jimmy. I owe you an amend."

"I'll take a pass. Don't do it again."

Two hours later, they checked into the Welcome Inn in Hagerstown, Maryland. Another room with two queen beds, this time a bit bigger and decorated with fifty shades of blue. Happy found a *National Geographic* laying on a side table. The magazine was devoted to the canals of Venice, Italy.

The existence of a one-thousand-year-old city built on water struck her as unearthly and incredible. Water busses? She couldn't imagine them. The photographs of gondoliers navigating the canals thrilled her. How hard would it be to become a gondolier?

Happy's eyes were tired. She closed the magazine and lay cross-wise on one of the beds. "Do you mind if I play some music?"

"No," Jimmy said, barely raising his eyes from his book.

"Now don't get mad. I'm going to listen to Bernie playing a melody he composed."

"Why?"

"Because I like it...the first part, anyway. And I'm telling you in advance so you won't think I'm manipulating you or something, OK?"

He shrugged an OK and returned to his book.

Happy listened to "Melody Rocks" on her iPad. Jimmy continued reading during the slow introduction. When the melody lurched into its surprising transformation, he placed the book on his lap, frowned, and squinted his eyes. The melody came to its sudden end.

He tossed his book on the side table. "Where did that come from?"

She explained the composition's history and finished with, "Let's listen to it again."

When the melody finished the second time, Jimmy renewed his frown and squinty eyes. "Who told you that was Bernie playing? I've listened to him play the piano well over two hundred times. That wasn't Bernie... maybe he played the introduction, but not the rest of it. He's just not that talented."

Happy propped two pillows against the bed's headboard and cozied into them. Jimmy's voice was harsh and unforgiving. He didn't like Bernie, period. His animosity bled onto Bernie's composition. "Nobody else has said that, Jimmy. Maybe your dislike for Bernie is getting in the way. What happened between you?"

"Nothing. I told you that."

"Bullshit. No wonder our friendship fizzled. It's a one-way street—I tell you my crap, you stay stoically silent about yours."

She inserted her earbuds, primarily to shut Jimmy out. She re-played Bernie's melody. Jimmy could be right. The styles were so different, there could be two pianists. The melody's lovely introduction appealed to her.

As she listened, a pleasant memory surfaced. She was little, maybe a toddler. Her mother sat on the edge of her bed, singing with a voice filled with smiles and love. When the song ended, Debbie whispered, "Go to sleep, Lucy. I love you." A kiss on the forehead. Lights out.

Happy wanted to stay wrapped in the memory. She re-played the introduction until her nodding head alerted her to imminent sleep.

Music off. Lights out.

Chapter 39

The next morning, Happy awoke in Jimmy's arms. They were tucked together under a warm, comfortable quilt. Her head rested in the curve of his neck. Her body rose and fell with his breath. She didn't know how they came to be in that position and didn't care. Physically, they fit well together—like the pieces of a jigsaw puzzle. It was unfortunate that when their puzzle pieces were assembled, they didn't compose a pretty picture.

Jimmy's cell phone sounded. He jolted to alertness and stretched for the phone, shrugging her from his shoulder. "Everything's fine," was all he said to the caller. After he disconnected, he returned to his sleeping position and gestured she could return to hers.

"I miss this," she said after getting comfortable. A mistake.

Jimmy sighed and shook her off his shoulder a second time. "I need to take a shower. Stay in this room and don't open the door to anyone."

She made coffee with the in-room pot and poured him a cup when he emerged, fully-dressed, from the bathroom. They sat in the two chairs by a circular coffee table.

He placed his cup on the table. "I didn't mean to mislead you. You were restless last night."

"I don't remember sleeping poorly. What was I doing?"

"Mumbling, mostly. Singing a little."

She gave him an open-mouthed stare, followed by a burst of laughter. Sometimes she talked in her sleep, but no one ever told her she sang.

"What was I singing?"

"Hard to tell. Something about treetops."

"I hope I didn't keep you awake. I've been told I can't sing."

He smiled wide enough to show his teeth. "You've been told correctly."

Happy's mood lightened. It'd been a long while since she'd seen that smile. She showered, wondering what she'd dreamt about. Treetops? Maybe her summer garden. She'd been planning it since the first snowfall. Stacks of horticulture magazines occupied the desk in her bedroom. Used too, anyway.

Refreshed and rested, she was ready to escape from the room and do something interesting. The Hagerstown Outlet Mall was down the street. They could visit the Antietam National Battlefield. Frederick, known for its shopping, Civil War history, and restaurants, was less than forty minutes away.

She picked up a hotel guide book. "What shall we do today?"

"More of the same."

"C'mon, Jim—"

"No arguments. You agreed."

She almost wished somebody *would* kill her. At least she wouldn't be bored to death. She logged on to her iPad and read the *Garrett County Republican.*

The paper's headline read, "Deep Creek Home Ransacked." There was no mention of the address or the identity of the residents. The story described the extensive efforts of law enforcement to identify the perpetrators. The length of the column seemed out of proportion to the crime. Either yesterday had been a slow news day, or the paper's editors sensed the story was important. She showed the iPad screen to Jimmy.

He had no reaction other than a wrinkled forehead; apparently, there was another matter weighing on his mind. "You were right. I don't like Bernie. But acknowledging that doesn't change my opinion about his abilities."

"Why don't you like him?" She asked a delicate question. "Did he hurt you?"

Jimmy shook his head forcefully. "Not in the way you're suggesting."

"Then, how?"

"I caught him kissing a woman who wasn't Olivia."

"That's it? People kiss for all kinds of reasons. How do you know it meant anything? Even if they were having an affair, how did that hurt *you*?"

"I was a kid, and he put me in the middle of an adult dilemma."

"How so?"

Jimmy took a sip of his coffee. "For my fifteenth birthday, my parents gave me a two-week summer baseball camp in Aberdeen. The program included an IronBirds game. I saw Bernie in the stands with the woman. All during the game, they were holding hands, hugging, and being affectionate. It made me sick."

Jimmy's soft voice reflected the conflict he'd felt as an adolescent. "I didn't know what to do. I took lessons at his house every week for five years. Olivia treated me like family. She was great. I had to decide—do I tell Olivia what I saw or be a silent accomplice? I couldn't stand the thought of seeing Olivia every week, knowing Bernie was cheating on her. He was sucking me into his betrayal. It was easier for me to avoid the issue, so I quit."

"But not before calling Bernie."

"Yeah, I told him what I saw." Jimmy's teeth clenched hard enough to grind gears. "He denied it, but I knew he was lying. Then he tried to confuse me. 'You didn't see what you thought you saw.' That's when I quit. Bernie...this man I liked and admired...he didn't care if I quit or not; he was only worried that I'd tell Olivia."

"Did you?"

Jimmy poured himself another cup of coffee. His answer waited until he added cream, sugar, and stirred it all together. "No. I talked it over with my parents. My mother told me not to say anything. She said Olivia probably knew. It was a marital problem they had to work out themselves."

"Was that the reason you didn't want to help figure out Bernie's surprise?"

"Partly. I was afraid it might take me down paths I didn't want to travel. I knew that if it was important, police investigators would figure it out."

"They didn't."

Jimmy shrugged. "Then it wasn't important."

"Unless it had something to do with him getting killed."

"Happy," Jimmy laughed a little. "You're getting carried away."

"Laugh all you want but take it from me—sometimes the truth comes out of nowhere and bites you on the ass."

Chapter 40

Happy returned to her *National Geographic*. Jimmy returned to his book. The room was quiet but for the sound of turning pages until Jimmy's phone buzzed. He glanced at the phone's screen with an expression that indicated he didn't recognize the incoming number. He answered in his usual way. "Bittinger."

A long period of silence followed while the caller spoke. Jimmy pressed the phone closer to his ear. Tilted his head. Pulled the phone away from his face and looked at it. Returned it to his ear. Leaned forward as if changing his position would improve his hearing. "Who are you, again?"

There was something in Jimmy's troubled voice that pulled Happy from her magazine. She saw the color drain from his face. He sank backward into the chair and placed his left hand on his forehead. His lips moved, but he verbalized nothing.

"What's happened?" Happy said, alarmed.

"Yes, I'm still here," Jimmy said to the caller.

"Who is it?" Happy said.

"Yes, she told me," Jimmy said.

"Jimmy!"

He handed her the phone. "Romero wants to talk to you."

She came on the line. No hello, no greeting of any sort. "What do you want?" Her voice was sharp and impatient.

"I was worried," Romero said. "I couldn't reach you. I sent you a phone—"

"Yeah, the burner phone. I got it. Along with the photograph."

"Why didn't you answer my calls?"

"The phone didn't ring."

"Oh. Something must be wrong with the phone."

"I'd say so. I threw it in the lake."

"Wha—"

"And I cremated the photograph in the fireplace. I told you not to contact me anymore. You promised me you wouldn't." Happy's voice got shriller with every syllable. "We're over. Over! I don't know how to say it any plainer than—"

"Yes, you were perfectly clear. I was worried. I found out your house was ransacked and—"

She gripped the phone tighter. "How'd you find out?"

"I read about it."

"Read about it? Where?"

"In the *Garrett County Republican.*"

"The paper didn't publish my address. How'd you know it was my house?"

"I figured it out from the land records."

She caught her breath before she hissed. "You're online, stalking me? How dare you?"

"Lucy—"

"Get out of my life!" she screamed. "Every time you get near me, my life turns to shit. Get out! Get out! Get—" She slammed Jimmy's phone onto the desk with every "Get Out!" until there was no more phone.

She awoke from her rage and found herself standing in front of the desk, staring into the mirror. Pieces of the phone littered the top of the desk. She lowered herself into the chair, rested her arms on the desk, and sat with intertwined fingers.

After a few minutes, she examined the desk for damage. No dings or dents. Her hands swept the phone's remains into the trashcan. She exhaled on the desk and polished a spot with a tissue. "Jimmy, I owe you another amend."

He answered with an expression she'd never seen on his face. Befuddled and confused. He said nothing.

Happy threw the tissue into the trashcan. "And a phone."

Within ten minutes, they were in Jimmy's Jeep heading down Route 40 toward the Verizon store. Happy stared out the passenger window, imagining she was in Venice, lounging in a gondola, gliding along a canal, and listening to the serenade of a gondolier. She glanced at the time on the dashboard. How many more hours until she could kiss WITSEC goodbye? Too many.

They waited side-by-side on a bench in the Verizon store while the saleswoman transferred Jimmy's data to his new phone. They didn't speak or look at one another. Eventually, Jimmy broke the silence. "Why didn't you show me the burner phone?"

"Our relationship was over. There was no reason to unless I wanted to say, 'I told you so.' And I didn't."

Jimmy looked at her for the first time since Romero called. "Happy, I should have believed you. I'm sorry."

"I understand why you didn't, I really do. Under the circumstances, I'm not sure I would've believed me either."

"But..."

"But you should've let me tell you about my meeting with Romero. I really needed you to listen." She unzipped her backpack. "So, let's do this—cancel the amends we owe each other and be squared up."

"You're very forgiving."

She gave him a sad smile. "A self-defense tactic. I need a lot of forgiveness." She took out her iPad. "I don't mean to be rude, but I want to listen to Bernie's melody."

She inserted the earbuds and before long, drifted back to Venice. Her muscles relaxed. She mentally hummed along with the imagined gondolier. When the introduction concluded, she hit replay, and she drifted some more. Life was peaceful as the gondola glided under the Rialto Bridge. Her ransacked home floated far away. Peeps vanished into the Grand Canal.

The melody soothed her into a space that allowed introspection. One day, she'd have children. She'd read them books between hugs and kisses. When it was bedtime, she'd play this soothing melody to lull them to sleep.

Happy sat upright and tore out her earbuds.

"What is it?" Jimmy said, now on full alert.

She didn't hear Jimmy's question. There was something important nipping at the edges of her mind. She was searching, hunting her mental files for a connection between one thing and another. What things? She moved from the bench to the store window.

The wind was picking up. Leaves blew across the parking lot. A few stubborn leaves clung to nearby pin oak trees. Then it hit her. *On the treetop.* That's part of a song. *Rock a bye baby, on the treetop.*

Bluesy Cruise was right; this melody wasn't intended to be sold. It was personal. Maybe a keepsake. Maybe a gift.

She turned toward Jimmy, now standing beside her. "The first part of Bernie's melody is a lullaby."

"And the rest?"

"Not exactly sure, but I think 'Melody Rocks' is part of a big secret. A secret his friends were hiding. One that Olivia knows nothing about."

Chapter 41

It was Saturday. Happy knew from her messenger days the Maryland state courts were closed for the weekend. She wouldn't be able to follow her hunch until eighty-thirty Monday morning. Not with a person, anyway. The internet was *always* open. Happy's energy was drooping, along with the power of her phone and iPad.

She yawned. "Can we go to Starbucks?"

Jimmy was more than willing to accommodate. After purchasing their lattes, they took seats at a long table with a charging station. She logged onto Case Search, a website operated by the State of Maryland. It was a tool she frequently relied upon in her messenger business; it was important she knew who she was dealing with. The website wasn't perfect—Romero's absence from it taught her that.

After she entered Bernie's full name and date of birth, the details of a lawsuit appeared on the screen; *OCSE v. Singleton,* Circuit Court for Harford County, Case Number FL103601. The Maryland Office of Child Support Enforcement had filed a child support action on behalf of Renee Atwater, the mother of a twelve-year-old unidentified female child. Renee and child resided at 9310 Elmhurst Drive, Aberdeen, Maryland.

Happy reviewed the short docket. The complaint for support was filed three months ago. Bernie requested court-ordered DNA testing. The genetic testing confirmed Bernie's paternity. A settlement conference was scheduled and postponed twice. The last entry was a notice of dismissal, filed by the OCSE, closing the support action because of the death of Bernie Singleton.

She mulled over the information until her head hurt. It was all very interesting, but not relevant in any way that she could see. Did Olivia know about the little girl? Even if she did, Happy couldn't imagine Olivia killing Bernie, no matter what the circumstances. Maybe Hank Tinker did. When she looked up from her iPad, she found Jimmy watching her.

"Figure out Bernie's mystery surprise?" he said.

"Not unless Olivia always wanted a stepdaughter."

They returned to the Jeep. Happy was explaining her discoveries when Jimmy's new phone chimed. His jaw line squared when he glanced at the cell's screen. Romero.

"Let me answer it." She gave him a reassuring smile. "I promise I won't break your phone."

Her anger at Romero had dissipated. She greeted him politely.

"What happened?" Romero said. "The phone disconnected. I couldn't get through."

"I broke it."

"You didn't break it against Jimmy's nose, did you?"

She almost laughed but didn't. No sense in annoying Jimmy further. "What do you want?"

"Come join me in Alaska, even if it's just for a while. You'll see I've changed. I realize my marriage proposal may have taken you by surprise. You can use me as a place holder while you look for someone who loves you more. I'm confident you will never find such a person."

Jimmy's jaw hung open. Apparently, he could overhear both sides of the conversation.

Happy answered without hesitation. "No."

Romero's tone became more urgent. "Promise me you won't leave WITSEC."

"I won't promise that."

"We had a deal, Lucy." Romero raised his voice. "I agreed to turn state's evidence. You agreed to go into WITSEC. Stick with the deal you made."

"Or what?" Happy's clenched her teeth. "The trial is over, and you're 'dead.' There's no reason for me to stay in WITSEC."

"You're forgetting about Peeps."

"I haven't forgotten. I'll go somewhere he can't find me."

"Let me guess. You told Jimmy I was alive, and he didn't believe you."

"I'm not talking about Jimmy."

"Well, that's a 'yes.' Now you're angry. Don't make a decision like this when you're not thinking clearly."

Happy imagined reaching through the phone lines, grabbing Romero by the vocal cords, and ripping them out of his throat. "Not thinking clearly? Don't you dare say that to me. I've got too many men who don't know squat telling me what's *really* going on inside my head. Give me a fuckin' break."

He put on a soothing voice. "You're right; I'm sorry. Tell me what's really going on inside your head. I want to know."

Happy didn't answer. She thought of Christine, her dear friend who lost her parents twice; once when they died and again when everything left of them was destroyed. The lies Happy told at Etchers's behest deprived Christine of the chance to protect what was precious to her. How could she ever make an amend for that?

The phone fell from Happy's hand into her lap. She wept into her hands. Jimmy circled his right arm around her shoulder and used his left hand to wipe her face with a warm, wet cloth.

She soon felt better; either from the nurturing or the warm cloth, she wasn't sure which. She took the cloth from Jimmy and blotted her eyes. The strong aroma of coffee rose from her face. She realized Jimmy had been wiping her face with coffee. "What the hell are you doing?"

"I'm trying to comfort you."

"By washing my face with—"

"My mother used to do this." He gave her a half-smile. "Whenever one of the kids started crying, she'd get a wet washcloth and wipe their face while she listened to their troubles. It became a family joke—we'd see Mom carrying a facecloth and ask, 'Oh, no. Who's crying now?'"

"What did your dad do? Make coffee?"

Jimmy's head tilted in apparent confusion. "Sometimes...if that's what he thought was needed."

"No facecloth?"

"Just once." Pain overshadowed Jimmy's confused expression. "I saw my father wash my mother's face. She'd just found out my brother had his third relapse."

"How is Nathan?"

"He's doing well. You're an inspiration to him."

Her eyebrows knitted together. "One thing I don't get—why use coffee to wash away tears? Wouldn't water be better?"

A stream of laughter poured from Jimmy's mouth. "No, it's supposed to be warm water on the facecloth, not coffee. I was improvising." He chuckled. "I wondered why you asked if my father made coffee."

Jimmy's clarification triggered a laughing spell. She doubled over and hooted between big snorts. When the spell passed, Happy spotted Jimmy's phone on her lap. Her stomach flipped. Had Romero overheard their intimate conversation?

She raised the phone to her ear. "Romero?"

"Still here. Are you feeling better?"

"Some."

"Good." Romero's voice turned business-like. "Let's get back to the topic at hand. If you leave WITSEC, where will you go? How will you support yourself?"

"I've given this a lot of thought. I'm going to be a gondolier in Venice."

"Happy!" Jimmy said, fed-up and frustrated. "Get serious, will you?"

While Happy's left ear listened to Jimmy's rant, her right listened to Romero's loud guffaws. The right ear won out. "Good luck with that," Romero said. "That's been a man's job for over a thousand years."

"We'll just see about that," she said.

"Listen to me, Happy. Gang members have a limited life span on the street. In the end, they get killed or jailed. It's inevitable. I want you to consider a compromise. Stay in WITSEC until Peeps is out of the picture, one way or another. It won't take long; I promise."

"I'll consider it. Romero, don't call or communicate with me in any way. Ever. I do not want you in my life. Are you clear on that?"

Romero's voice became quiet, almost pensive. "Yes. I won't bother you again. I will miss you. One last thing, don't ever forget who you are, Lucy Prestipino. Now, I'd like to speak to Jimmy."

She handed Jimmy the phone.

"Jimmy," Romero said, with a voice loud enough for Happy to hear. "You know Lucy's going to bail on WITSEC, don't you? That was a real nice story about your parents. Right out of *Happy Days*. Do you think your father would stand by and let someone kill your beloved mother? No, he'd do whatever it took to save her life. What about you? You've got a gun, a badge, and a database. You can find Peeps yourself and—"

"Romero!" Happy screamed. She yanked the phone away from Jimmy and disconnected it. She couldn't bear to hear Romero utter the words *kill him*.

Chapter 42

Happy's heart pulsed through her head and delivered a steady beat of searing truth she could no longer deny. Romero hadn't changed; he'd ruthlessly tried to use Jimmy's love for his parents to goad him into killing Peeps or, at the very least, to diminish Jimmy in Happy's eyes.

"Jimmy." Happy was pleading. "Don't listen to him. Get him out of your—"

He gripped the steering wheel with white-knuckled fingers. Red veins lined his neck. He turned to her with penetrating eyes that drilled into her heart. "How did you get mixed up with that low-life?"

"I told you already." Happy met Jimmy's eyes. "Now I have a question for you. You were at the proffer session. You learned everything there was to know about me and Romero. Afterward, you befriended me. You kissed me. You slept with me. So, how'd you get mixed up with *me*?"

"I loved you, Happy, from the very beginning. You're smart, funny, and hard-working, the bravest person I ever met. I spent months praying you'd forget about Romero. Then one fine day, you kissed me, told me you'd left him behind. But you weren't truthful with me. Maybe not even with yourself."

"Jimmy—"

"Why'd you answer the phone just now? Why'd you talk to him? You didn't have to."

"I wanted to make it clear to him we were through. I wanted *you* to hear me tell him to leave me alone. So, tell me…when I handed you the phone afterward, why did you take it? You didn't have to talk to him either."

Jimmy turned his eyes away and started the Jeep. He drove east on I-70, without speaking or glancing her way. After they passed Frederick, she asked where they were going.

"Aberdeen."

"Why?"

"You've convinced me Bernie's death was more than an accident."

If she'd thought Jimmy would welcome the gesture, she would've kissed him.

Happy was born and raised in Baltimore, but she'd never been to Aberdeen. The small city was twenty-six miles northeast of her home town. It sat near the top of the Chesapeake Bay, close to the point where the Susquehanna River flowed into the estuary. It was home to the Cal Ripken, Sr. Stadium and the IronBirds, the triple-A minor baseball league feeder to the beloved Baltimore Orioles.

Jimmy took the interstates—70-E to 695 to 95-N—until they exited onto Route 22. A few turns later, they pulled up to a two-story, aluminum-sided house surrounded by a quarter-acre of land. Dormant azalea and hellerei holly bushes landscaped the front. The bushes were oversized, reaching above the sills of the three front windows.

As they walked on a cement sidewalk toward the front door, Happy heard a piano resonating from the house. The sound grew louder and more ferocious with each step. Happy was about to push the doorbell when she decided not to ring it; she wanted to enjoy the concert she believed was a gift from her mother. The music was glorious.

Jimmy stood beside her, smiling, apparently sharing her joy. When the music ended, he let out a soft whistle. Happy blurted, "Wow!" and pressed the doorbell. A petite, tween-aged-girl, with chestnut hair and brown eyes, stood before them.

"Was that you playing the piano?" Happy said. "I was spellbound. Truly."

The girl blushed and nodded.

"We're here to see Renee Atwater," Jimmy said. "Is she home?"

The girl turned her head and bellowed in a voice loud enough to be heard across Baltimore's M and T Stadium. "Maaaaa! Some people are here to see to you."

Renee rushed to the door. "Melody! I've told you a hundred times not to answer the door to strangers."

The girl grimaced at the reprimand and returned to the piano. She played a mellow version of "Stairway to Heaven."

Appearance wise, Renee could have been Olivia Singleton's younger sister; same height, coloring, and posture. There was one physical difference between them—the placement and direction of facial wrinkles. Olivia wore hers downward, around her mouth; Renee's lines traveled upward from the outer corners of her eyes.

Renee planted herself in front of the open front door, blocking them from entering the house. "Who are you and what do you want?"

Happy introduced herself and Jimmy. "We're here about Bernie Singleton. Do you know—"

"He's dead? Of course, I do. Did Olivia send you?"

"No, Ms. Atwater. I'm the snowplow driver who found Mr. Singleton. The truth is, I felt so terrible about Bernie I offered to help Olivia. She fired me for getting too much into her business."

Jimmy's unblinking stare reminded Happy she'd never told him about her last conversation with Olivia.

Happy pressed on. "I'm here for me and me only—I need to find out how Bernie ended up under my snowplow blade. When I found him, the way he looked at me, the way his hands were, I swear he was trying to tell me something, something really—"

"Come in." Renee turned to her daughter. "That's enough practice for today. Go finish your homework." Melody closed the keyboard cover and bounced up the stairs, belting out "Single Ladies."

Jimmy and Happy entered a living room that could've have passed for an Ikea showroom. Every piece of furniture was white, Billy-style. The window coverings were made with the bright, festive colors of Ikea fabrics. Artificial plants, framed pictures, entertainment center, all Ikea.

Happy was impressed. "Who put together the furniture? My mother used to say, 'If you want to get to know someone, ask them to assemble Ikea furniture.'"

Renee cracked a small smile and directed them to the sofa. "Melody and I assembled everything but the bookcase. Bernie did that." She laughed softly. "When he finished, he handed me a bunch of screws. We're waiting for it to collapse."

"How long ago was that?"

"Three weeks ago, or thereabouts."

"You got back together?"

Renee shuddered. "Not hardly. He came by to see Melody, but she was at a music lesson. That was just like him. Pop on by without calling, like we don't have a life without him. I'm glad Melody didn't inherit his flakiness."

Jimmy joined the conversation. "Your daughter is amazing."

"She is, isn't she? She gets it all from her father. I have no musical ability whatsoever. I'd love to send her to Julliard, but I can't afford it."

"Didn't Bernie pay you child support?" Happy said.

"No. I didn't tell him about her until recently."

"Why?"

Renee sat still, with hands folded on her lap, and spoke matter-of-factly. "After Olivia found out about us, she showed up on my doorstep. She screamed at me, called me a slut. Told me if I ever went near her husband again, she'd kill me. She was so out of control, I was afraid she'd hit me."

Happy nodded comradery. "I've seen that side of Olivia, myself. It's not pretty."

"It certainly isn't. Until Olivia's tirade, I didn't even know Bernie was married. What an asshole. When I found out I was pregnant, I knew Bernie would want visitation. You know...a man with two sons and no daughters. Of course, he would. And I was OK with it. But I knew Olivia would make our lives miserable. I didn't want Melody getting caught up in the drama, so I just didn't tell him."

"What made you change your mind?" Happy said.

Renee smoothed her black skirt. "Melody's piano teacher said she's talented enough for Julliard. I finally got the gumption to fight for her. About five months ago, I called Bernie and demanded child support. He was shocked. A few days later, he came by to meet Melody. He said he was going to check his finances and get back to me." Renee shook her head with obvious disgust. "He never did.

"That made me spitting mad. I filed for paternity and support." The tone of her voice changed. The calm was gone, replaced by agitation. "He demanded a paternity test. I'm sure Olivia was behind that. When it proved he was Melody's father, he came by wanting to settle things. He said Olivia had total control of the family finances. All he got was a weekly allowance. He put up with it because he loved his boys."

Renee stood and paced the room. "I refused to drop the court case. We had a settlement conference scheduled with the court. It got postponed a couple times." The dark shadow of anger filled her face. "I'm sure Olivia was behind that, too...Anyway, we never had it. Bernie died.

"Olivia called me that very night to tell me—along with the fact that a child support obligation ended with Bernie's death. That wasn't the end of her news—everything Bernie had was jointly-owned. Olivia got it all. I consulted with a lawyer and what Olivia said was true. The best I could do was get support from the time I filed to the day he died. But I'd have to go to court. It just wasn't worth it."

Renee didn't spill any tears, but all Happy could think about was a warm washcloth. Bernie had left his talented daughter nothing but a melody with no commercial value. She caught herself short—Renee didn't need a warm facecloth. She needed a fierce kick-ass lawyer. And there was none fiercer than Minerva Wilson James, Attorney at Law. She'd been one of Happy's bike messenger customers. Minerva owed Happy a favor; she'd earned a lot of money representing Romero Sanchez at Happy's request.

Happy wrote the lawyer's contact information on a piece of paper and handed it to Renee. "She's a really good lawyer. Tell her I referred you. Call her today."

Renee nodded her intention to do so.

"Ms. Atwater," Happy said. "Do you know anything about a melody Bernie composed? It's called 'Melody Rocks?'"

Renee was quiet for a long while. "An accidental duet. It was recorded soon after he met Melody. He'd composed the beginning and wanted to teach it to her. He recorded the lesson. She sat beside him while he played. When he finished, she laughed and pounded out a riff. He wept when he heard her talent."

"At least I have something to remember my father by," Melody said from the middle of the staircase.

Renee patted the seat next to her on the sofa. "Come join us, Melody."

Melody curled into the seat and leaned close to her mother. "I gave my father a Ravens ornament for Christmas. Do you think he liked it?"

Happy remembered the ornament she found in Bernie's box. It explained the reason Olivia wanted Bernie's personal property destroyed; she couldn't bear to see reminders of Melody's existence.

"I know he did, honey," Happy said. "Your father kept it in his SUV so he could treasure your gift in private moments. He loved you. He really did."

Chapter 43

The injustice to Melody Atwater made Happy's stomach curdle. Olivia orchestrated a string of reprehensible delaying tactics to deny financial support to an innocent child. She was behind the demand for a paternity test, a transparent insult. Happy's disgust led her to wonder whether Olivia killed her husband out of spite.

Jimmy drove through Renee's neighborhood toward Route 22. His gaze roamed across the road in front of him, into the rearview mirror, the side mirrors and returned to the front. He could spot trouble ahead for a mile. Happy was reluctant to start trouble inside the Jeep, but she had to know what was on his mind.

"Jimmy, what're you thinking?"

He didn't turn in her direction but surveyed the road ahead. "Olivia fired you, and yet here we are. Have you no respect for boundaries? I'm thinking about every conversation we had since we left Deep Creek. I'm wondering how you sucked me into this shitstorm. This is exactly why I didn't want to get involved with the Singletons. There are some things I'd just rather leave be, some people I'd just rather not know that well."

She had the uneasy feeling that *some people* included her. If that's how he felt, why did he volunteer to protect her? She asked him.

"Etchers was bullying you, and I knew it would end in a gigantic backfire. You needed time to consider your decision. I couldn't think of any other way to make that happen."

She wanted to scream, *"I already decided! I didn't need time to consider!"* Instead, she said, "Thank you, Jimmy."

Five minutes elapsed before she added, "Sometimes you need to plow through a shitstorm to find the truth."

"So, tell me—what truth have we found?"

Nothing, but Jimmy's question renewed her determination to find it. "We're still plowing."

"No, we're not, Happy. We're done."

He pulled into the parking lot of the Aberdeen Holiday Inn. "We're staying here." He opened his door, put his left foot on the ground, and turned to face Happy. "And, if you say one more word about Bernie Singleton, I'll shoot you myself."

Checkout time was eleven o'clock the next morning. They were on the road to Deep Creek by eleven-fifteen. As they neared the outer edge of Aberdeen, Happy's stomach rang an early lunch bell. There was a strip mall on the right with a nail salon, Advance Auto Parts, tattoo parlor, Dollar Store, and deli. Jimmy pulled into a parking space in front of the Aberdeen Grape and Grub. A flag depicting grapes and sandwiches hung over the doorway. There was a large sign with a picture of a Powerball ticket attached to the front door.

Holder of $1M winning Powerball ticket! Where are you?

Happy halted at the door before entering. "Jimmy, did you know about this?"

"No. I don't pay attention to the lottery."

As they passed through the door, Happy inhaled the delicious fragrance of deli meats and dill pickles. A stocky woman behind the cash register greeted them. When Jimmy mentioned food, the cashier pointed to the glass case displaying an array of meats and cheeses. A deli guy wearing a gray bun at the base of his neck took their orders; a Rueben sandwich for Happy, ham on rye for Jimmy.

Jimmy's prickly mood telegraphed *don't bother me.* She was glad to oblige and wandered away for a self-guided tour of the deli. In the back of the store, she found a wine tasting program in progress.

"Would you like to taste some South African wines?" said a young woman with large, almond-shaped eyes the color of her chocolate-colored hair. She reminded Happy of an Almond Joy candy bar.

Would I ever! was Happy's mental response. "No, thanks," was what she said.

Happy continued her self-guided tour and found herself in front of a display filled with wine coasters, bottle openers, and corks adorned with crystal artistry. She studied a high-tech wine opener with wonder; wine accessories certainly had changed during her seven-plus years of sobriety. Jimmy called out Happy's name, his voice interrupting her musing.

She headed in his direction and passed a refrigerated display case stocked with desserts. The cakes and ice cream caught her attention. She decided she could use a little sugar solace. As she perused the selections, her heart raced, and the prickles rose on her neck.

"Jimmy!"

It must have been the tone of her voice. The almond-eyed wine pourer stopped speaking. The cash register stopped beeping. A customer ran from the store. Another ducked.

Jimmy materialized at her side. "What is it?"

She ran past him to the cash register. The cashier's eyes showed alarm as Happy stood breathless in front of her. "Hon, what's wrong?"

"When was the winning lottery ticket purchased?"

"A little short of five months ago."

Jimmy stood beside her, saying nothing, but intently watching and listening.

"Do you remember what the lottery customer looked like?"

The cashier shook her head. "Everyone keeps asking me that. I ring up hundreds of customers a week. Unless they're regulars, I don't remember them."

Happy opened her cell phone and showed the cashier Bernie's photograph. "Is this him?"

The cashier studied the photograph for a solid minute before she shook her head. "I can't say one way or another. I have no memory of the customer." The cashier held the photograph closer. "Do you think he bought the ticket?"

Happy bolted from the cashier and stood at the deli counter. She showed the deli man the photograph. Same questions, same answers. The wine pourer was next. No information. Frustration flowed into her.

She became aware of the aroma of wine surrounding her. She inhaled the scent; it smelled of a Baltimore block party on a balmy summer's eve.

The sign on the table offered free tastes of South African wines. She'd consumed lots of wine from lots of countries, but never South Africa. Would a little swallow matter?

She took a seat at the tasting table to contemplate the question. It took her a moment to answer it for the zillionth time in her life—for her, tasting a little wine would be akin to tasting a little drain cleaner. Toxic.

Jimmy took the chair next to her. She waited for him to say, "Don't drink" or "Let's go" or "Give up" or some combination. Instead, he studied her with his perceptive cop's eyes. "You're onto something, aren't you?"

Whatever the something was, it had evaporated into the ether. She'd lost her stream of thought. "It was there for a minute, but now it's gone."

"Come with me."

He led her to the display case. "You were standing here when you called my name. What was it about the refrigerator that prompted you to call out?"

She studied the refrigerator and its cache of desserts. Two chocolate Smith Island cakes occupied the top shelf. Her stream of thought began gushing again. "They sell Smith Island cakes."

Jimmy raised his eyebrows. "Explain."

"Remember when Olivia told us Bernie bought her a Smith Island cake for their anniversary? The anniversary was about five months ago... the same time he visited Renee for the first time and the same time the winning lottery ticket was purchased. Now the lottery winner has gone missing. Bernie's dead. Maybe he bought the ticket."

Jimmy nodded in apparent agreement. "A lot of customers buy lottery tickets in a day, but I'll bet only a few buy a Smith Island cake plus a lottery ticket. Maybe someone here remembers the man who bought the cake. Bernie was good at chatting people up. He might have said something memorable while he bought it."

Why didn't she think of that? Happy and Jimmy returned to the cashier.

Happy displayed Bernie's photograph a second time. "The man in the picture may have bought a Smith Island cake. Maybe he mentioned his wedding anniversary."

The cashier yelped recognition.

"What do you remember?" Happy said.

"He came in here for some reason; I don't remember why. He took a Smith Island cake out of the refrigerator. While he was paying for it, he mentioned it was his lucky day. His anniversary was the next day, and his wife loved Smith Island cakes, especially chocolate ones. They don't sell them in Cumberland. That's where he lived."

The deli man had been listening and join in. "I overheard the conversation. I told him, 'If this is your lucky day, you ought to buy a lottery ticket.' The customer laughed. Then he went ahead and bought one."

"Yes, I sold him the ticket," the cashier said.

"I hope he still has it," the deli man said. "Winning tickets have to be redeemed within six months. Time runs out on that ticket in a month."

Jimmy surveyed the walls behind the cash register. He pointed to the security cameras. "Would the purchase have been recorded?"

"It was, but it's long gone now," the cashier said. "The cameras run on a twenty-four-hour loop. Did something happen to the man?"

Happy couldn't hear Jimmy's answer because the voice inside her head was shouting, *"Yeah, something happened to him. He got murdered for the ticket."*

Chapter 44

Jimmy and Happy fled the deli when the employees reached a state of near-hysteria. Do you know the ticket holder? Where is he? Why hasn't he redeemed the ticket? As Jimmy merged onto I-70 heading west, he clutched the steering wheel with one hand and held his sandwich with the other.

The Rueben sandwich Happy raised to her lips had no appeal. Her appetite disappeared when she realized Bernie lost his life because of a lottery ticket. She re-wrapped the paper around her sandwich and returned it to the carry-out bag laying by her feet.

Jimmy wondered aloud why Bernie never cashed in the winning ticket. As far as Happy was concerned, the voluminous contents of Bernie's wallet explained it all—the man was disorganized. Even Renee Atwater described him as "flakey." He'd forgotten about the ticket and had no idea he won the lottery.

Unless he found out the day he died.

Instead of eating her sandwich, Happy chewed on another question: how and where did Bernie discover he held a winning ticket? She was certain the winning ticket was his surprise for Olivia. He attended the football game, desperate enough to ask his friends for money. Later, he called his wife in a state of elation. Somewhere between Pittsburgh and Somerset, he learned he was a millionaire. Did he find out at the gas station, inside the Explorer, or at the Somerset Bar and Grill?

Happy pondered for the next hour. Jimmy apparently noticed she hadn't touched her sandwich. "I thought you were hungry."

"Don't you see? Someone found out about the lottery ticket and killed him for it."

Jimmy shot across two lanes of the interstate to the next exit. They ended up in the parking lot of the McDonald's in Myersville, Maryland. He turned off the ignition. "Explain."

"I talked to his football buddies. At the game, Bernie was upset and hitting them up for money. Later, he called Olivia from a bar in Somerset. He was giddy about a surprise. What if, somewhere between Pittsburgh and the time Bernie called Olivia, he discovered he won the lottery? What if someone else found out about it and decided to steal the ticket?"

"Why hasn't that someone cashed it in?"

"That's where I'm stumped."

Happy's heart sank when Jimmy pulled out his cell phone. "Who are you calling?"

"Corporal Friend. Let the investigators figure it out."

She touched his arm. "Please don't call him."

He stopped tapping in numbers. "Why?"

"All we have are bits and pieces of a theory with nothing to back it up. Let's figure out a little more before you call him." She smiled at Jimmy. "Besides, it would be nice to pass the time doing something productive."

Jimmy's initial hesitation gave way to appeasement. He put the phone away. "All right. What's next?"

"Bernie probably carried the ticket around in his wallet for months. I'm sure he forgot all about it. After the football game, something triggered him to check his ticket. We need to find out where he was at that point. He might have blurted it out to someone."

"My money is on the Somerset Bar and Grill," Jimmy said. "He called Olivia from there. That was his last stop before running out of gas."

Happy considered. "What prompted him to check his ticket?"

"He could've read about the unredeemed ticket in a newspaper. Maybe there was a story on TV. It might be as simple as just finding it in his wallet when he paid the bill."

Happy weighed the possibilities. Bernie didn't buy a newspaper at Taste Buds; the receipt showed only a gas purchase. She didn't see any newspapers for sale at the Somerset Bar and Grill, so that possibility was out. Christine mentioned Bernie gave her a large tip. Surely, she would've noticed whether Bernie's mood had turned ecstatic. Bernie must've made his discovery after Christine left the bar. Happy surmised he saw something on TV.

"Jimmy, let's find out if there was a news story about the lottery Bernie might've seen."

They entered the McDonald's. Customers occupied every table. Some were holding trays and waiting for seats. A dozen children occupied a corner of the seating area, all wearing party hats and holding balloons. The noise level rattled Happy's teeth.

"We need to go somewhere more private," Jimmy said. "Ever been to the Hagerstown Airport?"

Happy smiled. A new airport to explore. Thirty minutes later, Jimmy parked in the expansive lot of the Hagerstown Regional Airport. It was now two o'clock. The airport was small compared to BWI, the only airport Happy had ever been to. The parking lot was nearly empty—no hustle bustle of drop-offs, pick-ups, taxis, and baggage handlers.

They entered the airport's lobby via a glass door, surrounded by a decorative cobblestone wall. A wine-colored canopy protected the entrance way. Cobblestone walls decorated the interior. The chairs in the passenger waiting area matched the color of the canopy.

In Happy's opinion, the airport was pretty enough to be featured in a home and garden magazine. There were only a few waiting passengers. It was oddly quiet. Happy felt the urge to whisper and tread softly.

She pointed to two large, white rocking chairs by the baggage carousel. "Let's sit there."

They rocked in tandem, their iPads in their laps while compiling a list of all television and radio stations broadcasting to Pittsburgh and surrounding areas. They planned to call the program manager of each station.

"We'll never get through these," Jimmy said. "We have to call Christine."

Happy frowned. "Christine?"

"We know the Somerset Bar and Grill was his last stop, right? Maybe he was sitting at the bar, watching TV, listening to the weather. Christine was there, so she would know what station was on."

"She won't talk to me," Happy said, picturing the ruins of Christine's beloved treasures littering the kitchen.

"You're probably right. Maybe she'll talk to me."

Christine answered Jimmy's call immediately. After a short greeting, Jimmy stopped mid-sentence to say, "Happy's fine." He handed her the phone. "Christine wants to talk to you."

Happy's hands perspired as she gripped the phone. She'd been in a lot of sticky situations before, but this was the first time she was afraid of a phone call. "Hi, Christine. I don't know how to tell you how sor—"

"No, no, don't be sorry. Deputy Etchers explained everything to me. How you helped get rid of Roach...and the terrible price you're paying—"

"I should've told you, I should've—"

Christine wept into the phone while Happy repeated, "Christine, Christine..."

When the tears slowed, Happy was finally able to speak her piece. "Christine, you have every right to be angry. I owe you an amend, a big one. Remember when I told you I always try to fix my mistakes? I will this time, I promise."

"You don't have to—"

"I do, and I will. Listen, Christine. Jimmy called because he wanted to ask you an out-of-the-blue question. When Bernie was in the Somerset Bar and Grill, was the TV on?"

"It's always on; customers want to keep up with the sports scores."

"What station?"

"Usually ESPN, but that night Al put it on the Weather Channel. After a while, Al changed it to CNN. He said he was sick and tired of watching the weather."

"Do you remember any of the CNN stories?"

"No, I was getting ready to leave, so I wasn't paying attention. How come you're asking?"

"We're just chasing down a hunch about Bernie Singleton. That's all I can say."

After they said their good-byes, Happy remembered Christine's dream to go to college.

Chapter 45

Happy and Jimmy hunkered down with their iPads to find CNN's program manager. The task was more difficult than anticipated; CNN was a sprawling, international corporation with numerous subdivisions and affiliates. Happy used her phone for telephone calls and her iPad for social media. While she waited on hold for a CNN information specialist, she posted her question on every social media platform she could think of: how do I contact the program manager at CNN?

Frustrated, she purchased two bottles of water from the snack bar. As she handed one to Jimmy, he let out a low chuckle. It rumbled slow and easy, like a finely-tuned dump truck. Smiling, he handed her his iPad. "Found it."

A video was primed on the screen, ready to be viewed with the push of a start arrow. In the background was an attractive woman, identified on the bottom of the screen as "CNN Business Correspondent."

Happy watched a short segment about unredeemed lottery winnings. Billions of winning dollars were lost by players who didn't thoroughly check their tickets. Players looked no further than the Powerball number before dismissing their ticket as a loser. Tickets with all correct numbers except for the Powerball number were million-dollar winners. It was possible to multiply the winnings by adding the power play option.

Jimmy pointed to the bottom left of the screen. "Check out the date and time the story aired."

CNN had broadcast the story ten minutes before Bernie called his wife. He'd had enough time to watch the story, remember the lottery ticket in his wallet, look up the winning numbers, and compare them to his ticket.

"How did you find this, Jimmy?"

"I searched CNN plus lottery tickets."

"Good thinking."

"We make a good team."

Jimmy's words hung in the air. He rose from his seat and stood in front of the window facing the runway. Happy left him alone while she considered the next step. Who did Bernie tell? She envisioned Bernie stunned by his discovery, not believing his own eyes. Maybe he let out a celebration whoop; maybe he asked someone to verify his winnings.

Jimmy turned from the window. "Something's not right here."

"Something more than a man getting killed for a lottery ticket?"

"No, in our reasoning process. The ticket is five months old. If Bernie misread the ticket and thought it was a loser, why didn't he just throw it away? He probably didn't toss the ticket because he never had it in the first place."

Happy joined him at the window. "Bernie was an organizational disaster, that's why. I sifted through two envelopes of clutter stuffed inside his wallet. Old receipts, loyalty cards, every credit card he ever owned—including expired ones. It's a wonder he could carry that thing around. He probably didn't even know he had the ticket."

"I never saw anything like that when I went for lessons."

"Why do you think that was? Tidy Olivia took care of things. She's a proud woman. She wouldn't let anyone outside the family see a messy house or a messy marriage for that matter."

She gazed through the window and watched a small plane roll down the runway, gather speed, and lift into the air. The wings wavered a bit as the plane caught a gust of wind. The plane climbed and slowly turned until it eventually disappeared. Her contemplative mood evaporated when she glanced at Jimmy's face. "Can we grab a breath of fresh air?"

They exited the airport and stood beneath the wine-colored canopy covering the front entrance. Happy resumed her sky-watching. She looked east, then west. Took a deep breath. Ran her fingers through her hair. Stroked the skin on her face. "A snowstorm is brewing. It'll probably start sometime tonight."

"How can you tell?"

"Something I learned during my messenger days."

The clouds began spitting tiny water droplets that tapped on the canopy. A memory transported her back to North Charles Street. She was pedaling through rain and gridlocked rush-hour traffic, calling her mother after every delivery. Why wasn't her mother answering? *Dammit, Mom! Pick up the fuckin' phone.*

The sound of her own rapid breathing shook her from the flashback. What had she been talking about? Oh, yeah. Olivia's need to keep her messes private.

"Olivia asked me several times why you quit guitar lessons. I think she was afraid you knew about Bernie's affair. When I got close to finding out about Melody, she fired me. She couldn't bear for anyone to know. That affair humiliated her. She kept going, but she never came to terms with it."

A chill ran through her, not because of the cold but because of the words she had just spoken. She had hurt Jimmy to the core. Jimmy would be civil to her, even kind, but he would never come to terms with the fact that she once cared for Romero Sanchez.

"What's next, partner?" Jimmy said, wearing a *hot-on-the-trail* expression.

"We go inside. You call Corporal Friend."

His face fell. "Don't you want—"

"To find out who killed Bernie? Find the ticket? Of course, I do. The ticket's going to expire in a month. We don't have the resources to follow through. It's not fair to Olivia. Our fooling around with this could cost her a million bucks."

She could see Jimmy's energy trickle away. He pulled out his phone and hesitated. She nudged his ribs with her elbow. "Go on, call him. I want to talk to him when you're done."

After a twenty-minute conversation with Friend, Jimmy handed Happy his phone. Corporal Friend quizzed her about Taste Buds. She explained her assumption he knew about the stop for gas. Yes, she would email him her digital folder, including the Taste Buds receipt. No, she had no theory about who or how someone might've killed Bernie. When he finished his questions, she asked her own. "Corporal, are there any new developments concerning my house?"

"The CSI's finished processing it this afternoon. There's a community clean-up in progress."

"At my house?"

"After word got out, your friends began cleanup efforts. Your co-workers, too. There's a crowd of people there right now. It'll be dark soon, so I expect they'll leave and come back tomorrow."

She almost gagged. A crowd of people handling her personal property? What friends? She didn't have any. While mulling over her own question, she handed the phone back to Jimmy.

"Any sign of gang involvement?" Jimmy said to Friend.

When Jimmy smiled, Happy understood the answer was negative.

If it wasn't gang-related, who ransacked her house? And why?

Chapter 46

Jimmy nixed her request to return home. "We're not going back until I can hand you off to Etchers."

"C'mon, Jimmy. There are people going through my things. Personal things. How am I supposed to face my colleagues knowing they've handled my bras and underwear? *Male* colleagues, I might add."

Jimmy was unrelenting.

She needed to throw the hunting dog a bone. She didn't know whether the bone she was about to throw had any meat, but she tossed it anyway. "Do you think the ransacking had anything to do with Bernie's death?"

His response was immediate. "Knock it off, Happy. I'm wise to your manipulations. I'm not taking you home."

"So why would someone wreck my house?"

"Maybe some kids found it empty, decided to party, and it got out of hand. I've seen it before."

No, that wasn't it. When she looked through the photographs, there were no signs of a party house. She knew what a party house looked like; as a young teenager, she'd been in plenty. There were always the tell-tale signs of drugs and alcohol left behind, if not physical damage. Bottles, cans, condoms, and marijuana roaches.

Before she got sober, her party remains included rolled dollar bills, razor blades, and mirrors. Once her mother literally dragged her by the hair from a party house. Happy squeezed her eyes shut to block the shameful memory. *Don't think of it. Don't think of it.*

"Happy?" Jimmy's voice snapped her into the present like a taut rubber band.

She answered by moving to the runway-viewing window. The clouds in the west had merged into a continuous, gray carpet. The brewing storm would be a bad one, maybe even a nor'easter. Did Jack know? The weather in Deep Creek was tricky. She had to warn him.

Jack answered on the first ring.

"There's a big storm coming," she said. "You'd better start preparing the roads."

He laughed. "Where have you been? The storm's been all over the news."

She realized she hadn't watched TV in two days. "Oh."

"Sorry about your house, Happy. The night drivers are there now, trying to save what they can before the storm hits. Don't worry yourself about the roads. We got this."

After she disconnected, she returned to the pair of rocking chairs. Jimmy followed her. They rocked in unison for a moment.

"What are you going to do?" Jimmy said. "Have you decided?"

"I'm getting out of WITSEC. I want to move forward, just like you always say."

He sat in the rocking chair, looking bereft. "You're going back to Romero."

"Jimmy! Romero's out of my life. For God's sakes, get him out of yours."

She stormed to a single lounge chair at the far end of the airport. A few seconds later, she saw Jimmy answer his phone. He didn't say much but nodded before disconnecting. Probably Etchers. She gazed at the arrival and departure boards from her lounge chair. Tomorrow she would be free of WITSEC. Where should she go? Orlando, San Francisco, Denver, Jackson Hole. The endless possibilities excited her.

She reached for her bottle of water. Not there. *Dammit!* It was on the table between the rocking chairs. The water bottle triggered a vague memory. She closed her eyes and concentrated. It was winter. Snow covered the ground. Her car was parked in the driveway. So was Jimmy's. She recalled the day Jimmy dumped her. What was she doing? For the life of her, she couldn't remember.

Happy made the long walk to the rocking chairs. Jimmy was immersed in his iPad and didn't look up when she approached. "Jimmy, the day you broke up with me, what was I doing when you first saw me?"

"I don't want to talk about our relationship anymore."

"Neither do I. That's not why I'm asking. Do you remember what I was doing when you first came down the driveway?"

He massaged his temples while he thought about it. "You were standing in the front of your 4Runner, looking at it. I don't know what you were doing. Maybe checking your lights. Now, I have a question for you."

"No more questions about Romero."

"Agreed. Why do you think there's a connection between your house and Bernie's death?"

"Gut feeling, I guess. I've been in plenty of party houses, and I know what they look like. My house wasn't a party house."

"I agree with you. Your house wasn't vacant or abandoned. It was clearly being lived in. And the intrusion happened in broad daylight."

Happy was back into her memory. "That's right. It *was* daylight. I wouldn't have been checking my lights in the daytime. Maybe I was looking for something."

Jimmy had the flame of pursuit in his eyes. "That makes more sense—somebody was looking for something in your house. And considering all the damage, that person was angry."

She paced around the rocking chairs. "That's what it was—I got in my 4Runner, and the water bottle was out of place. I always put it in the console by the gear shift. But that morning, I found it in the holder near the dashboard. When you pulled down the driveway, I was looking around the 4Runner to see if someone had broken into it. Somebody was searching for something and put the water bottle back in the wrong place."

"Whoever it was must've been watching your house. How else would they know when to come? Did you ever get a sense someone was watching you?"

"No. I'm sure Christine didn't either. She would've said something."

Then it hit her—Steppie knew. He tried to warn her the day she came home after giving Friend the smashed cell phone. He was out of control, barking non-stop. While she was gone, he scratched up the door and the walls beneath the windows. She thought he had a panic attack. Who knows what she would've walked into if he hadn't scared the invader away?

"Steppie knew. He tried to warn me, and I didn't pay attention."

"They tried again. Whoever it was waited until the house was empty and Steppie was gone. Any idea what they were looking for?"

She resumed sitting in the empty rocking chair. "The lottery ticket? But why would they think I have it?"

"You'd been asking around about Bernie. Maybe someone thought you found it. Who'd you talk to?"

Happy pulled out her iPad and reviewed her notes. She began ticking off names. "Olivia, you, Christine, Randall Kennedy, Al and Zeke Hershber..."

She paused to pull a stray thought together. "What if Bernie blurted out to one of the Hershbergers that he'd won the lottery? They could've cooked up a scheme, robbed him, killed him, and then somehow lost the ticket. Does that make sense?"

"Up until the part where they lose the ticket. After going through the trouble of killing someone, you'd think the ticket would be under lock and key."

Happy sighed. Yeah, Jimmy was right. That ticket would've been locked up good and tight. Besides, why would they think the ticket was in her possession? She hadn't seen the Hershbergers since they came to her house to visit Christine. Christine gave them a tour—a very thorough tour, come to think of it.

They'd asked questions about the police response time in case of an emergency. They wanted to know about the alarm system. Why? To make sure "their Christine" was safe, they'd said. The Hershbergers' concern for Christine was surprising; they were clearly fed up with her hoarding. Al's nasty note to Christine resounded in Happy's head. *Pack up your shit and get out.*

Happy sat upright in the rocking chair. "New theory. The ticket came to my house when Christine moved in. Remember when Violet arrived?"

"I'll never forget it. What an entrance." Jimmy slid from his chair with a perfect imitation of Violet alighting from the truck.

Happy bent over, held her stomach, and howled a laugh. She always loved the silly side of Jimmy. "Violet had just come from the Somerset Bar and Grill. Christine had some things there, and Al wanted them gone. Maybe the ticket accidentally got moved to my house."

The approval in Jimmy's eyes encouraged her to continue.

"And there's more. After Christine moved in, Zeke and Al visited. She gave them a tour. Maybe they were scouting the place out, looking for places the ticket could be. They asked how long it would take the police to get there in an emergency. Christine mentioned the alarm system."

Happy rocked faster in the chair as she recalled more of the conversation.

"Then Al noticed a smashed phone on the dining area table. Turns out Christine found it in the bar's parking lot after Bernie died. Al demanded we give him the phone. I lied and said I reported it to the police and they were expecting me to deliver the phone to them the next day. That shut him up."

"Assuming it's the Hershbergers, how did they kill him?"

Happy stopped rocking. "I don't know. But I'll bet you a million dollars I can figure it out."

Chapter 47

Happy wanted to search for the ticket. It had to be someplace inside her house. Maybe somebody already found it. She pulled up the website of the Maryland Lottery and Gaming Agency and checked the winning number. No one redeemed the ticket. It was still out there, probably tucked into some nook or cranny inside her house.

She pleaded with Jimmy. "Let's go to my house and look for the ticket. Just you and me. You can keep a lookout while I search. Besides, there wasn't a gang at my house. It was just someone looking for the ticket. C'mon, let's go. We can figure out how the Hershbergers killed Bernie while we drive. Please?"

To her shock, he agreed.

They traveled on I-70 for an hour, saying nothing. Happy was busy analyzing different murder scenarios. No theory was strong enough to verbalize. They merged onto I-68 and passed the small town of Hancock. She felt the engine kick into a lower gear as the Jeep climbed the steeply-graded highway up Sideling Hill. At the top, where I-68 sliced through the Allegheny Mountains, Happy marveled at the sight of the multi-colored, gradient rock that lined each side of the highway. Jimmy pulled into the rest area and parked near the vending machine building.

"Getting coffee?" she asked.

"No. We can get some if you'd like."

"Why'd you stop?"

"This is where we first met, remember?"

"Of course, I do. You gave me a traffic ticket." She flashed him a sly smile. "And I would've beaten it if the Marshals Service hadn't gotten it dismissed."

"No doubt." Jimmy opened the car door. "I need to stretch my legs."

He walked twenty feet to the deserted picnic area of Sideling Hill. He looked east at the ridges of the Allegheny Mountains, his back toward her. She watched him through the windshield. The view in front of him was surreal. Low-lying clouds settled over the Allegheny Mountains and obscured the mountain tops, giving the incorrect impression they were hills. Funny how you can look at something right in front of you and not see how things really are.

Jimmy returned to the Jeep and stood outside the driver's door while he unzipped his sweatshirt. The zipper stuck. He yanked and tugged on the zipper to no avail. Giving up, he pulled the sweatshirt over his head.

Happy held out her hand. "Let me fix it. Stay parked for a few minutes."

She focused her attention on the sweatshirt in her lap. She picked at the fabric caught in the zipper's slider for thirty seconds before she started chatting. "I keep thinking about Melody. It's hard when someone you love just up and dies. I lost my mind after my mother died, I really did. Rick McCormick said I was to blame for my mother's death…I believed him. Now that I look back, I don't know if he really meant it or was trying to manipulate me into turning against Romero."

She held the sweatshirt closer to her face to examine it. "Later, Romero got really angry with me because I lied to him. Next thing I knew, I was alone in a bathroom with two lines of cut cocaine sitting on a mirror. It was the most beautiful thing I ever saw." Happy tugged on the stuck zipper. "This darned zipper is being stubborn.

"Romero slapped the coke out of my hand and flushed it all down the toilet. I begged for it. I would have sold my soul for more. Romero could have taken advantage of me in a thousand ways, but he didn't. He took care of me until I got better. If it wasn't for him, I'd be dead. I know that as sure as I know the sun will come up again." She pulled on the zipper. "How do you thank someone for something like that? His request to see me seemed like such a small thing…I couldn't say no. Like weighted averages, you know what I mean?"

She looked up at Jimmy to confirm he did. His expression couldn't have been more intense than if he were watching her disarm a bomb.

Happy unsnagged the zipper and handed the sweatshirt back to Jimmy. "There. It's fixed. Let's go."

Jimmy turned the ignition and then turned it off. "Is that why you wanted to see him?"

"That's most of it...but the rest, I don't know why, exactly. Maybe I just needed some time to sort out gratitude from love."

"Did you?"

"That was the easiest thing I ever did. Romero was still handsome and charming, but those things didn't matter anymore. I didn't love him and never did."

Jimmy's posture relaxed. A slight upward curve formed on the edges of his mouth. "Now we can finally move forward."

Happy slowly shook her head. "No, Jimmy we can't. Don't you see? Romero did us a great favor. He saved us from becoming another Bernie and Olivia. A lifetime of unmet expectations, distrust, and blame. I don't want that. You and I will move forward, but not together."

Jimmy leaned back into the driver's seat and stared straight ahead. The clouds were thicker and totally obscured the mountains. "OK," was all he said before turning the ignition a second time.

There was no conversation until they crossed over Big Savage Mountain. Jimmy spoke first. "We'll be in Deep Creek in thirty minutes. Do you have any ideas about how the Hershbergers killed Bernie?"

"No, I'm still thinking on it."

Not really. All she could think about was an Irish car bomb. *Down the hatch.* She was a practiced drinker, skilled enough to keep the shot glass from hitting her front teeth. She imagined the combination of Bailey's and Jameson Irish Whiskey slipping down her throat. Next came the stout. Within seconds her toes warmed, her muscles relaxed. Maybe she'd have another. No, she wanted to sip on the next one.

Sip.

She awoke from her daydream. Her heartbeat accelerated. The answer was floating inside her fantasy shot of liquor. She corrected herself. The answer wasn't in the shot of liquor; it was in the drinking of it. How do you drink a shot? Guzzle, nurse, nip, savor, relish. None of these words grabbed her senses like the word *sip.*

Highway miles slipped by until Jimmy exited from I-68. "I need gas."

He drove into the nearby Pilot Service Center and pulled up to a gas pump. At the adjacent pump, a man fed gas into a red gallon container. He triggered the pump a few times to avoid an overfill. The hose jiggled with each pump.

She could hardly breathe. "C'mon, c'mon," she pleaded with her analytical self. "Figure it out."

There was an Arby's inside the service center. A woman walked out holding a bag of food with one hand and a large plastic cup with the other. She raised the cup to her mouth and sipped through a straw.

At that moment, Happy knew how the Hershbergers killed Bernie Singleton.

Chapter 48

Happy began explaining her theory as soon as Jimmy pulled out of the Pilot.

"Since Bernie bought gas in Pittsburgh, he still had plenty when he arrived in Somerset. There was nothing wrong with the Explorer. That left only one way for the SUV to run out of gas—someone siphoned it."

Jimmy glanced at her with raised eyebrows. "His SUV would be equipped with an anti-siphoning device."

"You're right. 'Siphoning' isn't the right word. Let's say you want to sell your car, but it's got a full tank of gas, and you want to empty the tank before selling. All you do is remove the pressure valve and attach a draining tube. Then you bypass the pump with an insert. The gas will drain out when you start the car. You're not really siphoning the gas; you're draining the tank. You can buy kits to make it easier. It takes some time, but—"

Some time. Happy's theory came to a full stop. What if you didn't have the time? How would you speed up the process? Sometimes it takes a while for the gas to start draining. Would someone be tempted to suck on the tube to get the gas to drain quicker? Risky business. Gas could get in the mouth and even worse, into the lungs.

Zeke Hershberger. He went home sick the night Bernie died. Ended up in the hospital with pneumonia. Aspiration pneumonia. Zeke claimed he aspirated a kernel of corn. She consulted her iPad. Can gas in the lungs cause pneumonia? Her friend Google answered immediately. *Yes.* Zeke didn't aspirate corn—he aspirated gas. He almost died. Was it worth a million dollars? She planned to ask him when he was in handcuffs.

"OK, Jimmy. Here's how it played out. Bernie discovers he has a winning lottery ticket. Blurts it out to Al, the bartender. Al tells Zeke, who at that point is in the kitchen. They cook up a plan. They send Christine home. Then Al feeds drinks to Bernie, steals the car keys, and Zeke drains the gas. But time is of the essence. Instead of waiting for the gas to drain, Zeke tries to speed things up. He siphons the gas right into his lungs and ends up getting pneumonia. In the meantime, one of them drives Bernie's Explorer until the remaining gas runs out; the other follows in another vehicle. They rob Bernie of the ticket and leave him to—"

Her eyes watered as the memory of Bernie's dead body resurfaced. The left hand frozen into the bizarre shape of an L. Panic-wide eyes. Open mouth. Now she understood what Bernie was trying to tell her.

"They leave Bernie to die. He tries to save himself. When he realizes he's dying, he does the last thing he can for his family: he sends a hand signal to the person who will find him. 'L' for 'lottery ticket.'"

Jimmy turned to her, his eyes reflecting the emotion she was feeling. "I think it all depends on whether either of the Hershbergers knows how to drain gas from a car."

"Let's ask Christine," Happy said.

He dialed using his Jeep's voice commands. Christine's voice came through the speaker phone. "It's Jimmy. Do you know whether either of the Hershbergers has experience working on cars?"

"They both do. Before they bought the restaurant, they owned a car repair shop. They lost it in the recession. They sure have bad luck, don't they?"

"Do you know where they are now?"

"Nope. The restaurant is all boarded up. The house they rented is empty. The last time I saw either of them was when they came to Happy's house. Why are you asking all these questions about Al and Zeke? Do you think they had something to do with Bernie dying?"

"No, no. Nothing like that. They might have some helpful information. I just want to talk to them."

When Jimmy disconnected, he turned to Happy. "I'm updating Corporal Friend."

While Jimmy spoke to the corporal, Happy thought about Jimmy's conversation with Christine. It was a revelation; his ability to tell a smooth lie rivaled that of Romero's.

Twenty minutes later, Jimmy eased his Jeep down Happy's driveway. There was a swarm of volunteers cleaning up her home. Happy recognized most of them—friends from AA, her neighbors, Pastor Nelson, and the night crew from Mountain Lake Landscaping, including Milo Sullivan.

When Milo spotted her, he gave her a hardy wave and opened her passenger door. "How are you doing, girl?"

She nodded an *OK* and introduced him to Jimmy.

"Police?" Milo said, glancing at Happy.

"State trooper."

"Is everything all right? I was just trying to help with—"

"Law enforcement is going to give this place another search," Jimmy said. "Has anyone reported anything of interest?"

"Like what?"

"Anything out of the ordinary. Something you wouldn't expect to find in the house."

Milo glanced at Happy, his face the turning the color of a tomato. "Happy, I'm sorry to say this...I really am." He turned toward Jimmy. "People have been speculating that Happy's a hoarder."

Happy's jaw dropped open. "What? That's not tru—"

Milo ignored her protest and continued talking. "Have you seen the shed? One of the bedrooms, too. It's like a waste dump. I'm really surprised. She's so particular at work...always straightening up the lunch room and hanging coats back up on the—"

"You're talking like I'm not here!" Happy said, nearly at shout level. "I'm not—"

Jimmy interrupted. "Anything interesting besides that?"

"No...not that I saw. And no one's said nothing to me about anything else. The only thing they're talking about is Happy's hoarding. What are you looking—"

"I'm not a hoarder!" Happy repeated, continuing her loud protest. "Don't be telling people that. It's not tr—"

"Happy," Jimmy said. "Get in my Jeep."

She stomped off and slammed the Jeep's door as she slipped into the passenger seat. After stewing a few minutes, she observed the investigation. Corporal Friend was talking to Jimmy and Milo. When did Friend arrive? The property bristled with law enforcement from the state police, the sheriff's office, and the Oakland city police. Through the leafless trees, she could see ten police vehicles parked along her street.

A trooper corralled the volunteers; two other troopers, holding notebooks, conducted interviews. The volunteers placed anything held in their hands onto the ground. After the interview, a deputy sheriff escorted each volunteer from the premises. The volunteers passed by Jimmy's Jeep as they exited. They offered her grim smiles and consoling words. She thanked each one, muttering to herself, "I'm not a hoarder." She watched for Milo. She wanted to explain the hoarder was her roommate, not her. He walked by the car with his head turned away.

Happy leaned back, closed her eyes and breathed deeply. She practiced conscious awareness exercises. She felt the warmth of her coat; inhaled the fresh air of the lake, heard the trees creak and sway in the light breeze. Calm overtook her. It didn't really matter what Milo thought or said.

By tomorrow morning, she'd be long gone.

Chapter 49

A series of quick knocks on the passenger window startled Happy from her transcendental state. Trooper Michael Rhodes opened the door. "It's cold. Go inside."

Snowflakes dotted the windshield. Why hadn't she noticed? She realized she'd been asleep for thirty minutes. Police were still combing the premises.

She stepped from the car. "Have they found the lottery ticket?"

"No."

"What about the Hershbergers?"

Rhodes's demeanor was somber as he gave her a report. "Pennsylvania state troopers picked them up. They denied everything. Said they didn't know anything about a lottery ticket. Zeke insisted his pneumonia was from swallowing a kernel of corn the wrong way. He authorized the police to look at his hospital records."

"Are they in custody?"

"No, there's nothing to hold them on."

She followed Rhodes inside her house. Officers were on hands and knees, searching every space, overturning rugs, emptying drawers and cabinets. Two deputy sheriffs picked through the property gathered by the volunteers. Corporal Friend stood in the kitchen directing the search.

"Corporal, no lottery ticket so far," said one of the officers.

Happy remembered Christine's bag of lottery tickets.

"Corporal Friend," Happy said. "Christine had a big bag of old lottery tickets. She was going to weave them into wallets. Has anyone seen it?"

A flurry of inquiries flew around the room, through the front door, and around the outside of the house. Five minutes later, the answer was negative. The bag was missing.

Something shiny in the corner of the great room caught her eye. She crossed the room to investigate. An empty beer can. She picked it up and gave it a little shake. There was a bit of beer inside, maybe a quarter cup. The scent of alcohol floating from the beer can tempted her to take a swallow. Did she want to break her sobriety streak with a gulp of beer dregs? Yuck, no.

As she reflected on the beer can, it was taken from her hand. "I'll take that."

Of course, it was Jimmy. She wasn't going to drink it, but he didn't know that. It figures he'd catch her in an ambiguous situation and assume the worst.

"The CSI's will want to test it," he said, apparently reading her mind. Again.

She nodded *thanks* and left the house. The sky was milky white. The tiny snowflakes fell and gently settled on the deck. It was getting colder. The snow was sticking.

Experience told her the snowfall would morph into a storm vicious enough to take down trees and power lines. There would be the usual heart attacks and strokes, topped off by weather-related traffic accidents. The snowplow drivers would risk their lives carving paths through snow and ice to allow first responders access to the emergencies. Maybe Jack would call.

She'd give anything to plow roads during an epic snowstorm.

Another vehicle descended the driveway. She was surprised to see Etchers; he wasn't supposed to come until tomorrow. After exiting, Etchers opened the passenger door and pointed to Happy. Steppie charged toward her. The dog rebounded off her knees and spun with delight. His relentless yapping echoed throughout the trees.

Happy tried to grab him, but he ran loops around the driveway. Finally, she caught him as he looped her way. He licked her face and settled into her arms. "Steppie, Steppie," she murmured between planting kisses on his forehead. "I missed you."

Etchers joined her on the deck. "He ought to be good and tired—he played with my grandkids, nonstop."

"Grandkids? All this time and you never mentioned—"

"I'll tell you about them over the next cup of coffee."

Steppie wiggled from Happy's arms and romped to Jimmy, who had just come from inside the house. "Happy, Corporal Friend wants to speak with you."

Friend stood in the middle of the great room. His overall expression was downward; his mouth, his eyes, his eyebrows. "There's no lottery ticket here. It was a neat theory, but it didn't pan out. Zeke's medical records verified his statement that a kernel of corn was removed from his right lung. The Hershbergers—"

She stopped listening. All she could hear was Steppie's happy bark. From the sound of it, he was running around, playing with the officers. She could hear their laughter as Steppie pandered for attention. His imagination for antics couldn't be beat. She'd rather be outside playing with her dog than inside, listening to Friend.

He was still droning on when she cut him off with a simple *thank you*. She left the conversation and headed for the door. Crunch. She'd accidentally stepped on the shards of Christine's precious Lenox vase. Goddammit! Happy bit her lip. Maybe she could glue the vase back together. It would never hold water, but it might be good enough for dried flowers.

It occurred to her that she hadn't seen the matching teapot.

"Corporal Friend, may I take another look at the crime scene photos?"

He handed her his iPad. "What are you looking for?"

"Christine had a teapot. I don't remember seeing it. Did she report it missing?"

"No."

Happy spent the next twenty minutes reviewing the photographs. No teapot.

She called Christine. "Sweetie, do you know what happened to your teapot? I'm at the house with the police and haven't seen it."

"It's in the breakroom at Discount Depo. Why? What's going on?"

"Probably nothing. Where are you now? Can I meet you at Discount Depo? I'll tell you everything then."

Christine was eating dinner at the nearby McDonald's. They agreed to meet in thirty minutes. Friend was no longer in the great room. Happy went outside and found him engaged in a serious conversation with

Jimmy, Rhodes, and Etchers. No doubt, the four men had been talking about her; the conversation halted as she approached.

"Who's protecting me at the moment?" Happy said to the group.

Etchers raised his hand. "That would be me."

"I need to go to Discount Depo. Want to come along?"

"Why do you need to go there?"

"There's been a new development. I need to look inside a teapot."

"Good Lord Almighty," Friend said, slowly shaking his head. "That girl never quits, does she?"

"No," said Jimmy, Rhodes, and Etchers in unison.

Chapter 50

Christine was waiting at Customer Service when Happy and her law enforcement entourage, plus Steppie, entered the store. Happy gave her a quick run-down about the lottery ticket that might have been purchased by Bernie Singleton.

"You think a million-dollar lottery ticket is in my teapot?" Christine said, her voice incredulous. "How would it get in there?"

A sparsely-haired man wearing glasses and a store badge approached the group. "May I help you, Officers? I'm the store manager. Only service dogs are permitted in this store."

Friend showed his badge. "Corporal Harold Friend, Criminal Enforcement Division, Maryland State Police." He looked toward Steppie. "The dog is part of our team. We'd like to go into your employee break room for a few minutes."

"Of course. Follow me."

The breakroom was large and equipped with a sink, a coffee pot, and a refrigerator. Employee lockers hung from every wall. A long table, surrounded by eight folding chairs, occupied the center of the room.

Once inside the breakroom, Christine led the group to her locker. Stickers of pink hearts, flowers and puppies covered the door. She turned the dial on the combination lock and opened it. Trash, magazines, and "good deals" crammed the locker's interior. The Lenox teapot rested on the locker's top shelf. The teapot's lid was taped shut.

"I keep the teapot here, so I can see it every morning, noon, and night," Christine said. "It makes me happy to look at it."

Friend studied the teapot without touching it. "How long has it been taped shut like this?"

"Since I packed it to move to Happy's house. I taped the lid on to make sure it didn't get broken in the move."

"Where'd you move it from?"

"I kept it on a shelf at the Somerset Bar and Grill. That's where I used to work."

Friend was clearly intrigued. "That's where you kept it? At the Somerset Bar and Grill?"

"Yes, sir. There's this decorative shelf near the ceiling. It's got all kinds of knickknacks on it. I put the teapot on the shelf next to Al's favorite baseball caps. That way I could look at it and not worry about it getting broken."

"Who exactly moved it to Happy's house?"

"My aunt Violet. The day of the move, Al called to remind me to pick up my belongings from the bar. Violet drove the rental truck, got my things from the bar, and then brought everything to Happy's house."

"Where were you at the time?"

"Waiting at Happy's house."

"Did Violet say if anyone else was there when she picked up your things?"

"It was just her. She was mad about it, too. She expected Al to help, but he wasn't there."

Friend snapped on some latex gloves and reached for the teapot. "May I?"

Christine nodded.

He turned to Rhodes. "Take a video while I open it."

When Rhodes was ready to record, Friend gently peeled the tape from the teapot. He held the lid in one hand while peering inside the body of the teapot. "Well, there's something in there."

Jimmy, now wearing gloves, took the lid from Friend and handed him a long pair of tweezers. Friend extracted a small, rectangular paper and studied it. "Well, how about that? A Maryland lottery ticket. Trooper Bittinger, do you know the winning number?"

"No, sir. I'm sure Happy does."

Happy glanced at Jimmy. He was lying; he knew the winning sequence as well as she did. His smile confirmed he wanted her to have the satisfaction of announcing the winning lottery ticket had been found. "7-12-22-10-3-16."

"I'm holding a million dollars," Friend said. "When's the ticket expire?

"In about a month," Jimmy said.

"Good," Friend said. "We have some time to sort this out, evidence-wise. Mrs. Singleton needs to cash in the original ticket. The State's Attorney may need it to prosecute a criminal case. I'll call the SA to figure it out."

Friend began hashing out a theory. "All right, we know Singleton probably bought the lottery ticket. Al Hershberger was the last one to see Singleton alive. The ticket was stored at his place."

Jimmy piped up. "We've been thinking about the Hershbergers as a pair. We know Zeke wasn't involved because his medical records prove where he was. But Al—"

"You're right. Zeke may not have known what his brother was up to." Friend then fired out a rapid round of orders. "Rhodes. See if you can track down the charge nurse who was on duty when Zeke Hershberger came into the hospital. I'm wondering whether Al stepped out for a while. If his continued presence can't be verified, he needs to be interviewed again...Actually, I'd like to interview him myself. I'll call my counterpart in Somerset if it comes to that."

"Bittinger. Log in the lottery ticket. Get the CSI's on it. We need fingerprints processed right away." Friend smiled. "And...good work. You too, Happy."

"Don't forget to ask Al about the Smith Island cake," Happy said.

Friend looked at Happy for a moment and then turned to Jimmy. "Bittinger, do you know what she'd talking about?"

"Yes, sir, I do," Jimmy said.

"OK. When you're done logging in the ticket, you come with me."

Christine, sitting in a chair at the lunch table, began to weep loud, messy sobs. She held Steppie to her chest while fat tears dropped on his fur. The movement in the room came to a standstill while everyone stared at her in surprise.

Happy took the chair beside Christine. "Sweetie, what's wrong?"

"It was Al, wasn't it? All this time, you got blamed for what happened to my things. But it all happened because of me. He was my employer. The teapot belonged to me. Now your house is wrecked. I caused all this, not you."

Happy circled her right arm around Christine's shoulder. She caressed Christine's hair with her left hand. "Oh, Christine. You didn't do anything wrong. All you did was move your things from one place to another. The only one who's responsible is the person who trashed the house. And we don't know for sure it was Al." She gave Christine's shoulder a squeeze. "You stay put a minute."

Happy turned on the sink spigot. When the water reached a warm temperature, she used it to drench a clean washrag. Soon, she was wiping Christine's face with the rag. "Shhh, Christine. Everything's gonna be all right." Happy combed her hair with her fingers. "Listen to me. We'll be leaving this room soon. You are *not* going to walk through your place of employment with teary eyes. Blow your nose. Dry your eyes. Put your chin up. You're leaving this place like a fierce warrior, even if you have to pretend."

Jimmy cleared his throat. When Happy looked up from her comforting task, his mouth curved into half-smile. He left the room before she could smile back.

Violet arrived a few minutes later. Happy watched as Christine exited the store like she was Xena, the Warrior Princess.

Within twenty minutes, Happy and Etchers were back at Happy's house. Etchers was inside warming up. Happy was outside walking Steppie and assessing the weather. The condensation floating from Steppie's mouth alerted her to the plummeting temperatures. It was twenty-five degrees. Snow covered the driveway. Snowflakes were smaller and falling faster. They were serious flakes.

Her cell phone rang. It was Jack. A driver called in sick. He was shorted-handed. The storm was shaping up to be another Superstorm Sandy. He ended the conversation with a plea, "Will you plow tonight?"

"Sure," she said. "Can I drive Mack the Knife?"

"I'll reserve that snowplow for you."

"One more thing—will you watch my dog?"

"You're killing me, Happy."

Chapter 51

Happy knew it would happen; Etchers had a fit when she informed him she was out of WITSEC as of that very minute, with or without the exit paperwork. She had made Etchers a cup of coffee with the only undisturbed appliance in her kitchen. They were sitting on the fireplace hearth when Etchers blew his stack.

"Goddammit, Happy!" He slapped the hearth with both hands, spilling the coffee onto the floor. "I thought Jimmy talked some sense into you."

"He tried." She shot an angry glare in his direction. "Now don't you try to weasel out of our agreement. I lived up to my end of the—"

He stood and paced through the debris on the floor, kicking bits and pieces out of his way. "You plowed up a dead body. That body belonged to someone who bought a winning lottery ticket. That someone was murdered because of that ticket. You led the police to the ticket. How long do you think it'll take the media to get ahold of that story? Your name and picture will be all over the internet. You'll have a big, fat target on your back."

Etchers had a point. The story would start with the *Cumberland Times* or the *Garrett County Republican* and go viral from there. Even the U.S. Marshals Service, with its magical powers, wouldn't be able to suppress it.

He returned to his seat beside her on the hearth. "What's this about, Happy?"

"I'm not WITSEC material. You said some people aren't and I'm one of them. It's as simple as that. If you have any papers for me to sign, it's now or never."

"No, there's more going on here. Tell me."

She stared into her cup. "The truth is, I hate Happy Holiday. I don't want to be her anymore."

"That's it? We can change your name easy enough."

"No, it's not just the name. I'm talking about the stupid twit who doesn't speak up and keeps making stupid mistakes, the girl who's afraid of everything...the one who needed a man to save her from a face-slap. Everything I liked about myself was inside Lucy. She was confident. Physically strong. Able to take care of herself. Now Lucy's just about disappeared, and I want her back."

To Happy's surprise, Etchers seemed to understand.

"When I first met you," Etchers said. "I sized you up as a tough cookie, from a tough neighborhood, who had a tough life. Maybe Lucy got you through all that. Your edges are smoothing, but you're not morphing into someone new.

"Let me remind you—you just solved a death mystery. And you did it by plowing over everyone's conclusions Singleton died because of a tragic accident. You're growing up, that's all. It's a hard process, and I don't doubt for a minute it's exponentially more complicated when you're also dealing with a new identity."

Happy's cell phone sounded. It was Jimmy. "Hey, the CSIs got a good print off the ticket. Guess whose fingerprint they found?"

"Al's?"

"Bingo. He's in custody. Friend is getting ready to interrogate him. Where are you?"

"At my house. Etchers is here."

"OK. I'll keep you posted."

Happy gave Etchers an update ending with, "You think I'm growing up? That's just silly. I've already grown up."

His mouth curved into a tentative smile. "I'm almost fifty-seven, and I'm still growing up. At the moment, I have three children in their twenties. It's not an easy time of life—coming to terms with "adulting," as my kids call it. Some have a hard time. Some fly through it easy-peasy.

"Think of yourself as a sliding scale between Happy and Lucy. As circumstances arise, slide toward the one who suits you at the time. Be patient with yourself. You'll be fine—as long as you're not dead. Think about what I said, at least until tomorrow."

What Etchers said made a certain amount of sense. "Well, I'll think about it. But if I stay in WITSEC, I want a new name."

"That's a given. This time, you won't have a choice, but what name would you pick for yourself?"

"Peter Pan."

Etchers rolled out his bouncy laugh. "That's the spirit."

"All right, we'll talk again tomorrow, but I'm plowing the roads tonight. I'm not gonna be one of those employees who doesn't show up when she's needed."

She rummaged through her backpack and pulled out an envelope. Inside was a gift certificate to the Pittsburgh Palace in an amount sufficient to cover the cost of a meal for Etchers's entire family. "I'm going to miss you, Uncle Peter. Have an awesome retirement. You deserve one."

Her eyes welled, and she kissed him on the cheek. "Uncle Peter...about the face-slap... thanks for the save. You're still pretty quick. Now I want to hear all about your grandchildren."

Happy's shift began at midnight; she had time to make a life-changing phone call. She tapped in the home number of Minerva Wilson James, Attorney at Law. During Happy's messenger days, the attorney gave Lucy her personal cell number with the instruction, "Call me any time." She hadn't spoken to Minerva since arranging for her to represent Romero.

A surprised Minerva sputtered a few seconds before Happy interrupted, "I need to talk to you."

"What do you need?"

"Two things. First, I'd like to set up a college scholarship for someone. I'll tell you the details later. Can you do that?"

"Yes, I can do that. What's the second thing?"

"Did Renee Atwater contact you?"

"Yes, but I couldn't help her. Her first lawyer was correct—"

"I have a story to tell you..."

Chapter 52

Happy gave herself an extra thirty minutes to reach the garage. Tiny snowflakes swirled across the roads in the ever-increasing wind, creating the disorienting appearance of snow-waves. She concentrated on mailboxes lining the streets to keep her 4Runner in the road. The weather report from radio station WQHJ warned that the rain/snow line was unpredictable. Western Maryland could be hit with snow, ice, or a mixture.

She arrived at the garage without mishap. Employees' personal vehicles filled the parking lot. Jack must've ordered everyone in. A long line of snowplows, waiting for a load of anti-skid aggregate, surrounded the garage. She parked her SUV and walked the dog across the parking lot to the entrance. Steppie did his part—he pranced like a show dog; chin up, tall and proud, wagging his tail along the way. The waiting drivers lowered their cab windows and shouted different versions of *welcome back*.

The greetings continued inside the building, along with the incredulous smiles from drivers when they spotted the dog. The employee breakroom hummed with activity. Drivers gathered outside Jack's office for their route assignments.

Within a few minutes, Happy stood in front of Jack's desk.

"Your route is Glendale Road," he said.

Happy was disappointed. Glendale Road stretched a mere six miles between Bittinger Road and Garrett Highway. The route was boring; mostly flat and straight, especially when approaching Bittinger Road. The only thrill was the steep slope and S-curve on the east side of Glendale

Bridge. The bridge itself could be a challenge if it iced up. Attentive and patient driving would thwart any possible adrenaline rush.

"What else?" she said.

"Nothing else. What were you expecting?"

"Backbone Mountain."

As usual, her joke fell flat.

"All nightshift drivers are on duty tonight. State and County, too. Short routes for everyone so we can keep up with the snow. Can you handle the bridge?"

"Yes, sir."

"Don't forget the expansion joints."

"I won't," she said. "What about chains?"

"We're going to avoid them as long as we can, so they don't tear up the roads unnecessarily."

She offered Jack the leash attached to Steppie, now sitting by her feet. "Jack, meet Steppie. Promise me you'll be sweet to him."

Jack bristled and looked at the dog as if he were a piece of broken equipment. "I'll be as sweet as a sirloin steak."

"Promise. He's all I've got in this world."

Jack picked up the dog and held him in his arms. "Don't worry about your dog. I'll take good care of him. You be careful and stay in touch."

It felt good sitting in her snowplow. She'd nicknamed it "Mack the Knife" for its ability to slice through ice and snow. The snowplow was sturdy, reliable, and safe; it would protect her from any danger that came her way. She stroked Mack's dashboard with affection. "Nice to ride with you again."

Happy joined the line of drivers waiting for their loads of anti-skid, a seventy-thirty mixture of limestone and salt. First, a sprayer coated Mack's empty bed with a mixture that allowed anti-skid to drop more easily through the snowplow's auger and spreader. After receiving the spray, Happy positioned Mack under a front-end loader. The snowplow jostled as ten tons of anti-skid dropped into its bed. Happy exited the garage and headed for Glendale Road.

The snow remained dry and swirly, but the wind was picking up. She preferred blizzard conditions to icy ones. If there was a snow white-out, she'd stop plowing until she could make out the road. Ice was sneaky.

Mack trucks didn't have four-wheel drive. If you weren't paying attention, you could drive too fast and end up in a ditch, if you were lucky, or slide backward down a hill, if you weren't. If your luck totally ran out, you could jackknife.

Happy drove ten miles to Glendale Road. The State and County snowplows had done a fine job of keeping up with the snow. She turned east from Garrett Highway onto Glendale. There were no hazards in sight. Glendale Bridge was in good shape; no ice. She raised the blade as she crossed over the bridge's first expansion joint, threw an extra batch of anti-skid along the bridge, and raised the blade again as she crossed the second expansion joint at the end of the bridge. The lake was frozen solid; even the fast-flowing channel of water beneath the bridge was still.

She threw extra anti-skid while climbing the S-curve following the bridge. After the road straightened, the climb continued upward for another half-mile. Mack forged ahead without a pause or slip. When the tricky part of the road was behind her, Happy patted the dashboard. "Good job, Mack."

The remainder of Glendale had some curves but was generally flat. She considered her return trip. The was no easy turnaround area at the intersection of Glendale and Bittinger. As she neared the end of Glendale, she turned right onto Hunt Valley Road, which looped to connect to Bittinger. Then left onto Bittinger, and left onto Glendale, heading west.

She called Jack. "Finished the first pass. No ice. No obstructions."

"Good. Steppie's sleeping like a baby on my lap."

"Thanks, Jack."

"What's with the scars on his stomach?"

She paused a moment. There was no longer a reason to deflect or lie. "He got shot trying to save my mother."

Silence.

"The snow's picking up," she said. "I'm starting the next pass."

"Um...Happy." Jack cleared his throat. "Trooper Jimmy Bittinger called. He asked for your route. He wants to meet up with you on your break. He said don't call back—he's in a spot with bad cell service."

Happy's spirits rose. "If he calls again, tell him I'll meet him in the parking lot of the Fireside Deli and Wine Shop. I'll aim for four in the morning."

She slogged down Glendale toward the bridge, smiling to herself. Why did Jimmy want to meet up? Give her an update on Al Hershberger's interrogation? Say a proper good-bye? Her imagination fluttered in all directions. It eventually landed on Jimmy's king-sized bed. She felt the weight of Jimmy's body on hers. He was caressing her face, kissing her neck. His hand skimmed her breast as it slid down...

Mack skidded on a slick spot in the road. She turned the wheel into the skid—only a tad, to avoid triggering an overcorrection and a slide in the opposite direction. When the snowplow straightened, she scolded herself. She'd been driving too fast, not keeping her mind on the road. No more thinking about Jimmy.

Two hours passed. The traffic disappeared; the governor must have declared a state of emergency for Western Maryland. The wind gained velocity. Strong gusts shoved Mack into slight swerves along the road. The snow morphed from tiny flakes to icy pellets that bounced off the windshield. Soon the pellets would stick to the road and encase power lines and tree branches. Happy settled into her seat and breathed deeply. She knew what was coming—an ice storm. And soon.

Jack called. "What are the conditions on Glendale?"

"Deteriorating, but manageable."

"Crews in Pennsylvania are reporting falling trees and power lines. If you see that, come in. We're not risking our crew. We'll clean up after the storm."

She crept down the S-curve and crossed Glendale Bridge, throwing extra batches of anti-skid along the way. At Garrett Highway, she eyed the conditions in all directions. No hazards, other than the icy snow. She deemed it safe for another pass. Made the turnaround. Headed east on Glendale.

Mack began slipping as it ascended the S-curve. She engaged the axel interlock. All wheels were now working together. She performed a dance of gears and clutches. The snowplow struggled through the curve. There was another uphill half-mile ahead of her before reaching the level part of the road.

The wheels slipped and spun. "You can do it, Mack," she whispered under her breath. Mack answered by sliding backward; just a few feet, but far enough to scare the bejesus out of her. She parked the snowplow, locked the brakes.

Out came the safety jacket. She exited the snowplow and retrieved a shovel from the storage area at the back of the cab. Next came hand-shoveling anti-skid from the bed and piling it behind the snowplow's back wheels. Tried again. The snowplow moved forward. There were no difficulties plowing the remainder of Glendale. She made her turns. Mack slipped again on Bittinger Road.

It was time to put chains on the back wheels. In fair weather, she practiced the procedure weekly—laying out the chains, checking for twisted links, positioning the chains around the wheel, tightening the cams. Practice made for speedy efficiency. Every second counted in bitter weather. For safety reasons, Jack wanted his drivers to put on the chains in the garage.

She called Jack. "I need chains. I'd rather not come in until I need another load of anti-skid. I can put the chains on in the Fireside's parking lot. OK?"

"All right," he said. "Call me when you pull over."

As she entered Glendale Road, skid marks swerving across the road greeted her. Her eyes tracked the fishtail path to the wheels of a Voyager trapped in a drainage ditch. When did that happen? She didn't see the accident; the driver must've lost control while she was plowing Hunt Valley Road.

Happy slowed as she approached the vehicle. There was no driver. Her stomach turned queasy. She parked. Put on her safety jacket. Grabbed the tire hammer from under her seat. Climbed out of the cab. Searched. No driver inside or outside the Voyager. She used her tire hammer to search the drainage ditch. Nothing. She shouted, "Driver! Driver! Call out!" No answer.

Could the driver be walking for help?

Suddenly, she was shaking. Bernie Singleton. No, no, no! It couldn't be happening again. She called Jack but couldn't control the quaking in her voice. "There's a stranded Voyager trapped in a ditch on Glendale. Near Bittinger Road. I can't find the driv—"

"I'm notifying the Sheriff's Department," Jack said. "They'll search. Listen up, Happy. Heavy ice is on the way. Trees will fall. They'll take out power lines. Get back to the garage ASAP."

"The driver might be walking. I need to look—"

"No! I'm ordering you to return to the garage."

"How will they get here to do the search? I need to keep the road clear. I should—"

"Get back here. Now! No arguments."

"Yes, sir."

She reluctantly returned to the snowplow and inched along Glendale, fretting about the missing driver. Branches of the trees lining the road began to droop under the weight of the falling ice. Ice collected on the windshield wipers. The snowplow skidded. Happy scolded herself, "Stop worrying and start driving."

A wind gust interrupted her renewed focus. The snowplow shook but continued its steady drive. She flinched when she heard the unmistakable crack of a falling tree. Her head swiveled. Where'd that come from? She braced herself. Could Mack protect her from a falling tree? A tree crash-landed in the nearby woods, about twenty yards behind her. Thank you, sweet baby Jesus.

She called Jack. "A tree just fell behind me."

"Take shelter," Jack said. "Then call me and tell me where you're at."

Happy didn't need convincing. The Fireside was three miles away. The owner would take her in; she might even feed Happy a panini. And cheese. And chocolate. Maybe Jimmy would be there.

The weather relented. She knew the calm was a temporary respite. The circular winds of the storm brought bands of weather. One band had just passed; another was on the way. There would be a few minutes of clearer visibility.

Happy spotted a pedestrian trudging along the shoulder. The missing driver? The pedestrian was bundled in a thick, hooded winter coat. From the size and portly shape, she guessed he was male. His walk was slow and deliberate. An older man. The pedestrian turned around, apparently having heard the snowplow, and frantically waved for her to stop.

She pulled beside him and lowered the passenger-side window. The hood of his green parka covered his head and obscured his face from the eyes up. He had ruddy cheeks, thin lips, and a drippy nose. He was shivering.

She shouted to the man, "Are you the driver of the Voyager?"

He tried to speak but nodded instead. After some effort, he said, "W-Will you help me?"

She hesitated. Could he be a Roach gangster? He seemed too old to be in a gang. On the other hand, she had no weapon, no way to defend herself if he meant her harm. One thing she was *sure* of—she wouldn't be able to live with herself if he died after she refused his plea for help.

"Of course, I will. Can you get inside the snowplow?"

He opened the door and, to her surprise, climbed the steps with ease. The man smiled with chapped lips. "Th-Thank you," he said, rubbing his hands together.

"You're welcome."

"Happy?"

Her stomach dropped. "Who are you?"

The man flipped back his parka hood and removed his black skull hat. "Milo Sullivan. Remember me?"

"Of course, I do," Happy said, relieved. "I didn't recognize you in your winter gear. Why didn't you identify yourself? You gave me a little scare."

"Sorry. The cold has made me lose my faculties."

"Is anyone coming for you?"

"No. The weather's too bad. Everyone's calling for tows. No one's coming for hours." Milo dropped his cordial smile. "Thank God you came by. I didn't want to freeze to death like Bernie Singleton."

"I'm heading to the Fireside to take shelter. You come with me. Put on your seatbelt; it's going to be quite a ride."

The transmission screeched as she raked the gears. Mack was stubborn; the gears wouldn't slide into place. She jiggled the stick shift into first gear and proceeded.

"These darn gears," she said, moving the gear into second, then to third. "Do you think the company will ever spring for trucks with automatic transmission?"

"Nah. It'll keep replacing these antiques with newer antiques bought at auction."

Happy quickly glanced at him with a friendly smile. "What in the world are you doing out on a night like this?"

"Meeting up with a woman."

"In this weather?" She laughed. "I hope she's worth it."

"She's worth a million dollars."

Her head spun in his direction. Milo jammed the muzzle of a pistol into her forehead. "Do what I say, or I'll blow your fuckin' head off."

Chapter 53

Happy couldn't breathe, or blink, or move her head to watch the road. All she could see was the malice in Milo's eyes as he pressed the gun's muzzle into her skull. The snowplow rumbled forward as the road curved right. The snowplow crossed the center line and veered toward the opposite shoulder.

Milo yelled. "Stay on the fuckin' road!"

"I can't...all I see is the gun."

She gingerly turned her head so she could see the perilous road in front of her. He pressed the gun into her cheekbone. She squeezed her eyes shut. Tears squished through her lashes. "I can't drive with a gun in my face."

He lowered the gun from her cheek and jabbed it into her ribs. "Open your eyes and drive."

She complied, tears streaking down her cheeks. "What do you want? Why are you doing this?"

"The lottery ticket. Where is it?"

Milo? What did he have to do with the ticket?

He hit her in the cheek with the gun. "I said, 'Where is it?'"

Happy's vision turned dark. Electric eels writhed before her eyes. Her stomach turned, and she retched. An endless moment passed before the steering wheel reappeared. "Milo, don't hit me again. Please. I almost passed out."

He raised the gun above her head, menacing another blow. "Then tell me where that goddamn ticket is."

He didn't know the police had the ticket. Once he knew she couldn't give it to him, he'd kill her then and there. He rammed the gun twice into her ribs. He intended to kill her. Lying was the only way to save herself. She had to dream up a good one—once he figured out she was lying, he'd kill her.

She thought of a lie that would bring her near the state police barracks. "My storage unit. You know, the self-storage place in McHenry."

"Drive." He waved the gun in her face. "No funny stuff with the snowplow. I've been a driver for longer than you've been alive. I know all the tricks."

It would take twenty minutes to get to McHenry. If she drove slowly, she might be able to draw it out to thirty. She needed time to concoct a plan. What could she do? He had a gun. The shovel was in the storage area behind the cab. The tire hammer was under her seat. Even if she could get to them, they were no defense against a bullet. *Think. Think.* She was too scared to think. She gripped the steering wheel to fight off growing panic. *C'mon, Lucy. Help me.*

As they rounded a curve, she braked without down-shifting. The snowplow swerved and skidded. She recovered with corrective steering. Milo jammed his right foot on an imagined brake. He may be an experienced driver, but he was a nervous passenger. Good information.

Her hands cramped from her tight grip on the wheel. Wait! She *did* have a weapon. One much bigger and more dangerous than a gun. She had Mack the Knife. Mack would take care of her. She just needed to tell Mack what to do.

"OK, OK. I'm driving to McHenry. But I'm warning you. The roads are getting worse. Can't you feel it? I gotta drive slow, or we'll wreck. And get that gun out of my ribs. I need to concentrate."

He jabbed her again with the gun.

"Listen, Milo." Her voice became stronger as her mind cleared away the panic. "We're heading toward Glendale Bridge. You know it's slippery. If that gun goes off, I'll be dead. There's no way you'll be able to drive this snowplow from the passenger seat over a dead body. It'll crash through the bridge's barrier rail. Fly into the lake. Break through the ice. You'll be trapped inside. Then you'll drown. Is that what you want?"

He moved the gun from her ribs but continued to point it at her. She got her first good look at the gun—it was hers. The decocker was off; the slide was closed. Milo's forefinger was not on the trigger but resting along the barrel. This observation told her Milo had both trigger discipline and experience with semi-automatic handguns. It also confirmed the gun was loaded.

"Stop pointing that gun at me!" She shifted down. "If you accidentally shoot me, you'll never get the lottery ticket. How did you get my gun anyway?"

Milo turned the gun toward the dashboard. "I happened to find it while searching your house for the ticket. Nice gun."

"How did you get in without tripping the alarm?"

"I have a jamming device. Next time, get an upgrade on your security system."

"Did you *have* to trash my house? Destroy my roommate's property?"

"A lying girl like you?" Milo smirked. "All full of mystery and secrets. It's as plain as day you have some serious shade in your history. I figured trashing your house would throw off the police. They'd spend their time looking into you."

Happy remained silent while she considered what Milo said. His reasoning was more right than wrong. She had no idea her efforts to comply with WITSEC made her look disreputable.

Milo settled into his seat. "Why didn't you redeem the ticket?"

Oh, boy. What kind of a lie would explain that? She remembered the CNN report, which included some financial advice. "I needed to see a financial planner. You know—should I take a lump sum or an annuity?"

"Shit." Milo rolled his eyes with contempt. "Stupid bitch."

There were headlights coming toward her. A snowplow. Followed by three police vehicles. It was the search party for the "missing" driver. Maybe she could throw some anti-skid. Hit every vehicle with flying aggregate. That would get their attention.

"Don't even think about it," Milo said, apparently reading her thoughts.

She leaned back into her seat to give the oncoming snowplow driver a line of sight into her cab. Maybe the driver would notice she had a passenger and report it to Jack. "How did you do it, Milo?"

When she glanced his way, she caught him smiling to himself. Apparently, planning and executing a million-dollar robbery was a source of pride. No matter that someone was killed. The self-pride was pathetic, but it was something she could use to save herself.

"Tell me. You must've devised a brilliant plan. Or did someone else think it up?"

He responded with ruffled irritation. "No, it was me. Singleton came into the Somerset Bar and Grill. He told Al he'd won a million dollars in the lottery. The dumbass even showed Al the ticket. Al called me."

"What's your connection to Al?"

"My cousin."

"I can guess the rest. You drained the gas out of the Explorer while Al got him good and drunk. Then Al offered to drive him home. He drove Bernie until the Explorer ran out of gas. Then he stole the ticket, and you picked up Al, leaving Bernie to die." She scoffed her derision. "But you fucked up, didn't you? Didn't drain enough gas. Al ended up driving over thirty miles."

Milo sat silent. There were no denials or explanations.

Happy put on her most sarcastic voice. "And you call me stupid. Tell me, who's stupider? You for not knowing how to drain a gas tank or Al for losing a million-dollar lottery ticket?"

Her cell phone sounded. It was Jack.

"Don't answer it," Milo said.

A moment later, Jack was on the radio. "Happy, what's your location? Ans—"

She glanced at Milo.

"Shut it off," he said.

She disconnected the radio. Good; nothing infuriated Jack more than a driver who was *incommunicado.*

They were now a half-mile from the Fireside. Maybe Jimmy was there waiting for her. He'd know something was wrong if she drove past without stopping or honking the air horn. Maybe she could threaten Milo with Jimmy's expected presence.

"My boyfriend's waiting for me at the Fireside. You met him—the state trooper. If I don't stop, he'll know something's wrong. He'll call SWAT. Tell them it's a hostage situation. That never ends well for the hostage taker, does it? Want to get shot? Want to die with bullets in your chest?"

Milo burst out laughing. "What a bimbo you are. I called Jack and pretended to be Trooper Bittinger. That's how I got your route. Your boyfriend's not coming. Not as smart as you think you are, are you?"

"You impersonated Jimmy?"

Milo threw back his head and laughed louder. Rage replaced her fear and disappointment. Now she was the one getting robbed—her last chance to see Jimmy before leaving Deep Creek just evaporated. And Milo called her a stupid bitch and a bimbo. Maybe she was, but now she was an angry, stupid bitch-bimbo.

She gripped the steering wheel and pressed on the accelerator. They passed the Fireside at thirty miles per hour, twice the maximum speed for plowing icy snow.

Milo stopped laughing and started hollering. "Slow down! The bridge is coming up!"

Glendale Bridge. It wasn't yet within view, but she could see it in her mind's eye. The steep S-curve. The expansion joints that allowed the bridge to expand and contract during Deep Creek's weather variations. The bridge's straight concrete surface. The slight rise of the bridge followed by the slight fall. More expansion joints. Exit the bridge.

She had a plan.

Chapter 54

"All right, all right, all right!" Happy geared down and feathered the brakes. The snowplow returned to a safe speed. "You made me mad, Milo. Keep your mouth shut so I can concentrate."

Her plan was tricky. It had to do with a physics principle she learned in a CDL class, the name of which escaped her. The snowplow's bed had to be empty; she couldn't risk tons of anti-skid crashing into the cab. Everything had to line up precisely—the speed, the snowplow's blade, and her nerve. It was going to get ugly.

Could she fool Milo? He claimed to know all the tricks. He might figure out her plan if he paid attention to her driving. Distraction was the key.

"I'm cold," she said. "Don't get excited…I need to reach for my blanket."

Milo watched as she retrieved the fleece blanket behind her, folded it with one hand into a protective square and covered her chest.

The snowplow entered the S-curve. She threw generous amounts of anti-skid as the snowplow descended the dangerous slope. "Milo, do you really think you can trust Al?"

"What are you talking about?"

She pressed on the accelerator. Threw some anti-skid. "Your dear cousin, your accomplice, your partner in crime. Do you think you can trust him?"

"Say what you mean."

She angled the blade a bit to the left. "Did I mention the police found the lottery ticket? It was inside a locker at Discount Depo, sitting as pretty as could be inside a tea—"

"Shut up! You're lying!"

"My whole life I've been told I'm a terrible liar." She speeded up a little more. "What do you think? Am I?" Milo said nothing about the snowplow's acceleration. "I watched Corporal Harold Friend pull the ticket from my roommate's Lenox teapot with a pair of long tweezers. Then he looked at the back of the ticket."

She glanced at Milo with a malevolent smile. "You'll never guess who signed the lottery ticket."

Milo's lips parted, but he remained silent.

"Go on, say it. You know the answer." She angled the blade a bit. "Surprise, surprise! It was your dear cousin, Al Hershberger. He was gonna cash it in himself and take off with the money. You're a chump."

The bridge loomed in front of her. Her blade was positioned exactly right—at its lowest level and angled to line up with the expansion joint. The blade scraped along the road's surface. "Know what else, Milo?"

No response.

The speed of Happy's lies was accelerating along with the snowplow. "Your fingerprints were on the ticket."

"No! That's not possible. I never touched the tick—"

"One last thing." Happy turned to him with the lethal eyes she'd seen on Romero. "You're a dead man."

Milo let out a terrified cry when he awoke to his surroundings. "Raise the blade! Raise the blade!"

Happy drove the snowplow over the expansion joint. The cutting edge of the precisely-angled blade dropped into the narrow slot between the concrete surface on each side of the joint. The gap captured the blade like a trap and wouldn't let go.

The blade lurched to an abrupt stop. The snowplow's front end kept moving until it smashed into the wedged blade. Happy's chest slammed against the seatbelt. Her head snapped backward when the snowplow's bed, also moving forward, rammed into the cab. The sickening sound of scraping, twisting, and grinding tore through the night air, punctuated by Milo's screams.

She had the odd sensation of climbing upward. Panic stopped her breath short. Was the snowplow climbing the bridge's barrier railing? For an instant, she envisioned herself inside the snowplow as it flew over the bridge, smashed through the ice, and disappeared beneath the frigid water below.

The snowplow came to a stop.

Happy gasped for breath as she pressed her foot on the brake. The explosive echoes of the crash bounced across the lake. It took another five seconds for her to realize the forward movement had stopped. She peeled her fingers from the steering wheel. They trembled but had no feeling. She held them in front of her face and counted. Yes, they were all there. Happy gazed through the windshield. She wondered why her body was tilted backward and she was viewing the snowy sky.

Her wits returned to her. No time to think. Find the gun. Get out of the snowplow. Run, hide, fight—the order of action she'd learned from her former AA sponsor, Floater. She unsnapped her seatbelt. Milo's voice was hoarse from screaming, but he continued to try. He no longer held the gun. Where was it? Probably on the floor at his feet. He was too large for her to lean over and reach the floor. He might grab her hair, beat her face, or strangle her with his bare hands.

She nixed the idea of getting the gun. Time to get out and run. She warily opened the door and discovered she was now six feet above the ground. Was the snowplow's cab hung up on the barrier railing? No, the bridge's road surface was below her. She retrieved the tire hammer from under her seat. Climbed one-handed down the wreckage.

Once on the ground, her wobbly legs wouldn't hold her. Happy fell on her hands and knees. "Let's go, Lucy," she said. Once she was upright, she stared at the truck. The blade was crumbled, twisted backward. The cab rested at a forty-five-degree angle on top of the blade.

The sound of the passenger door opening sharpened her focus on staying alive. She heard Milo rumbling around inside the cab, probably looking for the gun. What to do? The icy surface would impair her ability to run. If she fell, she wouldn't be able to defend herself. Running was out of the question; she needed to hide until she could fight.

Happy crouched behind the driver's side of the mangled snowplow while Milo maneuvered to exit the cab. He would soon be hunting her. She controlled her breathing so she wouldn't give herself away. Milo muttered curses as he began his descent down the wreckage. Happy knew the open passenger door would obstruct his line of sight to the front of the snowplow. She crept around the snowplow to an invisible spot. Hid. Waited. Peered beneath the snowplow.

She spotted Milo's left foot searching for the ground. The right foot was still on the cab. He was likely gripping the gun in one hand and holding on to the cab with the other. He would be off-balance.

Lights and sirens drew her attention toward the S-curve. The rescue snowplow. Three police cars. The first responders heard the crash while searching for the "missing" driver. They were on their way. She needed to stay alive a few minutes longer.

If the lights and sirens had gotten her attention, they would have had gotten Milo's. He would be looking in their direction. Distracted.

Happy darted from her crouched position to the passenger side of the snowplow. She leaped upward toward the open door, slamming her raised arms and hands against it. Milo fell from the cab, still holding the gun, and landed sprawled at her feet. Happy swung the tire hammer with all her might. Smacked the gun from Milo's hand as if it were a baseball. The gun flew ten feet and skidded across the icy bridge. Milo attempted to get on his feet. She kneecapped him.

Milo screamed.

"Thought you knew all the tricks, didn't you, asshole!" she said. "Who's the stupid bitch now?"

Emergency lights flashed in the distance on the western side of the bridge. She could make out the shapes of police cars and a rescue squad truck. Milo moaned and sobbed at her feet.

She hovered over him with the raised tire hammer, tempted to hit him again. All she needed was a reason. "Quit your cryin', you big baby, or I'll quit it for you!"

Police, snowplow drivers, and rescue personnel swarmed the bridge from both directions. Corporal Friend appeared at her side. She stood over Milo poised to strike him with the tire hammer. Friend gently removed it from her hands. "It's all right now, Happy."

Friend turned to the nearest state trooper and nodded toward Milo. "Arrest that murdering son of a bitch."

Happy pointed in the direction of the gun. "My gun's over there. He stole it from me."

Friend returned his attention to Happy. "You're hurt."

She touched her face. Blood. A flashback—Milo hitting her in the face with the gun. Dammit! She should've whacked him again while she had the chance. "Corporal, Milo helped kill Bernie Singleton. For the lottery ticket."

"I know. Al Hershberger confessed. His lies fell apart as soon as I asked about the Smith Island cake."

Friend gestured to the paramedics. "Check her out. She may need to go to the ER."

"Where's Jimmy?" she said.

"I sent him to Cumberland to give Mrs. Singleton an update."

She thought about her phone call to attorney Minerva Wilson James. There was going to be a shitstorm about the ticket. And Jimmy would be in its vortex.

The paramedics assisted her to a gurney near the ambulance. She balked. "Can I talk to my boss a minute?"

Jack was standing in front of the contorted snowplow. Happy approached him, a paramedic at her side. Jack ignored her. She walked around the demolished snowplow and quietly studied the damage. Her memory returned to her. *Inertia*—that was the name of the physics principle she'd been trying to remember. An object at rest tends to stay at rest; an object in motion tends to stay in motion. Dummy crash tests demonstrate what happens when force collides with inertia.

Her recollection triggered a slow-motion movie of the snowplow's destruction to play inside her head.

Once the blade fell into the expansion joint, inertia forced the truck's front end against the wedged blade. The blade crumbled and twisted backward under the force of the still-moving truck. The force continued through the push-frame at the blade's base and snapped the connecting A-frame. The two hydraulic cylinders operating the blade ripped from the connecting A-frame. The forward momentum continued and propelled the truck to climb the trapped, twisted blade.

She stroked the snowplow as if to comfort it. "I'm so sorry, Mack."

"Did you do this on purpose?" Jack said, now beside her.

"Milo had a gun on me. I didn't know what—"

"Quite impressive." Jack spoke in an academic tone. "I've seen drivers get blades stuck in a bridge expansion joint, but it takes excellent driving to do that on purpose."

Did Jack just give her a compliment? "Thanks…I think. Where's Steppie?"

"The little guy is in my snowplow. Hear him?"

Happy tried to smile at Jack, but her aching cheek kept her from doing so. She hugged him instead. "Plowing with a dog? Don't you know that's a safety violation? You could get fired."

The ER discharged Happy after five hours. She was home with Steppie, packing her suitcase, getting ready to leave for parts unknown. Etchers managed to get his SUV down the icy driveway. Happy was glad to see her former Uncle Peter. "I told you everything would be all right, didn't I?"

He answered with an unblinking stare that lasted a few seconds. "Stitches?"

"Three. I have some bruises where I hit the seatbelt, and I'm a little sore. Other than that, I'm fine."

"There's someone I want you to meet."

A moment later, a woman in her early forties came through the door. She was a petite brunette, with flawless olive skin, and dark eyes. Happy's stomach flipped, and her breath flew away.

"Happy," Etchers said. "This is Deputy U.S. Marshal Dottie Dixon."

Happy choked on her next words. "You look just like my mother." She turned to Etchers. "Was this your idea?"

"Maybe, maybe not." He half-smiled and then became serious. "We want you to stay in the program. I thought you might be able to relate better to a female deputy. By the way, the AG authorized us to kidnap you if necessary."

"Oh, stop it."

"OK, kidnapping you was Romero's idea."

Surprise took Happy's breath away for the second time in a minute. "Romero? You knew?"

"Of course. I know everything that might affect you."

"Are you mad I didn't tell you?"

"A little hurt...not mad. Or surprised. I told the AG you wouldn't tell. You can keep a secret, that's for sure."

Dixon spoke next. "Happy, Milo Sullivan groomed you for friendship. He tricked you into picking up him up on the side of a deserted road. He took advantage of your kind heart. Do you realize how easily you fell into a killer's trap?"

She knew the answer but couldn't say it out loud. She looked at her feet and answered with a silent nod.

"Give us some time to find Peeps," Dixon said. "It won't take long. Romero's assisting us."

"Where will I go?"

"Please trust us to place you somewhere safe and suitable for you."

While standing before the two deputies, Happy came to terms with the truth; she needed protection, and she needed to grow up. Her impulses were her worst enemies.

"I want to talk to Jimmy one last time."

"He's waiting for your call."

The deputies moved to the kitchen while she called. Jimmy answered on the first ring.

"You decided to stay in WITSEC?" he said.

"Yes. Thank you for giving me the time to sort it all out."

"You're welcome."

"Before I go, I need to tell you something." She braced herself. "I called Minerva Wilson James about the lottery ticket. I wanted Melody to get her share. You're gonna be in the middle of another shitstorm."

He laughed softly. "I know. I called Renee Atwater for the same reason."

"You did?" Jimmy had just surprised her, in a good way. She continued. "I don't think Olivia's gonna put up much of a fight. She won't risk Bernie's infidelity becoming public."

"Yeah. You did good, Happy."

"*We* did good. Both of us together. It was fun, don't you think?"

"Best time ever."

"I'm going to miss you. You stay safe now, you hear? Oh, one last thing... Jimmy, are we squared up, amend-wise?"

"Yes, we are. Take care of yourself, Happy."

She disconnected, took a deep breath, and joined the deputies in the kitchen. "I'm ready now. If you won't tell me where we're going, can you at least tell me our first stop?"

Dixon answered. "International Departures, Pittsburgh Airport."

Chapter 55

Six months later

No matter how much Lucy Holiday practiced, she couldn't master the *voga alla vanetta*, the basic oar stroke.

She could easily balance herself while standing on the stern of the flat-bottomed, asymmetrical gondola. Her experience as a bicycle messenger and truck driver gave her an excellent sense of spatial awareness. Not once had she bumped into another gondola or God forbid, a *vaporetti*—the water-buses that traveled down Venice's Grand Canal.

Kicking off against a corner building while turning into a narrow, interior canal was instinctive; she must have biked that maneuver a thousand times. Valentino, her gondoliering instructor, taught her to yell "Oe!" before rounding a blind corner.

It took a while before she learned how to keep the oar in the curved *forcole*. During the first three months of lessons, she'd dropped the thirteen-foot oar every week and watched helplessly while it floated away. She joked that the Grand Canal should be renamed the "Canal of Sighs" for all the dramatic sighs Valentino exhaled while retrieving a runaway oar.

She was making progress, but the complicated *voga alla vanetta* eluded her. She had to lean into the oar with all her strength while using the *forcole* as leverage. Next came the forward push, the oar twist, and the backward stroke. She had to be mindful of each maneuver while feeling for the tide and dodging obstacles.

Valentino's gondola weighed fifteen hundred pounds. It was an elegant structure carved of cherry wood, painted sleek black, and embellished with a brass *ferro*. The seats were red velvet.

Steppie supervised her from one of the velvet seats. He wore a life jacket and quietly watched the gondolas skim along the Grand Canal. After each lesson, Lucy and Steppie shared a gelato in the Piazza San Marco. The local gondoliers gave them nicknames: King and Lady Gelato.

"Lady Gelato, apply your force!" Valentino shouted from the bow as she threw her body weight onto the oar. She'd been applying her force to the stroke three times a week for four months. Her stomach's six-pack reappeared, along with her biceps and the cut between the shoulder muscles and triceps. Her extra ten-pounds vanished.

Another gondolier, Giovanni Vianello, guided his gondola until it was parallel to hers. "Lady Gelato, when are you going to quit?"

"The day I beat you at the Regata Storica race."

Giovanni guffawed as he glided his gondolier away with an efficient agility she could only envy.

The comradery of the gondoliers reminded Lucy of her bicycle messenger posse. They traded quips and barbs as they passed each other along the network of *rii*, the small canals leading off the Grand Canal.

A passing gondolier waved and shouted, "King Gelato!"

Steppie answered with the same joyous howl he had sung while strapped to Lucy's chest as she pedaled through the streets of Baltimore.

It was late afternoon when her lesson finished. It was a good day. No dropped oar and no hollers from Valentino to "Watch out!" She helped Val dock the gondola before walking Steppie to the Piazza.

It was her favorite time of day. The sun's reflections danced along buildings while the shadows from Venetian buildings grew long. The city sparkled a rosy gilt that reminded her of Jimmy's hair. She kept the memory of her sweet hours in Jimmy's bed close to her heart. Did he ever think of her? God, she missed him.

Lucy thought about prosecutor Rick McCormick. He'd been so certain Romero had killed her mother, but he'd been so wrong. She was haunted by the fact she'd done the same with innocent Zeke Hershberger.

When she discussed her mistake with Dixon, the deputy said, "Lucy, you had tunnel vision. Investigators are trained to avoid that. Listen, you have a knack for criminal investigation. If you want to know how to do it right, go back to school. And forgive yourself." Lucy decided she couldn't forgive herself unless she forgave Rick. So she forgave him—in her heart. One day, she would tell him.

Lucy ordered her usual vanilla gelato from the Favaretto Gelato, with a separate two-tablespoon serving for Steppie. The pair sat across from one another at an outside table. The dog finished his gelato with two slurps and waited patiently while she finished hers.

Her time in Venice was coming to an end. When she departed Deep Creek, Dixon was about to begin a sabbatical to study the Italian witness protection program. She agreed to become Lucy's handler. According to Dixon, Venice was Romero's idea. Lucy never heard from him again.

She liked Dixon. They'd grown close during a two-week biking trip as they traveled from Venice, along the Adriatic Coast, through Italy, Slovenia and Croatia. She told Dixon about her mother, Romero, and Melody Atwater. The tower of amends Lucy owed to her mother seemed to shrink with the telling.

Dixon's sabbatical was near completion; the deputy would return to her position at the U.S. Marshals Service in Denver, Colorado. Lucy opened her phone and re-read an e-mail she received a month ago; she'd been accepted by the University of Denver. In two weeks, she would begin coursework in criminology.

A month ago, Peeps vanished; the Marshals Service suspected he was dead. She agreed to stay in WITSEC until his death was confirmed or he was in custody.

Lucy finished her gelato. Faint sounds of a distant guitar caught her attention. The crowds of tourists obscured the melody, but she could piece together the notes well enough to hum along.

It was the lullaby portion of "Melody Rocks." Someone was playing it on a guitar, over and over.

She stood on her chair and surveyed the Piazza. She saw nothing but concluded the music was coming from the west.

"Steppie," she said as she jumped from the chair. "Let's investigate."

The music grew louder as she walked toward the Venice Archaeological Museum. Steppie strained against the leash. She struggled to heel the dog, but he would have none of it. He gagged as he pulled. Lucy worried he would injure his trachea against his collar. She quickened her pace to run with him. They darted between tourists until they reached the guitar player. Steppie leaped over the guitar case and into the lap of the guitarist.

The lap belonged to Jimmy.

He sat in a folding chair. The open guitar case rested on the ground in front of him. A few pieces of change sprinkled the inside the empty case.

"Steppie! I'm glad to see you!" Jimmy said as he looked up at Lucy.

Jimmy's hair was long, his smile wide, and his eyes bright. He wore khaki pants and a white shirt. She smiled back, unable to speak because of the endless questions leaping inside her head. She tossed two euros into the guitar case.

"*Chiao, signorina,*" Jimmy said. "What may I play for you?"

"A lullaby. It's called 'Melody Rocks.' Have you heard of it?"

"I believe I have. Long ago, a beautiful woman insisted I listen to it."

Using a pick, Jimmy played two repeats of the lullaby portion of 'Melody Rocks.'

"*Grazie,*" Lucy said. "The woman must have loved you very much to share such an exquisite melody with you."

"I pray every night she still does. It took me a long while to find her. I was hoping for a moment of her time."

"Perhaps we can share a ride in a gondola. You can tell me how you found her."

Jimmy put away his guitar. They walked through the piazza and reached the dock where Valentino was waiting for a customer to hire him. Lucy introduced the men to one another. "This is my old friend, Jimmy. This is Valentino, my new friend. Val, will you take us for a ride?"

"It would be my greatest pleasure, Lady Gelato."

Jimmy glanced at her with curiosity.

She attempted to hand Val the usual eighty euros, but he waved her off. "Where would you like to go?"

"Under the Bridge of Sighs. At sunset, if you can manage it."

Val raised his eyebrows, smiled, and nodded.

Jimmy and Lucy settled into two plush, velvet seats.

"May I?" he said.

When she nodded, he wrapped his left arm around her shoulder. The sun was low in the sky, throwing its golden lights against the thousand-year-old buildings lining the canal. She leaned against him. Val rowed the gondola down the Grand Canal toward *Rio di Palazzo*, an interior canal. As they turned into the *rio*, the water was serene and reflected the buildings that now glowed with rosy colors.

"You've taken up playing the guitar again," she whispered.

He laughed softly. "That's the only melody I know."

"How did you find me?"

His lips lingered next to hers but did not touch them. "The Marshals Service wouldn't tell me a thing. I called Romero. His number was still in my cell phone."

She pulled back, shocked. "You called *him*? What did he say?"

"First, he demanded I meet him in person. In Alaska of all places. I flew into Anchorage and ended up in a tiny town north of the Arctic Circle. We met at an outside bar at midnight. I had to wear my sunglasses because the sun was so bright. I asked him again where you were. He said if I had listened to you, I would know exactly where you were." Jimmy gave her a wry smile. "Then he told me I was an idiot. That was his answer."

She tsked. "Oh, for goodness sakes."

"It took me weeks to remember your conversation about becoming a gondolier. At the time you said it, I thought it was a joke and didn't pay attention."

Lucy became quiet as she processed the fact Jimmy had come to terms with her relationship with Romero. Otherwise, Jimmy would never have asked him for help.

Jimmy planted a soft kiss on her head. "Romero wanted me to give you a message."

"Do I want to hear it?"

"I think so."

"What's the message?"

"Romero told me Peeps is dead. He said you're free to live as you wish."

She pulled away and stared at Jimmy, astounded. "How does Romero know that?"

"He didn't say, and I didn't ask. I don't think you should, either."

The Venetian sun was sinking behind the buildings. It would soon be dark.

Lucy sunk into the warm crevice of Jimmy's shoulder. "You said you wanted a moment of my time. How long will the moment last?"

"For an hour, a night, a year. Maybe a lifetime. The moment will last for as long as you want it to."

"I can't make any promises."

The strong arm around her shoulder held her close. "Maybe one day you will."

They were now approaching the Bridge of Sighs. The enclosed bridge, built in the year sixteen hundred, spanned high over the *Rio di Palazzo.* It connected the Ducal Palace with an old prison, Palazzo delle Prigioni. It was said that prisoners, crossing the bridge from the interrogation rooms within the palace to the prison, would sigh as they looked, for the last time, at the beauty of Venice before their execution or incarceration.

Lucy preferred the romantic story of the bridge, inspired by the poetry of Lord Byron. If a couple kissed while passing under the bridge at sunset, they would enjoy eternal love. The powerful, romantic moment prompted their sighs. She didn't know whether she'd enjoy eternal love with Jimmy but thought she would try to tip the odds her way.

The sun disappeared. The bridge was overhead.

She used her fingers to tenderly turn Jimmy's face toward hers.

She kissed him.

There were still many questions. She had been so sure of her desired future—marriage, children, home—but now she didn't know what she wanted. She needed to figure herself out. College was the next step on her *adulting* path.

Right now, she'd enjoy the moment. She rested her head against Jimmy's shoulder. Steppie curled into her lap. The post-sunset twilight shimmered on the water.

It was a very good moment.

Acknowledgments

I am deeply indebted to my family and friends for their continued support of my writing efforts. Special thanks to my Best Buds and Denton Five pals, for their ever-present encouragement. Thank you to Harry Chan for suggesting that Happy Holiday expand her horizons.

I consulted with many professionals. My inquiries began with an explanatory e-mail and a request for help. Without exception, the replies were prompt and positive. The communications frequently led to better plot ideas than the ones I had dreamed up. Their willingness to share their time, knowledge, and experience gave me the courage to learn and write about unfamiliar topics. Any mistakes of fact, law, or procedure are mine.

Many thanks to the Public Roads Division, Garrett County Public Works. Paul Harvey, Roads Division Chief, arranged for me to take a ride-along in a snowplow. During night of the ride-along, Deep Creek's mountain roads transformed from snowy to treacherous. Thank you to the very capable snowplow driver, Darlene Jackson, for keeping me safe while explaining the fundamentals of plowing snow. Until I personally experienced time in a snowplow, I had little appreciation for the hazards of the job. I came away from the ride-along knowing it was the perfect occupation for the intrepid Happy Holiday.

After Mrs. Jackson retired, I needed additional snowplowing expertise. I discovered the blog of Ellen Voie, President and CEO of the Women in Trucking Association. She posted my request for help on the Association's Facebook page. Within minutes, I was in touch with Pam and Ted Kays, Over the Road Owner-Operator Team Truck Drivers, with many previous years of experience plowing snow for the Indiana Department of Transportation. During the course of many e-mails and telephone calls, Mr. and Mrs. Kays explained the nuts and bolts of snowplowing. They also suggested how Happy could rescue herself from her deadly circumstances.

Thanks to Scott Moorman, Director of Engineering at Buyers Products Company/SnowDogg Plows. Mr. Moorman provided me with insight and materials pertaining to municipal snowplows so that I could describe the novel's climatic action.

Thanks to the Maryland State Police for vetting my plot, providing information on death investigations, explaining how Garrett County's various law enforcement agencies work together, and providing information on law enforcement jurisdiction and procedure. Specifically, thank you to the former Lieutenant Joseph J. Gamble, Regional Commander and Commander, Homicide Unit, Criminal Investigations Bureau (now the Sheriff of Talbot County, Maryland) and Lieutenant Mark Rodeheaver, Commander, McHenry Barrack W (Retired). A special shout-out goes to the Assistant Barrack Commander, First Sergeant Bradley D. Williams who answered my endless questions and gave me a tour of McHenry Barrack W.

Thanks to the cheerful nurses and staff of Station B, Somerset Hospital, who enthusiastically brainstormed an illness for character Zeke Hershberger—a patient they understood was totally fictional.

Thanks to Melissa Holiday, Somerset Chamber of Commerce, for helping me select a likely site for the Somerset Bar and Grill. Ms. Holiday told me, as a youngster, she was called "Happy." I was thrilled to meet a real Happy Holiday.

Many thanks to John Longbottom, song-writer and composer, for his invaluable help in developing the "Melody Rocks" plotline.

There are no words to express my appreciation to my dear husband, Ron Crockett. I bombarded him with questions, plot ideas, and theoretical issues. Ron, a mechanical engineer, interpreted the reams of snowplow materials I gathered. He located my work-in-progress whenever the computer disappeared it into some weird place. On the night of the snowplow ride-along, Ron unstuck my SUV from our icy driveway so that I could make it to the long-awaited ride-along. He endured freezing weather and tromped through snowbanks to help me take winter photographs of Glendale Bridge. Ron frequently saved me from getting swept away while doing research ("Do you really need to know everything about socket wrenches?"). During our forty-plus years of marriage, Ron always loved and believed in me, no matter what ventures I chose to pursue.

CPSIA information can be obtained
at www.ICGtesting.com
Printed in the USA
LVHW012114110121
676215LV00041B/1130

For Ellen and John Warren, my parents of blessed memory